NEW STORY OF THE STONE

NEW STORY OF THE STONE

An Early Chinese Science Fiction Novel

WU JIANREN

Translated by Liz Evans Weber

Columbia University Press

New York

Columbia University Press
Publishers Since 1893
New York Chichester, West Sussex

Library of Congress Cataloging-in-Publication Data
Names: Wu, Jianren, 1866–1910, author. |
Weber, Liz Evans, translator.
Title: New story of the stone : an early Chinese science fiction
novel / Jianren Wu ; translated by Liz Evans Weber.
Other titles: Xin shi tou ji. English
Description: New York : Columbia University Press, 2025. |
Includes bibliographical references.
Identifiers: LCCN 2024053448 (print) | LCCN 2024053449
(ebook) | ISBN 9780231203463 (hardback) | ISBN 9780231203470
(trade paperback) | ISBN 9780231555067 (ebook)
Subjects: LCGFT: Science fiction. | Novels.
Classification: LCC PL2732.U24 X5613 2025 (print) |
LCC PL2732.U24 (ebook) | DDC 895.13/48—dc23/eng/20250131

Cover design: Chang Jae Lee

GPSR Authorized Representative: Easy Access System
Europe, Mustamäe tee 50, 10621 Tallinn, Estonia,
gpsr.requests@easproject.com

For Tom and Mari

CONTENTS

NEW STORY OF THE STONE AN INTRODUCTION TO THE TEXT

AVID READERS of Chinese literature may already be familiar with author Wu Jianren (1866–1910) as a literary giant of the late Qing period, primarily remembered today as a writer of fiction and essayist.[1] No less an authority than Lu Xun (1881–1936), himself considered to be the "father of modern Chinese literature," pronounced Wu to be one of the preeminent authors in the popular genre of exposé fiction that flourished during the late Qing period.[2] Part uproarious satire, part sci-fi fantasy, *New Story of the Stone* (*Xin shitou ji*, hereafter *New Story*) is a unique, important example of the genre in which Wu so excelled.[3] I am delighted to make it available for the first time in a full English-language translation.

The latter half of the Qing dynasty was a complex and fascinating period, generally characterized by instability and decline. Widespread official corruption had begun to weaken the empire both economically and administratively; at the same time, rapid population growth put pressure on arable land, leading to food shortages, inflation, and popular unrest, ultimately manifesting in a number of protracted and traumatic internal rebellions. It was this beleaguered and increasingly hard-pressed empire that would find itself mired in multiple foreign wars starting in the mid-nineteenth century—all fought on Chinese territory—with imperialist European powers and Japan. Suffering defeat after defeat, the Qing would find itself forced to sign a series of "unequal treaties" that imposed crushing indemnities upon China while simultaneously forcing Chinese territory open to foreign trade.[4]

Owing to these dramatic changes in China's geopolitical fortunes, the final decades of the Qing were a period of great intellectual ferment. In particular, China's intellectuals took up the task of attempting to chart a way forward for an empire that had ceased to be the awesome regional hegemon of its former, more glorious days. Their debates centered not just on concrete questions relating to military modernization and industrialization but on more abstract ones relating to statecraft, economics, culture, and "nation" as well.

By the mid- to late nineteenth century, many Chinese intellectuals had taken for granted the need for technological and scientific advancement in China; however, the question of how to implement such changes would prove thorny, for tied up in these debates were existential anxieties about history, culture, and civilizational identity. As a result, one of the major preoccupations of this period was the question of whether, how, and to what extent China could or should adopt Western technologies and ideological systems in their attempts to adapt to the contemporary geopolitical moment. For example, some were loath to accept new, foreign epistemologies at the expense of China's own native scholarship and hoped that Western technologies could be surgically and pragmatically adopted while leaving China's own cultural and intellectual code intact. (This doctrine is succinctly expressed in the oft-quoted slogan "Chinese learning as [intellectual] core; Western learning as [practical] tool" [*Zhongxue weiti, xixue weiyong*]).[5] In other words, they conceded that a certain degree of adaptation was necessary for China's survival but hoped to effect it in such a way as to leave China's social, moral, and intellectual fabric largely unchanged.

By the time China suffered its defeat at the hands of Japan in the 1895 Sino-Japanese War, however, the situation appeared desperate. Political activists became more convinced than ever that real, structural change was necessary if China was to avoid calamity—in other words, technological advancement alone had proved insufficient to overcome the many challenges threatening the weakened empire.[6] The Qing was facing a moment of existential crisis, and it seemed that a drastic rethinking of the political and intellectual status quo was called for. Emergent discourses of Social Darwinism that had begun to circulate in China—and which dovetailed in compelling ways with domestic Xunzian philosophy—asserted that the strength of a society lay in its ability to unite as a group (*qun*) and organize to counter external threats.[7] As a result, the formation of a unified Chinese "nation," composed not of passive imperial subjects but of politically active citizens, was increasingly posited as the key to China's survival.

In the years following the Sino-Japanese War, two basic ideological camps, revolutionaries and reformers, would assert distinct visions for the ideal form of a new Chinese nation-state. Revolutionaries such as Sun Yat-sen (1866–1925) would advocate for the total overthrow of the ethnic minority Manchu court and the establishment of a Han ethnonationalist republic.[8] By contrast, the reformers, led by Kang Youwei (1858–1927) and his disciple Liang Qichao (1872–1929) argued that the Manchu court could remain in power as long as certain changes were made to the functioning of the government. More specifically, they advocated for the implementation of a constitutional monarchy: on the one hand, they reasoned that the continuation of the monarchy would provide necessary stability as China took its first tentative steps toward representative government; but more important, they hoped that a constitution would "ensure the political participation of the majority of the people," which would in turn result in "the formation of a cohesive and strong nation-state."[9]

When, during a period known as the Hundred Days Reform, the reformers' efforts to win the progressive Guangxu emperor over to their cause began to bear fruit, a palace coup dethroned the emperor and installed the more conservative empress dowager Cixi in his place. In the aftermath of the coup, a number of prominent reformers were executed, while others, like Liang, were forced to flee. Undeterred from his mission, Liang would continue his work from his new base of operations in Japan, helming a number of influential journals that advocated for reformist goals, including *Qingyi bao* (The China Discussion) and *Xinmin congbao* (The New Citizen). (It is *The China*

Discussion, along with two of Liang's earlier publications, that so enraptures our protagonist Baoyu in chapter 7 of the present text.)

Aside from the need for governmental reform, Liang would also emphasize the importance of instilling a sense of political subjectivity in the people. He firmly believed that a unified Chinese "nation"—and the fostering of a politically active citizenry that was invested in and responsible for the fate of China—would be the key to staving off future foreign incursions and preventing further decline.[10] Liang had a clear idea of just how this could be achieved: in his influential 1902 essay "Lun xiaoshuo yu qunzhi zhi guanxi" (On the Relationship Between Fiction and the Governance of the People), Liang argued that fiction, with its unique ability to engage its readers as compared to other modes of writing, would be the perfect tool for constituting a socially responsible public. First, however, it would be necessary to reform China's fiction, so that its object was no longer mere entertainment but the delivery of clear moral and socially oriented messages to its readers. (In the same essay, he further argued that previous works of popular fiction that romanticized things like banditry or illicit love affairs had been responsible for leading generations of Chinese readers morally astray.)[11] In essence, Liang drew a clear and explicit throughline from literature to politics, asserting that socially aware fiction was the only way to national salvation.

The response to Liang's call to (literary) arms was resounding. Indeed, Wu Jianren himself was one of many moved by Liang's essay on the need for a new fiction, and it is partially for this reason that Wu turned his hand to the writing of novels.[12] As is the case with many other works of socially oriented fiction that emerged during this particularly febrile era of literary production, Wu's works often provide acerbic commentary on what he perceived to be a decadent contemporary society: corruption, venality, abuse of power, willful ignorance, and unthinking infatuation with Western culture, ideas, or values all come under fire in one or another of his works. An incisive humorist with a penchant for gossip and scandal, Wu entertains his readers with shocking anecdotes and tales of disgraceful carryings-on, revealing a morally bankrupt late imperial China in which petty self-interest, in its many possible manifestations, has gradually come to replace the more traditional moral code. Viewed in the context of Liang's cris de coeur, Wu's scathing social critiques must thus be understood not simply as indulging in lurid, sensationalist nihilism; rather they are intended to serve a didactic function, shocking the reader into contemplating and condemning the depredations of the late Qing society that they themselves inhabited.

■ ■ ■

In keeping with most of Wu's other works, *New Story* presents a trenchant indictment of the state of late Qing society and morality; however, there are two key aspects of *New Story* that mark it as quite unique both among Wu's own oeuvre and among other works from this period. The first has to do with the perspective from which Wu posits his critique: namely, he has borrowed his protagonist, Jia Baoyu, wholesale from a famous novel written well over a hundred years earlier: the celebrated mid-Qing novel *Story of the Stone* (*Shitou ji*), better known as *Dream of the Red Chamber* (*Honglou meng*), by Cao Xueqin.[13] Part of what makes *New Story* so remarkable is that Wu has selected as his protagonist one of the single most famous and beloved figures in all of Chinese literature, so that he might send him on a surprising series of adventures.

The unexpected and fantastical nature of said adventures is the second point of appeal of *New Story*. Wu does not simply pick up where the plot of *Story of the Stone* (hereafter *Story*) left off, restoring Baoyu to his familiar milieu somewhere in the mid-eighteenth century; rather, he transports Baoyu over a hundred years into the future (to the year 1900), thrusting him first into a decadent late Qing society that bewilders and infuriates him by turns, and later into a dazzling Chinese sci-fi utopia called "The Realm of Civilization." These two distinct realms are depicted in vivid detail and with keen imagination: one, the backward, degenerate "Sick Man of Asia" whose populace is too keen to emulate foreigners and turn a quick profit to notice that the empire is at risk of total moral and intellectual collapse; the other a technological superpower whose might—which is depicted as being vastly superior to that of contemporary European nations—is based on native Chinese epistemologies and the strong shared sense of moral solidarity that is lacking in its real-world counterpart.

These two elements contribute to making *New Story* a fascinating read for sinologist, science fiction enthusiast, and casual reader alike; however, the translator appreciates that Wu's decision to couch his message in these terms may require further contextualization. In particular, some background knowledge about the basics of Cao Xueqin's *Story* and a brief explanation of the message underlying Wu's choice of a Confucian utopia in the second half of the novel will be instructive in helping the reader better understand the intentions behind Wu's authorial choices. Therefore, the remainder of this introduction will be divided into two parts: the first seeks to situate the unfamiliar reader in the context of Cao Xueqin's original *Story*, the better to understand what Wu is able to accomplish by choosing to write his *New Story* as a "sequel" to this monumental work. The second part will then discuss the significance of the sci-fi utopia that features in the second half of the novel.

STORY OF THE STONE

To understand just how Wu is making use of Baoyu in *New Story*, it will be necessary first to explain the "baggage" that Baoyu carries with him from Cao's original novel (and with which Wu could assume readers of *New Story* to be familiar). On the one hand, Baoyu provides a crucial character archetype that Wu heavily reinscribes with the political preoccupations of his own moment; and on the other, he is a representative of a bygone age who must come to terms with how much China has changed in a fairly short period of time.

Cao Xueqin's *Story* paints a telling picture of the thriving mid-Qing China in which our protagonist Jia Baoyu grew up: the emperor and imperial household are always mentioned with reverence, and imperial envoys treated with solemn—if anxious—deference; royal gifts are bountiful and munificent, and the capital appears to be at peace.[14] There is no menacing foreign colonial presence to speak of, even as the establishment of European trade routes into Asia can be inferred from the presence of a European chiming clock and other imported trinkets possessed by various members of the wealthy Jia family.[15] Within the world of Cao's novel, all calamities brought down upon the Jias and their kin are due to individual greed or hubris, rather than any systemic failure or collapse on the part of the state.[16] In essence, we are shown the Qing at its cultural peak, from the perspective of a family well situated to enjoy everything that that entailed.

Within the context of the "high Qing," *Story* depicts in exquisite detail the ostentatious luxury enjoyed by the "Nanjing Jia" family, the meritorious service of whose ancestors has made them tremendously wealthy and ensconced them among the highest echelons of Qing society, where they frequently rub shoulders with all manner of princes and other nobility. Cao depicts their lodgings, their clothing, their food, and furnishings with keen painterly attention, overawing the reader with the sheer sumptuousness of the family's lifestyle and wealth. Indeed, even the servants are so elegantly dressed that a poor country relation mistakes a maid for one of the young mistresses of the family.[17]

The gilded halls and richly appointed boudoirs of the Jia mansions are no doubt a major part of *Story*'s appeal, rendering accessible to readers, albeit in fictional form, delights beyond their own imagining. Perhaps the single most memorable space is the family's beautiful garden, Daguanyuan (Grandview Garden or Grand Prospect Garden), which, just like the internal spaces of the Jia estate, is described in lavish detail. Indeed, this sprawling garden complex is so vast and so elaborately conceived that nearly an entire chapter is dedicated to its description. The garden is a richly textured and ingeniously realized space, whose construction has been undertaken with the greatest of care. The garden's paradoxically engineered "nature," with its winding paths, tranquil streams, and craggy rockeries, its thoughtful profusions of colorful plants in some places and eremitic austerity in others, is presented as a true artistic wonder. The young Baoyu of *Story* is deeply impressed by the garden and all of its complexity. (It is no surprise that when in chapter 10 of the present text Baoyu sees a British-style "garden" in Shanghai, which consists simply of a flat rectangular lawn surrounded by flower beds, he takes offense on behalf of the word "garden" for having been thus devalued.)

While the glamorous ostentation with which the Jia household is depicted creates a delectable sense of luxury, *Story*'s enduring popularity has more to do with its vivid and lively cast of characters—and in particular, its charming young protagonists and the intimate world they inhabit. Indeed, *Story* is perhaps most famous for its tender depiction of adolescent love. From the early chapters of the novel, Baoyu finds himself in an impossible triangle, caught between two beautiful, talented cousins: his paternal cousin, the frail, temperamental, poetic savant Lin Daiyu; and his maternal cousin, the staid, down-to-earth moralist Xue Baochai. Daiyu is the "perfect love" as viewed by the passionate young Baoyu; Baochai, on the other hand, is the "perfect daughter-in-law" as viewed by his Confucian parents. Daiyu and Baochai thus represent two different, competing versions of idealized femininity. Baoyu is fond of each of them but is naturally drawn to Daiyu; despite the fact that their relationship is tumultuous, filled with tantrums and misunderstandings, it is clearly the more heartfelt, more passionate of the two. (In fact, the two are predestined to come together owing to a karmic debt from their previous incarnations.) It is this relationship more than any other in the novel that has moved generations of readers.

However, while on its surface *Story* may appear to be concerned with romance and aesthetic grandeur, it has philosophical preoccupations that run far deeper. In fact, the "action" of the novel begins with neither a description of the fabulous wealth of the Jia family, nor a heartfelt plea about the nature of love, but with an abstruse framing tale about a lump of sentient stone (the titular "stone," in fact), set in a divine realm called Taixu huanjing (The Land of Illusion). Our stone, one of many thousands forged by the goddess Nüwa so that she might use them to mend the cracked vault of the heavens, is the only one ultimately not used in the goddess's endeavors; as a result, it has lain alone in idleness for millennia. When a Daoist and a Buddhist monk encounter the bored stone, they take pity on it and decide to send it into the "real" human realm where it might be incarnated as a human and experience the vicissitudes and vacuity of mortal existence. It is not until the following chapter, now set firmly in the human world, that we are told that a certain Wang furen (Lady Wang), the wife of Jia Zheng, has a young son who was born with a piece of jade in his mouth, the boy whom they have named Baoyu (Precious Jade).[18] Thus are we given to know that the stone has been successfully incarnated in the form of this scion of a wealthy house, this mysterious boy who has an otherworldly connection to the jade with which he was born.

The stone experiences a (brief) human lifetime as Baoyu, filled with love and disappointment, hope and heartache, which teaches him the illusory nature of attachment and of human existence. When, in the later chapters of *Story*, this enlightened version of Baoyu leaves home to take the imperial examinations (by this time aged nineteen), he suddenly vanishes from the examination hall, having been whisked away by the monk and the Daoist who have reappeared to escort him back to the spiritual realm. In the final chapter we are told that the entire story we have just read was in fact carved upon the body of the sentient block of stone itself, having since returned to its place of origin. (Wu Jianren borrows this device at the end of *New Story*, albeit with the added twist of an illusory message in English for those who are traitors to the nation.)

Paradoxically, the divine Land of Illusion to which the enlightened stone ultimately returns is what is actually persistent and eternal; it is the "real" human world, with its mundane concerns and petty desires, that has been an illusion all along. The overarching message of *Story*, then, is about neither worldly beauty nor romance; it is rather a Buddhist warning about the nature of attachment and illusion. The beautiful homes and possessions of the Jias, their power and social capital, their love affairs and friendships, the charming young women and handsome young men—these are as insubstantial as smoke borne on the breeze or moonlight reflected on water. None can last forever, and in the end to pursue any of them is vanity.

KEY CHARACTERS: FROM *STORY* TO *NEW STORY*

One of things that makes *New Story* such a fascinating sequel to its predecessor is the creative way that Wu appropriates certain of Cao's characters for his own ends. Jia Baoyu is of course the character upon whom much of the attention of *Story* centers: when we are introduced to him at the beginning of the novel, he is a precocious young boy of roughly ten years of age who is doted on and spoiled by his grandmother, but whose antics often get him in trouble with his parents. He is obsessed with all things feminine: he enjoys fine adornments, mischievously plays with and eats (!) various cosmetics when he can get his hands on them, and he prefers the company of his maids and female cousins to the sanctimonious scholars with whom his father would have him associate. To his father's chagrin, Baoyu is wholly disinterested in his studies and applies himself only in the poetic arts—an important skill for a young man in his position, to be sure, but by itself insufficient to pass the imperial examinations that promise the only path to official (and social) success. In the later chapters of the novel, after the family's precipitous decline, Baoyu becomes increasingly disillusioned in the human realm and begins to distance himself from worldly affairs. Though this disinterestedness does not prevent him from sitting for the imperial examinations, it is immediately after he completes them that he retreats forever from the "world of dust" to resume his original form and take up a life of eremitic seclusion.

Given the late-Qing zeitgeist discussed earlier, the reader may well wonder why Wu Jianren borrowed this particular character to serve as his protagonist. Wu himself points to his thinking in brief introductory remarks in chapter 1. There he discusses the prevalence of unofficial "sequels" to *Story* (what we might today consider "fan fiction"), usually written, according to Wu, for the explicit purpose of "fixing" what was to many readers the unsatisfying culmination of the love triangle between Jia Baoyu, Lin Daiyu, and Xue Baochai. Wu self-consciously contemplates what it means to participate in such a literary trend before going on to assert that his own approach will be quite distinct: "Every single person who has written a sequel to *Story of the Stone* uses this opportunity to bring Lin Daiyu back to life and writes endlessly of private affections between the sexes. But what if I merely write that Jia Baoyu hasn't died and goes on to take up some more respectable pursuits?" It is here that the crux of Wu's choice of protagonist lies: he is interested not in the ornate aesthetics or affairs of the heart that had captured the attention of so many readers of *Story*, but rather in the pedagogic possibilities afforded to him by choosing to take Jia Baoyu as his own protagonist. From the outset, Wu asserts Baoyu's former proclivities to have been insufficiently "respectable," and that *his* Baoyu will come instead to embody a new form of respectability. Indeed, Baoyu's former characterization is to be almost wholly rewritten: to start, this new version betrays no interest in women or anything remotely feminine or romantic.[19] And if Baoyu's previous romantic inclinations are not respectable enough for Wu, neither, it would seem, are his religious ones: the "respectable" events of *New Story* can only take place after Baoyu has abandoned his life of Buddhist eremitism, suggesting that neither was that the "correct" path to respectability. Wu clearly intends to illustrate that in spite of the popularity of Cao's Baoyu, such a person should never be taken as any kind of exemplar. Rather, it is the slow forging of Baoyu *into* an exemplar—the kind of moral and politically engaged person demanded by the exigencies of the contemporary age—that is to be the object of Wu's novel.

Though Baoyu might feel familiar to us at the beginning of *New Story*—he remains fastidious about grooming and cleanliness, for example—the longer Baoyu spends exploring late Qing China and the Realm of Civilization, the more he is radicalized by what he witnesses, and the less recognizable he becomes. In other words, Wu has chosen one of best-known characters in Chinese literature only to subvert the audience's expectations for how he should behave. In so doing, Wu criticizes Baoyu's former worldview and proposes an alternative: whereas the Baoyu of *Story* is bored to tears by any talk of politics or governance, in Wu's hands Baoyu is gradually transformed into an avid and opinionated reader of reformist political journals, a man who studies technical manuals and marvels at the benefits that new technologies can bring to society. Baoyu's fantastical journey, then, is not just an opportunity for Wu to showcase two different visions of China; it is also a means by which the formerly apolitical Baoyu is reinscribed with political subjectivity, as was demanded by contemporary discourses on nation, political modernity, and the obligations of progressive literature. Wu's reinscription of Baoyu with socially and nationally oriented values over his former aesthetic and romantic ones (or even the Buddhist disinterest he has achieved by the end of *Story*) asserts the primacy of politics over all else.

Leaving to the side the particularities of Baoyu as a character, he also fulfills an important narrative role: namely, he is a representative of a bygone era, an embodiment of the Qing at its cultural peak, who is alarmed to discover what life is like in this new, alien, semicolonial China. Where other characters, long inured to this state of affairs, are easily distracted from their troubling political reality by amusing technologies or opportunities for personal enrichment, Baoyu alone dares to question the new status quo and vocally express his disdain for it. Through Baoyu's reactions to the things or people he encounters, Wu renders "alien" or de-normalizes commonplaces that would have been readily accepted or taken for granted by large segments of the contemporary audience. Like the metaphorical frog tossed suddenly into a pot of boiling water, our time-traveling Baoyu is immediately shocked and distressed by what he encounters in the late Qing. His horror is clearly intended to alert his complacent, slowly stewing countrymen of the calamity that awaits them all if they remain calmly inside the pot.

■ ■ ■

While Baoyu is the most important figure Wu borrows from *Story*, Wu co-opts three further characters from that novel: Xue Pan, Beiming, and Zhen Baoyu. Each of these is important not just for the role he plays in Baoyu's arc or development but for the ways in which Wu uses him to posit additional social critiques.

Xue Pan is Jia Baoyu's cousin on his mother's side, and is the elder brother of Xue Baochai, to whom Baoyu is eventually married in *Story*. Xue Pan is the worst kind of buffoon: though he can be entertaining at times and is a generous friend, he is ignorant and jealous; he also has a voracious and unrestrained sexual appetite as well as a violent temper. More than once, he is responsible for the violent deaths of other men: early in *Story*, we are told of how he has arranged a conspiracy to callously kidnap a young woman named Yinglian to be his concubine after having her devoted suitor beaten so savagely that the young man eventually dies of his injuries. Owing to the tremendous influence of the Jia and Xue families, Xue Pan faces no consequences for his role in these events and easily skips town with the young woman in tow. The second instance, toward the end of the novel, comes about when Xue Pan, irritated by the behavior of a waiter, smashes a cup over the other's head with lethal force. Perhaps as a sign of the families' waning influence by this late point in *Story*, Xue Pan is actually arrested this time; the family then bribes witnesses into claiming it was a case of accidental death rather than murder, with the result that rather than being executed Xue Pan is merely held in custody until such time as the emperor announces an imperial amnesty.[20] It is to this latter case and subsequent release that Xue Pan alludes when we meet him in chapter 4 of the present text.

In the world of *New Story*, Xue Pan is clearly intended as a foil to Baoyu: he has been in "modern" Shanghai for some time, and rather than reviling it viscerally as his cousin does, he revels in its crass consumerist culture, immediately making himself as comfortable as the proverbial pig in shit. That a man of Xue Pan's ilk should be so impressed with Shanghai and its cultural life is a clear indication that these things are in fact to be condemned. He is furthermore a credulous mark, easily duped by flashy foreign technology, fast talkers, and big promises of personal enrichment; in this way, he also represents the kind of uneducated person who lacks the critical thinking to understand the true peril in which late Qing society found itself, allowing himself always to be dragged along by more sinister actors. Xue Pan's uncritical gullibility is highlighted to particular effect when he is taken in by the obvious charlatanism of the Boxer rebels toward the end of the first half of the novel: whereas Baoyu immediately dismisses the Boxers as an ignorant gang of thugs, Xue Pan is too credulous to doubt their professed abilities and too opportunistic to decline the (dubious) benefits that are promised him.

Shortly before Baoyu finds himself in the Realm of Civilization, he receives a letter from Xue Pan detailing how after fleeing the foreign armies advancing upon Beijing he has met up with a friend by the name of Liu Xuesheng (a pun for "Overseas Student") who has led him to a place called Ziyoucun (Freedom Village). Later, when Baoyu relates the contents of the letter to Lao Shaonian, his guide through the Realm of Civilization, Lao Shaonian exclaims that this Liu Xuesheng is a man of totally corrupt, immoral character and that any "freedom" he would enjoy can only be the basest, most bestial kind. This exchange is important for two reasons: first, it establishes that foreign ideas of "freedom" or individual liberty are inimical to the kind of socially responsible "moral freedom" that is enjoyed in the utopian Realm. But second, Xue Pan's fawning acceptance of Liu Xuesheng and his "immoral" idea of freedom reveals that Xue Pan has learned nothing whatsoever from his previous ordeals and will simply continue to follow one charlatan after another because he lacks the discernment or critical thought to look beyond the satisfaction of his own immediate desires. Writ large, a China populated with Xue Pans would be in trouble, indeed.

Beiming (Tealeaf) is Baoyu's page. In *Story*, Beiming is intensely loyal to Baoyu, defends him in schoolyard scraps, and helps him get away with his various intrigues. Though a good-natured boy, he is of a different class standing than Baoyu, so his language tends to be coarser and less polished; he often fails to understand Baoyu's lofty romantic or poetic intentions, but by the same token he is often cannier about certain mundane concerns than his young master. Beiming as written by Wu serves a few purposes: for one thing, he often provides comic relief, serving in a clownlike role, accidentally turning straightforward conversations into punny jokes as a result of his misapprehensions. More important, however, Beiming provides an alternative perspective on a number of the technological advances Baoyu witnesses in China, usually appraising them with uncritical wonder (I would call the reader's attention to the contrast in Baoyu's and Beiming's perspectives on matches in chapters 2–4, for example). Beiming is easily impressed by most of the new things he encounters and serves to remind the reader that we should perhaps consider them with a more critical eye as his master does. When Beiming is—somewhat startlingly—removed from the narrative prior to Baoyu's admittance into the Realm of Civilization, we should not wonder why: he is a faithful companion, but he is simple, credulous, and coarse, and thus unlikely to meet the Realm's rigorous standards of cultivation.

Finally, we come to Zhen Baoyu, a character who is simultaneously less prominent in *New Story* than Xue Pan and Beiming and yet paradoxically more important to the novel's message than either. In Cao's *Story*, we are told from quite early on that Jia Baoyu (our Baoyu) has a doppelganger of sorts: there is another young boy, named Zhen Baoyu, who is in all ways the double of the other, minus the fact that he has not been born with a piece of jade in his mouth. (That his surname is Zhen is significant: Zhen can be taken as a pun for "real," while Jia can be taken as a pun for "false"—thus the existence of two different Baoyus, the one "real," the other "false," plays into *Story*'s themes related to illusion versus reality.)

While the young Zhen Baoyu is likewise fascinated by women and is known to be a mischievous, troublesome boy, he eventually matures into precisely the kind of dull Confucian that Jia Baoyu tries so desperately to avoid. When the two Baoyus finally meet, Jia Baoyu is caught off guard by how trite and insipid Zhen Baoyu's thinking is, and notes with some disappointment that his clichéd, insincere-sounding comments reflect "the telltale rhetoric of the 'career worm.'"[21] It is this interaction that must inform our reading of Zhen Baoyu in *New Story*.

While technically no character by the name of Zhen Baoyu has so much as a line of dialogue in *New Story*, he does appear. It is eventually revealed to us that Dongfang Wenming (whose name means "Eastern Civilization"), the patriarch and now-retired former emperor of the Realm of Civilization, whose enlightened rulership and custodianship of the Realm Baoyu comes to deeply admire, is none other than Zhen Baoyu going by his true name. And whereas Jia Baoyu once reviled Zhen Baoyu's polished propriety as "careerist," it is precisely Zhen's "dull" Confucian tendencies—a commitment to ethics and the tireless determination of the dedicated public servant—that have enabled Zhen Baoyu/Dongfang Wenming to lead the utopian Realm into an age of peace and prosperity. Thus, Wu Jianren turns the interaction in *Story* on its head: where a reader of *Story* is inclined to empathize with Jia Baoyu and find Zhen Baoyu's moralistic simpering distasteful, in *New Story* it is Zhen Baoyu who has been correct all along. Measured against the duty-driven achievements of his namesake, the free-spirited, frivolous, apolitical dilettantism of Jia Baoyu's misspent youth can only be understood as a waste—and perhaps as precisely the kind of profligate, disengaged attitude that is responsible for China's decline in the first place. When Jia Baoyu laments that Zhen Baoyu/Dongfang Wenming has usurped his own long-cherished purpose of "mending the sky," we can conclude that the Baoyu with the clear sense of Confucian morality and social obligation has always been the "real" one; by comparison, Jia Baoyu has always been false, a hollow vessel containing no meaningful substance.

Wu essentially asserts that while Jia Baoyu might be our protagonist, he is not and has never been our hero. In keeping with Liang Qichao's criticism of the kinds of literature that led people astray, we can conclude that political paragon Zhen Baoyu's/Dongfang Wenming's gentle chiding of Jia Baoyu for his acts of apolitical escapism is meant to be taken as a criticism of the values of *Story* more generally, and of those readers who would, like Jia Baoyu, ignore politics in favor of romance, aesthetic indulgence, or religious escapism.

ON "THE REALM OF CIVILIZATION"

The fantastical Realm of Civilization, which sage authoritarian Dongfang Wenming has ushered into its current state of prosperity, is far from the first utopia in Chinese literature. The most famous classical example is over a millennium older and can be found in Six Dynasties poet Tao Yuanming's (365–427 CE) famous work "The Peach Blossom Spring." In the piece, a traveler happens upon an isolated community composed entirely of the descendants of refugees who fled the tyrannical Qin dynasty (221–206 BCE) hundreds of years prior, and who have since been living in total tranquility, untouched by the troubles of the outside world.[22] To this day, "Peach Blossom Spring" remains one of the most celebrated works in Tao's oeuvre. Importantly, this early example demonstrates that the motif of the utopia specifically as a site of social or political critique is one of long standing in the Chinese literary tradition with which Wu would have been familiar.

Of course, by the time of Wu's writing in the first decade of the twentieth century he would have been influenced not just by native examples but by foreign works that were by that time circulating in translation as well. Scholars have noted, for example, Wu's indebtedness to American author Edward Bellamy's 1888 socialist science-fiction novel *Looking Backward*, which was translated into Chinese in 1894.[23] Bellamy's protagonist, Julian

West, enters a trancelike sleep in 1887 and wakes up over a hundred years later in a future utopian United States wherein all problems of class inequality and labor exploitation—problems that West describes as plaguing his own era—have been resolved. Just like Baoyu in our novel, West is an "outsider" to this utopia, and his curiosity about how everything has changed provides the impetus for lengthy exposition from other characters. However, whereas Bellamy wrote his novel in 1888 about an imagined future year 2000, Wu's novel is distinct in that he writes from 1905 to 1908 about two possible 1900s—the one that was, and the one that *might have been*. In other words, the first half of *New Story*, set in Qing China, exists not just to posit a general critique of late Qing society, but to illuminate just what it is that the Realm of Civilization in the second half is defining itself against. Thus, the Realm's tremendous achievements must be read against the decadent late Qing China we have just been made to witness in the previous chapters. It is worth noting that the narrative dichotomy Wu establishes between China and the Realm is also a clear callback to that between the human world and the Land of Illusion in Cao's *Story*: in each pairing, the former is a land of illusory seductions, while the latter embodies a particular version of principled "truth" or "reality." (However, unlike the religious "truth" to be found in the Land of Illusion, that of the Realm of Civilization is secular and is defined instead in moral, scientific, and political terms.) Much like the community in "The Peach Blossom Spring," the utopian Realm of Civilization has been able to thrive precisely because it exists outside of the contemporary governmental and moral systems that have caused the decline of the real-world

Qing. For one thing, the Realm has maintained a strong belief in the morality that is largely absent in the chapters set in Shanghai and Beijing. For example, in chapter 22, it is revealed that each region of the Realm takes its name from one of the cardinal Confucian values, such as "Benevolence, Righteousness, Ritual, and Wisdom." From the very beginning of Baoyu's time here, then, we are to understand that this is a place steeped in the Confucian ethos. The strong moral code of the Realm, coupled with its enlightened, public-minded populace, stands in stark contrast to the crass, self-interested behavior on display in Shanghai (particularly in the persons of Xue Pan and his crony Bai Yaolian) or the laughable ignorance and superstition of Wang Wei'er and the Boxers in Beijing.

The state of technological development in the Realm is likewise far more impressive than that of the "real" China presented in the first half of the novel; rather than being dependent on European engineers or technology, the Realm boasts a host of ingenious scientists whose inventions are vastly superior to anything Europe can offer. From medical lenses that allow doctors to diagnose ailments at a glance to high-tech food essences that are totally free of impurities and wondrous innovations in civilian transport, Baoyu is treated to a fantastical array of devices and machines, each more splendid than the last. However, it is not just the general superiority of the Realm's technology that is worthy of note: most of it is derived from native epistemologies such as Chinese medicine or textual traditions rather than from foreign ideas, demonstrating that China is and has always been more than capable of innovating for itself. And not only are the Realm's inventions technically superior to the foreigners', but they tend to be morally superior as well: the Realm's technologies are almost always developed in the spirit of humaneness and public service. Indeed, here technology is inseparable from social welfare.

One of the Realm's greatest social projects is its production of knowledge for the edification of its people, perhaps best encapsulated in the institution of the public museum. While he is in the Realm, Baoyu embarks on two lengthy fantastical hunting expeditions, one in a flying car and one in a high-tech military submarine.[24] Upon his return from each journey, Baoyu and his team bring back precious natural artifacts to be displayed in the Realm's many museums. While the hunting trips might appear to be simple (and somewhat tangential) adventure scenes, there are in fact multiple layers of meaning contained therein. On the most basic level, Wu uses these journeys to demonstrate the sheer technological sophistication of the Realm's inventions; on the next level, these exploits verify the existence of creatures recorded in ancient texts like the *Shanhaijing* (Classic of Mountains and Seas), thereby legitimating once again certain of China's native textual and epistemological traditions as "real" knowledge; and finally, and most important, in capturing these specimens, the Realm establishes itself as a producer of the kind of knowledge formerly associated with European colonial expeditions.[25] The filling of the Realm's public museums with "foreign" artifacts is thus not just about knowledge on its face—it is also about power, and more specifically about who does or does not have the power to claim the right of colonial knowledge production. Every artifact brought back to the Realm's museums from outside its borders thus asserts the Realm's position within the global hierarchy of colonial specimen collectors.[26]

The Realm's achievements are not limited to the civilian sphere, however: perhaps its most impressive accomplishments are its overawing military technologies. Wu devotes several chapters to expounding upon these developments—clearly, military strength and readiness was a preoccupation for him. In light of the late Qing context of multiple foreign wars that resulted in crushing defeats, unequal treaties, and exorbitant indemnities, Wu's intention in granting the Realm devastating military capabilities is not difficult to surmise. Given its sheer military might, the Realm has nothing to fear from the West; even so, the Realm's confidence in its military strength does not lead to complacency: the Realm's highly skilled, highly disciplined soldiers and sailors engage in frequent drills to ensure that they are always prepared to defend the Realm from any potential attack.

Notably, however, when Baoyu muses that the Realm could use its awesome military technologies to simply colonize the world, he is told that the Realm has the capacity to do so, but that Dongfang Wenming has refused to permit the Realm to engage in forcible colonialism. Rather, it has always been his hope that the "civilized" Realm will set a positive example by which the other nations of the world might improve themselves. All of this is a fairly clear, albeit implicit, dig at the colonizing practices of "uncivilized" Euro-American powers. In his refusal to engage in forcible colonialism, Dongfang Wenming reinforces the Realm's claim to moral and civilizational superiority vis-à-vis the "barbaric" Westerners. Indeed, throughout the second half of the novel, inhabitants of the Realm continually mock Westerners' uncritical belief in their own civilizational supremacy and condemn foreigners' behavior and values as "barbaric"; this stands in stark contrast to the fawning deference with which foreigners are often discussed in the earlier chapters. The novel thus takes a clear stance against Euro-American colonialism and "civilizing" projects of the nineteenth and twentieth centuries.

Though Dongfang Wenming rejects the logic of outright colonialism, he still envisions an imperialist "civilizing" project of his own. Toward the end of the novel, he expresses a desire to come to the aid of the "red, black, and brown races [who] have long been mired in calamity" by providing them with education and a means of securing their own livelihoods. In the late Qing, it must be remembered, not only had the embattled Qing state found itself making constant concessions to foreign powers, but anti-Chinese racism had also reached a fever pitch in certain parts of the world.[27] To envision the Realm as a paternalistic "savior" of other races—in contrast to the Qing, a weak pariah state whose own subjects and emigrants were being terrorized and discriminated against—is clearly a kind of empowerment or reversal fantasy on Wu's part. Though Wu might feel a sense of common cause with other victims of colonial racism, the reader will notice that he still couches certain assertions in racist language and resorts to disparaging racial stereotypes, usually presented to justify the need for the Realm's paternalistic "civilizing" intervention in other parts of the world.

Most of these instances occur in the second half of the novel, with the longest sustained conversation reflecting such beliefs taking place in chapter 39.

In the final chapter of the novel, we are offered a brief glimpse of the kinds of possibility promised by the civilizing aims of the Realm: while he is a guest in the home of Dongfang Wenming, Baoyu dreams that he travels back to Shanghai from the Realm and is amazed to discover that Dongfang Wenming is now the emperor of all of China; as a result, China has not only earned the respect of the entire global community but has also achieved remarkable economic development. However, as this short-lived dream reaches its dramatic and emotional climax, Baoyu suddenly plunges through the floor and awakens back in his bed in Dongfang Wenming's guest room, where he must come to terms with the fact that none of what he has just witnessed of a thriving, powerful China has actually come to pass. This brief scene, which some readers may find bewildering, is nevertheless key to our understanding of the end of the novel. It has been pointed out that the dream sequence is a variation on the ending of Bellamy's *Looking Backward* wherein protagonist Julian West dreams that he has returned to the iniquity-filled nineteenth century and that the "future" social utopia he has just witnessed has never truly existed. However, whereas West's awakening from his dream is cause for relief, signaling that those bygone days of poverty and immiseration exist only in the mind of the last human to have experienced them firsthand, Baoyu's waking from *his* dream suggests something more troubling. Is the strong China he has just dreamed of truly achievable? Or is it merely a mirage that dissipates upon waking?[28] After all, the imperiled Qing China that has been the cause of so much distress for Baoyu remains just as it was before he fell asleep. As such, the euphoric dream and the jarring negation that comes with Baoyu's waking have been interpreted as a sign of Wu Jianren's ambivalence regarding the future of China, with scholars suggesting that the feverish optimism of the dream is a red herring: rather, the real emotive weight here is the quiet pessimism implied by the idea that such a beautiful dream may in fact be an impossibility.[29]

Ultimately, Baoyu is simultaneously so impressed with Dongfang Wenming's many achievements and so dispirited by his own failure to "mend the sky" that he decides, after waking from his dream, to submit himself to the elder statesman's tutelage. This is a far cry from the Buddhist messaging of the ending of *Story*, where Baoyu, despite having passed the official examinations that would have guaranteed him a career in public service, decides to remove himself from such mundane concerns to sit in eremitic meditation. Instead, by the end of *New Story* he has been persuaded that public service and the welfare of the people are all that matters, and that so long as there are leaders like Dongfang Wenming struggling to make the world better for its inhabitants (and the people of the Realm/China in particular), turning one's back on such endeavors would be shameful.

Before he departs to devote himself to his new mission, Baoyu gives his divine jade pendant away to Lao Shaonian, his erstwhile guide through the Realm, as a token of his appreciation. We are told that he gives it away because it is too painful a reminder of his failure to mend the sky; but the translator suspects that there is something more at play here—that his surrendering of the pendant marks Baoyu's severance from his divine origins, suggesting a commitment to never again retreat into that world. Rather, Baoyu is now fully committed to the world of humanity, and as such his pendant, its divine associations, and the "special" status it once conferred upon him are now meaningless to him. In other words, Baoyu's transformation into a humble but willing political subject is both complete and irreversible.

TRANSLATOR'S NOTE AND ACKNOWLEDGMENTS

MANDARIN *PINYIN* romanization is used throughout the text (with the exception of one case, marked in the notes, in which I found it necessary to venture briefly into Cantonese to execute one of the many name-based puns in the text). I have followed Chinese naming convention throughout, which is to say that surnames appear first, followed by given names: the surname of our protagonist, Jia Baoyu, is Jia, and his given name is Baoyu.

I have tried to the best of my ability to keep my translation faithful to the source text, but there are some departures from the original. In cases I considered to have deviated substantially from the source text, I have provided a note explaining my intervention; but in cases where the departure is fairly minor, I have not felt it necessary to provide notes. To my mind, such "minor" deviations include eliminating repetition of frequently used words or phrases which, though unremarkable in the

Chinese, may have come to feel redundant in English (e.g., using a wider range of speech markers than the original, which almost exclusively uses "said," *dao*, as was common at the time of writing); reworking or otherwise breaking up long multi-clause sentences for flow in English; and adding clarifying context in cases where I felt that a dedicated note was not warranted.

■ ■ ■

Translating *New Story of the Stone* has been a slow but rewarding process. Between a global pandemic, pregnancy, the birth of my daughter, Marianna, and the illnesses and passing of both my mother-in-law, Carolyn, and my own mother, Patricia, life has changed dramatically since I sat down to start translating chapter 1 six years ago. To me, this project is almost like a time capsule, in that it sometimes seems that it was a different person, living in a different world, who translated those first chapters.

I initially embarked on this translation in winter of 2018, during my second year at the University of Rochester, with the sole intention of creating a partial translation for use in my newly created course on late Qing literature. In the weeks before an excerpt of *New Story* was due to be discussed in class, I poured my nights and weekends into translating and was ultimately able to give my students the first seven chapters to read. The project then went into stasis for a little while, but by the time I taught the course again in spring of 2020, I was able to complete another seven chapters, for a total of fourteen (and, as it happened, bringing this second round of students well into the satiric Boxer Rebellion chapters, probably my favorite part of the novel). Translating during the semester required the sacrifice of much of my free time, but it was during those challenging semesters that the foundation for the book project was laid. I would thus like to start by thanking the University of Rochester for giving me the freedom to teach the class, and the students from all iterations of the course for having provided the impetus to initiate and continue work on the project.

There were others who played key roles in getting this project off the ground. I am especially indebted to my dear friend Clara Iwasaki, without whose encouragement this translation might never have made it beyond my classroom. When I first began, I had no immediate plans to seek publication; it was conversations with Clara and her eminently reasonable counsel that convinced me that I should try to bring the project to completion and share it with a wider audience. Her friendship and support have been very precious to me. When the project was still very much in its infancy, Ari Heinrich and Chad Post kindly provided much-needed advice on publishing in translation for which I remain grateful. John Givens and Ryan Prendergast, in their capacity as chairs of the department of Modern Languages and Cultures at the University of Rochester, have been supportive of my endeavors in literary translation and have likewise been indispensable sources of advice.

Peng-sized thanks go out to the people who have contributed to the improvement of the translation itself. My friend and colleague Ping Pian provided her insight on many challenging lines and passages; her careful, thoughtful explanations and clarifications were invaluable to my revision process. Theodore Huters, who first introduced me to *New Story* in a seminar at UCLA in 2010, reviewed the introduction and the entire draft manuscript, making meticulous comments and suggestions throughout. I am grateful for his linguistic, cultural, and historical expertise, as well as the context he provided both in his notes and in his correspondence. His encouragement has meant more to me than I can say. To the anonymous reviewers who read and provided their thoughtful feedback on either the translation or the introduction (or perhaps both), I likewise offer my sincerest thanks. One reviewer of the translation was particularly attentive; their efforts are very much appreciated. Nathaniel Isaacson and June Hwang provided valuable feedback on this introduction, and it is much improved for their suggestions.

I would also like to thank Columbia University Press and the members of the editorial team who helped realize this project. To start, Christine Dunbar has patiently answered my many questions and been a source of helpful advice as I worked to complete the manuscript. I am also grateful to Gregory McNamee for his meticulous and expert editing, as well as to Leslie Kriesel and Zachary Friedman for likewise helping to bring this project to fruition. I deeply appreciate the efforts of all of the aforementioned; of course, any inaccuracies or oversights in the text are solely my own responsibility.

To my knowledge, Sterling Swallow's translation of four chapters of the novel in *Renditions* 77 & 78 (Spring–Autumn

2012) is the only (partial) translation of *New Story* into English that has been published. Swallow's chapter 1 was a valuable reference while I worked on that chapter myself. Places where his interpretations were especially helpful are marked in the endnotes. (I did not come into possession of his other chapters until the present manuscript was complete and already in the final stages of being prepared to go to press.) I have relied on Richard E. Strassberg's richly informative *A Chinese Bestiary: Strange Creatures from the Guideways Through the Mountains and Seas* (a translation of and commentary on the *Shanhaijing*) more than once for identification of the various creatures that Baoyu and his companions encounter during their adventures in the second half of the novel; such instances are also marked in the endnotes. The masterful translation of Cao Xueqin's *Story of the Stone* by David Hawkes and John Minford, published in five volumes by Penguin, has also been an indispensable reference as I have worked to translate this sequel thereto.

Finally, thanks to family and friends who supported me in various ways during the project. Some listened and were happy for me as I excitedly told them about what I was working on. Others humored me by answering strange one-off subject-matter questions as I cast about for *the perfect word*. Heartfelt thanks as well to my husband, Tom—sounding board, support system, and sly humorist in one—and daughter, Mari, who make me laugh even on days when joy seems in short supply. It is to them that I dedicate this work, in acknowledgment of their patience as I shepherded it to its conclusion.

Special recognition should go to my beloved mother, Patricia, a fellow bibliophile and logophile, who was always game to offer her thoughts on my deliberations over various *not-quite-perfect words* or agonized ruminations on compromises and circumlocutions. I miss her dearly and am despondent to know that I will never again be able to pester her with my questions. There are traces of her here, too, and I must take some comfort from that.

NEW STORY OF THE STONE

Chapter One

Reencountering an old servant, affairs of the past seem strange and hazy

Reading over a newspaper, a startling date catches the eye

GENERALLY, IF a person, whether in establishing his career, or in writing essays, wishes to stand out from the crowd, he must be able to plant his own unique banner. If he instead chooses to loiter outside the doorways of others' accomplishments, he falls into the category of being what we would today refer to with the new coinage, "of a dependent nature." Nothing decent can come from such a person's efforts. Let us not speak for now on other matters of import but focus instead upon the realm of fiction, where the aforementioned is especially true.

If you don't believe me, just read the *Tale of the Western Chamber*, taking "Startled from a Dream" to be its true ending; later writers then continued it in all sorts of directions, only to be thoroughly censured for it by Jin Shengtan.[1] There was one *Outlaws of the Marsh*, but sequels like *Quelling the Bandits* came under criticism by those who came after. There was one *Journey to the West*, but hardly anyone even knows about the *Latter Western Journey* that followed it. This being the case, why bother appending a wretched dog's tail to the rear of a mink and making oneself the target of mockery?

At the present moment, as I for no particular reason draft this *New Story of the Stone*, am I not also adding feet to the snake? Ever since the publication of Mr. Cao Xueqin's original *Story of the Stone*, others have followed up with countless sequels: *A Continuation of the Dream of the Red Chamber*; *Further Dreams of the Red Chamber*; *Supplemental Dreams of the Red Chamber*; *Dreaming Again of Embroidered Chambers* . . . all types of fantastical and absurd stories, too many to list them all! Of those who have read them, not a single person has ever claimed they were any good. Surely my own present venture must also be committing the same error?

And yet, as I see it, when a person raises his brush to write, he must first have some kind of intention. As he sets his brush to paper, it's not necessarily that he hopes to earn the praise of those around him; rather, he acts according to his own motivations, simply writing what is in his own heart. Whether those who come after judge it harshly or not has nothing to do with him. And so I too harbored this idea, not hiding myself from any potential criticism that may result, and wrote this *New Story of the Stone*. Whether you, readers, praise it or condemn it, I shall not be able to hear in any case.

But let us speak no more of idle things and return our focus to the story at hand. Every single person who has written a sequel to *Story of the Stone* uses this opportunity to bring Lin Daiyu back to life and writes endlessly of private affections between the sexes. But what if I merely write that Jia Baoyu hasn't died and goes on to take up some more respectable pursuits?[2] Although it's a little absurd, it may yet elicit a few laughs. Readers, listen for a moment if you will, as I compose for you a prologue:

Settled the country; the state, at peace—
  fine youth, thine aspirations worthy indeed
But thy cosmos is merely the size of a bean!
  How can it resist the cruel winds of caprice?
From a dragon-spring blade of only three feet
  shines forth a dazzling 100,000-foot beam
'Tis a pity that 'tween the glorious gleam
  of celestial orbs and thee,
Lie demons and impediments two, three, hundred
  lay'rs deep
That harm men by filling them with yearnings keen,
  akin to lunacy!
Harm men by filling them with yearnings keen,
  akin to lunacy!
Dear little head, no place for thee
  to stop and think or lay thee down to sleep
Which leaves only the chestful of hot blood thou bleed'st,
  and the thousand trails of tears thou weep'st
Splashed out upon the eastern sea,
  in terrifying waves they surge and seethe
Turn thy head and suddenly:
  everything that came before is mere absurdity!
The most egregious, these:
  deeds literary and military; celebrity; prosperity
Considering what is yet to come, all are but entries
  in a muddled account book spanning centuries

■ ■ ■

Our tale begins in the year in which Jia Baoyu had brought Jia Lan with him to take the imperial examinations. Sometime after the third round of exams had finished and it was time to leave the examination hall, the numinous monk and otherworldly Daoist adept were already outside, waiting to lead Baoyu to return to truth and simplicity.[3] Thus, when Jia Lan turned around and looked, Baoyu was nowhere to be seen. You should know that Baoyu had already come to completely understand the cycle of causality and decided to free himself from it once and for all. So, no matter how the members of his family clamored about looking for him until all was in a state of chaos, he left everything behind without looking back. The monk and the Daoist first led him to the Piling post station so that he might bid farewell to his father Jia Zheng; they then deposited him beneath Greenridge Peak of the Great Barren Mountain, wove for him a thatched hut, and instructed him to begin the arduous task of self-cultivation.

Without knowing how many centuries or calamities passed him by in the outside world, Baoyu always remained detached, as if his heart were made of shriveled wood or dead ash. He watched hundreds or perhaps thousands of years pass as if they were a single day. But it was fated that something should happen, and one day Baoyu suddenly thought, "On the day that Nüwa forged the five-colored stones for the purpose of mending the sky, she used up 36,500 of them, and I was the only block that remained unused. Later, although I was imbued with sentience, all I did was spend several years gadding about with a bunch of girls, and never fulfilled my true purpose of mending the sky. How can I fulfill this aspiration? Even if I were to be transformed into ash or smoke afterward, I should no longer have any regrets."[4]

As these worldly thoughts took hold, the blood suddenly surged in his heart, and little by little he was engulfed by his fervent desires as by a growing flame. He completely forgot what he had learned about the cycle of causality and wished to return home just once, so that he might fulfill his aspiration. However, he also thought that he had already become a monk and shaved off his queue—how could he possibly go back looking so ridiculous?[5] Not only would his father be furious if he saw him this way, but if his sisters were to see him, they would be put off by his poor grooming. There was nothing for it but to wait a while for his hair to grow back before setting off. Having made up his mind, he waited day after day for his hair to grow.

Oddly, during his time of arduous self-cultivation, who-knows-how-many centuries and calamities had flitted by as quickly as a single day; and yet, now that he wanted his hair to grow, each day felt longer than a year. Every day he hoped that he would find his hair longer than the day before, but his hair stubbornly refused to grow as quickly as he would have liked. Exasperated, he spent his days in his hut, muttering and sighing. After an agonizing year, his hair had grown to be about a foot long—finally just long enough to plait! Delighted, he hastily threw his hair up in a braid. Opening his bag, he saw that the fairly newish set of layman's clothes he had brought from home to wear during the official examinations was still there. He pulled them out and put them on, tying round his neck his precious jade amulet. Somewhat absent-mindedly he pulled another object from the bag: taking it out and looking at it, he realized that it was the small mirror he had wheedled out of Daiyu's maid Zijuan back in the day. Giving himself a once-over in the glass, he felt that his appearance was much as it always had been. He then straightened his apparel, emerged from his hut, and, without even discerning which direction he was taking, he set off.

He hoped that he would encounter someone from whom he could ask directions. How could he have known that he would meet nary a soul along the way? The sun was already setting behind the mountains in the west, and though he didn't know how far he had come, he was pleased to note that his feet had not yet grown weary. Turning to look behind him, he realized that he could no longer make out even a dim outline of Greenridge Peak. He had no idea where he had gotten to.

Pacing back and forth in uncertainty, he suddenly raised his head and saw that a black cloud had formed above him, growing steadily in size as he walked. In a short while it began to pour down rain. Baoyu anxiously stamped his foot and said aloud, "I've really done it this time! There's not a house to be found anywhere around here, where can I go to get out of the rain for a bit?" Since no answers came to him, all he could do was take to his feet and run. As he ran onward, he eventually came upon a forest and quickly ducked into it, hoping that there might be a house among the trees where he could take shelter. Making his way into the forest, he raised his head and looked around him. While there were still no houses to be found, there was, fortunately, a dilapidated temple. Baoyu felt as though he had stumbled upon a great treasure and hurried into the temple yard. The temple gate had already fallen and offered no protection from the deluge, so Baoyu had no choice but to dash into the main hall.

The ancient trees surrounding the temple blocked out the sky in all directions, and as dusk had already begun to fall, the hall was shrouded in an eerie blackness. Baoyu had entered in haste, and as he ran into the passageway he caught his foot on something in the dark and tumbled to the ground. As he was about to pull himself to his feet, a voice suddenly cried out, "Who's the eyeless bastard who dares kick his own master?"

Baoyu was about to help the other person up, but upon hearing his voice found it extremely familiar. Unconsciously narrowing his eyes, he closely examined the person before him; the young man scrutinized Baoyu in turn. Suddenly, the other man drew closer and threw his arms around Baoyu, exclaiming, "Aiya! My ancestor and young master! You have finally reappeared! Your servant doesn't deserve to live!" As it turns out, this man was none other than Beiming, Baoyu's erstwhile page.

Baoyu was delighted and inquired, "What has brought you here? What is this place?"

Beiming replied, "How long has Master been walking? How is it that you are still dressed like that? Don't you even know where you've gotten yourself to?" As he spoke, he glanced outside. Amid the twilight he was able to make out the collapsed temple gate and was startled: "Oh no! My slumber has left me a bit addled—how is it that I've ended up in this place? Second Master, what time is it?"

Baoyu said, "You must be *very* addled, my lad! You've slept so deeply that you've forgotten what time it is? Surely it's twilight?"

Beiming replied, "Oh dear, I went to bed early last night. How can I have slept away the entire day?" He added, "This appears to be a rundown temple, totally abandoned. How can we get a fire started in here?" He thought for a moment, then was pleased to realize that his fire-starting kit was still in the bag that he carried on his person. He pulled out a flint and struck it a number of times. Despite the cascade of sparks that erupted, he was unable to get a piece of wick to light. He became impatient and began feeling about to find his way in the darkness. Feeling his way eastward along the wall, he came upon a door and pushed it open. On the other side there was another courtyard that let onto two small rooms. From one of the rooms shone a light.

Beiming happily thought, "There must be someone there!" and strode into the room. There was an elderly Daoist squatting on the floor, tending a fire. The monk raised his head and, seeing Beiming, uttered a startled "Ya!" before running to hide himself in the corner, where he repeatedly called out the name of the bodhisattva Guanyin.

Beiming was taken aback, and said, "I'm no villain! So why would you need to call out for the bodhisattva?"

The Daoist replied, "Aren't you the sculpture of the child-immortal that lay fallen in the hall?"

Beiming paid this no mind, and instead quickly became interested in the scent of porridge that he suddenly smelled wafting from the old man's kettle. He felt flames of hunger licking his insides and could barely stop himself from seizing the porridge and eating it. He then realized that Baoyu was probably hungry as well and thought it best to call him in. They could request a bowlful from the old man—hopefully, it would be enough to get through the night at least, and they could reassess things in the morning. Having thus decided, Beiming emerged from the room and went back for Baoyu; the pair then returned together.

Just as they reached the door that let into the courtyard, they suddenly saw someone coming out toward them. The figure brushed past, then darted off, disappearing like a wisp of smoke. Baoyu was startled and wondered what was going on. He then followed Beiming into the room. As Beiming looked around, he noticed that the old monk was now nowhere to be seen: upon entering the inner room, he saw that it too was empty.[6] Baoyu had by this time acquired a lamp and, glancing at Beiming, was shocked by his countenance. He asked, "My lad, what have you been getting up to that you're so grimy?"

"Grimy?"

Baoyu pulled out the small mirror and told Beiming to look at himself. When Beiming did so, he realized that his face was coated in dust and filth nearly an eighth of an inch thick. Beiming, too, found this both startling and a bit comical. He hurriedly set down the mirror and searched the premises for a basin and washcloth. He also located a pitcher of water, and without even bothering to heat it up gave his face a good scrubbing. He could feel that his entire body must be coated in dust. There was nothing for it but to strip down completely and shake out his clothes. As he did so he cursed, "That old bastard must have played some kind of prank on me!" After shaking out his clothes, he donned them once again. He then found a bowl and chopsticks, gave them a quick wash, and filled the bowl with the old man's porridge, which he proffered to Baoyu. Baoyu finished one bowl but ate no more. He asked, "Where did this porridge come from?"

Beiming answered, "Don't worry about it, Master. We'll get to that after you've finished eating."

Baoyu then asked, "What *is* this place, anyway?"

By this time Beiming was so hungry that he could hardly stand it, so he began to fill another bowl with porridge as he replied, "Ever since Master disappeared, everyone back home has been kicking up such a fuss that even the chickens were aflutter and the dogs couldn't sit still. Everyone from your grandmother all the way down was in tears. The servants like me have been running around every day searching for you. Afterward, they put up the notice board saying that Master had ranked seventh in the *juren* examinations."[7] Reaching this point, he exclaimed, "That's right! I still haven't congratulated you, Master!" Before he had finished speaking, he knelt and knocked his head against the floor. He then stood up and continued, "Back then, the family caused such a fuss that even the emperor knew about it! He issued an edict, ordering all of the *yamen* to investigate your disappearance together. But they still weren't able to obtain any information. Later, when your father returned from his posting, he said that he had seen you at the Piling post station and that you had already become a monk. Your mother believed it at first, but as time went by and she brooded on it more and more, she no longer did. She said that when your father had encountered the monk he supposed to be you, the monk hadn't actually spoken to him. She worried that perhaps his eyes had gone blurry, that perhaps he had misrecognized this person as you. And so she once again called for a search to be undertaken. The capital was searched in its entirety, as was a perimeter around it. She even sent people to go separately to search in the south—and so I was sent to Jinling. She worried that Master might have returned to the southern mansion to live for a while on a lark, and thus she sent me to come look.[8]

"When I entered the boundaries of Jinling, it was already growing late in the day, and since I was still over ten li from the city, I didn't think I'd make it to the city gates before they were closed for the night.[9] So when I arrived at a certain 'Jade Cloud Temple,' I decided to spend the night. That temple glittered with gold and emeralds—it was really very exquisite—and was home to over a hundred monks. They allowed me to stay the night in one of the wings. I've no idea how it is that once I went to sleep I managed to sleep until now, or how I managed to sleep myself into this strange place. I must be mixed up." He finished his porridge as he related all of this.

Baoyu was stunned and bewildered by this report and asked, "Whose porridge was this? How is it that there's nobody here?"

Beiming replied, "Master, for now it's best not to ask about it." He added, "There's a bed here, so we'll camp out here for the night. Tomorrow we'll go into the city and return to your family's mansion." Baoyu assented, so Beiming took the lantern from him and went into the inner room.

Baoyu followed him and noticed that beneath the window there was a square table across which were strewn a number of books. Baoyu sat beside the table, and casually reached out to pick up one of the books, thinking that he could sit and do a little reading to stave off boredom. He leafed through the first book and found that it was a volume of the Ming novel *Investiture of the Gods*. He quickly set it back down and picked up another book, which turned out to be a copy of *Immortal Footprints in Green Fields*. He had no interest in reading these; but then he noticed a small bundle of books that had been wrapped in paper imprinted with characters. He pulled the bundle over and opened it up—inside were merely a few volumes of the Classics. However, Baoyu felt that the printed paper in which the books had been wrapped was very strange, indeed, and spread the sheet out to look at it better. The word *NEWS* was emblazoned across the top. A small tear in the paper made it difficult to read what came after the word *NEWS*, but it did seem that there had been something else printed there. What that word was or should have been, however, Baoyu could not say.[10]

Farther down the sheet there were words in small print, which Baoyu pored over carefully. As it happened, it was an essay. When he read the other side, Baoyu found all sorts of current events detailed and began to feel darkly perplexed. Flipping the paper from one side to the other, he read through it over and over again. Some things he was able to understand; others he was not. He flipped it to the front page yet again and started when he discovered that the first line read: "Great Qing, Guangxu 26th year, such and such month, such and such day; Western Calendar: Year 1900, such and such month, such and such day, Sunday."[11] Baoyu couldn't help but be alarmed.

■ ■ ■

If you wish to know what so alarmed him, please listen to the explanation in the following chapter.

Chapter Two

Reemerging into the world of dust, he first enters the City of Stone

Remembering bygone events, he gloomily reads Dream of the Red Chamber

WE WERE speaking of how Baoyu had seized the sheet of printed paper and been stunned upon reading it.[1] He thought, "Just how long have I been away from home? Looking at this sheet of paper, it must be of a kind with the *Capital Gazette* I am accustomed to. But this doesn't just publish internal government documents—it also publishes current events, so naturally they print a new one every day. Looking at the date, it's obvious that the reign name changed sometime after I left home. It makes me angry to think that while I was muddling along in my 'self-cultivation' I became so addled that I never bothered to keep track of the date! And looking below the date there, what's this '1900' business? That's even further beyond me."

In the midst of these thoughts, Beiming entered giggling and said, "Master, look! What the heck do you think this is?" As he finished speaking, he produced a tiny box and handed it to Baoyu.

Baoyu took it from him and looked it over. The little box had yellow paper pasted on it; the top was emblazoned with the word "Xiechang," while on the reverse side there was a small, fine drawing. When Baoyu tried to open it, however, he found that the box had no lid; he turned the box over, examining all sides of it, before realizing that it was the sort of box where a small drawerlike tray was nested inside a hollow shell, and which could be slid open from either end. He slid the box open and found that it was filled with small sticks, each with a small red thing at one end. He handed the box back to Beiming, saying, "It's just something for children to play with."

Beiming took it back, and, taking out one of the tiny sticks, looked it over carefully. He muttered to himself, "But how do you play with it?" Holding the stick in his hand, he held the red dot idly over the lamp flame to watch it burn. Who would have expected that as soon as Beiming introduced the object to the flame it would ignite with loud HUFF, startling both men?

Baoyu scolded, "Stop playing with that. It must be a fire starter."

Beiming, of course, was unwilling to listen. "Such a tiny little head, but when it ignites, it makes such a big fire! Let's take the heads from all of them and pile them together in the courtyard to make a big fireball to play with!" As he spoke, he searched out a small nail on the floor. Crouching, he dumped out the entire contents of the box and began using the nail to scrape the red dots off the sticks. He managed to scrape the dots off the first two, but when he tried a third one, he wasn't sure exactly how, but with a PAH, that red dot had ignited itself!

Beiming was both startled and delighted. Meanwhile, Baoyu, with his head cocked to one side, watched from beside him.

"Quit playing around! Let me see."

Beiming handed one of the sticks to him.

"And the box?"

Beiming passed the box to him. Baoyu looked the box over for a second time and said to Beiming, "Look—the box is very rough on one side, as if made with sand. There are several lines of red powder visible on the rough surface, perhaps one is meant to scrape the red dots across this rough material in order to set them alight. Why don't you try one and see?"

Beiming duly took one of the sticks and scraped it firmly along the box's surface, but the stick only snapped in two.

"Dummy!" snapped Baoyu. "Lighter next time."

Beiming took up another stick and very delicately brushed it upward over the same spot. He made two such passes with no result, worried that if he exerted too much force, the stick would simply break again.

"Too light," said Baoyu.

Beiming gave it one last try, and sure enough, the stick ignited itself with a PAH once again. Beiming excitedly said, "Second Master is so wise! I could have tried for a whole lifetime and never figured out that this is how you're meant to light them!"

Baoyu replied, "Quick, pick them up! These things can make fire—be gentle with them, don't bump them on anything. You just saw that merely scraping them with a nail made them burst into flames!"

As he began to gather up the sticks, Beiming mused, "Making fire like this sure is a lot more convenient than carrying around a fire-starting kit! Since we've got these now, I don't need that old thing anymore."

Baoyu took up one of the burned-out sticks and examined it closely. The little red dot, once burned, had turned into ash. Picking up the box, he scratched the stick along the rough surface, but it immediately crumbled. He thought, "Ah, so a stick can be burned only once. It would be even better if it could be used multiple times!" He watched as Beiming continued to pick up the sticks from the floor.

Beiming said, "Second Master, please go to bed! Tomorrow we'll go to the family residence—I also have to return to the capital so I can announce the good news of your reappearance."

"Then I'll make do with this bed," Baoyu replied. "What about you?"

"Don't worry about me, Master, I've got a place to sleep."

At this, Baoyu lay down to sleep, still fully clothed. Beiming warned him, "If you undress to sleep, whatever you do, be careful you don't catch a chill!"

"I'm not like I was before—now I can make do with anything, whatever the circumstances. And my health is fine, I won't catch a chill."

Beiming closed the door, then pulled several chairs together in front of the doorway, aligning their seats to make a sleeping surface, and lay down across it.

"Why are you sleeping like that?" Baoyu asked.

"I'm scared Master will try to run away again. I simply couldn't bear it if you did!"

Baoyu laughed. "Relax, I'm not running off again."

Of that evening, we have nothing further to report.

■ ■ ■

Baoyu awoke at dawn the next day and called out to Beiming to run out to the outdoor stove and heat some water. Baoyu perfunctorily washed his face, then master and servant set out together. They passed back through the small door; outside they saw the three-room main hall, which was peeling and decaying; the two cloisters had already largely collapsed, and the sacred sculptures that ought to have flanked each side were strewn about haphazardly. Looking back as they passed through the temple gate, the wooden sign reading "Jade Cloud Temple" still hung, albeit crookedly, overhead.

Beiming felt in a bit of a daze as he thought, "The 'Jade Cloud Temple' where I spent the night had such beautiful carved beams and painted rafters. How is it that after sleeping for just one night I've awoken to find that it has changed so drastically?" He felt unsure and confused as they continued down the path. For his part, Baoyu had also been extremely unnerved by the date on that sheet of newspaper—moreover, he did not even know where they were—and so could only walk along aimlessly.

After they had walked four or five li, they reached a tiny village. There, they saw an elderly man approaching them, carrying a farming implement. Beiming went forward and inquired, "Please tell me, old sir, we are trying to reach the city of Jinling. Which way do we go? What is this place?"

The old man responded, "This is called Wuwei Village,[2] it falls under the administration of Jinling. If you wish to enter the city, just head east. In no more than ten li you'll have arrived."

Beiming thanked the old man, and together he and Baoyu went east. Gradually, they began to see houses emerging on the horizon.

Once they had entered the city wall, Baoyu said, "Well, we've gotten into the city—now where is the family residence?"

"Don't worry, Master," chimed in Beiming. "Our family is among the esteemed nobility, as soon as we ask someone, they'll be able to tell us." Saying this, he reached out and grabbed a passer-by and asked, "Where is the Rong Guo *fu*?"[3] The person did not know. Beiming went and asked other people. He asked five or six people in a row, but not one of them knew of the Rong Guo *fu*.

Baoyu cut in, "How can you expect random people on the street to know? Go into a shop and ask."

Beiming did as he was told and asked several shopkeepers—who, it turned out, did not know either. Baoyu was perplexed and wondered to himself, "Perhaps this isn't Jinling at all. Maybe we've come the wrong way?"

"We've walked half the day, and I'm exhausted!" moaned Beiming. "Does Master see those teahouses? Look how many people are there drinking tea—why not go in for a bowl and rest for a little bit before we continue?" Baoyu nodded in assent.

Baoyu selected a clean-looking teahouse and went in, choosing a seat for himself. Beiming found a seat beside him. The waiter brewed tea for them, and Baoyu slowly savored it. He ruminated that perhaps the fact that Beiming had asked so many people about Rong Guo *fu* without result was due to Beiming's lack of eloquence. But it would also not do for Baoyu to wander out into the street and ask himself. So he determined that the best strategy would be to use drinking tea as a pretext and wait for a convenient moment to ask someone in the teahouse. He waited a while until he saw that another customer—one of a relatively dignified demeanor—had taken the seat beside him. Baoyu thought, "He might know—I might as well try asking him." Thereupon, he stood up and folded his hands in a polite salutation before asking, "One who has lost his way requests to enquire whether thou, elder brother, might condescend to point out the way?"

The other party hurriedly got to his feet and returned Baoyu's greeting, then said, "If you need directions, I'll tell you if I know—there's no need to be so polite!"

Baoyu told him, "I want to get to Rong Guo *fu*, but I don't know which road I should take."

The man listened and gave Baoyu a once-over before replying, "Older brother, it seems that perhaps you don't get out much. I think your question is a little off."

"What do you mean?"

"I only know of a Ning Guo *fu*, I don't know of any Rong Guo *fu*."

Baoyu was delighted. "That's fine! If you can tell me where to find Ning Guo *fu*, I can find Rong Guo *fu* by myself."[14]

"That's even stranger—how is it that you can find your Rong Guo *fu* from Ning Guo *fu*?"

"Older brother may not know, but the inhabitants of the two *fu* are of the same family. If I can get to Ning Guo *fu*, naturally I can find my way home from there."

The man was beginning to grow impatient. "If you want to get to Ning Guo *fu*, you'll have to take a steamer to Wuhu to start, then hire either a private boat or a horse to go the rest of the way. You can of course get there that way, but why are you asking about it in Nanjing? You must know that Ning Guo government offices are in Anhui!"

Baoyu stared at him. "I don't mean the Ning Guo *government*! I mean the *mansions* belonging to the dukes of Ning Guo and Rong Guo."

The man shook his head. "Then I don't know."

Before Baoyu could respond, Beiming interjected, "Don't pay any attention to him, Master. Our Jia family residences are known to everyone in Nanjing and Beijing. If he doesn't know, he must be some kind of bumpkin, it's no use to keep asking him." The man overheard this but paid Beiming no mind.

Under his breath, Beiming continued, "Even an old woman like Granny Liu could find her way to our house! Of course, our southern residence couldn't have been forfeited or turned over to someone else without anyone knowing about it. What a strange business this is."[5]

The man, still listening, stared at Baoyu, then looked over at Beiming. Turning back to Baoyu, he asked, "What are you talking about?"

Baoyu replied, "No one's talking about anything. If you, older brother, can't answer my question, then let's be done with it. I'll come back and ask someone else."

"But just now, it sounded like maybe you're trying to find the home of Jia Baoyu from *Dream of the Red Chamber*?"

"Exactly so!" Baoyu was elated. "But I don't understand this *Dream of the Red Chamber* you mentioned."

"Reading too many novels has turned your brain to mush," the man laughed. "Did you just want to see the house? Or were you hoping to meet Jia Baoyu? Or maybe see Lin Daiyu?"

"But—I *am* Jia Baoyu."

Beiming interrupted, "Second Master is standing in front of you! Why are you addressing him by his given name rather than his title? It's inappropriate."

The man, still somewhat agog, pointed to Beiming. "And who is this?"

"He's Beiming, my personal servant," answered Baoyu.

The man raised his head, staring up at the sky in disbelief, then rubbed his eyes. "Oh dear! Either I'm seeing ghosts, or I've encountered a couple of lunatics."

As he spoke, another young man approached them. Seeing him, the first man bade the new arrival to come sit and said, "I've always said you young people shouldn't go about reading nothing but novels! Why, just as I would have expected, here's someone who's read them to the point of ridiculousness! Previously, I read some 'notebook' or other, and written on its cover was a line claiming that this book was just as full of romantic longing and feminine beauty as *Tale of the Western Chamber*, to the point that it was capable of causing melancholic pining. I thought it was meant as a warning to readers, but who knew . . .?" Having said this, he pointed a finger at Baoyu, and went on, "This guy is claiming that he's Jia Baoyu, and keeps asking about whatever Ning Guo mansion or Rong Guo mansion. Don't you agree he must have read *Dream of the Red Chamber* to the point of delusion?"

The man had raised his voice as he lectured Baoyu and as a result had captured the attention of the other customers in the teahouse, who all came over and gathered around Baoyu, staring at him. Baoyu found this quite uncomfortable and arose awkwardly. He told Beiming to pay for the tea they'd drunk, and once he had done so, they left. Baoyu then turned to Beiming: "I was already feeling a bit muddled, and now after listening to that man, I feel doubly so. It appears as though we may not be able to find our home as quickly as we'd hoped. Perhaps it's best to find temporary lodgings for now, and then we can continue discussing what to do." The two men found an inn and selected a tidy room to stay in, then got to work bringing in and setting out their baggage. Beiming first went into the inner room and took care of setting up Baoyu's sleeping mat before going on to straighten up the connected anteroom in which he himself would be staying. Baoyu then instructed Beiming to go out to buy some stationery, brushes, and ink so that he might use them upon Beiming's return. Beiming assented and went out.

In very little time Beiming had purchased paper, ink, an inkstone, and a brush—the "four treasures" of a scholar's study—and making his way back to the inn, he took the further liberty of buying the accoutrements for making tea. In his youth at home, Baoyu had enjoyed rich foods and fine literature, as well as the pleasures of face powder, greasepaint, rouge, and perfume. Once he'd left home, however, not only had he lived among stones and trees and wandered with deer and boars, but his ears had ceased to hear and his eyes ceased to see. He didn't know how many generations had passed, or how many calamities had occurred. But now, seeing how even the simple, functional objects his servant had brought him from outside now seemed so fine and delicate, he couldn't help but turn them over and over in his hands.

Suddenly his thoughts turned to the man they'd encountered in the teahouse and to this *Dream of the Red Chamber*, which was evidently some kind of novel. "He said I'd read it to the point of delusion," thought Baoyu, "which is why I claim to be Jia Baoyu. But I obviously *am* Jia Baoyu, and since when have I ever heard of any *Dream of the Red Chamber*? When I think back to my youth, meeting Zhen Baoyu—the boy who shared my given name, and even looked like me—was already strange enough![6] Did that man in the teahouse honestly mean to say that this *Dream of the Red Chamber* features someone with the same given name *and* surname as myself? Well, I simply must read it and find out what it's all about!" His thoughts ending here, Baoyu picked up a pen and wrote down the words "*Dream of the Red Chamber*," then sent Beiming off to a bookstore to purchase a copy.

Beiming returned a short while later with his purchase, and Baoyu saw that he had brought back a stack of books nearly a foot high. He didn't look them over closely but picked up the first volume, hoping to find a table of contents. He was surprised to find that this was an illustrated volume. Seeing the names of the characters listed under their illustrations, he silently thought that it was indeed strange. Flipping haphazardly through the pages to the end, he finally came to a listing of the chapter titles. Reading carefully through them, he was startled, suspicious, and unsettled. He read through all of the titles before moving on to the text proper.

He really only wanted to read about the character Jia Baoyu, so he skimmed haphazardly through anything that wasn't related to him, reading only the sections he thought were important. The more he read, the more unsettled he became. "As I read through the events of this novel," he thought, "and reflect back upon my own life, it all now seems as though it were a world away. Even if I look to the events of the novel as confirmation of how I've ended up in this situation, it still feels as though I'm dreaming." Unconsciously, the more he read, the deeper in thought he fell. And the more he thought, the more he kept reading, and as a result he became even more dumbfounded.

Suddenly he saw Beiming come back in, giggling to himself. "Master!" he called, "Guess how much money this thing is worth!"

■ ■ ■

If you wish to know what it is that Beiming had brought with him, please listen to the explanation in the following chapter.

Chapter Three

Hearing the name of a beloved startles the heart and adds to his bewilderment

When trying Western food, he is filled with wonder at its strangeness

WE WERE speaking of Baoyu, who had been pacing back and forth anxiously, when suddenly Beiming entered the room holding the yellow paper box they had found in the temple. Laughing, Beiming demanded that Baoyu guess how much the box was worth. Baoyu, too distracted by his own thoughts, completely ignored him. This state of abstraction passed after a little while, and Baoyu returned once again to reading. Beiming dared not speak again, so he stood there for a while before withdrawing from the room. Baoyu read on in total absorption, as if anxious to finish the entire book in one go. He read without stopping even to sleep or to eat, staying up through the night as though preparing classwork. Indeed, he read with even greater intensity than all those times he'd worked late revising his classwork in order to placate his father. He read for two half-days and an entire night before finishing, and when he had finally read the whole thing, he continued to sit stupefied, taking neither tea nor food.

Beiming was worried and had no idea what to do to help his master. He could only think of the last time he had seen his master go into this kind of fit—perhaps this was like that time, when Baoyu had gone comatose after losing his precious jade.[1] But this time, none of the girls was here at his side, so Beiming was at a loss. Several days passed in this way, and Beiming felt increasingly helpless. Finally, the only useful thing he could think to do was to go out and continue his inquiries into the location of the Rong Guo mansion. He had worked his way through practically the entire city of Nanjing but was unable to find so much as a trace.

One day, when he returned from searching, he said to Baoyu, "It's no good for us to stay here long term, it would be best to return to the capital for now. Your parents had great hopes that you would return, and my original intention was to seek out the southern family mansion, then get a few of the staff to help escort you back to the capital. But since we can't find it now, it's up to me to look after you."

Baoyu replied, "I'm still feeling quite out of it, as if I've lost control of myself. I just worry that if I go back to the capital with you, I might not feel up to seeing my family."

"Why would Master say something so unlucky? If you go into the capital and find your parents, can't you imagine how happy they'll be? When I was outside the second gate shortly after your disappearance, I heard an old woman say that after you left, the mistress had had some happy news.[2] Perhaps that means another young gentleman has been born into your family—if you go back to the capital now, you should be prepared to make the transition to being an 'old master' rather than a 'young master'!"

"Bah! Stop wagging your tongue! Go to the clerk's office and ask them to hire a horse or a boat for me, so we can go up to the capital." Beiming assented and went out.

A short while later Beiming led the clerk into the room, saying, "In response to your request, Master, they've said that we can take neither a horse nor a boat to go to the capital!"

The clerk said, "Our guest must be from the hinterland and so doesn't understand river and coastal transport! If you wish to get to Beijing, it's not worth going slowly waystation by waystation all the way north. All you need to do is take the steamboat to Shanghai; then from Shanghai, take another steamboat to Tianjin. From Tianjin, you can take the train to the capital. Once you're on the train, you'll be in Beijing in no time. Just now, when your steward came to inquire about hiring a horse, or chartering a boat—isn't that taking the hard road when you could take the easy one?"

Baoyu said, "How big are these 'steamboats'? How many people do they hold?"

"I couldn't tell you how big they are, but they can carry several hundred people per trip."

Beiming hastily interrupted, "Enough, enough! Not another word! No matter how big it is, if they fit several hundred people into it, surely it's unbearably cramped! My master is not accustomed to such crowded conditions."

The clerk replied, "You are unfamiliar with it, I see. If one rides in the steerage compartment, then yes, it may be crowded. But if one has a private cabin, it's much better. And if one stays in a 'stateroom' cabin, it's even more comfortable than being in one's own home! Just like home, it has a parlor for receiving guests, and the food is good! The ship's compradors come check in on you, and idlers are kept well away.[3] If you are enamored of quiet and cleanliness you can ride first class, where foreign-style meals are served, and you are served by waiters the whole way. I'm afraid you couldn't achieve such comfort even at home!"

Baoyu pressed him, "When were these steamboats invented? And what is a 'comprador'? What is a 'waiter'?"

The clerk silently thought, "Even if he'd never seen one before, surely he's heard other people talk about them! Is it possible that these two are complete simpletons?" But aloud, he merely gave a quick explanation of the origins of the steamboat and the types of work done by compradors and waiters.

"I don't believe it! Such a large ship would require hundreds of people just to row the oars or punt it along!" said Beiming.

"It runs on machinery. If it relied upon men rowing or punting, it wouldn't be called a 'steamboat.'"

To himself, Baoyu thought, "A long time ago, when I was at home in the Yihong courtyard,[4] I saw a tiny clockwork toy boat made by foreigners. But that was just a plaything for display! Besides, even though it was called 'automatic,' it couldn't actually move. How is it that they've made such a large version now? I'll not worry about it for now—I'll just give it a try and broaden my horizons!" Having decided this, he said to the clerk, "Since you put it that way, we'll take the steamboat. But I don't suppose there's one that goes directly to Tianjin? If there is, that would be even better."

"There isn't. They all have to go through Shanghai first. Would you like to take a private cabin or a stateroom?"

"You said that the 'first-class' cabins or whatever they're called are best—we'll take one of those."

The clerk confirmed his choice and asked when he wished to depart. Baoyu asked, "Does the ship travel back and forth each day?"

"How on earth could it do that? But there is one ship departing each day, so you can set out on whichever day you wish."

"All right, then we'll leave tomorrow."

The clerk then asked where they'd be staying once they arrived in Shanghai and whether they had anyone to help them make arrangements. "We have a partnership with the Changfa Inn in Shanghai," he explained, "so if you'd like to stay there for a bit, they will take care of you." They exchanged a few more words before the clerk finally went on his way.

But for now, no more retelling of this idle chatter. On the following day, Baoyu was preparing to rouse himself from bed. Beiming, meanwhile, had gathered the luggage and eaten breakfast, then gone to hire a horse. With Baoyu riding and Beiming and some hired luggage haulers walking behind, the procession left town and arrived at the riverbank.

On this particular day, the boat departing for Shanghai belonged to the China Merchants Group, and so they first proceeded to the China Merchants Group's landing stage, where they sat and waited in a reception room. A young porter had been dispatched to the reception room to wait upon them. After a while, they heard voices outside calling, "It's here! It's here!" Baoyu made his way outside, and leaning against the handrail, gazed off into the distance. He could make out a thick trail of black smoke coiling skyward in the distance; beneath the smoke, a ship was slowly cutting through the water. It was not long before the ship was close.

Baoyu turned to the porter and asked, "Is that the ship we'll be taking?"

"It is." As he spoke, the large ship drew ever closer. Upon the side of the ship were written the words *River Wide*.

"What is the meaning of having those characters written there?" asked Baoyu.

"That's the ship's name," replied the porter.

"Even ships have names!" Baoyu thought. "Truly, I've never heard of such a thing!" As he thought about this, he realized that the ship was traveling right past the landing stage, as if it weren't going to draw up alongside at all. "What's the meaning of this?" he thought. To his surprise, only after the ship had sailed off a way into the distance did it execute a wide turn and double back. It then began a slow approach from the other side and soon pulled up alongside them.

When it was time to board, the sound of voices grew chaotic. The porter handled the luggage and, with Baoyu and Beiming following behind him, squeezed through the throngs of people. They climbed a flight of stairs and entered their first-class cabin, where the porter dropped off the luggage before hurriedly disappearing. Soon, he came back with yet another person and explained, "This is the purser for this section. His job is to take care of the guests on board. When you arrive in Shanghai, give your bags to him—he'll make sure you have no problems."

Baoyu asked the man's name, and the man replied, "My surname is Bao; and because I am always very appropriate in my dealings with guests, some of them have been so kind as to give me the nickname 'Appropriate Bao.'[5] If you need anything, just send someone to come look for me in the steerage section." With that, the porter who had introduced him said goodbye and left.

A little while later the ship departed. Baoyu emerged from his cabin, hoping to go up on deck to see the river scenery. Every object he encountered on board the ship was entirely new to him—he'd never seen any of it before! Appropriate Bao accompanied him, gossiping and chatting about anything and everything. Baoyu pointed to various unfamiliar objects, asking Appropriate Bao about each one—one by one he learned about things like "sampans," "firehoses," "life preservers," and "steering mechanisms." He then went up to the window of the engine room and spent a long while watching the machinery in operation.

Once he tired of this, he returned to his own cabin to rest. As he would have felt too bored on his own, he brought Appropriate Bao along to chat with him. Baoyu asked Appropriate Bao to tell him all about Shanghai. Appropriate Bao, seeing that Baoyu was a refined young man, decided that he was likely a man of some distinction, and so told Baoyu how prosperous and bustling Shanghai was, and went on at length about what one could find there and what one couldn't. Gradually, he turned to more amorous subjects and explained that the four most famous courtesans in Shanghai were the "Four Temple Guardians."

Baoyu laughed, "They're just a few powdered prostitutes, how is it that they've come to be called the 'Four Temple Guardians'?"

"I don't understand either," admitted Appropriate Bao. "But since that's what everyone calls them, that's what I call them, too. Anyway, among these 'Four Temple Guardians,' the most famous is called Lin Daiyu."

These words gave Baoyu a jolt, as if he'd been struck by lightning. He heard a loud ringing in his ears, his whole body broke out in a sweat, and he sat, for a time, stunned. Appropriate Bao continued yammering on in an unending stream of chatter, but when he finally noticed that something had upset Baoyu, he assumed he'd lost interest and so made a quick excuse before taking his leave. Appropriate Bao had, with that one utterance, made Baoyu feel as though he was no longer firmly connected to his soul. Baoyu didn't know what to do—he was both outraged and suspicious. He was angry that a person like Lin Daiyu—pristine as ice and pure as jade—could even contemplate going into such a business; and he was suspicious because he remembered that Lin Daiyu had quite clearly died, so how could she possibly still be alive? He wondered, "Could it be that they buried an empty casket in order to deceive me? That they said she was dead, but actually secretly sent her to the south?" He could make no sense of it either way and couldn't help but get himself worked up.

After brooding for some time, he had just decided to go outside and have a look around once more when he saw a young man approaching with a square tray. The young man took a number of objects from the tray and set them out on a table, then invited Baoyu to dine. Baoyu approached the table and sat down, looking at what the young man had brought. He saw a shallow white ceramic dish half-filled with soup, as well as a silver spoon, and two flattish pieces of something resembling cake. In front of him sat a kind of silver rack, which held several glass bottles. Baoyu looked at all of this with rapt attention, completely bewildered. He sat stunned for a moment, then picked up the silver spoon and ate two mouthfuls of soup.

He felt that the flavor was all right, and so continued eating, one spoon at a time. As he ate, he thought, "This must be the 'foreign-style meal.' But who puts soup on a plate?[6] It's absurd! I expect they'll use bowls to serve their pickled vegetables?" Without noticing, he'd already eaten half the soup and set down his spoon. The young waiter immediately came over and cleared the dishes. Baoyu thought this, too, was strange. To himself, he mused, "They haven't even brought out the rice, and he's already taking away the soup! And only serving one type of food! This is all extremely odd."

He was still turning these thoughts over in his mind as the young man returned and set down another dish in front of Baoyu. He also laid out a small knife and a pronged metal stabber of some kind.[7] This stabber, to Baoyu, was an indescribably odd thing. Looking back over at the new dish, he saw that it was a roasted fish, covered in something that resembled soup but wasn't quite soup, and also resembled broth, but wasn't quite broth. It was snow-white in color. Since he had no chopsticks, Baoyu truly had no idea how to go about eating it. "Am I supposed to stab it with this stabber and stick it in my mouth?" he wondered.

Beside him, the waiter saw that Baoyu was staring hesitantly, and so he walked over and pointed to the glass bottles, saying, "This one is chili sauce, this one is fish sauce."

"Pour me some," said Baoyu. The waiter obliged, pouring him out a little. Baoyu then picked up the stabber, stabbed a piece of fish with it, and ate it. He actually felt that this was quite a handy way to eat and so continued intently eating his fish. When he had finished, the waiter brought out yet another dish. By this time Baoyu had come to understand how to use the knife and fork, one in each hand. He ate seven or eight dishes in succession, with the waiter clearing each course in turn. Finally, the waiter brought out a cup of tea, which he carried on a tiny ceramic plate, along with a tiny teaspoon. Upon the tiny plate were two snow-white, perfectly square cubes, a bit larger than a pair of dice. Baoyu looked at them uncomprehendingly. He picked up the teacup and took a sip. He furrowed his brow with distaste. "Ugh! It's too strong! Far too bitter!"

The waiter then returned, bringing a small ceramic bottle and asked, "Do you take milk in your tea?" Baoyu nodded. "And sugar?" Baoyu nodded again. The waiter deposited the two white cubes in Baoyu's teacup and stirred a few times with the spoon until the cubes had dissolved. Only then did Baoyu realize that they must have been sugar. After he'd finished stirring, the waiter poured in some milk. Baoyu took another sip and felt that it was no longer so acerbic. He gradually drained the cup, after which the waiter reemerged to take the empty cup and clear the table.

Baoyu thought, "So this is what it means to eat a 'foreign-style meal'! But it went on for ages, and there wasn't a single grain of rice! And as for those two little bits of cake, I still don't know what those were! I didn't even touch them." At this point, Baoyu was quite full and felt that he should go outside for a stroll.

He encountered Appropriate Bao, who was giggling to himself as he walked up. Appropriate Bao asked, "Had your dinner, sir?"

"I have. And you?"

"Indeed, I have."

"What kind of food do you eat in steerage?" Baoyu asked.

"I'll be honest with you, sir," said Appropriate Bao, "a few chaps from the bursar's office have been helping me out, so I've been taking my meals with them, which is pretty good. But the food they get in steerage doesn't even come close. The kitchen sends out a wooden barrel of rice, and everyone rushes forward to try to grab some. Some try to fill their washbasins with rice, some try to fill baskets. And there are no vegetables—if you want vegetables, you need to bring them on board with you. You haven't been away from home long, sir, and there is much you haven't seen; but people like me, always traveling back and forth, we're used to all of these things. Did you enjoy your foreign meal, sir? The chef in charge of the foreign meals is from Ningbo, he puts on a fine spread. And the steward is called Li, he takes excellent care of the guests. Have you encountered him, sir?"

As Appropriate Bao went on with his ceaseless yammering, there came suddenly and without warning a deafening WUUU WUUUUU sound from overhead, terrifying Baoyu.

■ ■ ■

If you wish to know what the sound was, please listen to the explanation in the following chapter.

Chapter Four

The clever "Spirit Jade" seeks new knowledge from one less wise than himself

The "Oaf King," in his cups, resumes his old ways

WE HAD just been speaking of Baoyu and Appropriate Bao, who were having a pleasant conversation when suddenly a strange WUUU WUUUUU sound came from overhead, startling Baoyu.[1] Appropriate Bao said, "We've arrived at Zhenjiang." Baoyu was about to ask a question when he was interrupted by two more WUUUU WUUUUs.

"What keeps making that noise?" he asked.

Appropriate Bao laughed, "That's the steam whistle. When we arrive at a port, the captain sounds it to warn smaller ships to get out of our way to avoid collisions." Only then did Baoyu understand. Appropriate Bao began pointing out landmarks to Baoyu: over here, Mount Jiao; over there, Mount Jin. By this time the sky was already turning dark, and Baoyu could see the ten thousand lights of Zhenjiang glimmering in the distance. A short time later, the ship drew up alongside the landing stage, and Baoyu could hear the bustle of murmuring voices below him.

Turning his head and looking back toward his own stateroom, he noticed that there was light coming from within. "I didn't see anyone go inside," he said. "Who lit the lamp?"

Appropriate Bao laughed. "It's an electric light, no one 'lights' it—it comes on and goes off by itself! The foreigners really are awfully clever, they made all of this!"

"Indeed. Actually, I'd like to ask you—a short while ago I saw two people whose bizarre attire I need not comment on; but even their facial features were quite strange: yellow hair, yellow beards, and green eyes! Could they have been foreigners?"

"Precisely."

Baoyu mused, "I've seen ceramic statuettes of foreign children before, and they looked rather similar, except that the children had wings as well! There's no reason that any human should grow wings! Now, seeing those men, I supposed they must be foreigners. But . . . do they really have wings?"

"Whoever heard of people growing wings? But many of their paintings feature people with wings—I've heard that those are simply their bodhisattvas!"

Baoyu had a good laugh at this, then said, "What are those two foreigners doing on the ship?"

"They're the bridge crew! And there are not just two of them on board—there are at least five or six altogether."

"Does this ship belong to foreigners?"

"No, this ship belongs to the China Merchants Group—it's Chinese. But there are two other companies—Jardine Matheson & Co., and the China Navigation Company—which are both foreign."

"If it's a Chinese ship," Baoyu started, "then why are there foreigners running it?"

"Chinese people are incapable of doing it," replied Appropriate Bao.

Shaking his head, Baoyu said, "That can't be! It's not as though the foreigners have an extra set of eyes or an extra pair of arms. What about it is impossible for a Chinese person to do? Surely it's just that they haven't learned to do it."

Appropriate Bao replied, "I'm afraid we're simply not as clever as they are."

"All people are equally capable of cleverness! It's just the case sometimes that one type of person has been held back by their own habits and can't extricate themselves. Moreover, Confucius once said: 'If another person can do it once, I shall do it a hundredfold; if another person does it ten times, I shall do it a thousand!' How can there be an 'unlearnable' knowledge? If we don't hurry up and learn it, what happens if we have a falling out with them and they're unwilling to do this for us? Wouldn't this enormous ship be reduced to a piece of flotsam?"

As he was speaking, Beiming walked over, giggling to himself as he handed a small box to Baoyu. "Here's another kind! They're bigger than the first kind we saw! The first kind we found cost three coppers a box! But these are four cents. I bought them downstairs so I could show young master!"

Appropriate Bao looked them over: as it turned out, it was a foreign brand of matches with a picture of a monkey on the box. He laughed, "These are called 'matches'![2] Haven't you seen them before?"

Beiming replied, "The first box we saw was smaller than this, and those ones had a red dot on the end."

"Give it a try," said Baoyu.

Beiming tried lighting one.

"It lights silently!" remarked Baoyu. "And it catches fire faster than the others." Turning to Appropriate Bao, he asked, "Are these made by foreigners, as well?"

"They originally came from abroad," answered Appropriate Bao. "These ones are Japanese. But I've heard that it was Chinese who invented them over there. At the moment, these are considered the best and are selling like hotcakes! Someone told me they make ten thousand crates every week, and every crate earns them a silver yuan."

"How many of these little boxes are in a crate?" asked Baoyu.

"You've got me stumped there, that's something I can't really answer. But the crates are about half the size of an eight-person table!"

"What about the smaller boxes of matches?" Baoyu asked.

"Those are made in Shanghai. There are many different brands, like Xiechang, Huachang, and Liechang."

"And are they made by Chinese, or made by foreigners?"

Appropriate Bao replied, "They're made by Chinese. At the moment, there are also people making them in Hankou and Hunan."

Baoyu clapped his hands. "Didn't I say so? Didn't I say there's no skill that can't be learned? If Chinese have learned to make such clever little things as these, how can you say they can't learn to navigate ships? But let's go sit inside, it's getting a bit chilly out here now."

By this time, the ship had already continued on its journey. The two men went in and continued chatting for a while before

Appropriate Bao eventually took his leave. Of the rest of this evening, we have nothing further to report.

▪ ▪ ▪

The next morning, Baoyu awoke early. As he washed his face, a waiter arrived with a cup of tea, and two more of the small, flattish cakelike things. One side was smeared with a chunk of a clear, yellowish substance much like lard in appearance. Moreover, there was another plate with two slices of ham and two soft-boiled eggs. Baoyu was not so uneasy as he had been the previous day, so he picked up his knife and fork and ate. He drank the tea as well. Afterward he went out on deck to have a stroll and look at the scenery. Appropriate Bao walked over to him and said, "You're up early, sir! We're making good time now—we should arrive in Shanghai by ten."[3] The two men chatted for a while, then Appropriate Bao gave Baoyu a tour of the lower-level cabins and the steerage section, after which they returned topside.

Before much time had passed they had already reached the mouth of the Wusong River near Shanghai. Appropriate Bao pointed out ships to Baoyu by their flags, saying, "That's a British warship; that one's French."

Baoyu was startled. "How can such enormous ships possibly give battle?"

Appropriate Bao replied, "They're actually very powerful! I haven't seen it myself, but I've heard that when they fire those big cannons, the shell can travel several tens of li!"

"But why are their warships in our territory? Are they fighting us?"

"Shanghai is a treaty port, so there are traders of all nationalities here. The ships have been stationed here to protect their traders."

"Have we got warships of our own?" Baoyu queried.

Appropriate Bao pointed out another two ships: "That's the *Haichou*, and that's the *Hairong*. They're both Chinese."

"Are they mechanical, like this ship?"

"They are."

"And do foreigners command them?"

"No, they're run by Chinese."

"There, you see! Yesterday you told me that Chinese weren't as clever as foreigners and couldn't learn to do it; so how is it that Chinese can operate a warship? Why it should be necessary that foreigners run this ship, I simply don't understand."

Appropriate Bao murmured, "That is so, that is so. Sir is very wise."

As Baoyu swept his gaze along the riverbank, Appropriate Bao pointed out one by one: "That's a textile factory; that's a distribution center; that's the waterworks." As Appropriate Bao spoke, Baoyu could see in the distance a thick trail of black smoke that sped across his view as if it were flying. "That's a train," Appropriate Bao added.

"Is it mechanical as well?"

"It is."

Baoyu clapped his hands and smiled. "Of course! As I was boarding the ship, I thought that if there were such a vessel for water travel, there must be some kind of mechanized carriage for the land!"

As the two men continued their chat, the ship pulled up alongside the pier. Appropriate Bao helped Baoyu with his luggage, then hailed a rickshaw and escorted Baoyu and Beiming, master and servant, to the Changfa Inn, where they selected a tidy room. Once Beiming had unpacked their things, he went out into the attached anteroom to rest. A short while later a waiter entered and served a meal, which Baoyu ate.

Appropriate Bao entered and said, "Sir will have to stay for a few days—there's no ship leaving for Tianjin for the next two days, but the *Baoding* will sail from here in three days' time."

"Why is there a ship named after a place?" Baoyu asked. "That's quite odd."

"All of the China Navigation Company's ships are named after places."

"Didn't you say yesterday that the China Navigation Company is owned by foreigners?"

"Yes."

"Does the China Merchants Group have a ship that goes to Tianjin?"

"They do."

"And when does it go? I will only take a Chinese ship!"

"Fine, fine. Sir will have to wait for the *Xinyu*, which is a top-of-the-line ship. Even the current governor-general of Guangdong and Guangxi, Grand Secretary Li Hongzhang himself, has praised it! You'll just have to wait for it—plus, it's not so bad to have two extra days to enjoy yourself in Shanghai. I'm sorry, but I've got some things to take care of, so I cannot accompany you any longer." So saying, he took his leave and departed.

This left Baoyu alone in the inner room, feeling quite lonely. He thought about going out and wandering around the city but was worried about not knowing his way. With no other way to stave off his boredom, he once again picked up his copy of

Dream of the Red Chamber and reread the parts he had skimmed over his first time through. However, it would have been better if he hadn't, for as soon as he started reading, it was as though his soul were dreaming. He himself couldn't quite express the feeling and passed the day frustrated and out of sorts.

After eating dinner he lit the lamp and lay in bed for a while. All he could hear were the chaotic sounds of horses and carts coming and going along the streets outside, so noisily that he couldn't sleep. As he lay there rather bored, he heard a sudden stamping of feet and the sound of someone striking a table in the neighboring room. Then, he heard a voice shout, "You son of a bitch! Are you fucking *blind*? You just spilled boiling water on your old man's foot!"

It seemed to Baoyu that the voice sounded very familiar, and he thought it must be someone he knew. But as he thought about it more carefully, he told himself that he didn't have any friends who were so boorish and uncultured. He heard another burst of cursing, and then the sound of footsteps racing out of the room. Hastily, Baoyu got out of bed and ran to the anteroom, where Beiming had already positioned himself in the doorway to watch the spectacle. Two men had already sprinted past by the time Baoyu got to the door, but Baoyu could see that in the lead was a waiter, pursued from behind by someone trying to beat him.

Beiming said, "The pursuer's face is awfully familiar to me. I'm not sure which young master he is—I just can't think of it at the moment."

Baoyu replied, "As soon as I heard him shout, I thought his voice sounded familiar, but I couldn't think of who it might be, either. I rushed out here to see, but he's already gone."

Beiming thought a while longer, then said, "Aha! I've got it! It's Master Xue!" Hearing this, Baoyu went to see for himself. Reaching the staircase, he saw that the man had pinned the waiter against the wall and was striking him wildly. Looking closely, Baoyu verified that it was indeed Xue Pan.[4]

"Stop hitting him!" cried Baoyu. "There's an old friend here to see you!"

Xue Pan raised his head to look and was momentarily startled. "Eh? Brother Bao! You've made your way to Shanghai, too? It's been a long time!" As he spoke, he came over to shake Baoyu's hand. Xue Pan's face betrayed his utter inebriation, and each time he opened his mouth, Baoyu was assailed by the alcohol on his breath. Xue Pan was obviously drunk, so Baoyu and Beiming guided him back to their room. Beiming then looked up at Xue Pan and asked after his health. Xue Pan laughed and said, "Just fine! And you, you little scamp, I see you're still with the Second Master?"

They walked into the inner room. Xue Pan looked about the place, and stared for a moment before going on: "Brother Bao, I know it's been a long time since we've seen each other, but how is it that your taste has become so spartan? There's not a bit of decoration in this room, how can you bear to live here? I don't even want to sit down! Come, come, let's go over to my room, and you can take a look." Without further ado, he grabbed Baoyu and pulled him along.

They went into the room next door. The whole place was agleam as if with brilliant red light, for all four walls had been done up in red wallpaper with a gold flower motif. Hanging upon the wall were a full-length mirror and a chiming clock; upon the table were a number of items that Baoyu didn't fully recognize. Xue Pan gestured to Baoyu to sit on the bed, and as he looked at the bed, Baoyu felt that he'd never seen anything like it, either—it was suspended upon four narrow cylindrical poles, and adorned with a bed curtain unlike anything he was familiar with.

Baoyu sat and said, "It's been a long time since we've seen each other! When did you come to Shanghai?"

"Hey, I didn't get a chance to ask you yet—your old man said you'd become a monk, how is it that you ended up here? How many years were you a monk? And when did you rejoin us in lay society?"

Baoyu replied, "How could I ever be a monk for very long? All I was doing was sitting in meditation for a bit, but then I missed home and decided to come back. But I'd shaved off my queue, so I spent over a year growing it back before reemerging. Then I got lost for a bit and wound up in Nanjing, and fortunately I ran into Beiming en route. We left Nanjing yesterday and just arrived in Shanghai today. That's the whole story so far."

"How strange! I don't think I've seen you ever since that time I got into trouble. After I was pardoned I came back, and within a few days I got into a quarrel with my mother. I was in a right temper, so I arranged with friends to meet at Taoran Pavilion Park at Jinqiu Hill for food, drinks, and a stroll. Who would have known that I would get drunk and fall asleep right there in the pavilion? I don't know how long I slept for, but when I woke up it was pouring rain. My friends had all vanished, but there was a new party of people taking shelter from the rain in the pavilion with me. The rain didn't let up, so I eventually got to chatting with them. As it turned out, they were merchants heading south to do business. I thought it over, and honestly, when I left the house after that fight with my mother, I had already decided not to go back, so I was carrying a few dozen taels of gold and a hundred strings of pearls on my person. It seemed to line up perfectly: I'd go into business with those men and leave Beijing. The weird thing is, it was just a little nap, so I don't know when they had time to make these 'trains'—which, by the way, are tremendously clever—but we got on board, glided along the tracks, and in an instant, we were in Tianjin. Then, we boarded a steamship and were in Shanghai three days later." He went on, "This place is great. I've already been living here for two years, and now that you're here, Brother Bao, you should stay with me a while. For the past two years, I've been selling various goods and making a bundle of cash. It was only in the early days, when I was selling books, that I lost any money. In fact, I still haven't managed to finish selling the books from back then."

Baoyu listened up to this point and suddenly remembered something. He said, "I want to bring something and show it to you, wait just a minute." So saying, he walked out.

■ ■ ■

If you wish to know what object Baoyu wished to show Xue Pan, please listen to the explanation in the following chapter.

Chapter Five

Seeking knowledge, he plans to borrow some new books

His concerns and remonstrations about foreign goods fall on deaf ears

WE WERE just speaking of Xue Pan, who was watching Baoyu hurriedly rush off and supposed that he must have gone off to retrieve something of interest. Xue Pan waited a bit, then saw Baoyu come back into the room with Beiming at his heels. Beiming carried a bundle of books and set them down. Baoyu pulled out a volume of *Dream of the Red Chamber* and showed it to Xue Pan, saying, "Don't you think this book is odd?"

Xue Pan took it from him and flipped through it, then tossed it aside on the table and said, "Ugh, so now you, too, are trying to taunt me with that obnoxious thing? I'm afraid you won't find it great reading either."

"I read it, and it's stirred me up a bit. When I think about the story, it seems like the events of another century; but when I think again, it seems like it happened just yesterday. When I reread it, it feels just like reading my own diary—except that the author has written about so many other things I didn't know about. Do you have any idea who this Cao Xueqin person is?"

Xue Pan replied with irritation, "Why ask about him? Just hearing the name infuriates me! If I ever meet him, I'll give him a real thrashing!"

"Why do you hate him?"

"One time at school I carelessly misread the name 'Tang Yin' as 'Geng Huang' and he had the nerve to write about it in his 'book'—it's embarrassing! Why wouldn't I hate him?" Saying this, he glanced up at the clock on the wall and said, "It's almost nine. Brother Bao, let's go for a stroll outside."

Baoyu replied, "None of your shenanigans, please, it's already late. It's been so long since we've seen each other, we should have a nice pleasant chat. And besides, you've been in Shanghai two years longer than I have, so you must be familiar with the people and culture here. Why don't you tell me what you know about it?"

"All right, but—where shall I start?"

"Just choose what you think is important and tell me a bit about it."

Xue Pan clapped his hands and said, "All right, I'll tell you, but you won't believe me!"

"I've asked you to tell me, why wouldn't I believe you?"

Xue Pan clapped again, and said, "I'll be honest with you, then: Shanghai is different from any other place. Besides horse racing, strolling in gardens, going to the theater, and perusing the brothels, there's nothing else to do! And even if there were other things to do, they would still be secondary to those four other things."

Baoyu laughed. "I asked about the people and culture of Shanghai, but you've just told me about your own predilections!"

Xue Pan jumped up and said, "If you don't believe me, then starting tomorrow, you and I are going to spend the next couple of months thoroughly exploring the city. Then you can tell me if what I'm saying is true or not!"

Baoyu did not reply, and instead asked Beiming to return the volumes of *Dream of the Red Chamber* to their room. Xue Pan looked at him, and asked, "We haven't seen each other for several years, how is it that all of a sudden you treat books like precious valuables? And what's so interesting about a crappy book like that, anyway?"

"When I read it, I thought it extremely strange, so I brought it to show it to you. I'd no idea you had already read it."

"So what? There are plenty of strange books. When I first started selling books, I bought lots of sample books from collectors, to make it easier for customers to place orders. Afterward, I had no use for them, so I sealed them up in four big trunks. Tomorrow, I'll have them all delivered to you."

Baoyu happily said, "I'd love to read some more books! But which ones do you have? If it's all just the works of the sages of the Zhou and Qin and the various Classics and Histories, I've read them all and don't need to read them again. What I want is more recent stuff."

"I wouldn't know 'more recent' from 'less recent.' You'll just have to wait until tomorrow to see. You can pick out and keep the ones you're interested in; the rest, you can get rid of—I haven't got any use for them anymore." Baoyu thanked him repeatedly. They exchanged a few more words, then Baoyu returned to his room. Of that night, we have nothing further to report.

■ ■ ■

The next day, Baoyu woke up early, washed, got dressed, then went in search of Xue Pan to request the promised books. Upon reaching Xue Pan's room, Baoyu found it locked. He thought, "Why would Xue Pan have gone out so early?" He could only go back to his room by himself and mope. Around nine o'clock, he finally heard boisterous laughter from the hall, as Xue Pan burst into the room. He exclaimed, "Brother Bao! I kept thinking about you, so I came back a bit early this morning."

"Where did you go so early?" Baoyu asked.

"What makes you think I went out early? When you left last night, I was awfully bored sitting there by myself, so I went out and spent the whole night just wandering around. Come on! Let's go over to my room." Saying this, he dragged Baoyu out into the hall.

A waiter had already opened Xue Pan's door. Baoyu and Xue Pan entered the room and sat down. Baoyu asked Xue Pan about the books. "Why so impatient?" asked Xue Pan. "You'll get them soon enough. First take a look at this!" He moved a large box over toward Baoyu and raised the lid. Inside, there was a cylindrical tube of smooth, polished iron, at one end of which two small, round discs were mounted. Baoyu had no idea of what this thing was, or for what it could be used. Xue Pan, meanwhile, had retrieved a cardboard tube and tipped out a glossy brownish cylinder from inside, which he then then fitted over the metal one. He also pulled out something that looked rather like a trumpet and rigged it up on top of the apparatus. Finally, he grasped a handle at the side and gave it several cranks. The small discs began to spin rapidly, as if they were flying, and the cylinder slowly began to revolve as well. Suddenly, a strange sound began to emanate from the trumpet. Xue Pan said, "Go on, listen!" Baoyu inclined his head and listened intently: one moment it was cymbals and drums, the next strings and woodwinds; then it seemed as if someone was singing; and, just as suddenly, it was silent again.

Xue Pan laughed, "Could you tell what song it was?"

Baoyu shook his head. "No idea."

Still laughing, Xue Pan went on, "You've seen lots of cleverly crafted things in your day, have you seen one of these before?"

"I haven't."

"It's called a phonograph. Someone sings a song once into a device like this, and then you can play it over and over and over. You could play it a thousand times, or ten thousand, and it comes out perfect every time. Wouldn't you say it's a clever contraption?"

"And what purpose does it serve?" asked Baoyu.

"What do you mean, 'What purpose does it serve?' It plays music. That's it." Xue Pan got up and went over to fuss once again with his machine.

"Don't bother," said Baoyu. "It doesn't sound human—it doesn't even sound like a braying animal. It's horrible. Spending money to buy a plaything like this—so pointless!"

Xue Pan replied, "The machine by itself was sixty-some taels of silver, but then you have to buy the wax cylinders, too."

"Where did you buy them?"

"I bought them in a foreign goods store—they're Western goods."

Baoyu picked up a wax cylinder and looked it over. "That someone can sell this kind of useless thing for money, and that there are actually people who would buy it, is truly bizarre!"

"You may say they're useless," cut in Xue Pan, "but some foreigners use them to record their wills; some even use it to record legal testimony."

"Ah, so that's how it is. Someone invents a good, useful item, and people like you take it and turn it into some kind of toy. What a waste!"

"How is it that you've suddenly become some kind of stick in the mud? I've never been on the brink of death, so I've never needed to record a will, have I? And as for using it for testimony, if I've got a written contract, why would I need to record it? I just want to listen to some music and have a bit of fun! One of these days when I go back up north, I'll bring a couple along so the boys up there can entertain themselves."

Baoyu was about to reply when he heard a man walk into the hallway, fling a newspaper into a vacant chair by the door, and walk back out. Xue Pan walked over, picked up the paper, and looked it over. After he'd given it a quick glance, he passed it to Baoyu, saying, "This is today's paper, take a look."

Baoyu took it in hand and saw that it was the same sort of thing he'd seen that day in the crumbling temple. He hurriedly looked to the top line and read: *Great Qing, Guangxu 26th year, 2nd month, 12th day.*[1] Silently, he thought, "How shameful! It's taken until today to find out the date!" He kept reading, and once again saw the words "Year 1900," but still didn't understand it, and had to ask Xue Pan.

Xue Pan answered, "Lucky for you, I've had a lot of interactions with foreign businesses, otherwise I'd be stumped. That's the Western calendar, which starts with the birth of Jesus—it's been 1,900 years since his birth."

"How many days are there in one of their years? How is it that the twenty-sixth year of Guangxu is the same as their 1900?"

"They have twelve months in a year like us, though their New Year starts in our eleventh month. This 'Year 1900' you're seeing started in our eleventh month of last year."

As he was speaking, a waiter entered and asked whether they wished for their meal to be served. Xue Pan looked at the clock and answered, "It's only 10:30, too early! And besides, we're not eating here—we're going out to eat."

Baoyu asked him again for the books he'd been promised, to which Xue Pan replied, "How impatient you are! Come on, then, let's go get you your books." So saying, he pulled Baoyu out of the room, then turned around and locked the door. Then, walking past Baoyu's door, Xue Pan called to Beiming, "They've already prepared a meal downstairs, you go ahead and eat. I'm taking your Second Master out for food."

Beiming assented, then took a step toward Baoyu and said, "The silver your mother gave you as travel money back in Beijing—I pulled it out and tried to spend it when we were in Nanjing, but it had turned black and quite a lot of it had corroded. With the expenses we've incurred to get here, I'm afraid there's none left. Please, Master, you must think of something soon!"

Xue Pan interrupted, "Think nothing of it, my lad! So you've got no money. What's the big deal? You've got me!" He then started off.

Beiming called after him, "Be careful, Master Xue! Don't lose our young master a second time!"

Xue Pan ignored him and pulled Baoyu down the stairs. As they passed the clerk's office, Xue Pan called to him, "Among the trunks I had sent downstairs for storage in the basement, there are four that are not labeled. Have someone bring them upstairs for me, and deliver them to"—here he pointed at Baoyu—"this gentleman's room." Without so much as waiting for a response from the clerk, he continued leading Baoyu to the front door.

"Slow down for a minute!" said Baoyu. "Where are we going?"

"I'll tell you on the way!"

They exited the inn and walked west along the riverbank.

■ ■ ■

In his whole life, Baoyu had never been in a place like this. Each time he looked up, he saw new things he'd never encountered before. He pointed out and asked about each one. Xue Pan said, "What's so special about these? If you like these things, I'll take you all over and make sure you've seen your fill!" They reached Chessboard Street and went to look at two foreign goods stores. Xue Pan had been dealing in merchandise for two years, so he knew most of the employees well. They greeted him and inevitably invited him and Baoyu to take some tea and have a smoke. When they heard that Baoyu wanted to "see things," they assumed that he was a merchant from out of town who wanted to inspect their wares. They pulled out clockwork music boxes, phonographs, clocks, and watches and placed them before him. They started everything up, and even brought over children's toys and spread them out in front of him. Baoyu looked them over one by one.

After visiting the two shops, Xue Pan announced, "I'm hungry! Let's go eat!" As luck would have it, there were two rickshaws waiting by the door. Xue Pan climbed up into one and told Baoyu to get into the other. The two rickshaw pullers ran as swiftly as if they were flying. After the amount of time it takes to drink a cup of tea had passed, they turned a corner and Xue Pan yelled, "Stop!" In a fluid motion, he handed over their fares and pulled Baoyu into a restaurant. As they climbed the stairs, Xue Pan explained, "This is Yijiachun, a very famous and well-established restaurant. Let me invite you to try it—my treat." When they arrived upstairs, they chose seats; then Xue Pan asked for "guest invitation slips,"[2] then turned to Baoyu and said, "I'm a bit intimidated by writing. Why don't you write them out for me?"

"What shall I write?"

"Invite Bai Yaolian from the Mackay Company.[3] Just fill in that information, it'll be enough."

Baoyu saw that the slips were ready-made with blanks for invitees' names. He filled in the few characters that Xue Pan had told him to, then added Xue Pan's name at the bottom. Xue Pan then had the invitations sent out to be delivered.

Baoyu asked, "So who is this Bai Yaolian?"

"He's a comprador for the Mackay Company."

"Ah, that's right—on board the ship I heard about these 'compradors.' It sounded like it must be a very respectable occupation. But then I thought that in our household we also had a 'comprador,' but his role was just to take money to go out and buy anything the higher-ups in the house wanted—he was more of a second-rate servant."

Xue Pan didn't wait for him to finish, and interrupted, "No, no, no! The compradors who work for the foreign steamship companies are completely different from the household buyers. They're extremely respectable, and many of them are able to make a huge profit from their work! This year, a foreigner called John Mackay came and wanted to establish a presence for the Mackay Company here. He invited Bai Yaolian to be his comprador, specifically to arrange imports. I wanted to ask him to bring some foreign goods for me, as well, which is how we got to know each other."

Baoyu replied, "Just hearing you say 'foreign goods' vexes me all over again! Today, when I saw all those things, somehow I felt anxious and furious all at once!"

"Why?"

"Walking along the streets just now, nine shops out of ten were selling foreign goods. It's as though we Chinese have no businesses of our own."

Xue Pan was startled. "How bizarre! How is it that you're preaching the gospel of business now?"

"It's not that I suddenly want to talk about business. I've just been thinking: if the foreigners are working tirelessly to keep bringing their products here to sell to Chinese, won't they just be siphoning off Chinese money to their own countries, year after year?"

"I'd say you're spouting off like an idiot again. There's open commerce between all countries now, why would you say something so ridiculous?"

Baoyu said, "Open commerce and international trade have existed for a long time, it's not anything all that new. But open commerce should be about exchanging what one has for what one lacks—that is real 'trade.' So tell me: with so many shops here selling foreign goods, are there any companies that sell our local goods to foreigners?"

Xue Pan stared at him. "There's no such thing."

Baoyu clapped his hands. "You see? And isn't that horrifying?"

Xue Pan slapped his palm on the table. "Wait, I was wrong—there is! Our silk and our tea—those two industries sell their goods to the foreigners, and in no small quantity!"

"Because they don't have these things—this is in accordance with the logic of 'exchanging what one has for what one lacks.' Though each party might be content with the exchanges being made, they should at least be sending us some useful things! For example, the music boxes and phonographs we just looked at are all completely useless! Just playthings! But the foreigners brought them here and want to sell them for a hefty price. They're certainly not anything you can't live without, so why should you go to all that trouble to acquire them?"

"You may not know," replied Xue Pan, "but those things are all selling tremendously well. You're the only person I've seen so unhappy about it!"

Baoyu considered this, then said, "Even so, why can't we learn to make these things ourselves?"

Just as he was saying this, an attendant came in and reported, "Your guest has arrived!" They saw a man striding in from outside.

■ ■ ■

If you wish to know who this person was, please listen to the explanation in the following chapter.

Chapter Six

Leafing through volumes of books, he is astonished that so much time has passed

Hoping for a quiet night, he must instead mollify a drunken lout

WE WERE speaking of the guest who had just then arrived—it was Bai Yaolian. After Bai Yaolian and Xue Pan greeted each other, Xue Pan invited Yaolian to order some food. Yaolian chose what he wanted; Xue Pan then bade Baoyu order. Baoyu said, "I don't understand the menu—you order for me." Xue Pan chose for him and handed their order to a waiter.

Bai Yaolian was wearing a plush official's jacket. Looking at it, Baoyu was not sure what kind of material it was but felt it impolite to ask, and so kept his puzzlement to himself. Yaolian then pulled out two Philippine cigars from his waist pocket and offered one each to Xue Pan and Baoyu. Xue Pan took his, lit it, and started smoking. Baoyu, on the other hand, set his to the side and listened to the two men talking about ordering goods and the latest gossip from the brothels. Baoyu, only half-understanding, sat silently without uttering a word.

A short while later the soup course was brought in. Baoyu had encountered something like this once already aboard the ship, and now, able to observe the other two eating as well, felt it was not so strange as he had thought it before. But suddenly he saw Xue Pan pick up one of the little cakelike squares, smear it with a purplish-black sauce, and eat it.

Unable to restrain himself, Baoyu asked, "What's that thing you're eating?"

Xue Pan replied, "It's a *mantou* that's been sliced apart and roasted. The Shanghainese call it by a transliterated word from a foreign language: *tuoshi*. That's why I say these big fancy restaurants would rather have literati like you eat here than merchants like us. Because they don't want us to come!"

Baoyu asked, "Why do you say that?"

Xue Pan laughed. "Why do they only serve *tuoshi* and not *tuoshang*?[1] Aren't they showing their disdain for us when we come here?"

Baoyu went on, "I didn't see this item listed on the menu."

"Toast is complimentary—you don't need to order it."

Yaolian interrupted them. "It seems that this is your kinsman's first time in Shanghai?"

"It is," answered Xue Pan.

Yaolian turned to Baoyu, and said, "Once you've been here for a couple of days, it will all seem more familiar. Then it will be easier. Shanghai is more exciting than any other place!"

Baoyu gave an indifferent half-snort in response. Soon they had finished eating, and Yaolian, saying that he had business to attend to, was the first to take his leave.

Xue Pan and Baoyu slowly walked out of the restaurant. Xue Pan was still smoking his Philippine cigar, so Baoyu asked him, "When you smoke that, the smell of the smoke is unbearably foul! What are you smoking it for?"

"You're just not used to it—it's actually very fragrant."

Baoyu thought for a moment. "I used to see Sister-in-Law Xifeng smoking orchid flower tobacco from her water pipe—now *that* was extremely fragrant. Not only are *these* things not fragrant, but to put it quite simply, they stink!"

Xue Pan laughed and tossed the remainder of his cigar to the ground. "Enough, enough! I won't smoke it anymore, that way the smoke won't contaminate you. But I have to say, while smoking orchid flower tobacco in a water pipe might be more fragrant, it's not nearly so convenient as these! You can smoke these while lying in bed or walking down the street!"

Baoyu said, "But wouldn't it be just the same to carry a little bag of loose tobacco and a pipe?"

"That's still not as convenient as these."

"All right," said Baoyu, "then maybe someone should figure out a way to roll up orchid flower tobacco like this. Wouldn't that be better?"

"Great idea!" said Xue Pan. "As soon as I'm back in Beijing, I'll get ahold of some orchid flower tobacco and have it rolled into cigars!"

"But you're a big businessman, why would you peddle something as trifling as tobacco?"

"That's big talk! You do still have the air of an official family about you! Do you have any idea how many foreign cigarettes are imported every year?"

"I don't." Baoyu shook his head.

"According to customs investigations, over four million taels' worth of cigarettes have been imported each year for the past two years," answered Xue Pan.

Baoyu sighed. "So we don't smoke our own tobacco anymore? Just think—in only this one industry, we give away four million taels a year!"

Xue Pan stuck up a thumb, and said, "That's why I always say we Chinese are loaded—in a year's time, we burn up four million taels, just in the name of smoking for a bit of fun!"

At this, Baoyu could only sigh.

Xue Pan brought Baoyu for a wander through the Fuzhou Road District, strolling past teahouses and smoking lounges. Baoyu saw someone smoking opium, which he thought exceedingly strange, so he stood watching for a while. Suddenly, a gust of wind buffeted the smoke into Baoyu, giving him a headache, so he hurriedly stalked off. He said to Xue Pan, "I'm a bit tired, shall we go back and rest?"

"Are you worried there's nowhere around here we can rest?"

"Where could we go?"

Xue Pan pulled out his watch and glanced at it. "It's a little after two. Let's wander over to a brothel. If we go now, we'll be just in time to watch them do their hair!"

"You're the same as ever!" said Baoyu. "You'll never be willing to change, will you?"

"It's like they say: it's easier to move rivers and mountains than to change one's character! Unlike you—you've become a completely different person than you used to be!" As he spoke, Xue Pan hailed a rickshaw to take them back to their inn.

■ ■ ■

Baoyu was keen to start reading Xue Pan's books, but they had not yet been brought upstairs. Xue Pan once again urged the staff to dig them out of storage immediately, then invited Baoyu to his room. Baoyu, still thinking about Xue Pan's desire to go to the brothels, suddenly remembered the "Four Temple Guardians" that Appropriate Bao had told him about. He then pulled Xue Pan aside and discreetly asked the reason for it.

Xue Pan laughed, "Now this is very strange indeed. Recently, the prostitutes in Shanghai have all been taking the names of our sisters from the Grand Prospect Garden—and not just Lin Daiyu! They've even taken the names of my two sisters! Once I even wrote a letter to my mother, telling her to notify the household—I wanted her to tell my uncle, hoping that he would write a letter to the local officials asking them to outlaw the practice. To my surprise, after sending two letters, I received not one character in reply! I was so angry that I stopped writing to her altogether. Anyway, don't worry about it. Sister Lin died a long time ago, how on earth could she be involved here?" In that moment, Baoyu finally came to understand something.

Just then Beiming entered and announced, "The trunks of books have arrived!" Baoyu ran over immediately, and asked the porter to help Beiming open the trunks. Soon they had all been opened, and Baoyu started pulling out book after book, inspecting each; however, they were all examination prep books, like *Major Themes in Literature and Governance* and *Minor Themes: 30,000 Selections*. He threw them aside without reading them. In the next trunk were large-typeface books, and so he ordered the porter to bring them into his room, trunk and all. Looking at the other two trunks, he found that the first of these, too, was filled entirely with practice essays for the imperial examination, while the second was not. He ordered the porter to carry the latter of these into his room as well.

Back in his room, Baoyu began unpacking the books, laying each out one by one upon an empty bed. Fortunately the room had three beds, and he only needed one to sleep in, so he was able to completely cover the other two beds with books. He was eager to inspect their dates of publication and so dumped out the contents of one trunk. However, he still couldn't find what he was looking for.

Xue Pan walked over and pointed at the books Baoyu was inspecting: "I brought those from Beijing two years ago. I couldn't sell them. Surely you've already read all the books available in the capital?"

Baoyu made no reply and continued digging through the books.

Xue Pan went on, "Bai Yaolian sent a letter inviting me out for drinks at a brothel at six. He asked me to bring you along."

"That's very kind, but sorry, I'm not going."

"Oh, come on, what's the point of this Confucian asceticism?"

"I'm not a Confucian; it's just that as soon as I looked that man in the face, his disgusting vulgarity was readily apparent. I found him to be simply detestable."

Xue Pan looked at Baoyu dully and walked out with long strides.

Baoyu, his head lowered as he kept inspecting his books, paid him no mind. Suddenly Baoyu came upon a set of *Chronologies of Famous Historical Figures*. Flipping through it, he found that it was arranged by year and month. He carried the set over to the table and started leafing through the first volume, which started in the Han dynasty.[2] Thereupon, he flipped through the remaining volumes. When he eventually got to the final volume, he saw that it gave dates in the current dynasty, so he slowed down and flipped through one year at a time. The book ended in the twenty-seventh year of the Daoguang reign.[3] He thought, "It's too bad that the book ends here. How can I find out about the things that have happened since?" Suddenly he realized that if he were to read the biographies of contemporary people, he might be able to fill in the gaps. He located a volume titled *Records of the Major Accomplishments of Lord Zeng Guofan* and felt as though he had found something extremely precious. He was in too big a hurry to read all of the detailed accounts and so skimmed through year by year.

Making quick calculations on his fingers, he was suddenly shocked. "So!" he thought. "I'm a person from an era many years in the past who has once again emerged into the world! How is it that it only seemed I'd been sitting in meditation for a bit, then spent a year growing out my hair, and yet so many eras have passed? And no wonder this *Dream of the Red Chamber* exists—the people of this age have turned my life into a story to tell one another! Moreover," he continued, "it's no wonder that person in Nanjing said I'd read too many novels when we asked him for directions to the family mansion. As soon as I tell anyone my name, the people of this age will think it bizarre—I'd better change it! After all, I never took a style name before." And thereupon he chose for himself the name Zhongying.[4]

He also thought of Beiming and Xue Pan: Where had they come from? Could it be that they, too, possessed the ability to pass through life's hardships without being ground to dust? Having thought this far, he then began to wonder if perhaps he wasn't dreaming. "Let's not mind that for now!" he thought. "Now that I'm a man of this era, I have to know more about the times I'm living in." And so, he flipped through several more recent publications, unaware that it was already growing late in the day. A waiter arrived, delivering dinner; Beiming took it and served it to Baoyu.

Baoyu asked him, "The day that you fell asleep at the old temple—how did you come to be there? How long before that had you left Beijing? Do you remember?"

Beiming replied, "I already told you, Master. After leaving the capital, I went directly to Jinling. I hardly stopped along the way and rested at the Jade Cloud Temple for only one night."

"After today, don't tell anyone that story again," said Baoyu. "And when we're in public, don't mention my name."

"It's not as though anyone's going to ask me!" retorted Beiming. "Who would I tell? And as for Master's given name, even though the young ladies in the garden might say it, what servant would ever presume to do so?"

Baoyu finished eating and went back to his books.

■ ■ ■

A short while later, as Baoyu—lamp now in hand—continued reading, Xue Pan came round again, wanting to drag him off to meet Bai Yaolian. Naturally, Baoyu was still unwilling to go. Just as they were arguing over it, Beiming entered, carrying a small calling card, and reported, "Someone just delivered this. He said he was sent to invite Master Xue and my master."

Baoyu looked at the calling card, which bore only the three characters "Bai Jianren."[5] He then said, "He wants to invite people out, but he hasn't written anything here—do you know where he is inviting us to go?"

"I already know," said Xue Pan. "I'll go with you. Anyway, don't blame him—he's illiterate. I imagine at the moment there's no one there to help him write, which is why there's nothing written on the card."

"How is it that a man who wears the long gown of an official can't write a single character? You must be kidding me! He must be able to write at least a little, like you!"

"I just write badly—and am slow with the brush. He simply can't write at all. What's more, with the exception of the few characters he sees regularly, he can't read, either."

"And this is the kind of person you make friends with?"

"His command of foreign language and foreign writing is, however, extremely good; you shouldn't look down on him so."

Baoyu laughed, "This is a case of ignoring one's own fields and weeding someone else's!"

"Quit worrying about whether he's wheedling or needling anyone else![6] In Shanghai, even those who don't know characters can strike it rich! Waiters, cart drivers—plenty have become rich men! But on the other hand, educated men like you—and I'm not trying to offend you here—well, I've never heard of even one striking it rich!"

"That's as may be. And that's why they are worthy to be called 'educated men.'"

"That's also strange," said Xue Pan. "Why is it that scholars are supposed to be poor?"

"It's certainly not that they're *supposed* to be poor—but a great windfall isn't likely to simply fall to earth from the sky. If you tell a scholar to search deep within himself and act based upon heavenly order and his own integrity, I'm afraid he simply wouldn't pursue such profit. A scholar who has achieved clarity of principle will choose to preserve heavenly order and maintain his own integrity—and that will prevent him from making a fortune!"

"If you put it that way, then where does your family's money come from?"

"From the meritorious service of my ancestors. They served as officials, received salaries, and gradually built up their wealth over time. That's a whole other matter."

"Fine, if you don't want to talk about it, then we won't. Let's go!"

Baoyu held firm and refused to go. Xue Pan thought for a moment, then said, "He's invited you, but you refuse to go. What if I invite you as *my* guest?"

Baoyu replied, "When the time comes that you're playing host, we'll talk about it."

Xue Pan recognized that there was nothing he could do, and so all he could do was depart, alone.

■ ■ ■

Baoyu returned to his reading as before. He could read ten lines at a glance, and since at the moment he was eagerly seeking specific information about the current era, he read exceptionally quickly. Gradually the sound of voices outside grew quiet, and he told Beiming to shut the outer door and go to bed. Baoyu then shut the connecting door between the rooms and went back to his books.

Sometime around midnight he heard someone banging on the outer door, followed by the sound of Beiming opening it, and finally a raucous pounding upon his own door.

"Who's there?" he called.

"It's me!"

Baoyu could tell it was Xue Pan and groaned inwardly. He thought, "That brute is drunk again! Best to ignore him."

He called back, "I've already gone to sleep, I'll see you tomorrow!"

On the other side of the door, Xue Pan gave a great guffaw. "I can see you reading through the crack in the door! Who do you think you're fooling?"

"I'm really very tired and was just going to sleep."

"Open the door. I just want to talk to you for a minute."

Baoyu, feeling he had no other recourse from Xue Pan's goading, opened the door. Xue Pan strode in, grabbed Baoyu, and blurted, "I'm inviting you." Having gotten out these three words, he began pulling Baoyu toward the door.

Baoyu said, "What is it? Tell me first, then we can go. What time is it? And where would we be going?"

Xue Pan pulled out his watch and looked at it. "It's only one o'clock! Still early!"

"Where are we going?"

"I'm inviting you."

"Inviting me to do what?"

Xue Pan plumped himself down heavily into a seat. "Inviting you to go drink at a brothel."

"Isn't it a bit late for drinking?"

"You don't get it!" said Xue Pan. "Shanghai never goes to sleep! Today is the celebration of the Birthday of the Flowers, so the journal *Play* has published a list of selected 'flowers.'[7] The girls on that list will probably be up entertaining till the break of dawn!"

"You're already drunk, and yet you're going back out for more? You won't be able to keep it down!"

"Why yes, I have had a bit already. Two rounds, in fact. When drinking at the brothels in Shanghai, one usually drinks four or five rounds in a night! But how could anyone drink the last two rounds? They're like a sacrificial offering, to be left on the altar! Just for appearances."

Baoyu laughed: "Pffft!"

"What are you laughing at?"

"I'm laughing because you have not, as yet, been bound up and brought to the execution ground; and yet here you are, already talking about making 'sacrifices' like you're some kind of martyr!"

"Anyway, you're not drunk, so you could drink them. And it certainly wouldn't make a martyr out of you! Let's go!"

Baoyu was still unwilling to go, and Xue Pan, growing angry, said, "When Bai Yaolian invited you, you said you despised his 'disgusting vulgarity.' Do you dare despise me, too?"

With this, Baoyu knew there was nothing he could do and could only go along. Baoyu said, "I'm grateful that you've invited me, of course! It's just that it's already too late—I'm tired and you're drunk. I would be even more grateful if we could go some other day."

Xue Pan paid him no heed and dragged him out of the room while calling to Beiming to lock the door and follow them out.

■ ■ ■

If you wish to know how this particular outing will play out, please listen to the explanation in the following chapter.

Chapter Seven

A glib response causes discord; angrily, he interrupts a conceited sycophant

An upright gentleman impresses with a wealth of sound counsel

WE WERE speaking of Xue Pan dragging Baoyu out the door. Xue Pan already had a sedan-style horse cart waiting outside—in fact, it was the one that Xue Pan had ridden in on the way there. Xue Pan pulled Baoyu into the cart, then said to Beiming, "In the north, a servant would ride straddling the cart poles; but the carts here have no poles to sit on, so you should stand at the back of the cart instead. There's an iron platform back there for you to stand on, and overhead are two leather straps. Hold on tightly with both hands, so you don't fall over!" Beiming obediently stood as he'd been told to. The cart driver snapped the reins and whipped the horses, who took off as though they were flying.

A short while later, the cart stopped, and Xue Pan and Baoyu descended. Xue Pan said to the driver, "We won't need you any-more tonight! Come back at three tomorrow to bring us back to our lodgings." The driver assented, and, with a crack of the reins, was off.

With Beiming following behind, Xue Pan led Baoyu into a *hutong* and around a corner before finally entering a doorway.[1] He told Beiming to sit on the ground outside to wait, then led Baoyu to the stairs. Just as they arrived at the foot of the staircase, Baoyu suddenly heard a strange cry from outside. He couldn't make out what was being said but thought it very odd.

When they reached the top of the stairs they were greeted by two women, who welcomed them into the room. There were already two other customers there, but they were strangers to Baoyu.

Xue Pan bawled, "Where is he?"

One of the women replied, "Elder Brother had an invitation from Gongyang Lane, he'll be here shortly."

"Who can be bothered to wait for him? Go write an invitation slip for him!" As he spoke, he had Baoyu write out the slip.

"I've never written one, though!" protested Baoyu. "I don't know what to write."

Xue Pan pleaded with him, "My fine brother, you can write essays and even earned a *juren* degree! How is it that you can't make out a simple invitation slip? Don't make things so difficult!"

As they were arguing, they heard another sudden, strange call from downstairs. Upon hearing it, all of the women in the room ran out. In a few moments they heard someone shout, "I'm late! I'm late!" Rolling up the entryway door curtain, one of the women announced, "Master Xue, your guest is here!"

Baoyu looked, and saw that sure enough, the guest was Bai Yaolian.

Xue Pan clapped his hands. "Fantastic! No need to write that slip now."

Baoyu had only just returned to his seat when the two strangers in the room came over to introduce themselves. As it turned out, one was Bai Yaolian's brother Bai Yaoming, and the other, a man called Wu Bohui.[2]

Seeing Baoyu, Yaolian said, "Since you didn't honor us with your presence earlier, I thought perhaps you had thought my invitation insincere. I will choose another day and invite you again with the utmost sincerity!" Baoyu had no choice but to exchange a few rounds of polite apologies and small talk.

Then, noticing Wu Bohui's dashing posture, exuberance, and proud, energetic spirit, Baoyu decided that he was a very different class of man from Bai Yaolian. And so Baoyu and Bohui took up conversation with each other. Only then did Baoyu find out that Bohui had previously been an accountant aboard the *Taishun* steamboat and had met Xue Pan when the latter was traveling on board. At the moment, however, he was unemployed and a man of leisure.

Baoyu asked him: "Which company owns the *Taishun*?"

"The China Merchants Group."

"And is the captain a foreigner?"

"He is."

"I don't understand!" cried Baoyu. "Why does it have to be foreigners helming the ships? Do you mean to tell me that Chinese are incapable of doing it?"

"How could they be incapable?" replied Bohui. "But there's another reason behind it."

As the two men were talking, Xue Pan had already given a series of orders to set the table. At this point, he crossed the room to ask Baoyu, "Which one do you want to call?"

"What am I calling? I don't understand."

"You and I would call them 'calling slips'—for summoning 'companions.'[3] The locals call it *jiaoju*."

Baoyu replied, "I don't know any of them! Don't you know that by now?"

"It doesn't matter if you know any or not, you can't not call one! I'll help you call a couple—what kind do you like? Fat, thin, round-faced, long-faced, big, small—hurry up and say the word! I'll call them for you."

"This is entirely your own foolish idea. I don't care in the least."

At this moment, Bohui had been commandeered by Bai Yaolian for the writing of slips. Once he'd finished writing them out, Xue Pan pronounced that they should all take their seats.

Having last eaten quite a while earlier at the inn, Baoyu was by now feeling a bit hungry, so he joined the others and ate a little. He then asked Bohui to explain what he'd said a few moments earlier.

"It's not that Chinese are unable to helm ships," replied Bohui. "But if a steamship company hires a Chinese crew, their insurance company won't be willing to insure them. That's the difficulty."

Baoyu didn't understand the word "insurance," so Bohui explained it to him in detail.

"Are all of the insurance companies foreign-owned?" Baoyu asked.

"There's only one Chinese company."

"And you mean to tell me that even the Chinese insurance company also imposes this restriction?"

"No—but even though it doesn't, it can't bear the costs of insuring an entire steamship company on its own. In addition to the goods, there's also the boat itself . . . and it's even harder when there are many boats involved!"

At this point Bai Yaolian interjected, "It's not just that the Chinese company can't bear the burden itself; it's really just that all things Chinese are unreliable!"

"What you do mean, 'All things Chinese are unreliable'?" asked Baoyu.

Yaolian replied, "Among the Chinese, there's not one who's dependable!"

Baoyu, not waiting for him to finish, smiled coldly and said, "Everyone sitting around this table with you today is Chinese, so perhaps we are all unreliable? It would be one thing for you to say that I am unreliable; but do you mean to say that you're criticizing yourself, as well?"

"Even though I *am* Chinese," said Yaolian, "I have a little bit of the temperament of a foreigner."

At this, Baoyu was enraged and blurted out, "Does the foreigner's shit smell like roses? It's a pity we're all so unfortunate—perhaps if we'd been born foreigners' dogs, we'd have the chance to eat it!"

He then turned to Xue Pan: "I told you I didn't want to come! And yet you insisted on dragging me here to listen to this garbage. Tomorrow you'll have to prepare some hot water for me to wash out my ears!" He turned again, this time to Bohui, and, taking him by the hand, asked for his address. "I'll call on you tomorrow. I'm sorry, but I must take my leave."

By now, several women had already arrived, and Xue Pan had set to pawing at them, oblivious to what else was taking place. Suddenly, he heard Baoyu taking his leave of Bohui, and, turning to look, saw Baoyu disappear through the doorway. Xue Pan rushed after him and stopped him. "Don't leave—you don't know the way. Come back, and I'll take you home later."

Without saying a word, Baoyu continued directly to the bottom of the stairs, where he summoned Beiming and left. Xue Pan had no choice but to follow them down the stairs and lead them back to the entrance of the *hutong*. There he called two rickshaws for them and told the pullers how to get to the Changfa Inn. Once he saw that Baoyu and Beiming had gotten into the rickshaws, he turned around and went back to the party. Rejoining the group, he said to Bohui, "I wasn't paying close attention, how did he get so out of sorts all of a sudden?"

Bai Yaolian replied, "Your kinsman sure has an odd temper! All I said was that I had a little bit of foreign temperament, and he got mad! Really, my temperament can be whatever I like it to be—that's my personal right! Why does he think he gets to judge me?" Without waiting for Yaolian to finish speaking, Xue Pan had once again turned to resume chatting and joking with the courtesans. After sitting for a bit longer, Wu Bohui also took his leave. The other three men remained, continuing their boisterous party until such time as they had to go their separate ways.

Xue Pan felt a nagging sense of concern for Baoyu. When he made his way back to the inn, it was already past three in the morning, and when he mounted the stairs, he saw that the door to Baoyu's room was open and Beiming was nowhere to be seen. Baoyu was, as before, sitting reading his books.

Xue Pan walked in and made a deep bow, saying, "My dear brother, you mustn't act out like that. Regardless of who it is who has offended you, please spare a thought for my own poor reputation!"

Baoyu could see that he was drunk and that there was no point in discussing things with him. So he simply said, "No one offended me, and I wasn't upset. I just wanted to read, so I left a little early, that's all."

Xue Pan was about to reply when Beiming returned to the room and reported to Baoyu, "The kitchen tea-stove has already burned out—the water has gone cold."

"You want hot water?" asked Xue Pan.

"I had a bit of wine, so I'm feeling thirsty. But there isn't any, so it doesn't matter."

"How could you expect there to be any hot water left at this hour? Here, I'll make some for you." So saying, he bade Beiming come over and help him pull out a piece of equipment. As it turned out, it was a wickless kerosene stove, of foreign make and only a few years old. Xue Pan lit it and instructed Beiming to fill a small kettle with water and warm it on the stove. Before long the water had boiled, and they made tea.

Xue Pan said to Baoyu, "Every time you see foreign goods you complain that the foreigners have given us useless products in exchange for our money. What do you think of this, then?"

"As I said before: foreign trade should be about trading what one has for what one lacks. Who wouldn't love a clever contraption like this? But on another level, it's certainly not a naturally occurring thing—it was made through human labor. And if they can make such a thing, why can't we? Why, it would take nothing more than to simply buy one or two of them, pull them apart and take a look inside. If we then made our own based on their model, wouldn't that be splendid?" As he spoke, Baoyu glanced over at Xue Pan, who, jaw slack and eyes closed, was teetering precariously where he stood.

"Please go to sleep," Baoyu urged him. "We can talk again tomorrow."

Xue Pan requested a mouthful of tea and drank it, then mumbled "See you tomorrow!" as he lurched unsteadily out of the room.

Baoyu went back to his reading. As it happened, upon his return from the brothel, he had pulled out from his pile of books a bound volume containing the full run of issues of *The Chinese Progress*, as well as a number of issues of *The Reformer China*.[4] Leafing through them, he felt that they perfectly suited his purpose. Yet there was something strange about them—as he read the essays, he felt they were saying things that he himself had longed to say, but that he'd never been quite able to express. How was it that these writers had been able to articulate it so well? He didn't completely understand the current events the papers mentioned, but after slowly reading through them from front to back he gradually came to understand more and more. The more he understood, the more he felt as though his spirit had been ignited.

Once Xue Pan had left, Baoyu had resumed his reading and had completely forgotten his own fatigue. He read through the night and was still reading after dawn had broken. When Beiming woke up and came in, he saw Baoyu, still sitting as he had been the night before. Surprised, he asked, "Has Master not slept?"

Seeing that Baoyu neither moved nor responded, Beiming grew anxious and thought, "Oh no, he's fallen into another stupor!" But he also didn't dare to approach, lest he startle him; so he stood to the side, observing. When he finally saw Baoyu turn a page, pause for a short while, then turn another, Beiming realized that Baoyu had just been absorbed by his reading. Quietly, he withdrew from the room, went downstairs, and asked a waiter to pour him some water. Beiming brought this back into the room, and gently called, "Please come wash up, Master." Only then did Baoyu reply. He washed his face, then returned to his pile of books and continued digging through them. Suddenly he uncovered a bundle wrapped in paper with four characters across the front, reading "THESE BOOKS ARE BANNED." Whatever was inside had been wrapped tightly. Hurriedly trying to remove the wrapping to see what it contained, Baoyu was surprised to find that he had to tear through layer upon layer of paper. He thought, "Maybe it's the *Tuibei Illustrations*! Otherwise, it's got to be the *Song of Shaobing*!"[5] He continued tearing away the paper as he thought, tearing away countless layers. In the end there were only three books inside: collected volumes one, two, and three of the journal *The China Discussion*.[6] He immediately grabbed a volume and started to read it, finding it somewhat richer in thought than *The Chinese Progress*. As he read, he grew happier and happier. Without even noticing, he had read through all three volumes and was disappointed that there was not a fourth or a fifth. Returning to his pile of books, he dug through it for what seemed like ages, but did not manage to find even a trace of more issues of *The China Discussion*. Soon it was time for breakfast. He ate, then went back to reading, flipping back and forth through the pages of the three different publications he'd found.

He continued reading for quite a while until he saw Xue Pan walk in draped in a squirrel-fur robe, its buttons still unfastened. In a drowsy haze, he walked over to Baoyu, saying, "Brother

Bao, what energy you've got! How is it you're already awake this early?"

"What time is it, that you're saying it's 'early'?"

"Two in the afternoon. Have you eaten yet?"

Baoyu laughed. "It's too early for dinner!"

Xue Pan mumbled something in response and left. A short while later he returned, having washed his face and combed his hair. "Brother Bao, are you hungry yet? Let's go out for dim sum."

"Can't you settle down a little bit? Let's just have a quiet day at home. There's certainly nothing important we need to do out there, why should we go out and wander about aimlessly? If you want dim sum, send someone out to buy something and bring it back! Isn't it exactly the same?"

"Actually, my jaw really aches," said Xue Pan. "I don't really want to eat—but if you don't want to go out, forget it. We'll just chat here. I drank so much last night that I've forgotten everything I did!"

Baoyu pushed his book to the side. "You're always getting drunk—that goes without saying. But the company you keep—people like that Bai Yaolian—why do you go out of your way to be friends with them? Usually when you make friends with someone, there's a reason. So what's the reason you've become friends with him? If you say it's to order foreign goods, you must be aware that there are many other lines of business in which one can earn money! You think only about how selling foreign goods earns you money, but you should also know that the foreigners earn even more than you do—and yet you still continue selling things on their behalf. On the other hand, if you were to sell domestic goods, you're still selling them for someone else, but at least the goods you're selling are made by our own businesses. Why do Chinese go to such lengths to make themselves the slaves of foreigners? And as for this Bai Yaolian fellow, why he's simply inhuman! With the least provocation, he's willing to paint all Chinese with the same brush, saying that we're all 'unreliable'! I asked whether he, too, was unreliable—and he had the nerve to say that he has the temperament of a foreigner. I don't know what sort of conscience a man like this is born with! Based on what he says, the values that our ancient sages used as the foundation of their teachings—'cultivation,' 'proper conduct,' 'loyalty,' and 'trustworthiness'—apparently no longer exist! If I had the right to kill with impunity, I would kill a bastard like him first!"

Xue Pan laughed, "Why go so far as that?"

"Based on what he says," Baoyu continued, "it seems anyone who is trustworthy and practices proper conduct can be said to have a 'foreign' temperament. Fortunately—according to him—all Chinese are unreliable; otherwise, if we all happened to learn to be more reliable, how could China not be converted into a foreign country? To put it simply, he's learned a little bit of foreign speech and writing, and instantly he thinks everything foreign is great and can't wait to start revering the foreigners like his own parents! Last night, I spent the whole night reading and learned that the foreigners think patriotism is the most important thing. I'm afraid that those foreigners who love their own countries so much would have no use for such an undeserving son!"

Xue Pan said, "Why get yourself worked up criticizing him with such venom?"

"He criticized every Chinese person in one sentence! Is that not venomous? Simply put, I only have one bit of advice for you: such a person is the most worthless, low-class, sort of thing! In the future, you'd do well to keep your distance. I'm certainly not trying to flatter you, but someone like you—without artifice or affectation—as long as you keep to the right path, it wouldn't be hard to come up with a tremendously successful career of your own, and then what need would you have for cavorting with that kind of person?"

When Baoyu had finished his lecture, Xue Pan didn't know how to reply, so he switched to small talk to cover the awkwardness. He asked, "Do you think those books will be useful?"

Baoyu replied, "You've got plenty of good books here. But that journal *The China Discussion* only had three volumes—do you know whether any more were printed?"

"There were. If you want them, I'll arrange to buy you copies tomorrow."

Just then, Beiming entered and announced that a guest had come to pay his respects. Baoyu went out to greet the visitor, and as it turned out, it was none other than Wu Bohui, which delighted Baoyu.

■ ■ ■

If you wish to know why Bohui had come, please listen to the explanation in the following chapter.

Chapter Eight

At leisure, they drink tea and chat frankly about "natural feet"

A shocking discussion on hunting prohibitions turns to matters of real estate

WE WERE just speaking of Baoyu who welcomed Wu Bohui and led him inside. Bohui greeted Xue Pan, and each man then took a seat. After they had dispensed with the usual pleasantries, Xue Pan said that he had completely forgotten everything that he had done after he'd gotten drunk on the previous day.

Baoyu quipped, "A pity you weren't that drunk when you made Bai Yaolian's acquaintance!"

Xue Pan replied, "My good brother, forget about it. From now on, I'll distance myself from him a bit, and that's that. I've had enough of your complaining."

Bohui said, "Actually, Shanghai is full of people who worship foreigners. That's not so bad in itself, but there are many who go so far as to take advantage of the foreigners' power to bully and oppress their own countrymen!"

Xue Pan clapped and said to Baoyu, "Didn't I say so? It's fine. Even if you want to get upset over it, there are simply too many people doing it for you to be sore at all of them!"

Baoyu responded, "Then you're taking after them already!"

"Though I haven't necessarily taken after them," said Xue Pan, "I also won't make the mistake of getting crosswise with them."

Baoyu was about to reply when he saw Beiming enter with another person in tow. It was Xue Pan's driver from the night before, announcing that he'd arrived with the carriage.

"Great!" said Xue Pan. "Today's Saturday, let's ride over to have a stroll in the Zhang Garden."

"If I'd known you'd hired a carriage already, I wouldn't have hired one myself," said Bohui. "I came in a carriage as well. Last time you entrusted me with finding a house, and today I heard that there is a foreign-style residence available out past the racetrack, so I came especially to ask you to go take a look at it and see whether it suits your needs."

Xue Pan wanted to drag Baoyu along with him, and Bohui agreed that it would be good for Baoyu to get out of the inn for a bit to dispel his boredom. And so the three men left together, with Xue Pan and Baoyu riding in one cart and Bohui in the other. The driver whipped the horse, and they turned out onto Nanjing Road toward the Nicheng Bridge.

■ ■ ■

It was not long before they arrived at their destination, and Bohui went in search of the house's caretaker, obtained a key, and opened the door. The three men entered the building and took a look around. As it turned out, it was a two-bedroom foreign house, surrounded by a green lawn. Xue Pan asked Baoyu,

"Is this house all right? If you find it suitable, we'll move in together and live here for a while."

"If you want to live in a house, why ask me about it?" Baoyu replied. "But no, I wouldn't want to live here. What would be the point of picking up and moving my things back and forth all over the place?"

"Just say whether or not the house is okay!"

"It's clean enough, I guess. It's also pretty open and spacious. But it seems to me there's something not quite right about it . . . though I can't say exactly why that is."

Bohui cut in, "It's only natural that someone who's accustomed to living in Chinese-style houses would see the differences in a Western-style house and feel a bit unaccustomed to them."

Xue Pan suddenly cried out, "Damn! I'm hungry! How strange, why is it that as soon as I'm hungry I'm *unbearably* hungry? Let's go find something to eat."

"I think it must be that you ate breakfast too early," said Bohui.

Baoyu laughed. "He hasn't had any breakfast yet today. He'd only just gotten up when you arrived."

As Baoyu spoke, Xue Pan had already seized him and pulled him out of the house, urging Bohui to come along. They climbed back into the carriages and told the drivers to take them to Zhang Garden.

They soon arrived, and their carriages stopped outside the entrance of a large foreign-style building. The three men descended from their carriages, then entered the building and chose seats. Xue Pan exclaimed that he wanted dim sum and ravenously worked his way through an assortment of fried noodles and boiled dumplings. When he'd finished, he gave a small stretch and declared, "That's a bit better. Just now I was so hungry that my legs were going rubbery, it was so strange!" Baoyu and Bohui exchanged a glance and laughed. Xue Pan stood up and strode off.

Baoyu and Bohui struck up a conversation, and slowly began to discuss the house they'd just been to look at. Baoyu said, "It was actually very odd. That house looked fine, but I felt that there were many things not quite right about it, which I found myself unable to express. It was truly strange."

"It's just because the design is different, that's all."

"Just so! You meet with stairs as soon as you walk in the front door—that placement is totally incorrect!"[1]

"Foreign houses aren't all that way—that layout was chosen to suit the building site. Still, in my view, foreign houses are generally the best. Leaving everything else aside, the first improvement is their smooth, flat ceilings. In a Chinese house, when you lift your head and look up, you see the beams and trusses—not very attractive."

"How do they make their ceilings flat?"

"Saying it out loud, it sounds ridiculous, but they nail up slats of wood, then plaster over it with paper pulp and lime."

Baoyu laughed: "Putting it like that, I'd say our northern houses are still better. They also have something like that, except that they use long beams and poles to make a frame, then they nail it up on the ceiling, and then glue paper over it. The paper they glue on is white with silver flowers, and you change it once a year, so every year it's brand-new."

"But I'm afraid it's not as sturdy as their ceilings."

"Why should a ceiling need to be sturdy? And besides, there's another benefit to doing it our way: if the roof leaks, you'll know exactly where it's leaking, and you can fix that spot, wherever it is. But if you were to use the foreign method, if the roof leaks, the rainwater will pool inside that flat ceiling first, and who knows where it will go by the time it finally leaks out! If you want to fix it, you won't actually know where the roof is leaking."

Bohui laughed, "Leave it to you to think of such a detail."

As they were speaking, the number of people outside was gradually increasing: male, female, elderly, young, all contributing to a hubbub of laughter and chatter. Suddenly, they heard a peal of laughter from behind themselves, and when Baoyu turned to look, he saw Xue Pan laughing and talking with a courtesan while leading her over by the hand. To Baoyu, he said, "She was to be your companion yesterday. But you got mad and left early, so I had to entertain her on your behalf. Today I give her back to you, and what happens now is no longer my business."

Baoyu reddened and did not say a word. Xue Pan and two other courtesans then sat at a nearby table and brewed some tea. A young servant girl set up a water pipe for Baoyu, but Baoyu shook his head and said he didn't smoke. The servant girl left.

Not long after, the two courtesans sitting with Xue Pan called out to some of the other women and abandoned Xue Pan, so he came over to Baoyu and asked, "Of those two, who do you think is better?"

"Forget about who's better—more important, why do they all have bound feet? It looks so repulsive! How are you even able to be near them?"

Xue Pan had not yet mustered an answer when Bohui cut in, laughing, "Another 'natural-foot' advocate!"

"What's a 'natural foot?'" asked Baoyu.

Bohui answered, "In the past three or four years, there has been a group of activists who established an anti-footbinding society and have been attempting to persuade women not to bind their feet. Later, because of the fallout of the Hundred Days Reform,[2] their members were harshly punished, and the society broke up. After that, there was a foreign woman who established a 'Natural Foot Society,' with the same goal of dissuading people from footbinding. It takes its name from the idea that an unbound foot is natural, so they're now called 'natural feet.'"

"In my view," said Xue Pan, "the bound foot is the one that should be called 'natural'!"

Bohui asked, with some astonishment, "Why?"

"I remember reading in some book or other that 'It is natural that one must tread through adversity.'[3] If you think about it, if 'natural feet' are those that are unbound, how can they be said to be treading through adversity?"

"How bizarre!" said Baoyu. "How is it that you've managed to come out with such an erudite joke?"

"What's so strange about it?" asked Xue Pan. "I'll remind you, I once came up with the line 'The girl's elated: the nuptial candles have burned low, her lust by new groom finally sated' during a drinking game!"[4]

Baoyu turned to Bohui and said, "I've read a good number of books over the past two days, and today I got up early and read a manifesto published by an anti-footbinding society, as well as several introductions to the topic. What they said seemed generally to be correct, but in my view the article only took up one perspective and set its ambitions too high. It seems to me that it's not yet time for their approach. They said that footbinding was cruel, which naturally is not wrong, but they only took the approach of advising women to stop footbinding. They didn't broach the subject of men, so of course, their argument couldn't but be a trifle one-sided. From the outset, they started in with things like 'women are the mothers of our future citizens, not men's playthings'; they also said something about 'men and women should have equal rights,' and 'women should be able to seek their independence.' I wouldn't dare to disagree with any of these things, it's just that it's too early for them. The horrific custom of footbinding, which has been going on for who knows how many millennia, and has converted women into the playthings of men, has long since become an ingrained part of the character of Chinese men. And women themselves have long been content to be the playthings of men. If we now want to eradicate this horrible custom, why don't we—in addition to trying to persuade the women—try to persuade the men, too?"

"Footbinding is a women's affair," said Bohui. "How would you go about persuading men?"

"If we start from the very idea of 'playthings,'" said Baoyu, "there are indeed ways we might persuade the men. Think of big-footed people like ourselves. We have to bathe every day; otherwise, if things were to get busy and one were to go two or three days without bathing, one's feet would begin to stink. How much more so if they were bound! Tightly bound in layer upon layer of fabric, even though they may appear to be fine and delicate from the outside, on the inside, the odor must be unspeakably foul! If one is to think of them as playthings, it is in appearance only; if they stink on the inside, what good are they to play with? If this message were spread widely enough, I believe everyone would come to a great awakening. It's like playing with a jadeite snuffbox: inside of course there must be snuff, otherwise it's just an empty ornamental box—but even in that case, you can still amuse yourself with it. But if instead it were filled with shit or filth, not only would no one want to play with it, but I'm afraid no one would even want to look at it. These beautiful, charming women carry beneath them a pair of stinking feet—how is that different from a snuffbox filled with shit?

"Moreover, the smell is not the only problem. Bound into that shape, the foot itself must become unbearably hideous. And so they adorn them by putting them in tiny, pointed shoes. I look upon them much as I would upon a twisted, gnarled old tree: as completely without natural charm. If we were to persuade men of this, as soon as they took it to heart, they would naturally revile footbinding. When going to look for a new plaything, they would look with a renewed eye. These women who subject themselves to footbinding are happy to be playthings, happy to please men. But if men were to no longer want them, they would cease footbinding immediately. If this idea were to get out, this cruel practice might gradually be abandoned.

"After that, we can discuss establishing women's education and wait until these women have some learning; then, even without having to teach them to, they will naturally want to establish their own independence. Right now, even this cruel practice has still not been extirpated; to suddenly start teaching women about equality and self-determination would be like taking an ill person lying sick in bed and, before even helping him to stand up, trying to teach him to run! How could it be made to work? In worldly matters, the greatest fear is inaction; but we should also be fearful of the possibility that something is undertaken too hastily."

Bohui nodded and said, "Your approach is quite right. Of late, I often see people trying to achieve things, and I think they try to jump ahead too quickly; however, it seems as though they have no clear plan, and often make mistakes. It is always because of this need for haste."

"That is not called 'making mistakes,'" said Baoyu. "That is called 'spoiling one's chances.'"

Xue Pan suddenly clapped his hands and laughed. "Previously, if someone read a couple more books than you, you accused him of being a sinecure-seeking insect; now you're talking about these matters of political economy, so let me ask: That makes you a sinecure-seeking what? Or what kind of insect?"

"That was then; this is now."

Bohui said, "This is a matter of 'the scholar has been gone for three days; it's only right that we should look at him with newfound respect.'"

As they conversed, within the foreign building people had started crisscrossing busily back and forth just like the shuttle in a weaver's loom. Baoyu began to feel somewhat fed up and urged the others to leave. Xue Pan summed up and paid their tab, and they all rose together. They circled round the patio and took their seats once more in their carriages. Xue Pan ordered the drivers to take them to the Yu Garden, where the three men entered and strolled around together. However, they did not even stay long enough to brew another pot of tea before they mounted their carriages once more and returned, with Baoyu and Xue Pan still in the same carriage. After circling twice through the streets, Baoyu declared, "The driver must be lost! Otherwise why would he be carrying us back and forth like this on these same two streets?"

"It's called 'driving around,'" said Xue Pan. "People do it in Shanghai."

"Well, it's utterly pointless."

"According to you, Shanghai is full of pointless things. By now, the guest house will already have finished serving dinner. Let's go have some Western food."

"Why bother going to so much trouble? Let's just go back."

Xue Pan, without heeding Baoyu's input, told the driver to take them to the Yijiachun restaurant.

The three men got out of their carriages and climbed the stairs; it was already time for the lamps to be lit. Xue Pan ordered food while preparing calling slips for the summoning of courtesans.

"This simply won't do!" cried Baoyu. "If you're going to be like this, I'm leaving."

"Why are you so upset?" asked Xue Pan. "I truly don't understand, when did you develop the temperament of an old stick in the mud?"

"It's not that I'm a stick in the mud; it's that after that conversation we just had about footbinding in the teahouse, if I see a pair of delicate little feet, I won't be able to help but think about the filth contained within those dozens of layers of wrappings. If you invite them to come here, you will just end up making me feel sick to my stomach."

"Even if you're not inviting any, I'm going to."

"If you invite them, I'll still have to see them. Forget it! Come back tomorrow without me, then you can invite whomever you want."

Xue Pan laughed. "If you're going to be in Shanghai a long time, you'll end up 'taking up' with one of them anyway."

Not understanding what Xue Pan was saying, Baoyu paid him no mind and instead observed Bohui as he ordered food. Bohui wrote out a request for partridge, but the waiter at his side announced, "We're out of partridge, there's a ban on hunting."

"If I remember correctly, the spring season doesn't start until the twentieth of the month," said Bohui. "How is it that hunting season has ended already? It certainly hasn't been in any of the papers."

"I don't know," replied the waiter. "Honestly, I don't know for sure whether hunting has been banned or not. But the men who provide our wild game haven't sent any over for the past two days, so I'm guessing that's why."

Bohui wrote out another menu item and handed it to the waiter. Baoyu asked, "How is it that hunting could be banned? Isn't that strange?"

"It's the foreigners' rule," said Bohui. "Hunting is prohibited between spring and fall, because that is the hatching season, and they're afraid that a hunter will kill a mother animal, and then her babies will die as well. It's been a long-standing policy."

"Are there hunting grounds within the foreign settlement?"

"No. In order to hunt, you have to go into the villages further inland."

"So that means that their prohibitions extend all the way to our inland regions?"

"The prohibition doesn't extend that far, no. But they have made it illegal to sell wild game within the foreign settlement, so naturally, no one goes out hunting. Since it's mainly foreigners who eat wild game, if they prohibit its sale, there's no one else to buy it. So even though the foreigners haven't prohibited the hunters from hunting, the hunters stop all the same."

Xue Pan added, "You shouldn't say that foreign rules don't reach inland, it seems like only a matter of time before they do. Two days ago, I met up with an official called Li from the Bureau of Foreign Affairs. He told me that already five or six hundred mu of land, comprising land held under ten or so different land deeds, all within the Chuansha department in Baoshan county, have been sold to foreigners, and the *daotai*'s office has to officially certify the transfer of title."[5]

Hearing this, Baoyu found himself in a state of shock.

■ ■ ■

If you wish to know why he was so startled, please listen to the explanation in the following chapter.

Chapter Nine

The clever "Spirit Jade" samples foreign alcohol at Yijiachun

The "Oaf King" buys books at the Jiangnan Arsenal

WE WERE speaking of Baoyu, who, having heard that foreigners had bought land in inland China, was shocked and said, "But—the foreign concessions! I thought the foreign concessions were just *rented* to them! How could they have been *sold* to them! And not just that, but we've let them buy land *outside* of the concessions?"

Xue Pan answered, "Back when I first started selling books, I chanced to leaf through a few here and there. Some book I read said that China's land comprises two hundred million square li—it's hardly as though they could buy it all up!"

"Even an area of two hundred million square li is finite. We can't conjure another three hundred million out of thin air! But on the contrary, time is infinite, so if we allow them to buy some this year and some next year, eventually the day will come when we'll have sold it all!"

Xue Pan guffawed, "You really are a myopic worrywart! By the time we've sold it all, as you say, we'll all have long since died and turned to dust, so why bother about something that won't happen for another thousand or hundred years? The way you worry, I'm afraid your hair will have turned white in a couple years' time!" As he finished speaking, a waiter delivered the soup course. "Eat up and stop worrying! If you keep being this anxious, I'm afraid you won't be able to get anything down!" At the same time, he called out for some alcohol: "Beer, porter, brandy, whiskey, champagne: brother Bao, which will you have?"

"I don't understand," Baoyu replied.

Xue Pan then asked Bohui, to which Bohui replied, "Whichever. I'm not much of a drinker."

Xue Pan called for a bottle of champagne. A waiter arrived with a bottle and used a corkscrew to open it. Baoyu watched fixedly and noticed that when the cork came out, a great deal of white foam bubbled forth from the bottle. The waiter hurriedly stopped up the mouth of the bottle with his hand, then crossed over to pour a glass for Baoyu first before pouring for the others. Xue Pan raised his glass to make a toast, at which Bohui took a sip. Baoyu, however, did not move.

"Why don't you try it?" asked Xue Pan.

"I suspect it's been contaminated," Baoyu replied.

Xue Pan was startled. "It's only just been opened! How can it have been contaminated?"

"When the wine spurted out of the bottle, he used his hand to try to stop it up! I don't know whether his hands are clean or not."

As Baoyu said this, waves of red surged into the waiter's face. He replied, "Our hands are very clean!" He then held up his hands, examining them himself, before holding them out for Baoyu's inspection.

"Not only that," went on Baoyu, "but since he poured for me first, surely all the filth from his hands is in my glass!"

"Everything else about you has changed from before!" said Xue Pan. "In every other regard, it's like you're a completely different person. So how come your bizarre stance toward hygiene–your fastidiousness toward cleanliness and strange fear of contamination—hasn't changed?"

"The desire for cleanliness is a natural inborn trait—in this, all people are alike. If you don't believe me, just look around."

Xue Pan hurriedly stopped him. "Enough, enough. Don't go into another of your treatises. I'll get you a new glass."

Upon hearing this, the server hurriedly pulled out a new champagne glass, wiped it thoroughly with a white cloth, then held it up to the light to inspect it before setting it down in front of Baoyu. Xue Pan poured him a glass of champagne, and Baoyu took a sip. He knit his brow and demanded, "How is this wine? Vinegar is more like it! And not only that, but it's full of bubbles—it's gone off!"

Bohui said, "It's an acquired taste. Once you get used to it, you'll enjoy it."

"If you won't drink this," said Xue Pan, "I'll have him open a bottle of porter instead."

The server immediately went to open a bottle of porter and poured some out for Baoyu.

"It's so dark in color!" said Baoyu. "It looks like medicine. And there's so much foam on top of it, how am I supposed to drink it?"

"You drink the foam as well," said Xue Pan. "That part is good, too."

Baoyu gingerly took a sip. He had only taken in about half a mouthful when he hurriedly spat it back out. "I'm not ill! Why have you given me medicine to drink?"

This caused Xue Pan to break out in a big laugh.

"It's both astringent and bitter at the same time! How could it not be medicine?" Baoyu continued.

"If it's sour you say it's vinegar; if it's bitter you say it's medicine!" remarked Xue Pan. "Fine! Fine! Open a few more bottles of different types, and we'll let him try them all." Thereupon a bottle of beer was opened. Baoyu took only a mouthful before pronouncing, "This one is astringent and bitter, too!" Xue Pan then asked the waiter to open a bottle of brandy.

"There's no need," interrupted Bohui. "If you open a new bottle and he won't drink it, it'll all go to waste. Just have him bring a glass of it, that's good enough."

"Fine," agreed Xue Pan. And so, he asked the server to bring a glass each of brandy and whiskey. A short while later, the server returned, carrying two tiny glasses of spirits on a white porcelain tray. Baoyu took a sip of each, furrowing his brow each time.

"Drinking these is like stabbing oneself in the throat with tiny blades! They're far too strong."

Xue Pan turned to call for more spirits to be brought, but Baoyu stopped him, saying, "Forget it. I won't drink any more." Xue Pan gave up on ordering anything else for him.

A short while later, they had finished their meal. Xue Pan wanted to go off to the pleasure quarters, but Baoyu firmly refused and dragged him into the carriage and back to the guest-house. Bohui accompanied them and sat with them for a while. While he was there, he noticed the large number of books that Baoyu had laid out and remarked, "You've been hard at work!"

"It's not that I've been hard at work," answered Baoyu, "I've just been reading them in my free time to stave off the boredom." So saying, he picked up two books and added, "I read these, but I didn't understand even a little bit. I'd like to ask for your instruction."

Bohui took a look at the first of the books Baoyu held out to him, which happened to be *Telegraphy: Updated Edition*. Laughing, he explained, "This is just a book of telegraph codes." He then went on to explain the ins and outs of modern telegraphy. Taking a look at the second book, it turned out to be an incomplete primer titled *Learn English Without a Teacher*. "The opening introductory material is all missing from this one. No wonder you couldn't understand it." He then explained the purpose of the second book.

"But what use is it to study this?" asked Baoyu.

"It's of great use," said Bohui. "Once you understand their speech, it's much easier to communicate with them. Or more ambitiously, if you rigorously study the written language, you can translate their more useful books."

"Is it possible to buy books that have already been translated?" asked Baoyu.

"Yes." Bohui then glanced at the issue of *The Chinese Progress* that was lying on the table, then picked it up and leafed through it. Pointing at one of the pages, he said, "See here next to this article where it says 'Translated from *The Times*'? *The Times* is the name of a big foreign newspaper. If you want to buy translated books, you'll at least have to be able to point out a title, even if you not sure of what kind you want."

"How could I know anything about them?" asked Baoyu. "But if we can find a shop that specializes in selling translated books, we can go pick some out and buy them."

"The Scientific Book Depot specializes in selling translated books, many of which were translated by translators at the Jiangnan Arsenal. If you want to buy one or two, we can go there. But if you want to buy more than that, it's better to go directly to the Arsenal."

"To buy the entire set of the Arsenal's books would cost only about five or six hundred strings of cash," said Xue Pan. "I've bought two sets there before. If you'd like, I'll go with you tomorrow morning to order a set."

"Don't be too hasty," said Bohui. "Tomorrow's Sunday."

"All right, then we'll go the day after. But they're pretty obnoxious there—it's bad enough they won't mark down the prices of the books, but they won't sell on credit, nor will they accept payment in bank drafts. They say it's because their location is too remote, making it hard to get bank drafts authenticated, so they insist on cash. Even if you wish to pay in foreign currency, it would still require several hundred coins—which would be extremely heavy! How could you possibly transport it? Not only that, but they're not willing to deliver the books once you've bought them! It's ridiculous! They have a woodworking shop there, and even if you're willing to pay them to build you a wooden trunk in which to carry your books, they're not willing to make it for you! If you want to buy a big stack of books, how are you supposed to carry them home?"

"Hire a handcart," answered Bohui, "and have them brought home that way. It's not that difficult."

"However!" Xue Pan was getting into it now. "The first time I bought books there, I did hire a handcart to carry them home. But two of the books got damaged en route. I couldn't sell them like that, so I ended up having to go to the Book Depot to replace them. Actually, the Book Depot isn't that much more expensive, but you can't get the complete set there." Saying this, he strode off into his own room, returning a few moments later with a bank draft that he handed to Bohui. "If it's not too much trouble, could you exchange this for several hundred in banknotes by tomorrow morning? Otherwise, it will be far too heavy to pay in foreign pound coins, and I truly can't imagine how we could carry them all."

Bohui took the draft from him and looked it over. It was made out for eight hundred taels. "I'm afraid I haven't got that much to hand!" he protested.

"Whatever you have convenient at your office would be fine," said Xue Pan. "Otherwise talk it over with some of your buddies to see whether they can do anything."

Bohui assented. He chatted with them for a little bit longer, then departed.

Xue Pan drew out a gold pocket watch, gave a quick twist on something on its side, then held it up to his ear. A series of chimes—*ding dang ding dang*—rang out, which even Baoyu could hear.

"I didn't realize it was already 10:45," said Xue Pan. Saying this, he then opened the watch to take a look.

"How do you know that?" asked Baoyu.

"It's a chiming watch. I bought it for two hundred yuan, which was pretty cheap." He held it out for Baoyu to look at. He twisted the small key on the side of the watch again, then handed the watch to Baoyu so he could hear the chimes once more.

"Why, this is something a woman would use!" Baoyu exclaimed.

"You mean that men are too crude, and that such a thing doesn't suit them?"[1]

"No, that's not what I mean. Have you never heard the saying 'Works of gimmicky technology and excessive cleverness are used to entertain women'? Obviously, only women take delight in such things. Doesn't this watch fall into the category of 'gimmicky technology and excessive cleverness'? That's why I said this device is something a woman would use."

"So everything that is a bit clever is necessarily for women's use?"

"Allow me to make a distinction: something that is clever but useful cannot be called 'excessively clever'; something that is clever but useless—something that is made specifically to delight the senses—now *that* I would call 'excessively clever.' Take clocks and watches as an example: they are indeed 'clever' things; but when a clock is placed in the home, the whole family can know what time it is; a watch is worn on one's person, so that when you go out and are walking around, you can still know what time it is. That is a case of clever things being useful. But as for this chiming watch . . ."

Xue Pan grabbed it back from him and said, "What, it can't tell time?"

"No, that's not it! But even if it didn't chime, you would still be able to tell what time it is. So why does it need to chime at all? And if you were a little further away, maybe just a little over ten feet, you wouldn't even be able to hear it. If you want to know the time, just open it and look—why do you need to hear it? Besides that, by the time you've counted the chimes to find out the time, you could easily have just looked at it! Not to mention that there must be times when one counts the chimes incorrectly!"

"At night when the lights are out, is it not useful to be able to listen for the time?"

"At night when the lights are out, aren't you asleep? Why should you need to know the time?"

Xue Pan stood dully for a moment, then responded, "I'll give it back tomorrow, then. If I return this lousy thing, I can spare myself another round of criticism."

"I'm not criticizing you, I'm just criticizing that thing. Compare it to the electric lights and coal-gas lamps along the street that light the streets up as bright as day. Isn't their fabrication extremely clever? And yet they are extremely useful—they cannot be considered items of 'excessive cleverness.' That day when I was at the foreign goods store, I saw a small electric lamp in the shape of a bamboo tube. You twist it in your hands, and it gives off a beam of light that looks like a little white bean.

But what is its purpose? If you were to use it while walking along the street at night, it is not as bright as a lantern; and what use could it be within the home? This is a case of 'gimmicky technology' being 'excessively clever,' something you would give to a bunch of girls to entertain them."

Xue Pan clapped his hands. "Oh, but it *is* useful! At night when you're lying in bed, if you get bitten by a bedbug, you can use it to find the bug. Otherwise, you'd have to take the time to strike a match and light a lantern, and by then, there's no telling where the bedbug might have gone!"

Baoyu couldn't help but laugh. "Anyone who can spend so much money for the apprehension of bedbugs would be better served by cleaning his house; then he wouldn't have to worry about getting bedbugs in the first place."

Xue Pan rose, saying, "Enough! Enough! I can't outtalk you, so I'm just going to stop talking. I'll see you tomorrow!" And so, he left.

■ ■ ■

At this point, Baoyu continued reading as before. He approached the pile of books and turned up several about current affairs. As he read, he gradually felt that he was beginning to understand them. Suddenly he heard a voice from Xue Pan's room—it was the phonograph, playing song after song. The more Baoyu listened, the more irritated he became, and so he rose to his feet, intending to go over and shut it off. He walked over to Xue Pan's door and tried to push it open, but it was locked. He then retreated to his own room, where he was forced to listen to the phonograph continue singing for some time, until finally he could bear it no longer. He walked back over to Xue Pan's door and knocked twice.

"Who is it?" called Xue Pan.

"It's me."

Xue Pan opened the door. "You're not asleep yet?"

"That thing of yours makes such a racket, how could I possibly sleep?"

"I couldn't sleep either," said Xue Pan. "That's why I pulled it out and set it playing." As he spoke, Xue Pan ushered Baoyu into his room and bade him be seated. Baoyu reached out a hand to still the record spinning on the phonograph.

"Don't touch it!" cried Xue Pan. "I'll put it away." So saying, he fiddled with part of the mechanism, and the unit ceased playing immediately.

Raising his head to look at the time on Xue Pan's clock, Baoyu saw that it was already 1:30 in the morning. He said, "At this hour, surely the people in neighboring rooms have already been asleep for some time, and yet you decided to play that thing, which is so noisy no one could possibly sleep through it. They might not say anything to you, but I can't imagine how much they must resent you in private!"

"Haha! How strange! There you go again, trying to teach me the ways of the world."

Baoyu laughed, too. "It's not the ways of the world I'm interested in. It's more a question of 'doing unto others as you would have them do unto you.' For example, if you were sleeping here right now, and the person next door had turned this thing on, squawking and chirping endlessly, wouldn't you resent him?"

"In fact, not only would I not resent him," responded Xue Pan, "I would feel *grateful* to him, since just now I want to listen to a bit of music."

"I'm afraid you're the only person who feels that way."

"Let's speak no more of it. I'm so thirsty—can you call Beiming to bring back the foreign kerosene stove I lent you earlier?"

"What time is it? He's already gone to sleep. In the time it would take to go wake him up, you could already have retrieved it yourself."

"Fine! Fine! Let us take care to 'show compassion for our social inferiors.'" As he spoke, he crossed to Baoyu's room and retrieved the stove, then brought some water to boil.

Not sticking around to drink tea with Xue Pan, Baoyu bade him goodnight and returned to his own room. He had only just briefly drifted off to sleep when the sky once again grew bright. He dressed, then washed up and combed his hair. He didn't see any sign that Xue Pan had yet awakened, but he heard someone knocking at Xue Pan's door, followed by the porter telling someone, "He's not up yet, just leave it there." Baoyu assumed it to be Bohui, but when he emerged to look, it turned out to be a newspaper deliveryman instead. Baoyu called out to him to wait, then looked over the papers he was carrying. Taking one of each, Baoyu instructed the man to return each day, bringing the same papers. The man assented, then left. Baoyu then pored over each newssheet one after the other. Xue Pan didn't wake up until sometime after one in the afternoon—after Baoyu had already eaten lunch—and then immediately went out, not to return for the rest of the day. Baoyu paid this no mind, absorbed instead in thoughts of buying books on the following day.

By the evening, there was still no sign of Xue Pan. The night passed, and it was not until after daybreak the following morning that he finally came running in, asking, "Has Bohui come?"

"No," said Baoyu.

Xue Pan pulled out his watch and glanced at it. "It's just gone 7:00, he should be here any time now." He had not yet finished this sentence when Bohui walked in.

"All right, let's go!" said Xue Pan, pulling Baoyu behind him.

■ ■ ■

If you wish to know whither he intended to drag Baoyu, please listen to the explanation in the following chapter.

Chapter Ten

A debate on "civilization" versus "barbarity" touches on the topic of gardens

Examining industrial artisanry, they tour the Arsenal's factories

WE WERE speaking of how Xue Pan had dragged Baoyu away, when Baoyu said, "Where are we going? If you just told me, it would be easier."

"Didn't you say you wanted to buy books?"

"Sure, but why the hurry? It's still early."

"Yesterday Bohui was talking to me about you, saying that you're so fastidious in all things. He really respects you. Today you want to buy books, and he knows some people who work at the Arsenal, so he's going to accompany us there for a tour to see the machinery. But it's a long way to get there, which is why we have to leave early."

Baoyu was greatly pleased by this, and so he left with the others, bringing along Beiming as well. As before, they took two separate carriages to their destination.

They had not been in the carriages long when they suddenly stopped. Xue Pan pulled Baoyu down from their carriage, and Bohui stepped down from his as well. The party then entered some kind of establishment; upon entering, they were assailed by the smell of oil and smoke, and the building itself was unbearably dark. As they ascended the stairs, a blast of stiflingly hot air threatened to roast them alive. Truly unbearable! Arriving at the upstairs level, Xue Pan and Bohui chose a table and sat. Baoyu, still standing, asked, "Is this the Arsenal?"

Xue Pan laughed. "How could there be an arsenal that looked like this? This is a Yangzhou restaurant called the 'Eternal Flower.' We're just going to have a little dim sum first, then we'll go to the Arsenal."

"You two go ahead," said Baoyu. "I got up early and have eaten already. I couldn't have anything else right now."

Bohui said, "Just try a little bit—this is a famous Yangzhou restaurant, it's the only one of its kind in Shanghai."

"Truly, I couldn't possibly eat anything else," answered Baoyu. "But please go ahead." Saying this, he then walked over to the railing overlooking the street, where he stood for some time watching the goings-on below.

As the three companions were chatting, a server came and brewed them tea.

"If you won't eat anything, at least have some tea," entreated Xue Pan.

"I'm not thirsty either," said Baoyu.

In the end, there was nothing for Xue Pan and Bohui to do about his refusal. For themselves, they just ordered two bowls of noodles, which they ate hurriedly before going back down the stairs and paying their bill.

When they had first set out, Bohui had hoped to ride with Baoyu, but Xue Pan had dragged Baoyu into his carriage, depriving Bohui of the opportunity. Now, it was Baoyu who dragged Xue Pan into their carriage. The driver cracked the reins and off they went. As they rode away, Baoyu repeatedly spat into the street, saying to Xue Pan, "It's just like you to go to such a place, much less eat the food there! It was filthier than a dog's burrow! While a dog's burrow might smell just a bit worse, that place not only positively stank of coal smoke and frying oil, but the tables, chairs, and benches were all completely coated in a layer of oil, which is why I didn't dare to sit down. Just watching the two of you eating and drinking there made me feel revulsion on your behalf! I wanted to spit to get the bad taste out of my mouth, but I didn't dare."

"That's odd. Why didn't you dare to spit in there?" asked Xue Pan.

"If I were to spit in there, wouldn't it just make my saliva as filthy as everything else in there?"

Xue Pan covered his ears and exclaimed, "Stop it! I'm afraid you've gone back to being an idiot today. People take you to a nice restaurant, one which plenty of people of good standing have praised, and yet you say things like this!"

"If you say that makes me an idiot, then I'm an idiot! Meanwhile, you go along with it and aren't an idiot at all! But from now on, don't take me to places like that. Yesterday, across the hall from my room, there were a few people loudly discussing and debating ideas like civilization and barbarity and went on to speak more specifically about 'material civilization' and 'sartorial civilization.' They also said that Shanghai can be considered the most civilized place in China. I've gone with you into a teahouse and eaten two Western meals with you. Thinking of it, they were in fact cleaner than the restaurants I've seen in the north. In Nanjing, I went into a teahouse as well, and that one wasn't nearly so open and bright as the teahouses here. So I did indeed think that Shanghai was terrifically civilized; who would have thought that it would also have this kind of filthy place in it? And on the subject of 'barbarity,' it seems to me that in the parts of the world that are so barbarous that people live in caves in the wilderness—why, even they have clean air, and don't have to breathe in such foul fumes."

"Slow down," said Xue Pan. "When did I go with you to a teahouse?"

"The other day after we took the carriages to go look at houses, didn't we go to a teahouse?"

Xue Pan heaved a great guffaw at this. "You and your big eyes! That was Mr. Zhang's Weichun Garden! It's a garden, why did you think it was a teahouse?"

Baoyu stared at him for a moment. "I refuse to believe that was someone's garden. If it were a garden, regardless of anything else, there should at least be a few pavilions, viewing platforms, and towers, as well as winding paths and curved railings. There should also be some craggy rocks and trees, and one should be able to make out hills and dells. There was nothing winding or curved about that place! It was just a big open field with a big house built in the middle. If that can be considered a garden, I might as well go out and find myself a flat bit of wilderness on which to build a house, and that, too, could be considered a garden."

"It's a foreign-style garden," said Xue Pan. "So it has to have some open lawn, to keep the space feeling open and free. There is also a pavilion in that garden, as well as two rocky hills, but we didn't walk to them that day. Didn't you see the three big characters saying 'Weichun Garden' nailed up at the entrance?"

"And in that building," Baoyu continued, "they had laid out row upon row of tables, obviously set up for selling tea to patrons. Why would a garden be laid out in this way? Say what you will—if you tell me that 'Weichun Garden' is the name of a teahouse, fine. But if you insist that it's a garden, I simply must protest."

Xue Pan replied, "You're being strange again, why should you feel compelled to protest? It's got nothing to do with you."

"Leaving to the side the question of whether a garden should be a place of carefully manicured artificial mountains, forests, hills, and dells—even if we start with the assumption that that place is indeed a 'garden,' once they starts selling tea there, it should be considered a teahouse. Isn't the word 'garden' too noble suffer this kind of abuse?"

"You're full of idiotic rants today, I can't even listen to them anymore. Bohui apparently respects you, why don't you go tell him all of this after we get back?"

They stopped talking for some time, before Baoyu pointed outside the carriage, saying, "Look, there's another garden."

Xue Pan raised his head to look. "Ah! We're almost there. And that's Gaomao Temple, not a garden."

Baoyu laughed. "But didn't you say a building sitting in the middle of a flat empty yard is called a 'garden' now?"

"Take it up with the foreigners. I don't understand it either."

"It's too bad I don't understand a foreign language. And even if I wanted to study it, there's not anyone who can teach me."

"There are plenty of people around here who teach English, and for as little as one or two kuai for a whole month."

"I wonder how many months of study one would need in order to become proficient?"

"I don't know either," answered Xue Pan. "Ask Bohui after we get back, he's great at speaking and writing in foreign languages. But I don't know how long he had to study for."

"I'll ask him tomorrow if he can give me some guidance."

As they were speaking, the carriage pulled in through a gate. To their left stood a building over the door to which hung a sign reading "Artillery Shell Factory." The carriages continued forward, eventually pulling under an archway and turning a corner before coming to a rest. The three men descended from their vehicles, with Beiming jumping down behind them. Bohui had also brought his own servant, Huang Fu, who at this time also came over to attend upon his master.

Bohui said, "Shall we go buy books first? Or take a tour of the factories?"

Xue Pan replied, "To compile a whole set of books takes quite a while. Let's first go and tell them we wish to buy the books and ask them to put together a set. After that, we can stroll around the factories. By the time we're done exploring, the books should be ready. Isn't that the best solution?"

Baoyu and Bohui both heartily agreed.

And so, Xue Pan led the way, with Baoyu and the others following him, through a shedlike structure. The first thing that met their gaze was a large, black-faced clock hanging high above, which read 8:15 a.m. precisely. After turning a corner, they continued walking, passing beneath a tall building.

"That's the office of the General Manager," said Xue Pan. They continued walking a little further, along a path lined with green sheds. Xue Pan said, "Here's the Clerk's Office. This is where they sell the books." Even as he said this, however, he did not approach the Clerk's Office, entering instead a building on their right. This building had two large green doors, currently closed; but inset within one of these was a smaller door, which stood open. Outside the doors hung a sign reading "Department of Illustrations and Maps."

Baoyu was perplexed by this, and asked, "Why is the place where they sell the books called the 'Department of Illustrations and Maps'?"

Xue Pan pushed open the small, nested door and entered. Baoyu and the others followed him in. In the center of the room there was a large, broad table, at which sat Zhu Kun, the man in charge of selling books. Xue Pan expressed that they wished to buy some books, and in response, Zhu Kun asked, "What books do you wish to buy?"

"We want a complete set of your offerings," said Xue Pan. "I've bought books here twice before. You must recognize me."

"I do," said Zhu Kun. "I'll start putting them together for you."

"Then we'll go tour the factory while you do that. Once we've returned, we'll look them over and settle the tab." To this, Zhu Kun agreed.

As he was preparing to leave the building, Xue Pan realized that he had lost sight of Baoyu. As it turned out, further along that long table was a glass box in which there sat a tiny model steamship. Seeing it, Baoyu had been swept back into his memories of the small clockwork steamship he had played with back at his residence in Yihong Courtyard, which was very similar in appearance to this one. He was stunned.

When he finally turned away from this boat, he noticed that in another part of the building there were a number of plank tables. Sitting beside one of them was a person who appeared to be teaching pupils—children of a range of ages—who were gathered around him, reciting their lessons.

They were too far away for Baoyu to hear what they were saying, and so he could only watch dumbly as their mouths opened and closed incomprehensibly.

Xue Pan walked up and started to pull him away. "Let's go!" It was only at this point that Baoyu turned his gaze away from the children at their studies.

Bohui said, "Even though I have some acquaintances here, I don't know the place that well. We should get some directions before we head out."

Zhu Kun, who had just opened his bookcase and begun to extract books, asked them, "Where do you want to go?"

"The Boiler Works," replied Bohui.

"Once you've passed through the fence, walk toward the river. When you reach the dockyards head west, and you're there."

Bohui and the others followed these instructions. When they arrived at the Boiler Works, Bohui pulled one of the grunt workers aside and asked, "Where is the Accounts Office?"

The worker replied, "You've gone the wrong way. The Accounts Office is above the General Affairs Office."

Bohui looked confounded for a moment, then tried again. "I'm looking for Master Feng of the Boiler Works."

At this, the worker pointed to a nearby building and said, "He'll be in there."

Bohui led Baoyu and Xue Pan into the indicated building. There, they saw the bespectacled Feng, busily writing. Seeing

Bohui, Feng hurriedly set down his brush, took off his glasses, and stood up to welcome them. He greeted all of them, then asked Baoyu's and Xue Pan's family and style names. Baoyu gave the style name he had chosen earlier—Zhongying.

A short while later, after Feng had brewed some tea for them, Bohui said, "This is really very impolite of us. Today, these two friends of mine made plans to come see the factories. It goes without saying that they wanted to see your esteemed factory! I unfortunately haven't got connections at the other factories, so I am trying to come up with a way for us to get in to see them as well."

"Fine, fine!" said Feng amiably. "Please feel free to start here at my humble factory."

Bohui stood up and followed Feng, who accompanied them. Upon entering the factory proper, he pointed things out to them one at a time: "There's the manual workshop; there's the machine shop. That's the compound furnace, the most recent model—it takes up a little less space than the old one." He also led them to the machine shop, pointing out even more things: "That's the drill; that's the grinder; that's the iron-cutter." Feng called over a worker and instructed him to pick up a piece of scrap iron to demonstrate the cutter for his guests. The worker picked up a piece of scrap iron about an inch thick and ran it through the cutter. In a short time, it had been divided into two pieces.

Baoyu stuck out his tongue in amazement and gasped, "Astonishing!" He asked the worker to cut another piece, then bent at the waist and put his face close to get a better view of the process. Straightening back up after the cutting was complete, he remarked, "I thought it must be a very fast knife of some kind, but in fact there is no blade involved. There is instead a chisel about an inch wide. It's not so much being sliced into two as being split apart by force. But still, the power required is quite impressive!"

Feng then led them into the neighboring Underwater Mine Factory. The machinery here was all much more refined and sophisticated, very different from the machinery in the Boiler Works. Feng picked up one of the detonator needles to show them and explained that the copper exterior housed a filament made of platinum, an excellent conductor. Once fitted to the exterior of a mine, it would require contact pressure of only about four liang to detonate .[1]

Baoyu had never before heard the words "platinum filament" and tried to get a look at it, but it was not visible in the needle. Feng called for a worker and asked him to bring a piece of the platinum filament to show Baoyu. Baoyu quietly marveled at this filament, thinner than the silk of a spider. Once they had finished this inspection, they departed.

"I have a few unfinished tasks to attend to at the moment," said Feng. "So I can no longer accompany you. But I will call a worker to take you wherever you want to go and show you around. When the workers go on break, come back here for lunch."

"Wonderful, wonderful!" said Bohui. He instructed Huang Fu and Beiming to wait for them in Feng's office. Feng then summoned a laborer to lead the men on their tour.

Thereupon the men followed one another out of the Boiler Works and made their way back to the building on which hung the large clock—which turned out to be the Machine Factory. The worker escorting the party entered the building and approached someone, saying, "Master Hua, these friends of

Master Feng have come to tour the factories, so I have come to ask for your instructions."

"Of course, of course! Proceed however you wish. Unfortunately I have matters I must attend to here, so I am unable to accompany you."

And so the worker led the three men through each section of the factory. But it was only when they had gone upstairs and could look out over the floor that they could see the machinery in its entirety. The overseer of the machinery section, seeing that they were respectable people, pointed things out to them one at a time—the boiler, the cold vapor pipe, the hot steam pipe—explaining each one in turn.

The worker then led the three men out the rear exit, and a few moments later they arrived at the Refined-Iron Works. Because much of the factory was occupied by an enormous coal furnace, burning hot enough to turn the iron a bright, molten red, they remained by the entryway gazing in. The craftsmen were raising hammers and bringing them down, spraying sparks in all directions. There was nothing much worth seeing here, with the exception of a giant hammer that stood near the entryway. This hammer was clearly not for human operation but instead was designed to raise and lower itself.

"What is that called?" asked Baoyu.

"That's a steam hammer," replied the worker.

Having said this, he then led the trio to go take a look at the Firearms Factory.[2] Upon entering, they noticed a number of rifles piled near the door. The worker went on ahead of them and returned shortly thereafter. Soon a supervisor by the name of Wan came out to greet them. First he showed them an array of machinery similar to what they had seen in the machine factory. Then he had them each pick up an unassembled rifle barrel and look through it toward one of the bright areas of the factory—the interior was mirror-bright, and it seemed to them that they must be looking through a thick glass lens. However, upon blowing through the barrels, they found that they were indeed open on both ends.

Xue Pan remarked that this was strange, but Baoyu said, "This I actually understand! They have polished the interior of these barrels to be so incredibly smooth and slick, that when you look through it at a well-lit area, the whole interior of the barrel is illuminated by the reflected light. Isn't that so?"

"Yes, that is so," said Supervisor Wan.

A nearby worker cut in, "Exactly right!"

After this, Wan led them upstairs, where they looked around before departing. As they reached the door, Baoyu halted, looking at the rifles. Supervisor Wan walked up beside him and picked one up. Baoyu thought Wan was going to fire and retreated several paces.

■ ■ ■

If you wish to know whether Wan fired the gun to give Baoyu a demonstration, please listen to the explanation in the following chapter.

Chapter Eleven

Observing the manufacture of foreign weaponry, he is leery of technology shared

The chiming watch is relinquished, and conversation turns to the topic of gamblers

WE WERE speaking of Supervisor Wan, who had picked up a rifle. He then handed it over to Baoyu to let him appraise it. "This is the new model previously fabricated by General Manager Liu. It can fire thirty-five rounds per minute."

"How far can it shoot?" asked Baoyu.

Supervisor Wan paused for a moment, then eventually replied, "We haven't yet tested that."

Baoyu then asked the names of all of the different types of firearms, and Wan pointed them out: "This is a thirteen-round Mauser; this is a five-round Mauser; this is a Remington; this is a Martini-Henry; this is a Hotchkiss."

"What's the name of the one created by General Manager Liu?"

"Back when we first made it, it didn't have a name. But we sent some to Beiyang for Governor-General Li Hongzhang to take a look at, and he tested them out. He gave them the name

'String-of-Pearls Rapid-Fire.'" After this, the three men bade him farewell and left.

The worker accompanying them gestured to a building to the west and said, "That's the Crude-Iron Works, not much to see there. Let's skip it."

"We're already here," said Baoyu. "Let's go take a look and find out whether there's anything to see or not." And so they continued west.

When they arrived they saw a sign over the gate reading "Iron Foundry." The worker went in ahead of the others, who heard someone say from inside, "There's nothing interesting here, but you're welcome to take a look."

When the three of them arrived at the factory door, they saw that it was simple and shoddy. The men working inside had disheveled hair and filthy faces, covered in a layer of orange dust. Baoyu was startled to recall the state in which he had first encountered Beiming not too long ago, and without realizing it, became lost in thought for a moment.

"You're so afraid of getting dirty," said Xue Pan, "how is it that upon seeing this filthy place, you're practically spellbound?"

"When you look at what it is that is making them dirty," said Baoyu, "you realize that they aren't dirty by choice; to earn their livelihood, they must toil until they look like this. But they are willing to do this to themselves, so that they can support themselves with their own labor! Having seen them, I feel that they are both pitiable and worthy of respect!" So saying, he turned and exited the building. The party then resumed their original path along the side of the firearms factory. Xue Pan suddenly exclaimed, "The sun is so bright today—how can it be raining?"

The worker explained, “That’s the condensation from the Firearms Factory’s steam pipes; it’s not rain.” Indeed, Baoyu and Bohui had also felt water dripping upon their heads.

As they turned a corner, Xue Pan unexpectedly caught his toe on something and nearly tumbled to the ground. The object that had tripped him up turned out to be an iron rail.

“Is there a train line here?” asked Bohui.

“We didn’t used to have one, but General Manager Liu had one built. It’s only used in the transportation of cannons. As for that rail there, it isn’t for a train; it’s for workers to push carts of goods along.”

As they continued walking, they passed the Machine Factory once again and proceeded to the Woodworking Factory to have a look around. Inside, there were two racks of tools for such tasks as sawing and lathing wood. They had a cursory look before exiting.

Looking at the large clock, they saw that it was already eleven. The worker said, “Let’s go back to the Boiler Works room for a rest—it’s just about time for the workers to go on break.” The three men complied and returned to the Boiler Works.

By this time, Feng had completed his work and greeted them. He asked Xue Pan—who at this moment was bent at the waist, rubbing and complaining about his sore toe—what had happened.

“I believe it’s because he stubbed his toe on the iron rail,” said Bohui.

Baoyu laughed. As the group began to chat, he heard a loud rumbling sound from outside. He stood up and went to the window to look out—the sound he had heard was that of a cart loaded with iron beams being pushed past by two people along the rails. Baoyu commented, "Those rails do indeed seem to save quite a lot of labor!"

Hearing this, Xue Pan and Bohui also stood and crossed to the window to have a look.

"No trains run within the Arsenal, so they built the rails just for this purpose. Isn't that a bit of a case of 'exerting great talent for petty use'?" asked Bohui.

Feng replied, "In the first year of Guangxu,[1] the foreigners built the Wusong railway. The Shanghai *daotai* bought the route back from them, and since there was no use for the torn-up rails, we brought them here and installed them."

"Of course it is right to have bought back the rail line that the foreigners built," said Baoyu. "But why tear up the rails?"

"Because at that time, people were still afraid that peace between China and the foreigners couldn't last, and that if foreign battleships arrived in Wusong, their troops could travel easily by train into Shanghai. So the rails were torn up."

"But isn't there a rail line between Wusong and Shanghai again now?" asked Baoyu. "Is it that there is no more fear of war between China and the foreigners?"

Feng answered, "The outlook changes from one moment to the next. But the reality is that if they were able to land in Wusong, even if there weren't a railroad, would it really be all that difficult for them to get into Shanghai?"

As they were discussing this, they heard the loud *wuuuuu wuuuuuuu* of a whistle outside announcing the workers' lunch break. Feng strode outside and stood by the door, and the other three men followed. They saw a group of craftsmen emerge in single file, walk to the gate, and hand a token to an overseer before exiting. Soon they had all dispersed.

When lunch was served in the office, Feng urged his guests to be seated. After eating, Baoyu wanted to go back to see whether his books had been compiled. Feng asked, "You're buying books? That office won't be open now, you'll have to go back after the break has ended." And so the men sat around chatting, inquiring about the history of the Arsenal.

They waited until the break ended, at which time Feng ordered the worker to accompany them to see more of the factories.

"Let's just get the books and leave," said Xue Pan. "What else could you want to see?"

"How many factories are left?" asked Baoyu.

Feng listed them off: "There's the Large Artillery Factory, the Artillery Shell Factory, and the Steel Mill, you can go see those. Besides that, there is no machinery in the Engineering Department or the Steamboat Factory, so those, you can probably skip."

Baoyu wanted to see the first three factories suggested by Feng, but Xue Pan firmly declared that he was not willing to look at anything else. There was nothing Baoyu could do, and in the end he bade farewell to Feng. He summoned Beiming, as Bohui did Huang Fu, and they returned together to the Department of Illustrations and Maps.

Zhu Kun had already compiled a set of all of the texts. He presented an index to Baoyu and asked him to inspect it. Included in the index were such texts as the *Four Books* and the *Book of Changes*. Baoyu was surprised and asked, "Are these considered translations?" He quickly leafed through, and of course they were not translations—they were in fact old Chinese texts, which had simply had new printing plates cut at the Arsenal.

"No matter," he said, "include those as well, if it makes the set complete."

Once Baoyu had given his approval, Xue Pan calculated and settled the bill. Bohui then sent Huang Fu to summon a cart. Zhu Kun took out some thick paper and carefully began to wrap the books one by one. Huang Fu returned a short while later with a pushcart and bearer, but seeing that the books would not all fit in one cart, he went to fetch another. Bohui instructed Huang Fu to stay behind to help escort the loaded carts back to the Changfa Inn. Baoyu left Beiming behind as well. Baoyu, Bohui, and Xue Pan left the enclosure of the Arsenal, climbed into their carriages, and rode swiftly back to the inn.

When they arrived at the inn and stepped inside, the porter handed a slip of paper to Xue Pan. It turned out to be a note from Bai Yaoming, saying, "No matter what time you get back to the inn, I hope you will come immediately to my home to speak with me. I have an important business matter to discuss with you." The porter then added, "He came to see you once this morning himself, and later on, sent this message. After that, he sent a messenger two other times to inquire as to whether you had returned."

"What could be so urgent?" asked Xue Pan. "I need a rest first!" The porter withdrew.

At that moment, someone came in from outside, and it was, as might have been anticipated, Bai Yaoming. Now, when the men had first returned to the inn, they had at first all gone to Xue Pan's room. But when Baoyu saw Bai Yaoming arrive, he pulled Bohui into his own room and invited him to take a seat. Baoyu ruminated on the fact that all of the machinery they had seen at the Arsenal that day had of course been purchased from foreigners, and wondered whether China could make such things itself or not. Bohui said, "I think it's possible to learn the skills; but I'm afraid that our tools are not as good, so we would ultimately be unable to make machines. It's difficult to say that Chinese would be unable to learn to do this; however, even though we didn't see any today, I do know that there are a good number of foreign craftsmen working in the Arsenal."

"This is another thing that puzzles me," said Baoyu. "These techniques are all foreign, and yet they are willing to teach them to us? Making guns, making cannons—if we ever learn to make them on our own, against whom are we likely to use them? If there ever is a day when the peace between us is no more, wouldn't we turn around and use these weapons to attack the foreigners? I've thought of a few sayings that describe the situation: 'punishing the jailer with tortures of his own design,' and 'using the other's methods to deal with him.' You could even call it 'using the master's methods to harm the master.' Do you mean to tell me that they think we Chinese are all as righteous as the servant of the Duke of Yu?[2] Indeed, I do not understand this."

"How could that be the case? It's that their capacity for invention is boundless: the things they make this year are more refined than those they made last year, and the things they make next year will be even more so. If we decide we want to make firearms and ask them to show us how, the guns they show us how to make will be able to shoot at a range of one li, but the guns they make for themselves will already be capable of shooting at range of one and a half li. By the time we've learned to create a gun that shoots at a range of one and a half li, theirs will have a range of two li. So why should they be afraid of teaching us?"

Baoyu nodded. "Ah, so that's the reason. But why can't we do our own research and try to catch up to them? In most things, the most frightening stage is when one has no experience at all; but since we already have some expertise in this, it shouldn't be too difficult to simply continue along the same path, attempting to further refine the technology."

"How could it not be so! What I hate is our bad habits. We cling desperately onto established practices. When we hear about a new way of doing things, if we don't criticize it as absurd, we complain that it is unnecessary. Only after other people's new methods yield results that we can see for ourselves do we believe in them. So by the time we get around to actually *learning* how to do these things, it's already too late. Take those books you bought today—most of them were translated ten, twenty years ago. To the foreigners, they're already unbearably old, but to us, they are secret treasures to hide under the pillow at night!"

Baoyu replied, "If you put it that way, then these books are all useless!"

"That's not entirely true. Many of the books are on scientific topics, and if you wanted to use them as a basis to go and run experiments, then yes, the methods contained therein are already dusty relics. However, right now, we don't understand *any* of their science, so as long as one can use these texts as an entry point into understanding, there's no reason not to read them."

"And if I wanted to understand their more recent methods? What books should I get?"

"In my opinion, when it comes to this sort of thing, it's not the case that you can just read about it and understand it completely. They have specialized schools for the instruction of science, where students go from elementary school to secondary school, and then university, moving from general education to specialization; each field requires over ten years of study altogether before graduation. If it were possible to learn these skills just from reading a couple of books here and there, they wouldn't need to establish these schools."

After Bohui's explanation, Baoyu began to look somewhat dejected. "If you had said as much earlier, I wouldn't have let Xue Pan waste all that money on such useless objects."

"It's not true that they're useless," said Bohui. "If you start with the books you got today, you will learn the fundamentals, which will then enable you to go on to study current scholarship in more depth. If, on the contrary, you were to start with the most recent and advanced textbooks and methodologies, it would be too confusing."

"You say that, but if I want to seek out translations of newer materials after I've read these—will any even be available?"

"We'll just have to make some inquiries. But start with these, and we can discuss it again once you've finished them."

As they were chatting, Beiming and Huang Fu returned, escorting the books. With the help of the two pushcart bearers, the books were unloaded and delivered upstairs one parcel at a time. Baoyu instructed Beiming to gather up the older books for which he no longer had any use, bring them into the outer room, and place them back in the trunks in which they had previously been stored. He then began to lay out his new purchases. Bohui also instructed Huang Fu to help in the tidying and unpacking. They were at this for quite a while before things were adequately arranged.

Just then Xue Pan angrily entered the room and blurted with frustration, "Whoever heard of such a thing?" The others then inquired as to what had upset him.

Xue Pan turned to Baoyu. "It's about that chiming watch, the one you were so critical of. I decided not to buy it. It was Bai Yaoming who was selling it, he said it belonged to a friend. Because the friend had some expenses come up, he wanted to sell it for two hundred kuai. I was merely charmed by it at that moment and took it to look it over, but I had planned to get it appraised and find out whether it was worth actually buying. Who would have guessed that before I was able to do that, you would go into your whole spiel about 'gimmicky technology' and 'excessive cleverness,' and it being a thing for a woman to use? So yesterday I gave it back to him."

He then turned his head and addressed Bohui: "Can you guess why's he just come here? To have it out with me! He said I'd already agreed to his terms, so I couldn't return it now, and tried to force me to take it back! Do you think I'd be willing to stand for such an attitude? So I laid into him pretty good, cussing him out. When he saw that I wasn't about to give in, he changed his tune: he said that the guy selling it was in a real desperate situation and had begged for me to buy it. It would be doing a good deed, he said. At first I felt my resolve softening a bit, and I was about to just give in and buy it, but I hadn't yet said as much out loud. Then he suddenly said, 'Actually, the watch is worth over three hundred *taels*, but he's selling it at a price of two hundred kuai—so you're really getting it at half price!' That's when I got irritated. I had been on the verge of pulling out the two hundred kuai to buy it, if only to help someone out of a jam; but then he went and added that last bit, as if to say that *I'm* the one taking advantage! So in the end I refused, and he became hostile. Isn't it bizarre?"

"Is it the same watch I saw you give back to him yesterday?" asked Bohui.

"Of course."

Bohui laughed. "What happened to the watch chain?"

"There was no watch chain when he gave it to me," Xue Pan answered.

Bohui laughed again. "When he tries to start trouble with you again, tell him 'Mo Daochuan and I have already come to an arrangement,' and he won't have anything else to say."

"What are you getting at? You'll have to explain."

"Would you say that the brothers Bai Yaolian and Bai Yaoming are good people? They're both gambling shills, who specialize in tricking out-of-towners into local gambling halls. They use all kinds of different strategies, like 'the Heaven-upending seal' and 'taking off the boots backward' to cheat people out of their money.[3] That chiming watch was something one of their ilk, a man called Mo Daochuan, won off somebody. The watch and chain together were probably worth about three or four hundred—it belonged to a visitor who was passing through Shanghai and got taken advantage of by them. When he lost more than he could pay for, he put the watch up as collateral for eighty kuai, but in the end he lost that, too. The visitor wanted to try to put up a few more yuan, but they weren't willing. Later, when they divvied up the night's spoils, Mo took the watch in his share, valuing it at eighty kuai. Recently, I've heard that this Mo has been hard up, so he was willing to sell the watch at the same price he got it for. Bai Yaoming took advantage of Mo's straitened circumstances and paid him sixty up front for it, still owing twenty, which he said he would pay off in installments. And then, he took the watch and tried to use it to make a bit of cash off you!"

"What was the watch chain made of?" asked Xue Pan.

"Foreign gold. But the quality of foreign gold is quite poor—so even though you pay a lot to buy it, you usually take a substantial loss when trying to resell it."

Xue Pan leapt to his feet. "So the thing was only worth eighty yuan altogether, *and* he took the gold chain off it to boot, yet he wanted to sell it to me for two hundred! How can someone be so greedy?"

Just as he said this, a messenger from the Wu household arrived, seeking Bohui. Bohui stood up and bade Baoyu and Xue Pan farewell.

■ ■ ■

If you wish to know what happened after Bohui left, please listen to the explanation in the next chapter.

Chapter Twelve

Oppressed by arrogant bullies, Wang Wei'er suffers humiliation

His enemy lying in wait at the roadside, Yang Shizi meets with disaster

LET US speak for the moment of the novel as a genre: when things happen, one writes at length; but when nothing happens, there is not much to write about.

Ever since Baoyu had arrived in Shanghai and met Bohui, the pair had instantly become like old friends. Baoyu sought Bohui's advice on all things and even asked Bohui to teach him English. Bohui instructed him to buy and read *The Spelling Book*, explaining that this was a good primer to start with. Baoyu bought it and read it, and one day while Bohui was teaching him from it, said, "This isn't working. It's like our *Three Character Classic* or *Poems of Child Prodigies*, only of use if you start with it as a child. If we go on like this, who knows how long it's going to take to learn anything! A foreign text with footnotes in Chinese would allow me to study at a faster and more appropriate pace. Even better would be having something like a dictionary I can look things up in, as well. I think something like *Learn English Without a Teacher* would be better!"

"That one's no good," answered Bohui. And so he instructed Baoyu instead to buy *Introduction to English Writing* and a copy of the *Chinese-English Dictionary.* Baoyu bought them, and asked Bohui to resume his instruction.

Baoyu divided his days into different tasks: in the morning, he would read the Chinese translations of foreign texts he had purchased from the Arsenal; and in the afternoon, he read English. He was, after all, a uniquely clever person, and once he was shown where to start, he quickly became adept. He came to rely on the dictionary at his side—whenever he encountered an errant piece of paper with foreign writing on it, he looked the words up letter by letter. As a result, he made rapid progress. He eventually shelved his plans to travel to the capital, focusing the entirety of his energies on his studies instead.

In this way the days passed almost without notice, and it was suddenly the middle of the third month. One day Xue Pan rushed into Baoyu's room, saying, "Brother Bao, when you first arrived in Shanghai, you said you wanted to go to the capital. Why is it that you no longer mention it?"

"And what if I did mention it?"

"I just received a letter from the capital, summoning me there urgently. If you want to go, you can leave with me tomorrow."

"What's so important that you're heading off so hastily?"

"I'm making this trip to take up an official position," Xue Pan answered. "If you want to go, we should be able to find something for you, as well."

Baoyu laughed. "Congratulations! But unfortunately, one: I have no ambition of obtaining an official position; and two: I am still reliant upon Bohui's instruction in my English lessons. Although I would like to travel to the City, I am currently unable to leave."

"What will you do here by yourself if I leave?"

"It's strange, but when I first came to Shanghai, I certainly hadn't planned on meeting with you."

Xue Pan mulled this over for a moment. "The two hundred kuai I gave you before—how much of it have you spent?"

"Not a penny. If you need it for travel expenses, please go ahead and take it back."

"I don't need it for travel expenses, it's just that I'm leaving in such a hurry, I was hoping you could help me settle a few things for me here."

"What kind of things?"

"First, I'm unable to carry all of my luggage with me, so some of it will need to stay here with you; and second, I've got twenty thousand taels in the Hong Kong–Shanghai Bank. If you come to Beijing, please have it remitted to me. But when do you think you might come?"

"It's no problem to take care of your luggage, but I've never remitted money before—that's a task better left to someone else."

"Other than you, who else can I trust with it? If you don't understand how to do it, just ask Bohui, he'll know. When I come back, I'll give you the bank book."

Baoyu had all the while been focused attentively on his English studies and had no more patience for Xue Pan and his deliberations. In the end he distractedly agreed to do both things.

Xue Pan did indeed leave, and eventually day passed into night. Xue Pan returned with a foreign-style bankbook, as well as a paper luggage receipt, and gave these to Baoyu.

"So you're really leaving?" Baoyu asked.

"Of course."

"But really, what could possibly cause you to leave so urgently?"

"I can't explain it to you right now. When will you be coming to Beijing? When you get to Beijing, I'll be able to tell you."

"I've been thinking I should go," mused Baoyu. "The only thing is right now I can't just leave my foreign books behind, so for now I should stay here and study them a little while longer. Once I've gotten to a point where I've more or less understood them and have a solid enough grasp to study on my own without needing a teacher, then I will come join you."

"I don't understand you," replied Xue Pan. "A little while ago, there was nothing you hated more than foreign goods, so why is it that recently you're suddenly so interested in reading foreign books? And not only that, but you're putting so much effort into it! Are foreign books not foreign goods?"

"What I said to you before was that foreign goods can be classified thus: useful versus useless; beneficial versus not beneficial. These foreign books are useful things, so naturally I want to read them!"

"All right, I don't really care about all of that. When will you come to Beijing?"

"I don't know yet. At earliest perhaps in a fortnight or a month; at latest perhaps a year or six months. We'll have to see."

"Come as early or as late as you wish—I've entrusted all of my affairs to you. Take good care of that bankbook; and the items listed on the luggage receipt are all stored downstairs in the accountant's office. We should get up early tomorrow to meet with him, so I can turn everything over to you in his presence. I've got to go to bed now, I've got something to do first thing tomorrow."

"What is this really all about?" asked Baoyu, smiling. "What could possibly have you running about like this?"

"I absolutely cannot tell you right now. If you come to Beijing, I can tell you then. But I promise that it's something you would agree with."

At this Baoyu stopped asking, and Xue Pan took his leave. Let us speak no more of the rest of that evening.

The following morning Xue Pan came into Baoyu's room and instructed Beiming to run down to the accountant's office to ask someone to come upstairs, so that all of Xue Pan's stored belongings could be made over to Baoyu. Xue Pan then said to the accountant, "When he's ready to leave the city, turn it all over to him so he can bring it to me." The accountant agreed to do this and left.

Xue Pan then handed a key to Baoyu and told him to move into the room that he himself was vacating.

"I couldn't live in your room—the wallpaper is so dazzlingly red, I'd never get used to it."

"All right, then you should at least move all of the odds and ends I'm leaving behind in here with you."

"Tell the porter to move them over here."

And so, Xue Pan returned to his room and packed the remaining odds and ends into trunks, then called the porter to carry anything that didn't fit into a trunk over to Baoyu's room. Besides these objects, two trunks were also left in Baoyu's custody. All day the hall was filled with the sound of bumping and scraping as trunks were moved from one place to the other.

As it happened, on this particular day, the steamboat *Anping* was sailing for Tianjin, and would leave the port around 4:00 p.m., taking advantage of the evening tide. And so, Xue Pan hurriedly went about settling his affairs, and finally boarded the ship a little after 2:00 p.m. Baoyu did not see him off very far, only walking with him as far as the entryway of the inn before turning back inside. After this, Baoyu felt a great sense of joy and lightness. But let us not speak of that for now.

Let us speak instead of Xue Pan. Having boarded the steamship *Anping*, he was now as anxious as an ant on a hot skillet, unable to calm himself for even an instant, impatiently awaiting the moment of arrival. However, the ship encountered a persistent wind and was delayed in its arrival by a day. By the time Xue Pan finally arrived at Tanggu in Tianjin, it was already too late to go out about his business. He was so tense he was on the point of bursting, but had no choice but to wait until morning; and so he spent the night in a state of growing agitation. The following morning, as soon as the first light of day broke across the sky, he hired a small boat to take him ashore, then proceeded to the train station. He boarded a train for Fengtai, where he alighted and hired a mule-drawn cart to bring him into the city so that he could seek out an old friend.

Just who do you suppose this friend was? His surname was Wang, and his name was Wei'er. He was a renowned ruffian from Beijing. When it came to eating, drinking, whoring, and gambling, there was nothing he wasn't up for. One day, because he'd had a bit of business to take care of, he'd gone to Xuanhua County to visit a relative. The relative had put him up for several days, and a bit of social boozing had been unavoidable; Wang Wei'er had gotten drunk and gone out for a stroll. Before he knew what had happened, he had bumped into another man, who also happened to be in his cups. When the two parties collided, one drunkard into the other, it all blew up into quite a row. The passers-by on the street stopped to watch things play out, observing silently as the two men fell into a heap of flailing limbs, each suffering minor injuries. Eventually an elderly man emerged from the crowd and separated the two brawlers. He turned to Wang Wei'er: "Older brother, I'm afraid this must be your first time in our town. There's an old turn of phrase that captures the current situation well: 'When entering a new country, inquire about the customs; when crossing a border ask what is forbidden.' You didn't ask around, but this gentleman Master Yang Shizi is one of the most eminent stalwarts in Xuanhua city. Even the local officials and elites are a little careful around him. What kind of backup have you got that you would dare fight with him, rather than make haste to admit your wrongdoing?"

This infuriated Wang Wei'er. "I don't know any Master Yang Sheep-zi or Master Yang Cow-zi.[1] Now I, Master Wang, was born and raised in the capital. With the exception of the emperor and the royal family, if any Manchu nobleman were to so much as take one look at me, he'd bow his head outta respect! So what the hell could this guy possibly be to me? And not just him—why, I reckon no one in this whole city could stand a drubbing from me. Three punches and a couple of kicks, and you'd all be turned into pulp!" So saying, he flung himself at his nemesis once more, and the two of them were soon rolling around on the ground again.

As the men continued to tussle, it seemed it would be impossible to pull them apart. Suddenly the *Tang! Tang! Tang!* of a gong rang out, and the crowd that had gathered parted with a murmur. Two men then strode forward through the gap and gave a loud shout before seizing the combatants. As it turned out, the county magistrate had happened upon the scene. His runners, seeing that a fight had broken out in the street ahead of them, had first yelled at the men to stop; but since this was not successful, they had rushed forward and subdued them. They then dragged them before the sedan chair in which the magistrate was seated.

From inside the chair the magistrate asked, "How is it that you can't behave yourselves properly, and must instead fight in the streets and start trouble? Even when the county magistrate arrives, you don't have the sense to make way! It's simply despicable!" The magistrate then shouted out to his runners that each man was to be given twenty blows with a bamboo rod. As the runners were just about to start carrying out the punishment, the one named Yang fell to his knees, inched forward and pleaded, "I humbly petition your excellency: I am a Christian resident of this city, my surname is Yang, and my given name is Shizi."[2]

Before the man had even finished speaking, it was clear that the magistrate was growing enraged. He ordered his runners to drag Wang Wei'er closer, then demanded, "You bastard son of a turtle! Where are you from, that you dare to come into my jurisdiction and wreak such havoc?"

"Your servant is called Wang Wei'er, from Wanping County. I came here to visit a relative. When I ran into this Yang guy . . ."

Before Wang was able to get another word out, the magistrate interrupted: "Despicable! Take this one back for questioning. This has nothing to do with Yang Shizi—he is free to go." At this, Yang thanked the magistrate and left. The runners put Wang Wei'er in chains and led him back to the *yamen* offices.

Back at the *yamen* the magistrate, seated in his court, called out, "Bring him in!" Then, without asking for a single detail of the matter, he ordered his men to administer one hundred strokes to Wang Wei'er.

"Injustice!" screeched Wang.

"You beastly mongrel who doesn't know up from down! I will have you beaten to death! Is the place you're from not good enough for your trouble-making that you had to come to my jurisdiction and offend a Christian? Do you have any brains in there? Your dog life isn't worth the trouble! I'll tell you: my future prospects are not to be played about with by the likes of you! And yet you still dare to cry out that I am being unjust! I'll have you beaten till that dog's jaw of yours is dislocated and your dog teeth are all knocked loose! Then we'll see whether you still feel like crying out!"

The runners, hearing this, came forward and delivered fifty slaps—*slap slap slap*—across his face. Wang Wei'er's cheeks grew red and swollen, and blood began to seep through his teeth. The magistrate added, "Fit him up with the heaviest cangue we have! Then lead him back to the scene of his crime to make a public example of him. After a month give him another two hundred strokes and drive him out of here!"

Having been on the receiving end of this outpouring of bile, Wang Wei'er was full of resentment but had no way to seek redress, and so had no choice but to accept his bad luck. Fortunately for him, his relative borrowed some money and so was able to pay a number of bribes, ensuring that Wang's experience was not as miserable as it could have been. After a month Wang did indeed receive the promised two hundred further strokes, after which he was immediately escorted out of the county by two bailiffs. He was not even permitted to go back to his relative's place to apologize for everything that had happened. Covered in wounds from the beating, he limped haltingly along his way. As soon as they had left the jurisdiction of Xuanhua, the two bailiffs dumped him on the ground and left him. Poor Wang Wei'er slowly made his way back to the capital, begging for food along the way.

Dear readers! Just think: having borne such horrendous treatment, such injustice—how could he not be filled with resentment? The primary target of his resentment was the magistrate, but eventually he came to hate Yang Shizi as well. But because he was without any means of taking action, he realized that vainly hating them from afar was more or less useless.

Three or four years passed, and these events gradually faded from public memory. Wishing once again to visit his relative, Wang Wei'er made his way back to Xuanhua and stayed there for a little while. When it came time to return to the capital, he borrowed his relative's donkey and rode it out of the city. He had not traveled very far when he found himself face to face with Yang Shizi. For Wang Wei'er, it was a case of "when encountering an old nemesis, one sees with especial clarity." For his part, Yang Shizi seemed not to notice or care; he had long ago learned to take advantage of the magistrate's fear of Christians, and so every time he got into trouble or took someone to court, the ruling was always in his favor. His scuffle with Wang Wei'er had been the result of a chance encounter, so the incident was easily forgotten afterward—why should he remember it? And so he took no notice whatsoever of Wang Wei'er.

Indeed, he was quite unlike like Wang Wei'er, who, having borne such brutality, had thought ceaselessly and obsessively of his nemesis, even when eating or sleeping. Over the course of these three or four years, had there ever been even a moment when this resentment had been forgotten? This is why, upon encountering Yang Shizi, Wang Wei'er saw him with such clarity. He carefully observed Yang Shizi: the black donkey he was riding was equipped with a saddlebag, and Yang Shizi himself was wearing a straw hat—it appeared that he was embarking on a long journey. Without even thinking about it, Wang Wei'er pulled his own donkey's reins and fell in behind Yang Shizi, following him at a distance. When Yang Shizi stopped for a rest, Wang Wei'er stopped; when Yang Shizi found lodgings for the night, so did Wang Wei'er.

Eventually they crossed into Huailai County and found themselves in a deserted place with no trace of human activity. Only now did Wang Wei'er urge his donkey to catch up to Yang

Shizi's. When the two donkeys were side by side, Wang Wei'er recklessly raised the butt of his whip over his head and cracked it down ferociously on Yang Shizi's skull. His aim was perfect—he struck Yang Shizi in the temple, immediately stunning him and causing him to tumble headlong from the donkey. Wang Wei'er hurriedly leapt down from his own mount. Standing over the dazed Yang Shizi and pinning him down with one hand, he began to beat him in a frenzy, never addressing even a word to him.

"Who are you? Why are you attacking me?" Yang Shizi groaned. "I haven't done anything to you, I was just minding my business traveling along the road. If you must attack me, at least tell me why first!"

Through gritted teeth, Wang Wei'er replied, "You blind turtle's spawn! You might not recognize your master, but your master recognizes you! You, Yang Sheep-zi, your master is Yang Cow-zi! Today I have followed you to find out whether your sheep's horns are a match for my cow's horns! And since they are not, I'm afraid I must ask you to take a little punishment." As he spoke, he delivered several punches directly to his enemy's face, causing sparks to burst across Yang Shizi's field of vision.

"Spare me!" cried Yang Shizi, before adding, "At least tell me why you are beating me! I don't think I've ever done anything to you!"

Wang Wei'er struck him again and laughed. "All this punching is starting to hurt my hands!" He then changed tactics, grabbing Yang Shizi by his queue and alternately lifting his head and smashing it back into the ground. Yang Shizi struggled mightily for a time, then gradually grew weaker and eventually stopped breathing.

When Wang Wei'er had finished this round of beating, he noticed that Yang Shizi was no longer moving. Letting go of Yang Shizi's queue, Wang Wei'er pulled himself away and stood back up to survey his work. Yang Shizi's body lay flat out on the ground, his eyes staring fixedly into the sky. Noticing a heap of donkey or horse dung along the side of the road, Wang Wei'er picked up a clump and stuffed it into Yang Shizi's mouth before remounting his donkey and turning back toward the city.

He had ridden about as far as an arrow might be shot when he suddenly realized that having committed such an atrocity, it was not advisable to return to the city—it would be best to head elsewhere for a short while to avoid the fallout. Once he'd made up his mind, he pulled the donkey's reins to turn it once again, then gave it a quick flick of the whip and off they sped toward the north.

■ ■ ■

If you wish to know more about how Wang Wei'er's journey proceeded, please listen to the explanation in the following chapter.

Chapter Thirteen

Generous Xue Pan provides travel expenses to one in need

In a demonstration of his sorcery, Wang Ming dances with a blade

WE WERE speaking of Wang Wei'er, who had pulled his donkey's reins to continue riding north. He once again passed Yang Shizi's body at the side of the road. Looking at the body, Wang Wei'er realized that he had done extensive damage to it. He thought, "I've taken my vengeance, but this could have disastrous repercussions for me. Where can I go to hide away for a little while?" He continued thinking as he traveled along, when suddenly he noticed a black donkey braying at the side of the road. As it happened, this was the donkey that Yang Shizi had been riding—when Yang Shizi had fallen to the ground, the donkey had bolted in fear. Its reins, however, had gotten caught in the branches of a roadside jujube tree; unable to move, it stood there, crying out.

Wang Wei'er dismounted and approached the black donkey. He dug around in the saddlebag it carried and pulled out a string of large coins as well as a handful of miscellaneous bits of silver and three or four account books. Opening the books and leafing through them, he discovered that they contained logs of the high-interest loans Yang Shizi had given out. Wang Wei'er thought, "Perhaps Yang Shizi was on his way to collect interest payments, but as it happened, he met with me instead! His debtors are getting off easy. That he met this fate today is surely karma for his usurious lending practices and using his power to bully others. He can't blame me for it!" He then ripped the account books into shreds, pulled a box of matches from his pocket, lit one, and burned the scraps of paper, saying, "Even if you hadn't died, you would have come to misfortune and lost your money one way or another." He then took the cash and silver and fastened them about his own person. He didn't dare take the clothing and bedding that were in the saddle bag, so he left these, climbed back onto his own donkey, and left.

That night he stayed at the Huailai post station. Because he still hadn't firmly decided on where he wanted to go, he boarded here for two or three days without venturing out. One morning startling news was delivered to the post station: a homicide had taken place within the county. The deceased was a visiting merchant traveling through the area. He had been beaten to death, with a black donkey and a saddlebag left behind. From what the local constable had reported to the county, he had verified definitively that the victim had died from the wounds he had sustained. The report went on to say that marshals would be sent out immediately to aid in the apprehension of the guilty party.

Upon hearing this, Wang Wei'er was terrified out of his wits. He immediately settled his bill, got back on his donkey, and fled. Only once he was on the other side of the Huailai County line did he begin to breathe a bit more easily. He continued speeding along until he had passed through Zhangjiakou. Along the way, he sold the donkey for a few strings of cash to cover his travel expenses, which enabled him to drift around outside the Great Wall for a few months. He eventually crossed into Shanxi, after which he steered himself toward Shandong. Along the way, he engaged in a bit of petty trading, and in this way was able to keep himself fed.

One day, as he arrived in Dengzhou, he encountered a date seller from out of town who was looking for a companion who would be able travel with him to deliver some dates to Yantai. Wang Wei'er threw in with him and minded the cartful of wares for the whole trip. The stranger's name was Wang Ben. The two men struck up an amiable conversation, and Wang Ben began to tell Wang Wei'er his life story. As it happened, Wang Ben had been a *wuju* and a resident of Yuncheng County, Shandong.[1] For the past few years he'd been embroiled in a lawsuit with another party. He didn't know what kind of sorcery the other party had used, but they were able to procure a letter of support from a foreigner to give to the magistrate. Because of that, not only did Wang Ben lose the case, but he'd been stripped of his rank as well. He was so enraged that he left his hometown behind, choosing a life on the road with a new profession—that of traveling merchant. Hearing this tale, Wang Wei'er couldn't help but feel that he and Wang Ben had suffered from very similar circumstances, and so he shared his own story with Wang Ben.

Wang Ben was overjoyed. "Now that you've thrown in your lot with me, you've got yourself back on the right path! I won't lie to you—there's something big brewing right now. If you're willing to join up with me, I guarantee that not only will you be able to take your vengeance, but you will be able to get rank and fortune out of it as well!" Wang Wei'er was delighted and asked what exactly he was talking about. Wang Ben whispered in his ear at length, and whatever it was he said made Wang Wei'er so happy that he waved his hands and tapped his feet in glee. From this point on Wang Wei'er resolved to learn martial arts from his companion.

When they arrived in Yantai, they stayed for a fortnight. They would be selling the dates to a traveling merchant from the south—arrangements for how everything was to be sold on in Shanghai had already been settled. On the day, they delivered the goods aboard a steamship. Suddenly the other merchant came striding over and told them that they were short ten bags of dates. Wang Ben then asked Wang Wei'er to go aboard with the merchant to make a recount. As it happened, Wang Wei'er had just thrown back a few cups of liquor and had to marshal all of his forces to get up and board the ship. Who could have known that by the time he and the merchant had gone aboard, the merchant's assistant would have completed a recount and found that not a date was missing? Wang Wei'er was so outraged at having been inconvenienced that he started to argue with the merchant; but because he'd been drinking, now that he'd arrived at the wharf and been buffeted by the ocean breeze, he gradually began to feel that he could barely keep himself upright. And so he found an opportune moment to sneak off to a deserted corner at the prow of the ship and lay himself down for a little nap.

By the time he awoke, the ship had already been underway for some time. Wang Wei'er jumped up in alarm. When the deckhands aboard the ship noticed what was going on, they thought he must be a thief, and so, without further ado, they tied him up and brought him to the comprador. Fortunately, the comprador was a kindhearted man, and upon hearing the reports of the deckhands, he asked Wang Wei'er the circumstances of his presence on the ship. Wang related the whole story of having gotten drunk then come on board to count merchandise. The comprador instructed some of his men to keep a watchful eye on Wang, saying that they would figure something out once they'd arrived in Shanghai. As a result, Wang did not suffer any hardship. When the ship finally arrived in Shanghai, everyone else aboard the ship had his own duties to tend to, which left no one watching over Wang, who took advantage of everyone's distraction to slip ashore.

Shanghai is of course far more splendid than other places, and so Wang Wei'er was quite dazzled by what he beheld. He couldn't help but gaze this way and that, trying to take it all in. Not stopping to ask for directions, he decided to make his way for whatever area seemed to be the liveliest. Suddenly he felt quite an urgent pressure in his bladder, and so he undid his drawers and began to urinate by the roadside. A police officer ran up shouting and tried to stop him, but the urine had already begun streaming out and could not be bottled back up. The police officer grabbed Wang Wei'er and started to drag him along. Wang shouted, "What are you grabbing me for? If you've got something to say, say it!" as he struggled to break free.

The police officer raised his hand and gave Wang a great slap across the face. By now, a sizeable crowd had begun to gather around them. "I must make a fine punching bag!" cried Wang. "After what happened in Xuanhua County, I'm back in the same situation!" Wang then raised his own hand and was about to return the courtesy to the police officer when suddenly someone emerged from the crowd and stayed his hand, saying, "Sir, you don't seem to understand what's going on. This must be your first time here."

Wang Wei'er heard that someone was addressing him and raised his head to see who it was. The man's dress suggested that he was someone of high standing, and he spoke with a Beijing accent, so Wang thought that he had found an ally. "I came from Yantai, only just arrived," Wang explained. "All I did was take a little leak, and all of a sudden this guy grabbed me!"

"There's a rule here, public urination gets you a fine of three foreign jiao. But if you start fighting with him, that's a much bigger offense. You must stop immediately."

"But I haven't even got half a jiao in my pockets!" Wang complained. "How can I pay the fine?"

"Don't worry. I'll give it to you." The man drew three jiao out of his pocket and handed them to Wang. He then pointed down the street: "That's the police station. Hurry up and go with him to pay the fine. I'll be waiting for you here when you come out."

Wang Wei'er agreed to this and went off with the police officer to pay the fine.

Dear readers! Who do you suppose this stranger was? Why, it was none other than the "Oaf King" himself, Xue Pan. Even though he was born a bit slow, on those occasions when he got it into his head to become a righteous do-gooder, he could be extremely generous to those in need. And while he was actually born in Nanjing, he had spent quite a lot of time in Beijing and had regularly gone about with a group of locals there. After he'd arrived in Shanghai, it was very rare to come across a real Beijing accent, since most of the speech one overheard was a mixture of northern and southern tones. Today, suddenly coming across Wang Wei'er spouting a mouthful of Beijing-*hua*, Xue Pan had been moved and decided to call out to him. But let us not linger on details already discussed.

Let us speak now of Wang Wei'er. After he had paid the fine, he emerged from the police station, and as expected, saw Xue Pan standing off to the left waiting for him just as he'd promised. Wang crossed over and called out to him.

"You said you'd only just arrived. Where's your luggage?"

"I don't have any." Wang then proceeded to share once again the story about having gotten drunk and fallen asleep on the ship.

Xue Pan was moved to sympathy and invited Wang Wei'er back to his inn. He asked Wang his name, then said, "You're lucky you met up with me today, otherwise you would be in a pretty hard spot right now. You don't know the rules in Shanghai—foreigners run everything here. The guy who grabbed you today is called a 'police officer.' If you had actually struck him, who knows what they might have done with you! I won't lie to you, I did it once myself. We were about to get into a scrap, but he was no match for me. What I didn't realize was that he carried a tiny copper pipe—it made a terrible racket when he blew into it. If one of them can't subdue you by himself, he blows into his pipe and other police officers will come from nearby when they hear it. No matter how quick-witted you are, you can't get away. When they caught me, they brought me in and made me spend the night in the police station. Then I had to wait for it to be resolved in court. I was nearly locked up for a three-month sentence, but luckily I had a lot of friends on the outside who were able to post bail, so in the end I was fined only a few dozen kuai, and that was it. If you had actually committed such an offense, can you imagine how terrible it would have been for you?"

At this point Xue Pan summoned the accountant and asked him to make out a steamship ticket for Yantai so that he could send Wang Wei'er back home.

Wang Wei'er cut in: "My partner Wang Ben told me that once he'd sold the dates, he was planning to go to Beijing to look around. If you are willing to help me, it would be even better if you could give me a ticket to Tianjin." Xue Pan agreed to this.

As it happened, there was no ship for Tianjin that day, so it was necessary to wait a day or two. Xue Pan put Wang up at the inn, during which time Wang told Xue Pan all about his past, without hiding any of it. As a result, the two men came to think of each other as the closest of friends.

Two days later there was a ship sailing for Tianjin. In addition to covering the cost of the ticket, Xue Pan also gave Wang Wei'er several yuan, a few sets of clothing, and bedding for the trip. Wang departed, full of gratitude for his host's generosity. From then on the two had no further contact.

A year had already passed by the time that Xue Pan told Baoyu that he had received a letter summoning him urgently to Beijing. The letter was in fact from Wang Wei'er, and it was for this reason Xue Pan set about finding him as soon as he arrived in Beijing. When they finally met up, each greeted the other as long-parted friends would do. Wang Wei'er reiterated his thanks for Xue Pan's previous kindness and—after he readied a room for Xue Pan to stay in—treated him with the utmost attentiveness, slaughtering a chicken and a duck as well as buying some fish and pork with which to feast his arrival. Wang Wei'er's wife, Ms. Ba, also came out to greet Xue Pan and busily set about laying out his bedding and unpacking his luggage. They insisted that he stay with them.

A little while later, as the meal was being served, Wang Wei'er ceremoniously toasted Xue Pan with a cup of liquor: "When I was in Shanghai, I was greatly dependent upon your kindness. Even if I were to grind my body into dust and smash my bones, I could not repay that debt. After I returned to Beijing, the little problem I told you about before quieted down quite quickly, so I was able to relax and settle down. Wang Ben came to Beijing as well, and I put him up for a few days. He's a very skilled martial artist, and because I had studied with him for a couple days, I took him as my teacher and master. It was his suggestion that I send that letter asking you to come."

"Why not invite him to come over so we can meet?"

"He has now been given the title of master and spends every day giving instruction at his altar, so it is not easy for him get out and meet with people. When I decided to invite you to come, I discussed it with him first and got his approval—that's the only reason I dared to write the letter. Today we must endeavor to feast and drink in his honor, for tomorrow we must begin three days of fasting before we will be permitted to go pay our respects at the altar. For better or for worse, let's focus on what comes next. We can talk about it later."

"But isn't fasting a lot of bother? I'm not used to it."

"It's not as though we're *really* going to fast. We can still gorge ourselves on fish and meat; as long as we don't eat anything pungent like onions or garlic, it's not like he'll find out."

"I can't make head or tails of this whole thing. I had been thinking of coming to the capital anyway, and when I received your letter, I decided to come a little earlier. Tell me everything there is to know. How can I get an official position out of this?"

"Right now there is an elderly sage whose magical arts have spread throughout the regions of Shandong and Zhili. He has established a new religion, called the 'Militia of Righteous Harmony.'[2] His teachings are spreading everywhere, and have the ability to summon heavenly generals and heavenly soldiers with the intention of 'upholding the Qing and exterminating the foreign.' He already has 3,600 disciples who have themselves been given the title of master. Wang Ben is one of these. Those who have been made a master must establish an altar and seek new recruits to whom to pass these magic arts. Those who wish to join must first fast for three days, then go to the altar to offer prayers. If their obeisance is accepted, they may become senior disciples. Once they have learned the master's arts, they will be able to lead troops."

Xue Pan was greatly surprised by this. "I don't know much about it, but I have heard that any kind of organized society is illegal. If the authorities find out about it and catch you, at best it's a beating across the backside; at worst, they'll chop your head off! How can you possibly think this could work?"

"That's what you say! This is different from in the past: Heaven has already approved of our movement. The princes and grand secretaries already know about it, and not only have they not forbidden it, they are in fact pleased by it! Last month two senior disciples were invited to teach their magical arts at one of the palaces on the eastern avenue."[3]

"What magical arts? I've heard of paper cutouts that turn into horses, or scattered beans that turn into soldiers, but those were just stories from fiction! They're not necessarily true."

"That's what you say! The Iron-Helmed Prince on the southern avenue has in his possession a beggar-beating staff. The staff has been passed down from the Zhou dynasty, when Jiang Ziya vested the gods with their divinity. Having been passed down for several thousand years, it has fully absorbed the essences of heaven, earth, sun, and moon, and now it serves as a conduit for communication with spirits. Last month when our Master saw it, he said it was a precious magic relic: if an incantation is spoken, one staff becomes ten, ten become a hundred, a hundred become a thousand, and a thousand become ten thousand. Its usefulness is infinite! Right now, a talisman has been used to seal it, but it has been displayed prominently in the palace, just waiting to be put to use."

Xue Pan half-doubted but half-believed what he heard.

■ ■ ■

Sometime after dinner was finished, Wang Wei'er went to see Wang Ben. Meanwhile, Xue Pan went out for a stroll. However, he was in the kind of mood where everything around him looked wrong, and he was unable to snap himself out of this state of distraction. He walked for a while but returned in low spirits. By the time he returned, Wang Wei'er had already come back; beside him there now stood a boy of perhaps eleven or twelve years old. Wang Wei'er pushed the boy forward to meet Xue Pan: "This is my son, who has recently been studying the magical arts at the altar. Just now when I went to see the Master, I decided to bring the boy along home to meet you."

"What's his name?" Xue Pan inquired. "How is it that he's studying the magic arts at such a young age?"

"The younger they are, the easier it is for them to learn. His name is Wang Ming."[4] Wang Wei'er added, "I'll ask him to demonstrate his technique for you." As he said this, he pulled down a broadsword that had been mounted on the wall and began mumbling something under his breath.

A change slowly crept over the boy's face and his eyes became fixed. Suddenly, with a cry, he picked up the sword and ran out to the courtyard with it, where he began move swiftly and gracefully, showing that indeed he had no small amount of skill. The sword was both long and heavy, far too heavy for a child of eleven or twelve to dance with so gracefully. Xue Pan couldn't help but watch in stunned amazement. Suddenly the boy put the sword down and, using both hands, picked up a millstone that must have weighed sixty or seventy jin.[5] Xue Pan was so startled that he involuntarily let out a "Ya!" before adding, "Be careful! You might break a bone or strain a muscle!"

■ ■ ■

If you wish to know whether or not the boy did indeed strain a muscle, please listen to the explanation in the following chapter.

Chapter Fourteen

Receptive to idiocy, Xue Pan prays at the sacred altar

A grand secretary taken in by heterodox teachings attacks an embassy

WE WERE speaking of Xue Pan, who, having seen how such a tiny lad as Wang Ming was capable of dancing about with a large sword and picking up such a heavy millstone, began to believe what Wang Wei'er had told him.

"What kind of mystical technique is this?" he asked.

"We have taken enough of the hairies' abuse," replied Wang Wei'er. "Not to mention that of the hairies once or twice removed, who are more than happy to betray their countrymen! The solemn oath laid down by my Master is to 'support the Qing and exterminate the foreign.' In coming days, after he has performed this meritorious service, he will surely be ennobled or even made a minister. We are just venting the spleen that has built up over our lifetimes."

"What are 'hairies' and 'hairies once or twice removed'?"

"The foreign devils—we don't consider them people, so we simply call them 'hairies.' Those of our own Chinese countrymen who have cozied up to the foreigners are called 'hairies once removed,' while those who curry favor with the 'hairies once removed' are called 'hairies twice removed.'"

"This seems like such an enormous task. What is your plan?"

"Right now, the heavenly soldiers and the heavenly generals have not yet all come together. Once that happens we can strike. At this moment, numerous princes and grand secretaries are already making preparations. As soon as they receive word that our army is complete, the orders will be disseminated from on high. That's when we will make our move."

"But the foreigners' guns and cannons are so powerful. What means do you have to resist them?"

At this, Wang Wei'er burst into laughter. "If we were afraid of their guns and cannons, we wouldn't be doing this! All one needs to do is go to the altar and pray to the Ancestral Teacher and to the Master. Once he has done that, no matter what kind of guns or cannons they use, they won't be able to hit him!"

As the two men chatted, Wang Ming continued to hold the millstone in his hands, while his body, unmoving, remained perfectly erect.

"That's enough," Xue Pan called out to the boy. "Set it down."

"How could he possibly stop?" asked Wang Wei'er. "I haven't yet dispelled the charm." Turning to face Wang Ming, Wang Wei'er mumbled some nonsense. Wang Ming finally set down the millstone and walked over to the men, not a bit out of breath. Xue Pan felt increasingly that this was quite marvelous and could hardly wait to go to the altar to take a look.

As soon as they had completed their three days of "fasting," Xue Pan began pressing Wang Wei'er to take him to the temple.

"It's too early, the Master won't have arisen yet. And even once he gets up, he'll first need to take his Paste of Prosperity and Longevity."

"What's that?"

"It's the same as opium, but opium is foreign, so we don't use it. We make the Paste of Prosperity and Longevity ourselves, and taking it can augment one's prosperity and longevity—that's how it got its name."

Xue Pan had no choice but to wait. Only after they had eaten lunch did Wang Wei'er finally pick up a bag and lead Xue Pan off to the altar.

The altar was enveloped in the smoke of incense and candles, which drifted into the sky. In the center, there hung a yellow curtain, behind which all was black as a cave. Who could say what kind of idol was housed within? A number of weapons were arrayed along both sides.

Wang Wei'er knelt, set his bag upon the ground, and opened it. He pulled out a strip of red cloth, which he tied around Xue Pan's head; pulling out another strip, he tied this around Xue Pan's waist. He then tied a piece of cloth around his own head, donned a red vest, and tied a red belt around his torso.

Looking at Wang Wei'er, Xue Pan noticed that sewn onto the back of this vest was a circle of white cloth, just like on the uniforms worn by imperial soldiers. Upon the cloth circle were written in black the characters for the name "Sun Wukong."[1]

Xue Pan was taken aback at this. "What does that mean?"

Wang Wei'er waved his hand without giving an answer. "We can talk about that after we leave. For now, don't ask." He then led Xue Pan over to a prayer mat. Wang Wei'er first knelt three times and knocked his head against the ground nine times, then instructed Xue Pan to do the same. At that point Wang Wei'er entered the space behind the curtain. After a short while, he emerged and bowed to the heavens before taking a knee and calling out loudly, "We humbly request to see the Master!" With Wang Wei'er's voice still ringing in the air, the yellow curtain opened, and a figure stepped out from behind it. His face was a sickly greenish-yellow, and his eyes were half-closed. He was dressed the same as any normal person, with the exception of a strip of red cloth tied round his head and a red belt around his waist. While he wore the long robes of the scholarly class, on his feet he wore rough straw sandals. On his sallow face one could just make out a faint air of malevolence, while his heavy-lidded eyes betrayed a vicious gleam.

Wang Wei'er called upon Xue Pan to come pay his respects to the Master. Xue Pan had already been completely taken in by their malevolent influence, so he promptly prostrated himself in front of the Master. The Master, for his part, merely folded his hands together in response.

When Xue Pan stood up after completing his prostrations, Wang Wei'er told the Master, "This is Xue Pan, whom your disciple has brought as a new recruit. He has fasted for three days and has come especially to pray to the Ancestral Teacher and the Master. I hope that the Master will be willing to take him in."

The Master appraised Xue Pan for a moment. "Are you brave enough to commit yourself earnestly to being a member of our brotherhood? You should know that in our teachings, we specifically observe the practice of 'supporting the Qing and exterminating the foreign'—it is not permitted to have any dealings with the hairies. Anyone who has had any kind of dealings with them is a 'hairy once removed.'"

"Yes, I'm aware of that," replied Xue Pan.

"As long as you know that, then you are suitable to take in. However, the decision is not mine to make. I must pray to the Ancestral Teacher and request his sagely decree. It will depend upon your fortune." He then approached the incense table, burned a bundle of incense upon it, and mumbled a few words, pulling a face as he performed this tomfoolery. He stood like this for some time before kneeling and then prostrating himself on the ground. Wang Wei'er hurriedly pushed Xue Pan to kneel. The Master prostrated himself thus for quite a while before finally rising. He then picked up a piece of yellow paper and burned it over one of the candles. Cradling the ashes in his hands, he made a show of looking into them.

"Fine!" he announced. "The Ancestral Teacher has awarded you the position of senior disciple. Quickly, show him your gratitude!"

Wang Wei'er once again pushed Xue Pan down onto the prayer mat to knock his head against the ground.

"From today forward," the Master continued, "you are to come here to fulfill your duty every day. You cannot miss even one day. Once you have performed some meritorious service in your new role, I will recommend you for a promotion and request an official title for you."

Xue Pan vigorously—and respectfully—assented. He and Wang Wei'er then departed together.

■ ■ ■

When they reached the entrance, Wang Wei'er removed his red headband and belt, then took off his vest as well. He also instructed Xue Pan to take off his headband and belt and put them back in the bag. This completed, they left.

"What did the Master mean just now when he said he'd request an official title for me?" asked Xue Pan.

"Like the name written on my vest—that's my official title."

"And how did you end up with 'Sun Wukong'?"

"Most of the titles are the names of ancients, the most common one is 'Great Sage Equal to Heaven.'[2] Because he had the ability of body multiplication, this title confers the ability of body division. Actually, if you rely on doing your job to get a title, you'd have to fulfill your duties for at least three months before getting one. But if you were to grease the Master's palm with a few taels of silver, you could get one in a matter of a few days!"

"And what's the use of getting a title?"

"It's the same as being an official. Once you've got a title, your status improves a bit, and you'll be much more respectable!"

"How much would I have to spend?"

"There's no set price. But a few taels should do it. If you gave him ten, the process would go even faster."

Xue Pan went to his luggage and pulled out a silver ingot weighing ten taels, then handed it to Wang Wei'er, asking him to serve as middleman. After a short while, a gleeful Wang Wei'er returned, vest in hand.

"You were really lucky today! I was able to get it straight away!"

Xue Pan glanced the vest over—it appeared to be the same as Wang Wei'er's, except that on the cloth patch on the back were written the three characters "Xue Rengui."

"Congratulations, sir!" Wang Wei'er went on. "You will now have the strength of nine bulls and ferocity of two tigers! That comes from the *Account of the Eastern Campaign*,[3] I didn't make it up myself."

"If that's so, then you must be capable of seventy-two transformations!"

Wang Wei'er grew very serious. "As long as one is willing to study, there is nothing that can't be learned."

From this day on, Xue Pan went each day with Wang Wei'er to the altar to fool about and to study silly incantations.

■ ■ ■

More than a month slipped by in this fashion. One day there came a sudden rumor that the Red Lantern Women's Auxiliary had used their magical powers to set fire to and sink several dozen foreign military vessels outside the Dagu Forts.[4] Wang Wei'er was beside himself with excitement and rushed to the altar with Xue Pan in tow. When they arrived, they saw that the altar was already completely packed with throngs of senior disciples. Amid the hubbub of voices, the Master was giving commands, instructing some to go burn down churches, others to go attack foreign embassies. When his eye fell upon Xue Pan, the Master instructed him to go with Wang Wei'er and set fire to the railroad. The two men accepted their orders and led a group of others to the train station in order to set it ablaze.

They quickly burned down the two station buildings but were faced with a conundrum: How could one burn a railroad? The two men went back and forth as to how they should proceed.

Xue Pan hesitated for a moment, then said, "I've got it!" He led the group of men to break into a foreign goods store. He told them to set fire to the foreign goods while at the same time quietly instructing them to carry off any kerosene they might discover. They were able to lay their hands on a few dozen barrels, which they brought back to the railway. Xue Pan ordered the barrels to be opened one after the other and poured over the rails. Once all had been thus prepared, they set it alight with a torch. As the fire rose, crackling ferociously, the wooden railway ties all ignited. The men clapped their hands and shouted with glee.

As a result, the men immediately started a rumor: "Senior disciple Xue Pan's magical might is indeed strong! He merely recited a few incantations, and the railroad burst into flame all on its own!" When Xue Pan heard this, he was very pleased with himself.

■ ■ ■

After this, Wang Wei'er went with Xue Pan back to the altar to request recognition for their meritorious service. When they arrived at the altar, they saw veritable mountains and seas of people, packed so closely together it was almost unbearable. They asked a member of the crowd why there were so many people, and it was explained to them: in the past few days, a senior disciple had killed a "Japanese hairy," while another senior disciple had killed a "European hairy." Upon hearing this, one of the princes had selected today—being an auspicious day—to come to the altar to personally kowtow to the Ancestral Teacher as a show of his thanks. The prince had only just left, but the crowds had followed along to watch the spectacle.

The two men were able to squeeze their way through to the altar, where they reported that they had set the railway on fire. They omitted the fact that they had used kerosene and said only that they had recited some incantations. The crowd upon the altar cheered boisterously at their success.

As Wang Wei'er and Xue Pan were about to start pestering the Master for better titles, they saw that one of the senior disciples had nabbed someone's servant and was declaring that he'd caught a "hairy once removed."

Glancing over at them, Xue Pan became alarmed. "That's not a 'hairy once removed'! Please hand him over to me."

"Do you know him?" asked the other disciple.

"How could I not? He's my cousin's servant."

For his part, the servant, having been seized and brought to the altar, was scared witless. Not only was he too stunned to recognize anyone, but his whole face had broken out in a cold sweat. Only upon hearing Xue Pan's voice did he dare to open his eyes and look. Looking fixedly at Xue Pan, he appraised him for a moment, then cried out, "Yi! Master Xue is here! Master Xue, save me!"

"Beiming, how have you ended up here?" Xue Pan asked. "Has Second Master come as well?"

"How could I have come without him? We've already been in the capital for some time, he sends me out every day to see if I can find news of your whereabouts. But I was never able to find anything out. I never expected to bump into you here."

Xue Pan turned to a group of senior and junior disciples: "Turn this servant over to me for now. Let me take him—then we can go talk to my cousin and I can recruit him to join the movement." He then took Beiming with him and called out to Wang Wei'er to follow.

When they were about halfway to their destination, Wang Wei'er said that he had something he needed to do and had to return home. Xue Pan didn't try to detain him.

Xue Pan then asked Beiming, "Where is Baoyu staying now?"

"When we first arrived, we were staying in the Guangsheng Inn. But we were there for less than two days when things became tense in the city and the landlord wanted to close his doors, so all of the residents had to move out. Second Master then moved into a room at the Jiangning Association Hall and has been there ever since."[5]

As they were chatting, they eventually arrived at the Jiangning Association Hall. As soon as Baoyu saw what Xue Pan was wearing, he was stunned. Without first asking so much as how Xue Pan had been or commenting on how long it had been since they'd seen each other, Baoyu demanded, "How can you have gotten yourself involved in this? Is this the reason that you were so impatient to leave Shanghai for Beijing?"

"And if it was?"

Baoyu paused for a long while without saying anything. After a few moments he replied, "Do you know just what it is that you're doing?"

"We're the 'Militia of Righteous Harmony.' Everyone knows that."

"Hmph! You're dreaming! Everyone else is calling you the 'Boxer bandits.' How did you get yourself into such an idiotic situation? Just you wait and see—when you've caused enough trouble that the foreigners finally decide to fight their way into the city, where will you all flee to then?"

"We have the magical art of the divine fist on our side! We don't fear guns and cannons; how could the hairies advance against us? It is *we* who are going to drive *them* out! Just look—didn't we attack their embassies again today?"

From the side, Beiming interjected, "Actually, I heard today that a 'Grand Secretary Goon' was going to lead the 'Militia of Righteous Harmony' to go attack the embassies. That's why I went out to the altar to have a look. But they said I was a 'hairy once removed' and captured me."

"Why did they capture you?" Baoyu asked. "And how did you manage to escape?"

"I don't know why they said I was a 'hairy once removed,' but they caught me and were just about to kill me. Luckily, Master Xue was there and saved me."

Baoyu was thoughtful for a moment. "Right now, there is no grand secretary by the name of Gun unless the Boxer bandits are using their own presumptuous nomenclature."

"We're all 'disciples,'" said Xue Pan. "No one is called a 'grand secretary.' But today, Grand Secretary Gang did come to the temple."

"That's right!" Beiming cried. "It was Grand Secretary Gang I'd heard about. But they scared me so badly that I misremembered and confused it for Grand Secretary 'Goon.'" Baoyu and Xue Pan both had a good laugh at this.[6]

Xue Pan returned to the matter at hand. "As soon as you saw me, you didn't ask a single question. You just launched straight into criticizing me and calling me foolish—as if you've already got everything all figured out. But the princes and grand secretaries all believe in this. Does that mean that the princes and grand secretaries are lacking in insight compared to you? Right now, there's also a Grand General Li who is going to bring his troops into the capital.[7] If he were to come aid us, I bet that not a single hair from a hairy's head would remain in the capital!"

"Since you really believe that, there's no point in my arguing with you. We'll just have to wait and see," said Baoyu.

"Since you're already arguing, I'd actually like to ask you to explain things for me. If what you say does indeed make sense, then I'll rely on your judgment and give it all up."

"Where is there to argue about? As I see it, this is all like a child's game that has somehow blown up into something far bigger. Why, the claim that you don't fear guns or cannons—that alone is pure absurdity!" Saying this, he went into his luggage and pulled out a six-shot revolver. "I asked someone to buy me this in Shanghai. If you're not afraid of it, then are you willing to let me take a shot at you?"

"I've never tested it out before," said Xue Pan. "But from what I've heard them say, it's all true, with lots of evidence to support it. Do you mean to say they're all lying?"

Baoyu was just about to reply when they heard a burst of chaotic shouts from outside the main entrance. Among the voices was Beiming's. Baoyu stood, about to go out to see what was happening.

■ ■ ■

If you wish to know what the shouting was about, please listen to the explanation in the following chapter.

Chapter Fifteen

The Boxers wreak widespread havoc in the capital

The "Oaf King" absconds to the Changxin Inn under cover of darkness

WE WERE speaking of Xue Pan and Baoyu. Xue Pan, seeing that Baoyu intended to go out and see what was happening, rushed out in his stead. Seeing that Xue Pan had already hurried out, Baoyu decided to stay where he was. He abhorred Xue Pan's absurd getup and had no desire to be seen with him. He waited a short while, after which Xue Pan escorted Beiming into the room. They were followed by a man carrying a basket of watermelons. The man set the basket down and left.

"What was all that ruckus about?" asked Baoyu.

"For the past couple of days, Master has said he'd like some watermelon, so I went out looking for one. Who would have known that after searching all around, I couldn't find even one! But just now, outside the gate, two big carts full of melons pulled up. I asked them to sell me a couple. If they had just said they were not willing to sell, fine. But one of them went so far as to say that the melons had been bought by some grand secretary or other, and what kind of little ruffian was I that I would attempt to force him to sell?"

"Then they must have been ordered by someone. It doesn't matter whether it was a grand secretary or not, you can't just demand that the seller sell them to you. You were in the wrong."

"But I didn't know anyone had ordered them! That's why I asked. If someone else had ordered them, fine, don't sell them, and that's the end of it! Why'd he need to bring a grand secretary into it and scare me half to death? If he really is so fearsome, then how come when Master Xue came out he not only gave him some without daring to ask for a cent—he even came in and delivered them himself?"

Xue Pan explained, "It's because the grand secretary bought them with the intention of making a gift of them to the embassies—that's why the deliverymen didn't dare to sell them."

"Then how were you able to buy them?" asked Baoyu.

"If any of us senior disciples says we want something, who would dare not give it to him, much less ask for money! Who cares if it belonged to a grand secretary—even if it belonged to the emperor himself, if I said I wanted it, I would get it!"

"You've just said that it was a grand secretary who led the attack on the embassies, and now you're saying that one of the grand secretaries is sending gifts of watermelon to the embassies. What does it all mean?"

"How could you understand? What reason would they have for sending the foreigners watermelon, except as an opportunity to poison them?"

"That's very odd. How can you poison someone with a watermelon?"

"You can't poison someone with a watermelon alone—but you can fill it with poison! Then, naturally, they will die."

"But if you are sending them watermelon as a gift, surely you send the whole thing intact. How do you introduce poison into an unsliced watermelon?"

"With magic, of course."

Baoyu sighed. "Why do you continue to persist in these absurd beliefs? I don't have the energy to discuss this with you anymore. Do what you want."

"Let's not talk about it anymore," offered Xue Pan. "How about you tell me all about how you got here?"

"All I can focus on is that outfit of yours. Just seeing it irritates me."

"If it irritates you, I'll take it off." So saying, he removed his headband, pulled off his vest, and untied his belt. As he did so, he said, "You may not be able to stand looking at this outfit, but you should know that we are flourishing these days! When we go out in public, there's no one who doesn't show us a bit of respect. The princes and the grand secretaries salute us as equals; but when others, like monks and *yamen* heads, see us in the street, they get down from their carriages and dismount from their horses as a sign of deference. So I really don't understand your temper about all of this. In Shanghai, whenever you saw foreign goods, you despised them; but now that we have taken the hairies as our enemies, you still disapprove! Do you mean to say that even if we were to completely rout the hairies and remove all foreign goods from the country, we would still not meet your approval?"

"How can you be so muddleheaded? When I said I hated foreign goods, it was just that I hated the useless junk they were exchanging for our very useful money! And I hated that our own people were unwilling to take it upon themselves to learn how to make things. As for the foreigners, why should I hate them? As I see it, your militia is composed of those who were incited into it, but why should *you* go to the trouble of joining them? You must know that all the talk of making paper cutouts that turn into horses and scattering beans that turn into soldiers is just nonsense taken from random novels, how could it possibly be real? That kind of talk is good for tricking women and children, but who would ever have thought that a person like you would fall for it? Think about it: heroes have been taking up valiant callings since ancient times—but when has there ever been even one who relied upon heterodox arts? . . . "

Xue Pan interrupted him with a great laugh. "Ha! It's unfortunate that you are so well-read, and yet you've never read even one part of *The Investiture of the Gods*. Do you mean to suggest that when Jiang Ziya assisted King Wu of Zhou in pacifying all under heaven, he didn't rely upon the magic power of the heavenly bodhisattvas?"

At this, Baoyu snorted out a laugh before sighing. "Enough! Enough! Do what you will! I've tried to convince you, but there's nothing left for me to say. But I do have something serious to ask you: when I left for Beijing, I originally wanted to have the money you left in my charge remitted up here to you, but I heard Wu Bohui say that two of the remittance banks had already stopped transferring funds because of the bad news from the north. There were two other banks that hadn't stopped, but I didn't know whether or not they were reliable, so I didn't have the funds sent. Bohui said that if things calm down up here, you need only send a letter when you require the money, and he would work on your behalf to find a way to get it sent. What do you think?"

"I don't need it now anyway, so if you haven't remitted it, that's fine. Otherwise you can take it and use it yourself, it doesn't really matter."

Baoyu was about to respond when he suddenly heard shouting from outside. The shouting seemed to be growing closer and was much more agitated than the ruckus just now over the watermelons. Just as Baoyu was beginning to grow alarmed, a group of men, most of them wearing red headbands and belts and brandishing single-edged knives, swarmed in from outside. The one at the front of the pack was wearing a vest with a round cloth patch that read "Sun Wukong." It was Wang Wei'er. As soon as he saw Xue Pan, he cried, "You've made me look all over for you! I've looked everywhere, and yet you're hiding out here of all places! Go! Go! Quick! Quick! Something's happening at the altar!" Saying this, he grabbed Xue Pan and dragged him away. Xue Pan didn't even have the chance to say goodbye to Baoyu—he only just managed to snatch up the headband, belt, and vest he had taken off before he was engulfed by the crowd. With a roar, they left.

■ ■ ■

Baoyu could only shake his head and sigh. Back when Baoyu had departed from Shanghai, the atmosphere there was already tense and uneasy as a result of what was happening in the north. Bohui had urged him several times not to go; however, as Baoyu was anxious to see the situation in the capital, he was insistent upon going, and Bohui was ultimately unable to detain him. Leaving in Bohui's care all of the large, heavy items that Xue Pan had left behind, as well as all of the books he had already read, Baoyu took Beiming with him and left.

When they arrived in Tianjin, the atmosphere was even more tense than in Shanghai. According to people at the inn there, it seemed likely that the train to Beijing would stop running any day. As a result, Baoyu dared not linger in Tianjin and hurried on to Beijing. When they put up at the Guangsheng Inn, Baoyu noticed that all of the other guests were people who were checking out; after all, why would anyone still be trying to check in? The few people attempting to take a room found that new guests were no longer being accepted. Because Baoyu had already made arrangements through the Changfa Inn in Shanghai, the inn here was compelled to provide him with accommodation. Two days into his stay, all of the inn's remaining clientele had already fled, and the proprietor decided to close it down so that he too could escape the looming violence. After this Baoyu had moved into the Jiangning Association Hall.

When he had first moved into the hall there were a few other visitors living there. But before too many days had passed, they had all fled as well. From this time on he heard screaming every night and occasionally the sound of people scurrying across the roof. He began to think of moving to yet another place, or even of leaving Beijing altogether. A few days later someone told him that the majority of the people who had attempted to flee had gotten stuck partway to their destinations and were now unable either to advance or retreat. Moreover, there had been two cases where people had been slaughtered along the way by robbers. Baoyu reasoned that it was safer to wait it out quietly than to attempt to move on, and so he decided to stay put for a while before reevaluating the situation. However, staying on his own in such a large hall, it was inevitable that he should begin to feel lonesome, and he eventually decided to make inquiries as to Xue Pan's whereabouts so that he could invite him to come stay with him. Even if the two of them had nothing in common, it was still better than being alone with his shadow! But the capital being as large as it was, Baoyu was unsure as to where he could start looking for Xue Pan. Although Xue Pan had provided an address just before he had left for Beijing, Baoyu was unable to find it in his belongings. He then thought of how much Xue Pan had enjoyed trading in foreign goods in Shanghai and realized that he must be able to find someone who'd had dealings with Xue Pan among the local foreign-goods shops. And so he sent Beiming out to make inquiries among the shops.

Beiming dutifully went out and spent a quite a while asking around, but he was unable to obtain the desired information. On one particular day, as he was walking along outside Qianmen, he saw a large foreign goods shop sitting closed up and silent. He thought, "I've walked past so many times, but never noticed this shop before. Even though the door is closed, there might be people inside. I might as well go knock and ask." He strode forward and knocked on the door, not anticipating that a group of Boxer bandits would arrive at this precise moment. Seeing Beiming knocking on the door of a foreign goods shop, the Boxers declared that Beiming was a "hairy once removed" and trundled him off without letting him explain. Luckily, it was at this point that they had run into Xue Pan, who had saved his life. Since the rest of these events have already been described, there is no need to go back over them.

Let us speak instead of the fact that ever since that day, the Boxer bandits had been growing increasingly brazen, pushing their way through the streets in large groups or companies. If they encountered someone whose clothes they thought were just a bit too closely fitted, they immediately declared him to be a "hairy once removed." Beiming was so terrified that he dared not leave the association hall. Almost all of the hall's staff had left, with the exception of an elderly man called Zhang who remained in the porter's room taking care of association business.

When evening fell, the Boxer bandits would begin to chant their bizarre incantations. Even more bewildering were the strange, fantastical orders they were issued, which changed from day to day. For example, one day a sudden order was given that the eating of "unclean" foods was forbidden; on another day that it was forbidden to sleep; on yet another day that it was forbidden to bathe as well as to leave women's clothes to dry in the sun, since the offensive stink of it might impede the magical powers of the Red Lantern Women's Auxiliary. Every day, whether early or late, two or three different fires would be set. Watching the red glow illuminate the sky was truly terrifying. However, since Baoyu was surrounded by this chaos on all sides, there was nothing for him to do but wait patiently and calmly. Luckily the Boxer bandits did not come to harass him, so he passed the time as best he could. Only Beiming continued to be afraid.

One day the porter, Old Man Zhang, was sweeping out the inner courtyard as Baoyu stood on the steps looking around. Noticing the silvery hue of Old Man Zhang's mustache, Baoyu casually asked, "How old are you this year, sir?"

"I am eighty-five."

"So hardy for your age!"

"The past two years haven't been great, but before that, even though I was already over eighty, I could still run around to the tune of 110 li in a day!"

Baoyu then asked him for news about what had been going on in the city for the past couple of days. Old Man Zhang sighed. "What news could there be? They're still out there wreaking havoc! When the foreign armies finally come, won't it be just like the looting of the Old Summer Palace in the tenth year of Xianfeng?[1] I was only forty-five back then, so if you do the math, it's been exactly forty years. I guess they're so tired of peace that they'd rather bring the foreign militaries down upon us to trample the whole place again."

"What happened in the tenth year of Xianfeng? Although I've read about it a little in books, that doesn't provide as clear a picture as hearing it from someone who witnessed it himself. Would you tell me a bit about it?"

"It was a long time ago, so even I'm a little hazy on it now. But the most remarkable part was when the Xianfeng Emperor fled to Jehol. How pitiful! Once he ran off, he never returned to the capital. When the foreign armies forced their way in, it was because they wanted to negotiate some treaty or other with the emperor, but who would have known that their efforts would be in vain? Now, wouldn't you say that this part was strange? If it were we Chinese who had laid waste to the enemy's capital, and their emperor had fled, leaving his palace for the taking, wouldn't we seat ourselves at the throne? Who would have expected that the foreigners had no desire to install an emperor and instead just set the Old Summer Palace ablaze? They just burned it to the ground and left."

Baoyu smiled gently and asked, "And you saw this with your own eyes?"

"Indeed."

Baoyu did not pursue the topic further, and instead asked once again for news about what had been going on outside for the past few days.

"There is a little news, but you can't go talking about it willy-nilly."

"Why's that?"

"Because if the Boxers hear it, they would say that we're 'hairies once removed' and are spreading rumors about them. But the day before yesterday, a friend of mine returned from Tianjin and said that Tianjin has been thrown into such a state of upheaval that the soldiers all are running amok. The Dagu Forts have been taken, and the city has fallen. There is a foreign general who has brought lots of troops with him, preparing to fight his way into Beijing. They'd gotten as far as Yang village, but weren't able to advance past there, so they retreated to come up with a better strategy before trying again. They may be advancing as we speak. When they do arrive, won't it be just like the tenth year of Xianfeng?"

"Since you know all of this and are a Beijinger yourself, why don't you try to persuade the Boxers to stop?"

"How could I possibly get them to listen to me? Even my own grandsons and great-grandsons are out there being Boxers. If I was unable to stop even them, how much less successful would I be in trying to convince other people! What do they understand of it? Even an old man like me, why, previously I was also muddled about these things and didn't really understand what 'foreign countries' were. But because a certain Master Guo was dispatched overseas as imperial envoy, I once accompanied him to England and then to France. After I'd returned, I accompanied a Master Zhang to America; only after all that did I really understand it.[2] If I hadn't, I would still think that China was one country and 'foreign country' was another. I never would have known that there were so many different countries out there!"

"No wonder you speak with such understanding—you have truly seen the world," replied Baoyu.

As they were talking, they heard a burst of distant gunfire outside. Baoyu said, "Recently I've been hearing gunshots every day, and people have said that it's Boxers attacking the embassies. These simple little embassies have been under attack for such a long while now without being overrun—so one can imagine the actual efficacy of this Boxer 'magic'!"

Old Man Zhang laughed. "You're exactly right! They always say that they're not afraid of being shot, but who knows how many have been shot and killed in their siege of the embassies! It's funny to think that they are really only deceiving one another—in their demonstrations, one man picks up a rifle and shoots at a compatriot to prove the latter's defensive magic, and of course the target is not killed. The people watching believe this all to be real. How could they know that the bullets are loaded backward into the guns and can't be fired out, so it's essentially the same as firing an empty gun? The onlookers are totally taken in by it. That's all well and good, but of course, eventually, they also come to not fear being shot. The most ridiculous thing is that when they attack the foreign embassies, of course the foreigners return the courtesy. Although the embassies do not hold great stores of guns or ammunition, they seek ways to purchase them from outside. And so the Boxers will actually *sell* Mausers to the foreigners, justifying it to themselves by saying that the guns are incapable of killing any of their own lot while happily taking the foreigners' money. Isn't such idiocy pitiable?"

"If you have taken someone as your enemy, it makes no sense to trade with them at the same time!" replied Baoyu.

"And how could it just be guns? Aren't they also the same people who supply the embassies with food, coal, and water every day?"

He had not quite finished speaking when they saw Xue Pan come running up frantically. Xue Pan grabbed Baoyu and pulled him inside.

▪ ▪ ▪

If you wish to know why he did this, please listen to the explanation in the following chapter.

Chapter Sixteen

The Boxers' buffoonery is made fully apparent

Wang Wei'er's evil heart is suddenly revealed

WE WERE speaking of Xue Pan, who had come racing in in a frantic state. Baoyu was greatly startled by this, and forgetting Old Man Zhang, he followed Xue Pan inside. Xue Pan took a moment to catch his breath, then began: "Brother Bao, do you know why I've come?"

"You've come here in such a frenzy—and yet you would waste time making me guess why you've come! Quickly, tell me!"

"The foreign armies are going to fight their way into the city. I plan to run away—that's why I've come especially to tell you."

"What about your 'magical arts'?"

"According to the Master, the Heavenly Soldiers and Heavenly Generals haven't yet finished amassing themselves. He says that once they are ready, the Boxers will be able to snatch up all of the foreigners with one strike. But I've been mulling over what you said last time and am worried that what they say isn't reliable. I can't help but feel afraid. So I've decided that the sooner I get out of here, the better."

"Where did you hear that the foreigners are going to fight their way into the city?"

"It's a long story! There's a foreign goods shop in the city—the owner is a southerner, too. Since I started trading in foreign goods, we've had a fair number of interactions. Last year when he returned to the south for a visit, he passed through Shanghai and he and I spent a few days together, and so got to know each other better. Now he's here, and he and some others have formed a group to pool funds especially for the purpose of hiring a few people to go out and gather information. So the report is very reliable—he told it to me himself. He also told me that out past the Changxin Inn there's a place called the Peaceful Refuge. It's a great spot, perfect for hiding out. There have never been any reports of floods, fires, or thieves there. He wanted to go himself some time ago, but couldn't just abandon his business, so in the end, he never went. But he has told me to go, so I plan to go stay at the Changxin Inn for a few days first, waiting to hear news of what's going on here. If the news is good, I'll come back; if it's bad, I'll head to the Peaceful Refuge. I want to make arrangements for us to go together."

Baoyu laughed. "I've already had to put up with so many frights here! If you wanted to leave, we should have left earlier! Why wait until this moment? Please leave at your own convenience! Just send me a letter from wherever you end up."

"You're staying on here, then?"

"Not necessarily. I really wanted to come see what had been going on around the city recently. But I didn't expect that as soon as I'd arrived, I would meet with the current situation, and not be able to step even an inch out the door! Once things have settled down I'd like to spend a few days wandering around and taking in the city. Then I'd be willing to leave."

"And where will you go?"

"I'll just go back to Shanghai, of course."

"What do you have left to do there?"

"I don't have a real reason for going back, it's just that it's easier to get reliable information there, so I had a better sense for what was going on."

While the two men were talking, dusk began to approach. Xue Pan stood up and took his leave, saying, "In leaving like this, I'm deceiving the others. The last time I was here, there was a man who came looking for me. His name is Wang Wei'er. After I leave, he may or may not come looking for me again. If he does, please just tell him I haven't been here recently." The men shook hands and parted. Xue Pan hurried out of the city and made his way straight to the Changxin Inn where he planned to stay. But of that let's say no more.

After Xue Pan left, things were much the same for Baoyu, with the Boxer bandits carrying on outside as before. As Xue Pan had anticipated, Wang Wei'er came looking for him on two occasions, but Baoyu sent him away, saying he didn't know anything. Roughly two weeks had passed, when suddenly one day Old Man Zhang ran up in a panic and announced, "The foreign armies have arrived! They're going to enter the city any minute now!"

"If they enter the city, they enter the city. What are you so worked up about?"

"We need to make preparations to flee!"

"When the foreigners enter the city, will they kill people?"

"That's hard to say."

"You've been overseas before—do you understand any foreign languages?"

"I can speak English all right."

"Since you can speak with them, then it'll be easy enough. As I see it, we don't need to leave. It's unlikely that the foreign soldiers will start shooting people willy-nilly."

Just as he was saying this, they heard the sound of artillery streaking through the sky and a roiling commotion of voices from outside. Old Man Zhang ran out, and even Baoyu couldn't help but take up position in a doorway to look out. He saw throngs of people—men bearing one another up, women being carried—rushing in an endless stream through the street; the cries of parents searching for their children and children for their parents rang unremittingly in his ears. He truly could not bear to witness the scene before him.

By this time Old Man Zhang had also come to stand in the doorway. Suddenly someone ran up and grabbed hold of him, asking, "Both royal households have fled, why aren't you leaving too?"[1]

Old Man Zhang replied, "It's not as though the royal households have ordered me to escort them! Why should I flee along with them?"

"That's not what I meant, I'm just telling you to get out of here! Who says you're worthy to serve as an escort?"

Baoyu interrupted him, "What you just said about the two royal households fleeing—is it true?"

"A thousand times true! I just saw Grand Secretaries Rong and Gang, along with a number of others of high rank. They're all fleeing one after the other! *That's* the royal escort! Anyway, since the two of you won't leave, I'll be off!" So saying, the man disappeared into the crowd like a wisp of smoke. Old Man Zhang closed the main door.

After three or four days passed, the cries of people in the street gradually quieted. Old Man Zhang came to Baoyu and said, "All right, by now, wave upon wave of foreign soldiers have arrived. They have reached an agreement to divide the city into sections governed by each, so it is now safe to go out into the streets again. I'm just afraid that anyone who doesn't understand foreign languages might find themselves in a sticky situation with the foreign soldiers."

Hearing this, Baoyu went out for a stroll outside. Because he hadn't been outside for such a long time, when he stepped out into the street, he felt as though the complexion of the whole world around him had changed. He walked along at a leisurely pace, noticing small flags bearing messages like "Obedient Subjects of Mighty England" and "Obedient Subjects of Mighty Germany" sticking out from the doorways of each home that he passed. Along the road there were many foreign troops on patrol. If it happened that Baoyu stopped to look at something for a moment, a foreign soldier would immediately come and question him. Fortunately, because Baoyu had received two months' tutoring in foreign books from Bohui and because he was an exceptionally clever person—and was moreover willing to exert himself in his studies, such that even while living here, not a day had passed where he hadn't been studiously reading the dictionary—he was able to respond fluently with no effort or confusion whatsoever.

When he arrived in one particular part of the city, he saw a formation of dozens of foreign soldiers advancing down the street. Kneeling along the roadside as the soldiers passed were about ten locals; sticking out of the backs of their shirt collars were more small flags. Upon these, too, had been written "Obedient Subject of Mighty England" and "Obedient Subject of Mighty France." There were flags appealing to "Mighty America," "Mighty Germany," and "Mighty Japan," as well, with "Obedient Subject of—" invariably stitched at the top of each. The people kneeling at the roadside were proffering trays of *mantou*, plates of piping hot plump chicken, or choice cuts of meat. Among these locals Baoyu clearly recognized Wang Wei'er, which caused him to give a small involuntary laugh. The foreign soldier in command of the passing formation stopped in front of Baoyu and demanded, "What are you laughing at?"

In English, Baoyu replied, "I am not sure which country your esteemed army is from, but seeing those people kneeling there to greet your troops with those flags with 'England,' 'Germany,' 'France,' 'America,' and 'Japan' written haphazardly on them made me laugh."

The foreign soldier laughed too, and said, "We're English." Then, pointing to the flags, he asked, "Which one says 'England'?"

Baoyu looked, and as it happened, the flag that Wang Wei'er was bearing said "Obedient Subject of Mighty England," so he reached out casually and pulled it off him, then pointed out the word "England" for the soldier. The soldier looked it over, then looked back at Wang Wei'er. Seeing that he had now prostrated himself there on the ground, the soldier strode over, placed his fingertips under Wang Wei'er's chin, and told him to raise his head. Who would have expected that Wang Wei'er was by now so afraid that his face had completely drained of color? The soldier gave a great guffaw, shook hands with Baoyu, and walked off to resume his position overseeing the formation.

Baoyu continued walking and had barely gotten as far as an arrow can be shot when he heard from behind a voice crying out repeatedly, "Venerable Master! Venerable Master!" Baoyu turned to look, and saw that Wang Wei'er, his face completely bathed in sweat, was approaching. Baoyu was surprised by this, so he stopped and waited.

When he finally came up beside Baoyu, Wang Wei'er threw himself down to his knees, mumbling unintelligibly, then began to knock his head against the ground—*kebeng!*—*kebeng!* He then began to murmur, "Venerable Master, spare me!"

Baoyu was startled, and asked, "What do you mean? I don't understand!"

Wang Wei'er now began to weep. "If Master doesn't spare me, I'll bludgeon myself to death right here!" Saying this, he continued bashing his head against the ground. The skin was already broken, blood starting to flow.

"How bizarre!" said Baoyu. "If you're going to ask me to spare you, you have to tell me why! Moreover, I certainly have no intention of taking your life, so how exactly would you have me go about sparing it?"

Still weeping, Wang answered, "Although your humble servant has been to Master's home two or three times, luckily I have never caused any offense to you. But I didn't actually know that Master was friends with mighty Mr. Englandman. I hope that Master will treat me mercifully."

"The more you say, the less I understand. Just tell me once and for all why you've come after me."

"Just now, didn't Master tell mighty Mr. Englandman to kill me?"

"That's even stranger! Who is this 'mighty Mr. Englemann'? I don't know any such person."[2]

Wang Wei'er's cries continued unabated. He then shuffled clumsily forward on his knees and threw his arms around Baoyu's legs. As Wang's wailing increased in intensity, Baoyu was rendered quite speechless. At this moment there were several pedestrians passing by, all of whom stopped in their tracks to observe the scene. Baoyu didn't know what to do, so he stamped his foot and said, "Where is all of this talk coming from? And you're not even willing to explain yourself! If you would only explain it all clearly, I might be able to do something!"

Seeing that a crowd was growing around them, Wang Wei'er was even more reluctant to speak. Baoyu began to grow angry: "Let me go now, I don't have time to fool around with you!"

Wang hurriedly released him, then resumed knocking his head against the ground. "Master, take pity on your humble servant! My only son has already died! Spare me!"

At no point in the conversation had Baoyu come to grasp Wang Wei'er's meaning. Finally, he glibly replied, "All right, I spare you! Now get up!" Wang was overjoyed, and, wiping away his tears, began knocking his head against the ground once more. "Thank you, Master! I'd like to invite Master back to my home, so that I may offer you some tea."

"I don't have the time. I've already spared you. Be on your way."

But of course Wang Wei'er was unwilling to let him go and grabbed him. "My home isn't far, it's just up ahead. Please, Master, honor me with your company." So saying, he began to drag Baoyu away with him.

There was nothing Baoyu could do but go along. As Wang Wei'er had promised, they arrived after a short walk. Wang pushed open the door and invited Baoyu to enter first. After they were both inside, Wang carried a chair into the center of the room and set it down, then bade Baoyu sit. Once Baoyu had sat down, Wang then began as before to knock his head against the ground and called his wife to come out and do the same. These antics had the effect of making Baoyu feel that he must be dreaming. Only when Wang's fussing over Baoyu—now offering to make him tea, now offering water—had finally quieted, did Baoyu speak up: "At no point today have I come close to understanding why on Earth you should have asked me to spare your life. If you would only tell me plainly, I might be able to do something about it!"

Wang Wei'er started at this. "So Master is not willing to spare me after all?" He began to kneel once again. Beside him, his wife pleaded ingratiatingly that he be spared: "Venerable Master, please take pity on this poor woman!" She then pointed at Wang and added, "This wretch! Somewhere he met with a gang of bandits who claimed to have magical powers. They said they weren't afraid of guns, and that they were going to exterminate the 'hairies.' He even ordered me to learn how to be part of the Red Lantern Women's Auxiliary. In the evenings, I was to take up a lantern and climb up onto the roof. He taught me to recite some incantations and said that this would enable me to float up into the clouds and ride the mist; once riding along on the clouds, I would be able to use the divine fire within the lantern to go and burn the 'hairies.' Who would have guessed that despite muddling along for quite a while in this manner without it ever working at all, he didn't blame himself for having been taken in—oh no! He blamed his poor little wife, saying I hadn't been sincere enough in my efforts! He even brought our son to go study the 'magical arts.' Unfortunately, he was shot and killed the day they attacked the embassies. Even then, my husband didn't blame the bandits' 'magic' for not working! Instead, he said that because my hands were unclean when I braided my son's hair that day, the magic spell had been broken.

"Only in the past few days, since the foreign troops have fought their way into the city, have the bandits finally realized how fearsome the foreigners are and scrambled to tear off their red headbands and belts in their rush to surrender! Since then, there have been foreign troops walking past the door every day, so he goes out to kneel for a few hours, offering up liquor and meat in order to communicate that he was absolutely not a Boxer bandit. Unfortunately, if you don't understand how to talk to them, you can talk until your lips crack and the foreigners will act as though they haven't even heard you. But just now when he came home from his stint at kneeling, he was so afraid that it was like he'd lost two of his three *hun* souls and six of his seven *po* souls![3] He said that some venerable master who was friends with mighty Mr. Englandman was speaking with mighty Mr. Englandman, and that it was possible that the master would reveal with truth about him. Then I asked, 'How could he know the truth about you?' It was only then that the wretch told me that you were a friend of Master Xue and were living at the Jiangning Association Hall. He said in looking for Master Xue he'd ended up going there twice, and you, Master, would recognize him. That's why he begged you to spare his life. For better or for worse, please don't tell the truth about him in front of the foreigners. It would be a great mercy on your part if you didn't."

Baoyu listened to this speech and finally understood. "But you're the same as me—we're all Chinese. How could I ask the foreigners to cause trouble for you? Don't worry, I won't say a word, and that's that. And moreover, I am certainly not that foreigner's friend. I just gave a casual answer to something he asked me, that's all."

Wang Wei'er once again knocked his head on the ground and uttered his thanks. His wife had by now served tea. Baoyu stood up, intending to leave, but of course Wang Wei'er was unwilling to let him go. "Just now, if it hadn't been for Master's magnanimity, that foreigner could have shot your humble servant dead ten times and it wouldn't have been enough! I'm just preparing a cup of meager liquor as a token of my respect. I beg Master to do me the honor of having just a little. After all, there will be many times in the future when I shall have to rely upon Master."

Baoyu made repeated efforts to leave, but how could he withstand the pair's determined efforts to detain him? And so, he could only sit back down and watch them as they hurried about, setting up the table and chairs, then laying the table until it was full with dishes of chicken, goose, fish, and pork. Wang Wei'er and his wife each made a toast to Baoyu in turn. Privately, Baoyu found this all quite comical. He thought, "I would never have expected to be party to such strange doings today! It's really too funny that the very people who just a few days ago desired to kill the 'hairies,' are so terrified of the 'mighty foreigners' today! Today, seeing me converse briefly with that foreigner, they are so full of respect; but had it happened a few days ago, I would have been a 'hairy once removed'!"

As he was thinking this, he suddenly heard a voice yell from outside: "Wang Wei'er! Hurry! Hurry! The mighty foreigners are here!"

Wang ran out, leaving just his wife and Baoyu inside. Wang's wife poured more liquor and raised Baoyu's cup to his lips herself. With a demure sideways glance, she said, "Master, please drain your cup."

Baoyu thought, "Enough! How have I gotten myself into this situation? I can't let this turn into something like what happened with Qingwen's cousin-in-law. That would be too unseemly!"[14] As he thought this to himself, he took the cup and drank about half of it before pushing it away, claiming to be drunk. He then slumped onto the table and pretended to be asleep. Wang's wife took the remaining half-cup of liquor and drank it herself. She then began to prod Baoyu:

"Master, wake up! How is it you're drunk already?"

Baoyu did not respond and continued pretending to have fallen asleep. Wang's wife bent at the waist and closely scrutinized Baoyu's face for some time before venturing, "If Master wishes to sleep, then let me help you to the *kang*."

Baoyu still did not respond. A short while later Wang Wei'er came back into the room. Seeing Baoyu asleep at the table, he asked, "What happened?"

"He's drunk."

Wang Wei'er approached Baoyu and gave him a couple of shakes, but Baoyu still did not move. Wang then signaled with his hand for his wife to approach and whispered quietly to her, "To let him live would be planting the roots of our own future calamity. We might as well take advantage of his being drunk to do away with him!" Wang's wife tried to wave off the idea.

■ ■ ■

If you wish to know whether Baoyu was to lose his life or not, please listen to the explanation in the following chapter.

Chapter Seventeen

Two speeches at Weichun Garden

A night of simple conversation at the Changfa Inn

WE WERE speaking of Wang Wei'er and the fact that he was, fundamentally, a man with a wolfish, savage heart. Seeing that Baoyu was drunk, he discussed with his wife his desire to end Baoyu's life. His wife hastily waved her hands, saying, "He's just spared your life, how could it possibly do to not spare his in return?"

"'To know someone is merely to know his face, never his heart.' Even though he agreed just now not to tell the foreign devils the truth about me, who knows what might happen once he leaves? Besides, now he knows where we live—I'm afraid he'll lead them right to us!" Hearing this, his wife grew silent.

How could they have known that Baoyu was only pretending to be drunk, and that in spite of their hushed voices, he had already heard most of what they'd said? He thought, "The savage nature of people like these is indeed difficult to tame! In the blink of an eye, he's already come up with a plan to murder me! Luckily, I am only pretending to be drunk—if I were actually drunk, how could I but fall victim to this evil plot?" He then made a show of stretching and yawning before rising. He gave a little cough and spat, then exclaimed, "I'm parched!"

Hearing this, Wang Wei'er's wife hurried over with a cup of tea. Baoyu used it to rinse out his mouth. Wang Wei'er once again approached him solicitously.

"Thanks very much," said Baoyu. "I had too much to drink and unintentionally showed a lack of propriety. But I've just realized that there's an important matter that I must tend to, and so now I really must take my leave." Wang Wei'er tried his utmost to detain him, but Baoyu was insistent upon leaving. He thereupon made his goodbyes, exited, and went in search of the road back.

Along the way, he thought, "People like Wang Wei'er are truly devious, treacherous, indecent, and shameless—all in one! It seems to me that the Boxer bandits are all like this. But why would those in power suddenly trust and make use of them, and allow things to deteriorate like this? It is truly incomprehensible! Now, although I have heard that Li Hongzhang, the governor-general of Guangdong and Guangxi, has been sent to the capital to negotiate for peace, I haven't seen him show up! I honestly don't know when this catastrophe will be rectified." He then thought of Wang Wei'er's wife, who had turned out to be absurdly shameless. He continued turning these thoughts over in his mind as he walked and returned to the association hall feeling depressed and dispirited.

When his depression became insupportable, Baoyu ventured outside for a leisurely stroll. However, whenever one went out now, he would invariably be met with scenes of commoners kneeling to greet the foreign soldiers like obsequious slaves or servants, calling to mind the phrase "greeting the king's army with baskets of rice and jugs of drink." When the foreign soldiers were in a good mood, they simply passed straight by, ignoring the peasants on the side of the road; but if they happened to be in a foul mood, they would grow angry that those kneeling on the ground were hindering their movement along the road and would lash out, striking or kicking them. Those who were thus beaten still, perversely, turned up smiling faces to greet the foreigners. Baoyu thought, "It goes without saying that these miserable curs were previously Boxer bandits who wanted to kill 'hairies once removed.'" Seeing them thus actually made him feel quite sullen. When he looked upon the various national flags that had been erected atop the city wall, he grew even more despondent. He found himself deeply regretting his decision to go out for a walk, and after ruminating on it, decided it would be best to leave the capital.

Once he had returned to the association hall, he called Old Man Zhang to come in and talk things over. Old Man Zhang said, "Right now, you could say that the city has been pacified—but outside of the city, it's still a bedlam of soldiers and horses. Yesterday I heard it said that the two royal households are planning to flee to Shanxi, but the roads are quite dangerous. Luckily, when they arrived in Huailai County, the magistrate rode out to meet the royal carriages. Because he executed his duties well, he has been well rewarded. He has now been promoted to *daotai* out of nowhere and will escort the empress dowager and emperor together to Shanxi. Everyone is pleased for the former magistrate, but as I see it, it would have been better had he not been promoted."

"What do you mean?" Baoyu asked, startled.

"Since he's been promoted, the position of magistrate is now left vacant. And if he travels with the emperor to Shanxi, well, that *sounds* well and good, but with so many princes and grand secretaries also traveling along in attendance, what chance does the new *daotai* have of ever being noticed? At least in his position as magistrate, when there was nothing much to do, he could enjoy the simple pleasures of seizing commoners and having them caned a couple of times or sending them out to dig ditches!" This made Baoyu laugh.

Baoyu then continued, "According to you, then, it's not possible to travel just now?"

"When is it ever impossible to travel? I'm just afraid that the roads will be dangerous."

Beiming, sitting beside them, scratched his head. "Didn't you tell me earlier today that someone whose surname has hooves would come rescue us?"

Baoyu responded, "What surname has hooves? You're confused again."

"He's the one who said it! It wasn't 'cow' . . . or 'sheep' . . . he did say it, but I can't think of what it was."

Old Man Zhang laughed. "I did tell him something of the sort! In Shanghai, an aid society has recently been established, and people have donated money to hire a steamship to come up to Tianjin to rescue refugees and evacuate them back down south. Right now, all of the gentlemen who are hiding out in the capital and unable to return to the south themselves are eagerly waiting for its arrival. But I don't know whether it's coming or not. I've heard that the organizer is also a *daotai* by the surname of Lam."

"You see?" exclaimed Beiming. "A lamb does have hooves! I would never misremember it!"[1]

Old Man Zhang addressed Baoyu: "Previously, when everything was chaotic and upside down, and everyone else was so frantic to leave the city, you were so relaxed about it! You've already held out this long, why the urgency to leave now? Wouldn't it be better to stay for a little while longer and wait for the outskirts to calm down before leaving?"

"It's just that I've become unbearably bored staying here. When I go out for a stroll, there's nowhere worth going. But if there's nothing to be done, then I'll wait a bit longer." And so Baoyu could only remain at the association hall. Since no newspapers were being delivered, he had no knowledge whatsoever of what was going on outside. He passed each day in a dull stupor, as though he were dreaming. Luckily, he had brought a good number of books with him from Shanghai, and so he read every day to dispel his boredom.

It is true that time passes quickly, and before he knew it, the last vestiges of fall had given way to winter. It was then not long before the final month of the lunar year had passed, and spring had returned. By now, things had generally quieted down outside, and Baoyu completed his preparations and left Beijing. Along the route he saw crumbling walls and broken tiles, with few traces of human activity; of the wheatfields he passed, most had been abandoned. When he arrived in Tianjin, he felt that the cityscape had changed drastically from when he had first come, and he could not help but sigh. After arriving once again in Shanghai, he took up residence as before in the Changfa Inn. Once he had finished putting away his luggage, he went out to visit Wu Bohui, and the two men were glad to be reunited after such a long parting. Baoyu informed Bohui of Xue Pan's activities, and both sighed with regret.

Then Bohui said, "You've come just in time! There is a debate in the Zhang Garden today at 2:00 p.m. We can go watch together."

"What's being debated?"

"We've been hearing that China and Russia have agreed to a secret treaty that will allow Russia to annex our three eastern provinces for itself.[2] That's what everyone will be discussing. It's already almost time—let's get going."

And so, they climbed together into a horse carriage and hurried straight off to the Zhang Garden. As it happened, it was still early, so the two men stopped to have some tea on the porch of the old foreign-style building. They had been sitting for a little over an hour when they saw the other attendees begin to stream into the building. Roughly twenty or thirty people now gathered together in the meeting room. A long banquet table had been placed in the center of the room, with the first speaker now standing to take up the central position behind it. Baoyu observed him closely. The speaker's eyebrows were tightly knit, his eyes lifeless. His complexion was darkish, but not "dark" per se; greenish, yet somehow not quite "green," either. It would have been incorrect to describe him as either fat or thin. The worried brow and embittered gaze that were a natural part of his countenance gave him an air of demoralization and despondency.

He began to speak: "I know it was difficult for the assembled gentlemen to gather here today, but it just shows how enthusiastic you all are. Recently, we have heard that our government has agreed to a secret treaty with Russia—it goes without saying that this secret treaty is of great consequence. All of you gentlemen have assembled here seeking to discuss what we can do to prevent it." Having said this, he retreated a few steps. The members of the crowd then made a great show of making way and allowing one another to step up.

Eventually another man stood at the center table. This man had a yellow face and could not have been more than twenty years old. His hair was quite long, and at the front of his scalp it had grown out like that of a man in deep mourning.[3] Standing firmly, he said, "That the government has established a secret treaty with Russia is a matter of national importance. What's the use of someone like me getting up here and talking? What good does it do? But as I see it, we are all Chinese, and so everything that concerns China is our business. And since this particular treaty was made in secret, it's clear that the government isn't willing to tell us what's in it. But after the uprising of the Boxer bandits, when Prince Qing and Grand Secretary Li went to the capital to negotiate for peace, the Russians wanted to include the matter of General Shou Shan instigating that conflict in Heilongjiang last year as a further grievance to be considered in their negotiations.[4] So it's obvious that this secret treaty has to do with the three eastern provinces. Gentlemen, last year, the Russians abused our brethren in Heilongjiang—they marched several thousand people to the edge of the Heilong River and forced them to throw themselves in. In no time at all, the bodies of Chinese clogged the river and began to drift downstream. Gentlemen! Do not mistake yourselves into thinking that the affairs of the three eastern provinces have nothing to do with us! If we just keep concerning ourselves with muddling along as if drunk or in a dream, then what happened at the Heilong River is sure to set a precedent for what happens at the Yangzi River!"[5] When he had gotten this far, a number of people eagerly clapped their hands, after which the speaker then stepped down. Again, the crowd deferred and made room, and so the first speaker—the one with the worried brow and the embittered gaze—returned to the front once more and said, "Today, we must discuss measures that we can take—perhaps we could draft some telegrams to send to the government and to the various provincial officials, urging them to do their utmost to put a stop to this. What do you gentlemen think?" Again several people applauded. The speaker continued, "There are too few of us here today—but as we have already agreed to hold a large meeting the day after tomorrow, we will arrive at a decision about what to do at that time." Thereupon the crowd began to disperse. Baoyu and Bohui climbed back into their carriage and returned.

Baoyu made a date with Bohui to return for the larger meeting the day after next. When the day arrived, they returned and found that the atmosphere was greatly changed from previously. The meeting had been relocated to a large foreign-style building. In the middle of the meeting room two square tables had been pushed together, with a third table perched atop these. Arrayed in front of the tables were row upon row of chairs, numbering over a hundred in total; beside the tables a booth had been erected where attendees could sign up to join the cause. People were arriving in droves. The man with the worried brow and embittered gaze who had spoken at the previous meeting did not speak this time; instead, he paced back and forth agitatedly, letting out numerous sighs of varied intensity, stamping his feet and wringing his hands. At the start of the meeting someone climbed up onto the square tables and gave a brief explanation of their goals, after which another man got up and began to speak. Unfortunately, the audience today was much larger than before, and the hubbub of chattering voices made it impossible to hear the speaker clearly. Indeed, by the time this man finished speaking, even more people had come in, adding to the din.

Dear readers! You should know that this Zhang Garden is a place for parties and leisure, and that anyone is allowed in. And so a large number of brothel-going dandies, and even carriage drivers and prostitutes, had wandered in; meanwhile, others had come in thinking that they were catching a sermon about Jesus. Amid the racket of their talking and laughing, how could anyone hear? Suddenly, a man dressed in a foreign-style suit leaped onto the platform with a shout. Brandishing a wooden cane in his hand, he bellowed, "Today's meeting is for serious discussion, not for shooting the breeze! I suggest you all quiet down. You shouldn't be engaging in barbaric activities in such a civilized assembly hall as this!" Having said his piece, he leaped back down as suddenly as he had leaped up. When Baoyu scrutinized him more closely, he realized that it was the young man with the yellowish face who had spoken at the previous meeting. Seeing him today, dressed as he was in a suit, Baoyu realized that the young man hadn't been in mourning, as he had supposed based on the fact that the man was letting the hair at the front of his scalp grow out; rather, he must have been growing it out so that he could more easily get a short Western haircut.

After this a large number of people came up, one after the other, to speak. Unfortunately, none of them could be heard either. Baoyu was growing impatient and wanted to leave, when he suddenly heard a thunderous burst of applause. He hurriedly raised his head to look and saw that a girl of perhaps fourteen or fifteen years of age was now standing upon the platform. Baoyu was surprised by this, and thought, "Ah, so women like this have actually emerged now! Such things don't come about easily!" And so he cocked his ears and listened.

She began, "A person's being born within a particular country is rather like a hair growing out of one's head. If a person attempts to solve a country's woes by himself, it of course cannot be done—it would be like attempting to lift a person by pulling on a single strand of hair! How could you possibly lift him up? But if you were to take all of his hair into your hand at once, then of course you could lift him up. So if you want to solve this country's problems, you must first unify with a single purpose all four hundred million people who make up the country—indeed, once this has been achieved, is there any problem that couldn't be solved?" Hearing this, the audience burst into applause again. After this the voices of the audience members became increasingly boisterous, so much so that the speaker could no longer be heard. She spoke for a little while longer before climbing down from the platform.

Suddenly a monk came to the fore. Baoyu thought, "This monk must certainly have some marvelous message to impart, and is certain to speak in beautiful, evocative terms." He tried to listen intently, but when other members of the audience saw a monk standing before them, they all began to exclaim how bizarre it was. Some even wrapped their arms round their stomachs and doubled over with riotous laughter. How could Baoyu hear even a word? When the monk had finished speaking, he folded his hands in a parting salutation and stepped down.

After this, another man quickly took the stage. He began to shout in great, thunderous roars. His face was contorted with rage, and he slammed the table with his hand as he spoke, as if he were upbraiding someone. In his slamming of the table, he managed to upset a teacup, and very nearly sent the table itself tumbling over. Two other men then came and stood at either side of the table to hold it in place as he continued speaking; but this only allowed the speaker to strike the table all the more viciously. The man's voice was so powerful that he ought to have been heard clearly, but who would have guessed that as he raised the volume of his voice, so too would the noisily chattering audience? And so nothing of this speech was to be heard, either. Once this man had finished his tirade, another man climbed up, raised his hand, and announced, "The speeches are now concluded." At this point the audience began to disperse, though a good number of people had gathered around the sign-up booth.[6]

When Baoyu and Bohui walked past to look, they saw that a collection was being taken up to help pay for the cost of sending telegrams. Some people were giving eight or ten yuan, others were giving one or two. On one side stood a Korean who had also signed up and donated a few yuan. Because of the barrier in spoken language, the man had taken up the paper and brush and written: *Having seen the assembled gentlemen participating in this meeting, I say their enthusiasm is to be admired! Because of linguistic differences, I can't participate in the talks myself; but I offer my sincere assistance in paying for the telegrams* . . . and so on. Upon seeing this, Baoyu was deeply moved. Suddenly he heard a voice call out from behind, "Why don't you sign up, too?" When he turned to look, he saw another person respond, "If you ask me to donate a couple of coins, why, sure, that's fine. But I won't sign my name!" Baoyu couldn't help but sigh. Bohui smiled at him, and the two men exited the building together, climbed back into their carriage, and headed directly back to the Changfa Inn.

By now it was already late, so Baoyu asked Bohui to stay for dinner, adding, "I've been away from Shanghai for so long. When I was living in the capital, the chaos that broke out meant that there were no newspapers to be had, so I've been living like a deaf man. If you've nothing else to do, please stay and have a long chat with me tonight. You can tell me a bit about what has happened since we parted." Bohui had always enjoyed chatting with Baoyu, and so he agreed to stay. After dinner Baoyu told Bohui about what had happened with the Boxer bandits in the capital and said, "It goes without saying that the ignorant Boxers simply lacked the intelligence to know any better; but how is it that the princes, dukes, and grand ministers were all taken in so easily? It's incomprehensible."

Bohui laughed. "Don't talk to me about the capital—such a stubborn, ignorant kind of place! Why, Shanghai is much more enlightened, and last year even people *here* were praising Prince Duan's so-called 'statecraft'!"

As they were talking, Bohui suddenly thought of another matter.

■ ■ ■

But if you wish to know what it was he thought of, please listen to the explanation in the following chapter.

Chapter Eighteen

After apposite quotation of texts ancient and recent, a dumbfounded student flees by night

Cruelly imprisoned, the blameless "Spirit Jade" meets with calamity

WE WERE speaking of how Bohui was casually chatting with Baoyu when suddenly he remembered something and said to Baoyu, "Last year when all that chaos broke out in the north, so many people tried to flee to the south, but were forced to turn back after suffering all kinds of miseries and hardships. There were many who weren't even able to return and perished along the way. The fact that you were able to reside safely in the capital is really extraordinary. The southern provincial officials all had to sign treaties with the foreigners, saying that the foreigners were to be protected as before; the governor of Shandong was also captured and executed.[1] Since the Boxers were unable to make their way down south, the area ought to have been relatively tranquil! But the people of Shanghai still evacuated, saying that the Boxer bandits were bound to come. As if that weren't enough, people living in the hinterland then fled in droves *into Shanghai*! Just thinking about it is enough to make one laugh!

"But who would have known that there would indeed be a disturbance in the south, as well—one that nearly destabilized everything? In Hunan there was a scholar living on a government stipend who heard that the north was in such an uproar as to be completely unrecognizable. He wanted to start an armed militia in Hubei that would fight on behalf of the emperor. But when the local officials found out about it, they captured the scholar and executed him."[2]

Baoyu was shocked by this. "But fighting for the emperor is a good thing! How could they have killed him?"

"The local officials said only that he was an 'insurrectionist,' and so he was killed. A good many other scholars were implicated as well. Even now this matter has yet to be made totally clear. The officials say that this group of men are vile brigands, but according to public opinion they are men of integrity. We still haven't been able to reach a verdict as to the truth and falsity or rights and wrongs of the situation, and so we can only wait for future writers to 'grasp the writing brush of history' and make sense of it."

"Of course, 'justice' exists in the mind of the people. But I'm afraid that the 'writing brush of history' will be impossible to extricate from today's—"

Baoyu had not yet completed his thought when Bohui's servant, Huang Fu, hastened in to deliver a telegram. Bohui accepted it and as he looked it over, he noticed that it had been sent from Wuchang. Quickly leafing through his copy of *Telegraph Codes: New Edition*, he decoded the message. Sighing, he explained to Baoyu, "It is precisely because of the affair I was just describing to you that I am being summoned."

"What is it?"

"I have to go to Hankou, it's best that I leave immediately." As he spoke, Bohui slipped the telegram into his pocket. Pulling out his watch, he remarked, "It's already midnight, so there *would* still be time to leave tonight if I departed immediately; but how can I possibly pack everything so quickly?"

"What is so urgent?"

"It's because of that case last year in Hubei I was just telling you about. A friend of mine has been caught up in all of it for no reason and brought into the *yamen*. He's just sent this telegram asking me to go figure out a way to help him. It's a duty I can't refuse. But unfortunately, the telegram has arrived so late that I will have to wait until tomorrow to depart." He then told Huang Fu to head out, assigning him the task of returning to the house and beginning to prepare the luggage for departure. "I intend to leave tomorrow," he added. Huang Fu agreed and left.

"How can they still be carrying on about a case from last year?" asked Baoyu.

"In such affairs involving officials, it's not as though they need to rely on evidence! Once they have decided that you are their enemy, they could carry on a case for a thousand years and still not be done with it. Their minions will act according to the one-sided account they get from the officials, and that's that. Right now they do not look upon me as an opponent, but should the time come that they do—even though I am a law-abiding sort and thus there is no real case to make against me—it would not be hard for them to claim that I am a descendent of Wu Sangui and that I was plotting against the government.[3] That would be enough."

Baoyu laughed. "If you put it like that, it must be perilous indeed to be a commoner!"

"How could it not be? Right now, given the tensions between the old and new factions, it's even more dangerous than usual! There's nothing officials hate more than a new faction—if you give off even a whiff of novelty, they will immediately set to thinking of ways to deal with you."

"Speaking in terms of our current situation, it seems to me that reform cannot be delayed any longer. Do you mean to tell me that the officials are completely unable to see this?"

"You wouldn't know," replied Bohui. "'Reform' is in and of itself a positive thing; but once you attach the word 'faction' to the end of it, well—its membership is somewhat motley, so officials of the conservative faction will use that as an excuse to suppress them. After the start of the Hundred Days Reform movement in 1898, who wasn't saying that they'd like to go to the capital and prostrate themselves in front of the imperial palace to present a memorial to the emperor? Who wasn't saying that they would draft memoranda and present them to the provincial governors, so that they might in turn memorialize the emperor? But once the coup took place, all of those men were so terrified that they went so far as to change their names, then made an about-face and began vociferously criticizing the new faction. Was the determination that drove such men forward throughout the entire affair ever rooted in anything but their own aspirations to be promoted to officialdom and eventually strike it rich?

"It would be impossible to fully describe in one sitting the strange details of these events, but let me tell you about just one of the people involved. There was a man called Zhang Bosheng who had achieved a title of the fourth rank and was serving as a petty functionary in some bureau in Shanghai. He was also involved in this case in Hubei last year. If you think about it, the idea of an outlaw hero organizing to fight on behalf of the emperor can in fact be considered quite 'new,' too! And since he was involved, he was of course considered one of the 'new faction,' as well. After everything happened, he managed to escape the fallout. The people around him all thought that the members of the reform faction were unrivaled heroes and upright gentlemen. But how do you suppose this 'hero' behaved? He had been working in his bureau for several years, and so knew a few things about the dishonest practices that went on there. When Zhang found out that the general manager was selling off leftover supplies and pocketing the profits, he wanted a share of the proceeds. The manager was unwilling to cut him in, and the two men found themselves in a standoff. Zhang then submitted a report on the affair to the office of the governor-general of Jiangnan and Jiangxi. When the manager learned of this, he became anxious. He tried to reach a compromise with Zhang and promised to share a certain amount of silver with him. But there was nothing to be done, for the report had already been sent. For its part, the governor-general's office had already decided to send an officer to investigate and settle the matter. Having already received the payoff in silver, what could Zhang now do? He sent another report to the governor-general, saying that it was not he who had sent the previous missive. He said he didn't know who had wrongfully used his name to send the report and requested that the governor-general's office investigate and punish whoever the culprit was. How could anyone possibly look up to someone whose comportment is so base as this?"

Baoyu sat silently for a moment, deep in thought. "But surely it's not necessarily the case that all members of the reform faction are like this?"

"Of course, one can't paint them all with the same brush, but to have a man such as this among their membership does make things difficult." Having said this, Bohui then indicated that he needed to take his leave: "Originally I had hoped to spend the whole evening chatting with you; but because I must now depart tomorrow, I'm afraid I must return home to make my preparations."

Baoyu could see that it would not do to detain him and merely saw him off as far as the stairway. Bohui then said goodbye and departed. He had already reached the front door and was waiting for the porter to open it when Baoyu came running after him and asked, "Will you still come again tomorrow?"

"Do you need me for something? Then I shall come as soon as I can."

"That's not what I meant. I want to leave with you tomorrow for Hubei, so that I may explore a bit. That's why I'd like you to come here before you go."

"If that's the case, then I shall come tomorrow." At this the two men parted.

On the following afternoon, Bohui did indeed come. When he saw that Baoyu had already packed up all of his luggage, he laughed: "My, but you're anxious! We won't board the ship until evening."

"It makes no difference if I'm ready to go a bit early."

"I don't know how many days I'll need to stay over on this trip," Bohui cautioned him. "Are you sure there won't be anything you need to do here?"

"There's nothing I need to do. No matter how many days you need to stay, I can make do."

The two men continued their discussion so as to settle any other issues, and in the evening they boarded their ship. But of their journey we have no record.

■ ■ ■

After a few days' travel, they arrived in Hankou, where their ship moored along a wharf. Had it been up to Bohui, he would have immediately hired a rowboat to take him across the river to Wuchang; but because he also had Baoyu and Beiming with him, it was not convenient to simply call a boat and leave them there. As a result, the party disembarked and headed to the Hong'an Inn for a brief rest. Once he was sure that the other two were settled, Bohui left with Huang Fu to take a boat across the river. They did not return the whole of that night, nor had they returned by the second night. Growing bored, Baoyu went out for a stroll.

On the afternoon of the following day, Bohui returned. "I assume that your business here has already been resolved satisfactorily?" Baoyu inquired.

"It can hardly be called 'satisfactory' yet. No, I've only just started making the right connections. Tomorrow my efforts will begin in earnest, but I'm still afraid that nothing will come of them. Have you not been going outside to stroll around the city?"

"Bah! Don't start! I have long heard that Hankou is one of the four greatest trading hubs in China. That's why I came here so excitedly to stroll around. I went out this morning to have a look, and truly, hearing something a hundred times can't compare to seeing it yourself! When it comes to filth, Hankou may in fact be *first* in China! I was nearly suffocated to death by the stench of the privies!"

Bohui laughed. "As it happens, the nickname 'Rank-o Hankou' is somewhat famous. Anyway, I've come because there's something I'd like to discuss with you: the leads on which I must follow up are in Wuchang, so it's not convenient for me to lodge here. But if I were to leave you here alone, it would be quite lonely for you. It's better if we all relocate to Wuchang. That way, when I have free time, we can go out together and visit the historical landmarks. Unlike Shanghai, it has plenty of famous attractions."

"It's fine with me either way—moving to Wuchang is all the same to me."

And so they rested that evening, and early the following morning they summoned a rowboat to carry them to Wuchang. There they moved into the Liansheng Inn in the Doujiying neighborhood. Bohui once again set off to see about his business and returned only after quite a long while, reporting that a possible resolution to the affair was near at hand and that he now needed to await a response to his inquiries. He thereupon took Baoyu out to visit the Yellow Crane Tower and the Zhuodao Spring. They also went to Hanyang to climb Qingchuan

Pavilion, then amused themselves at Boya's Stage and paid their respects at the tombs of Mi Heng and Lu Su. They spent several days exploring in this fashion until Bohui once again had to leave to attend to his friend's situation.

Left to his own devices, Baoyu once again felt bored and went to pass his time sitting idly in the inn's common sitting room. As it happened, another lodger of the guest house—a student, judging by his dress—came over to Baoyu and began chatting with him. Baoyu couldn't help but ask him about the educational situation in Wuchang, and the student briefly told him a little about it. The student then added, "This afternoon, the superintendent of education is giving a talk, and all of the students from the various schools are going to listen."

"The learning of the superintendent must be great indeed," replied Baoyu. "How else could he attract the students of all of the schools?"

"That goes without saying! Why, here in Wuchang, even the provincial authorities all respect the superintendent! All of the students in the province consider ourselves his pupils, so we all call him 'Master'; some also call him 'Teacher.'"

"We are not students. I don't know whether it would be possible for us to attend?"

"As long as you wear a suit of student clothing, you can pass for students."

"But I haven't got such an outfit. Might it be possible to buy one outside?"

"Since you only need to wear it a short while, I can lend you one."

Baoyu was greatly pleased at this. By the time he had finished eating lunch, Bohui had still not returned, so Bayou changed into the borrowed clothes and left with the student.

When they arrived at the school, they saw that a considerable number of people had already arrived. A dais had been erected at the center of the main hall, and below it were crowded row upon row of chairs. Baoyu and the student squeezed in and sat together. After a short while the superintendent arrived, and the entire crowd rose to their feet to welcome him. As the superintendent mounted the dais, he gave the audience a quick bow, and the audience once again took their seats. Baoyu scrutinized him closely: he was a man of lofty, imposing bearing, with a chubby face the size of an ice tray. A black beard hung on his cheeks, his eyelids were creaseless, and he wore spectacles with lenses that were as large around as a teacup. The gown he wore had sleeves that were over twelve inches wide; on his head, he wore a brand-new dark blue cap. Standing there at the center, he straightened his posture, then pronounced in a booming voice: "'The Way of Great Learning!'" He sighed, then continued, "'The Way of Great Learning' is a subject that we could discuss our entire lives and never finish. But allow me to give you all a very rough and superficial explanation that will be easy to understand. This 'Great Learning,' if focused externally, can unite the family, govern the country, and pacify all under Heaven; if focused internally, it can help one cultivate himself, rectify his mind, be sincere of intention, and expand his knowledge via observation of foundational principles."[14]

Having heard this much, it was all Baoyu could do to stifle his laughter. After this point he no longer made even an attempt to pay attention. To himself he lamented, "This again! I thought that he would have some great knowledge of statecraft, but as it turns out, he's just like a country scholar giving a lecture. When I was a child, I heard so much of this that I couldn't bear to hear another word." And so his thoughts began to wander.

The superintendent continued droning on for what seemed like ages. Baoyu lowered his head with the intention of catching a quick nap. Suddenly there came the jarring thump of someone pounding on a table, which startled him into raising his head to take a look. The superintendent was saying, "Recently, a group of young graduates have begun to seize upon the idle comments of certain Japanese, and constantly declare themselves to be 'reformers,' while accusing others of being 'conservatives.' Since when have we Chinese ever had such words in our lexicon? This group learned them all from the Japanese! However, over time, they have now become an indelible part of our own vocabulary! I have settled upon another idea: I shall support neither reform nor conservatism, and shall instead choose only the most central, most correct, reasoning and will comport myself accordingly. You students must also do the same. Whether now in applying yourselves in your studies, or in the future when you set off into the world to become officials, when the time comes for you to choose a course of action, you too must act in accordance with the most central, correct path. We must completely rub out these ideas of 'reform' and 'conservatism.' Only *then* can we be considered true accomplished ministers of Confucian ethics!" Having finished speaking, he descended from the dais with his head held high. The audience then drifted out of the hall.

Baoyu and the student returned to the Liansheng Inn. Bohui had returned some time before, and upon seeing that Baoyu had changed his outfit asked the reason for it. Baoyu explained, "I went to listen to a talk. But who could have known that by the end, I wouldn't have heard a talk at all—just a lot of jokes."

The student was surprised. "What jokes did you hear?"

Baoyu called for Beiming to bring a set of his own clothing and began to change there in the sitting room.

"Yes, what were the jokes?" Bohui asked.

"Why, everything he said was a joke!" answered Baoyu. "The talk was to be delivered by the superintendent of education, so I thought it would be about statecraft or other kinds of important knowledge. But who'd have known that it was just like being stuck on a cold school bench listening to another stale lecture. He brought up the 'Way of Great Learning' and claimed that one could talk about it all his life and never finish. Later on, he started saying some even stranger things. He said that the two words 'reform' and 'conservatism' had both come from Japan, and that we Chinese had never had such words of our own. Apparently he's never read a book! Wouldn't you say it's strange? Isn't that a joke?"

"So according to what you say," began the student, "the words 'reform' and 'conservatism' aren't Japanese, and are in fact, Chinese?"

"Unless all of China's Classics and Histories were imported from Japan, I am comfortable making that assertion, yes."

"There's no need to debate that point! But then I would simply ask you this: in what Classics or canonical Chinese works would one find the words 'reform' and 'conservatism'?"

"In the *Book of Documents*, it is written that 'those who have long been stained by their filthy manners will be allowed to reform themselves.'[5] And would you also claim that the line in the *Classic of Poetry* that says, 'Although Zhou is an ancient nation, its mandate is reformed' originated in Japan?[6] And who knows how many historical imperial edicts have used the word 'reform'? One surely couldn't count them all in one go."

The student flushed. "And do you mean to say that there are also places where 'conservatism' makes an appearance?"

Baoyu lowered his head and thought for a moment, then quoted, " 'Because he was conservative and lacked nuance, his arguments were impoverished and weak in spirit'—that's from *The Biography of Ouyang Xiu*, so I'm afraid that *History of the Song* must also have come from Japan."

The student was rendered speechless and made no reply. He hurried back to his own room.

Baoyu instructed Beiming to return the borrowed set of clothes to the student, then followed Bohui into his room. "Have you resolved your business?" he asked Bohui.

"Just about. Within another three to five days, he should be released." They then chatted for a little while. Since it was already rather late, we have no further details of their evening.

When they awoke the following morning they found that the student had already moved out of the inn, but Baoyu was not terribly bothered by this. Bohui, as usual, went out to tend to his business. Two more days passed. On the evening of the second day, the men had just adjusted the lamp wick to brighten the room so that they might sit and chat together. Bohui announced that his affair was finally resolved. He had had to pay out a substantial bribe, but it was likely that the prisoner would be released the following day. He had not yet finished telling the story when two government runners burst into the room and demanded, "Which of you is Mr. Jia?"

"My surname is Jia," answered Baoyu. "What's this about?"

One of the runners then pulled out a document and flashed it quickly under the lamplight. It happened so quickly that Baoyu was not able to make out which *yamen* the runners had come from, nor why they had come for him. The runners lowered their heads, then violently dragged Baoyu away with them.

■ ■ ■

If you wish to know why this was happening, please listen to the explanation in the following chapter.

Chapter Nineteen

Courting disaster with his careless words, he finds himself detained in prison

When nefarious schemes are commonplace, life is as inconsequential as a molted feather

WE WERE speaking of how Baoyu and Bohui had trimmed the lamp for a late-night chat when suddenly two *yamen* runners had come, asking their names. Without allowing any explanation, they dragged Baoyu with them and left, running off like the wind. Baoyu's heels never even touched the ground as he was dragged this way and that. Moreover, since it was the middle of the night, he was unable to see anything. The trio eventually entered the grounds of a *yamen*, at which point the runners led Baoyu around a corner and stopped under a covered entryway. One of the runners stood guard over Baoyu while the other went inside to report. After a short time, the latter reemerged and said, "No interrogation for now. We're to take him in first." At this, the two men once again dragged him along until they had reached a place that appeared to be a jail. They turned him over to the jailer and immediately departed.

The jailer shoved Baoyu into a barred holding cell. He had no more than crossed the threshold when he found himself swarmed by a number of men who surrounded him and searched him for anything he might be carrying. As Baoyu looked at them more closely, he realized that this grimy, tangle-haired mob were also prisoners. He thought, "Why would the prisoners want to search me?" He was glad that besides a few loose coppers, he had not carried anything else on his person. Once the swarm of prisoners had searched out these few coins, they abruptly dispersed.

When Baoyu looked further into the cell, he saw that it was pitch-black and that the prisoners were all lying on straw mats on the floor. He looked about for an open mat upon which he could seat himself, but in the end could not find one. Not uttering a word, he stood, feeling somewhat dazed—in his heart, it felt much like he was having some kind of dream. He thought, "What could the reason possibly be that I've been seized out of nowhere like this today? I've never broken the law, so who could possibly have lodged a complaint against me here? And what *yamen* is this?" After a few moments, he was still unable to reach any conclusion, and when he looked around for someone whom he could ask, he found that there did not seem to be any such person. He then resumed his silent thinking: "The reason Wu Bohui came to Hubei this time was to save a friend; just when the news came that there was some hope for this friend—that he might be released within the day—these men unexpectedly appear to cause trouble and throw me in jail, too! I expect Bohui will now have to take up on my behalf as well!" Having thought this far, he suddenly remembered something Wu Bohui had said: that once officials decided to treat a commoner as the enemy, they could stick a charge on him easily enough. "Perhaps the officials have decided that I am an enemy? And yet I have no quarrel with or resentment against them, so why should they go out of their way to harm me? Moreover, I don't know a single person in this city! So how do they even know who I am? It's all very strange!" He turned these thoughts over and over in his mind but was still unable to think of an explanation for it all.

Beside him, the other prisoners had been watching him standing there at length without moving. They all thought it must be the case that he was terrified to the point of distraction. Some made passing comments about him; others mocked him. However, Baoyu did not hear any of this: rather, he began following his feet further into the cell in hopes of finding some unoccupied gap on the floor where he might squat down. As he ventured deeper into the cell the light grew dimmer, and he was assailed by a wave of foul stench. As it happened, this was where the nightsoil pail had been placed. Baoyu stopped in his tracks. Beside this fetid pail there lay a number of prisoners with a small lamp, toasting and smoking opium. Baoyu retraced his steps and, looking now through the bars to the outside of the cell, saw that there hung on the opposite wall a bowl of oil that, having been set alight, served as a lamp. And yet within the cell there was no such light source. If it hadn't been for the prisoners on the floor smoking opium, there wouldn't have been so much as the shadow of a spark within the cell.

Seeing that there was nowhere to sit, Baoyu began to pace back and forth instead. He paced deep into the night, until after the rest of the prisoners had fallen asleep, sprawled haphazardly across each other. Some snored thunderously; some cried out feverishly in their sleep; some even wept as they dreamed. Baoyu suddenly thought of Bohui's friend, who had not yet been released from prison. Was it possible he was in there, too? And so, in the half-light of the cell, he began surveying the faces of the other prisoners. He thought, "Although I don't know what he looks like, he is after all a friend of Bohui's. And given the lengths to which Bohui has gone to save him, he's obviously a close friend. I think it's fair to assume that he won't look anything like the average prisoner!" So he thought somewhat numbly to himself, looking at one face after another—but how could he possibly recognize him? And yet he could not help but harbor these wild hopes. Fortunately, he was not in the least bit anxious and went about the task calmly and silently, for if the men surrounding him had realized that he was sizing them up, those prone to cowardice would have grown fearful, while those prone to violence—well, who knows what kind of rage they might have flown into? But Baoyu was just as calm and self-possessed as he would have been on any other day. The only difference, perhaps, was the air of doubt that had attached itself to him. However, even this small trace of doubt was sufficient to give rise to an endless stream of chaotic thoughts, with the result that he was unable to fall asleep all night. After the human activity within the cell had finally ceased and all had grown still, there was nothing to be heard but the snoring of the prisoners in concert with the knocking of the watchman's wooden clapper. Hearing this, Baoyu gradually came to feel a sense of calm and serenity.

Suddenly, outside, the knocking of the watchman's clapper grew increasingly urgent, and the booming of a cannon was heard shortly thereafter. As Baoyu raised his head, he saw that it was already growing light outside. Soon the other prisoners began to rouse themselves. By now it was broad daylight outside, though the cell continued to be bathed in incomparable darkness. Some of the prisoners had food being delivered; others handed over money to have people go out to buy snacks for them. Since Baoyu had neglected to wear a watch, he didn't know what time it was and found it disorienting. All he could do was observe his surroundings in a daze.

Suddenly the jailer called out to him from outside the cell. As Baoyu approached the bars, he saw Bohui standing on the other side, with Beiming behind him.

"I've put you to so much trouble to come see me," said Baoyu. "As for what crime I'm meant to have committed, I still haven't got the slightest idea."

"Indeed, I don't understand it either," answered Bohui. "I spent all night last night rousing various friends and have been at it all morning today as well, but in the end I have been unable to make sense of it. The first strange thing is that there is no plaintiff."

The jailer, standing to one side, let out a cold laugh. "It's the local officials who decided to take him into custody—so of course there's no plaintiff. I'm afraid it looks like your friend is involved in a serious case!"

Bohui hurriedly followed up: "Might you know what the case is? Why not tell me—I will thank you handsomely for your help."

The jailer gave another cold laugh. "Why don't you ask yourselves what it is you've been getting up to? I'm just in charge of watching the prisoners. How could I go out and snoop into the ins and outs of the case on your behalf?"

Addressing Bohui, Baoyu said, "Don't worry about all that right now. More important, this place is unbearably filthy."

"Try to bear it a little while longer," said Bohui, "and I'll try to figure out something for you when I come back. I just wanted to come and see you first, and thought I might as well take the opportunity to bring Beiming along so that he could learn the way here. If something comes up, it will be easier to send him to deliver a message to you, since I am still occupied with my other business." He added, "If you're brought out for questioning, be careful with what you say."

"I'm not concerned with being 'careful' or 'careless,' since I didn't commit any crime! What have I to be afraid of?"

"It's not convenient to talk at length here. We'll talk about it later." And with that, Bohui took his leave.

When Baoyu had heard that there was no plaintiff, he began to grow increasingly uneasy. He thought, "According to what the jailer said, it was local officials who had me arrested, but I certainly haven't done anything wrong! And besides, I've only been in town a few days! Today they still refuse to bring me in for questioning—if they asked me a few questions, I might have some clue as to what's going on."

A short while passed, and Baoyu saw the jailer open the door to the cell. He was followed by Beiming, who was carrying a set of bedding. The jailer called out to one of the other prisoners and told him to move somewhere else to make some space.

As this was happening, Beiming surreptitiously passed Baoyu a strip of paper. Baoyu understood his meaning and concealed the paper in the breast of his gown. Beiming had only just arranged the bedding for Baoyu when the jailer hurried him back out of the cell. Now that Baoyu finally had some space to himself, he promptly sat down. He was pleased that Bohui had paid such attention to detail in his arrangements—he had even stuffed a few books inside the bedding! Baoyu lay down and began reading, then casually pulled out the piece of paper that Beiming had delivered and slipped it between the pages of his book so that he might stealthily read it. The note read:

> *It is because you courted disaster with verbal indiscretions that you are now in your current predicament. This morning, I learned that the person who has it in for you at present is in a state of absolute outrage, so it will be difficult to approach him. We must bide our time and strategize carefully. You should be especially careful of your language while in prison—there are snarls of thorns at every step. Your situation is extremely perilous.*

Once he had finished reading Bohui's note, Baoyu ripped it up into tiny pieces. He was beginning to feel increasingly depressed. He thought, "I've never been one to say more than he ought. So when did I say whatever it was that could be considered 'courting disaster with verbal indiscretions'? And who is it that holds this grudge against me? He's powerful enough that he can order the local officials to arrest me, so he must be someone very important! But how did I manage to offend such a person? It's all very strange!" He then methodically thought back through everything he had said before his arrest but could still not think of what could have been the cause of all this. Without noticing, he had stretched out on his bedding and gradually drifted off to sleep.

He didn't know what time it was when the jailer called out to wake him. The jailer led him out of the cell, where two bailiffs had been waiting for him for some time. Baoyu assumed that these men wished to question him, and so he willingly followed them. But who could have known that, after having turned a couple of corners and arriving in a new place, the bailiffs would simply deliver him into someone else's custody before departing once again? This new jailer then dragged him into a room. There were no other prisoners in this room; neither were there tables, chairs, benches, bunks, or any kind of furniture: the room was completely empty. The man pushed Baoyu into the room, then locked him in with a quick turn of the wrist. As with the other room, here the entrance was a gate made up of a row of bars. By now Baoyu was even more bewildered than before, but by the time he thought to question the new jailer, the jailer was already too far away.

As dusk was approaching, Bohui reappeared with Beiming following behind, carrying Baoyu's bedding. The jailer opened the door for them. As Beiming brought the bedding into the cell, Bohui also entered to speak with Baoyu.

"I don't understand what you wrote in the note you sent," said Baoyu. "When did I ever 'court disaster with verbal indiscretions'?"

"Let's leave that aside for now," answered Bohui. "Right, now, your case is becoming increasingly pressing. The place you were brought to last night was the *yamen* jail, but for reasons I don't know, they've transferred you to an external prison today. I have to go try to make some arrangements on your behalf. Try not to be too anxious."

"I'm certainly not anxious! It's just that I am so very *confused*. You've got to tell me *something*!"

Bohui didn't respond, and instead walked to the door to confer with the jailer. After they had spoken for a little while, he turned back toward Baoyu and said, "I've entrusted all of your care here to him. He's the head jailer of the external prison; if you want tea or water, you need only ask him."

"I asked, with no small amount of urgency, you what you meant by 'courting disaster with verbal indiscretions,' and yet you only respond thus! What did you mean by it?"

"This whole nightmare is a result of something someone heard you say when you went to listen to that talk the other day."

"How strange! I didn't open my mouth the whole time I was there, how could I have offended anyone?"

"It was the critique you delivered upon your return to the inn that was the root of your current predicament."

"But even in the inn, I didn't ever say anything that could cause anyone to take offense!"

"Didn't you challenge that student's ideas on 'reform' and 'conservatism'?"

"But how could that have offended anyone?"

"I had to ask quite a few people, but I finally got an answer: that student is a favored disciple of the superintendent of education. Now, what the superintendent likes best is flattery; what he hates most is when people challenge his ideas. He never stops to consider whether such challenges might have merit—he assumes that anyone who challenges his ideas is slandering him. So when this favored disciple heard you criticizing the superintendent's ideas, he went and told him—and who knows how much embellishment he added to the story. That's why all of this has come about."

Baoyu was taken aback at this. "The law here must be quite singular!"

"Why do you say that?"

"I made a couple of comments, and he rousts the officials to have them grab me and put me in prison. Wouldn't you call that singular? Certainly nowhere else has such a law!"

"Of course they can't legally put you in prison for making a couple of comments. Who knows what spurious charge he's stuck you with!"

"If he wants to stick me with a charge, then he'll still need proof for it."

"Once again you've got an outdated understanding of how things work! The case will be decided among other officials. Won't they act based on what he says? What evidence do they need?"

"Then what charge has he stuck me with?"

"I haven't been able to find that out yet."

"What do you plan to do?"

"I think we may find success in the strategy of 'Letting he who fastened the bell upon the tiger be the one who unfastens it,'" replied Bohui.

As they conversed, the jailer instructed two runners to move a plank table into the room, along with a couple of stools. They also put together a bed for Baoyu, upon which Beiming laid out the bedding. The jailer had moreover sent in a red clay teapot.

Baoyu smiled. "This is almost like an inn now! I could live like this a few more days quite comfortably."

Bohui smiled, too. "Only you could stay so calm and composed—anyone else would have died of anxiety already. Why, it seems I'm even more anxious than you are at the moment!"

"Once one has seen through the illusions of life, death, fortune, and disaster, he need never be anxious again," replied Baoyu.

Bohui then led Beiming out of the cell, and they took their leave.

■ ■ ■

From this point on Baoyu felt quite at peace. The only real shortcoming of being in the prison was that the door was locked, so he couldn't go outside. Each day Beiming delivered three meals—it goes without saying that this was owing to Bohui's having bribed the jailer. Since Baoyu had nothing else to do, he sat quietly reading his books. When newspapers arrived from Shanghai, Bohui dispatched Beiming to bring them for Baoyu to read. Thus his time in prison was not so trying as it might have been.

Three days passed in this fashion, and Baoyu had not been questioned once. One day, as he sat in a state of bemusement over his fate, Bohui walked in and said to him, "This case is truly full of all kinds of strange twists! Can you guess what charge they have leveled against you in the end?

They've declared that you are one of the remnant 'Boxer bandits.'"

"That's even stranger," replied Baoyu. "Without even a shadow of proof! How on earth did they come up with it?"

"Truly, it's amazing what they come up with! And where do you suppose they got the idea? Because you speak with a Beijing accent, and they said that the 'Boxer bandits' are all northerners. How can you possibly defend yourself against such an unjust charge?"

As they were speaking, they saw the jailer arrive. He said to Bohui, "If you, sir, are going to come up with a way to help the gentleman, you'll want to do so sooner rather than later. Since I have accepted your 'gift,' it would be wrong of me not to let you know: just now, they've sent down instructions saying that tomorrow, I'm to report that he's 'fallen ill.'"

Bohui was startled by this. "Really?"

"Why should I try to deceive you?"

Hearing this, Bohui stood up hastily and left without even taking his leave of Baoyu.

Baoyu, failing to understand what was happening, asked the jailer, "What did you mean when you said that you're to report that I have 'fallen ill'?"

"I'd rather not tell you," he answered.

"Don't worry, just tell me."

The jailer was still unwilling to explain, but Baoyu questioned him persistently, and even promised him a further bribe. Only then did the jailer say, "If I tell you, you mustn't be afraid. When we are told to report that a prisoner has 'fallen ill,' it really means he's done for."

"What do you mean?"

"You're a clever man, how can you not understand what it means? Back when Qin Hui wished to harm Master Yue, didn't he use this very strategy? Just think about it."[1] Having said his piece, the jailer relocked the door and left.

Baoyu thought over the jailer's words very carefully. He thought, "Then they obviously mean to kill me. In making a simple, two-sentence comment, I have brought a death sentence down upon myself. Under such circumstances as these, my death cannot but be less significant than a wisp of goose down. But I don't know how they intend to kill me. If Bohui is unable to come up with a way to save me, then perhaps I'll give death a try—if I end up being a ghost, it will at least give me a chance to further expand my horizons! Luckily I have already lived through so much that really, I have nothing to fear." Having proceeded thus far in his thoughts, Baoyu actually became calm.

On the following day Bohui returned, and Baoyu told him what the jailer had said.

"It won't necessarily happen as he says. I have already been doing everything in my power to get you out of this," Bohui replied. "If it should happen that I am unable to find a solution in the end, it would be to my great shame."

"I have brought this upon myself and should thus bear the burden; it's nothing to do with anyone else. I am already unspeakably grateful to you for the way you have been running to and fro these past two days."

Upon hearing this, Bohui grew somewhat pained. Observing Baoyu, however, he noted that his color was much as it ever had been and betrayed no trace of anxiety. Bohui then said goodbye and left.

Without Baoyu's realizing it, another five days passed. On this particular evening Baoyu had already fallen asleep, and at some point as he dreamed, he felt himself being lifted up and carried. Just as he was about to open his eyes to look, he suddenly felt a tremendously heavy object pressing down upon his face. As he still lay face-up, as he had in his slumber, this object was now preventing him from drawing breath. Frantic, he tried to push the object aside, but he found that his hands were also pinned down; when he tried to struggle with his legs to flip himself over, he found his legs similarly weighed down. He thought, "Of course. This is how they have decided to kill me."

And so, calmly and patiently, he awaited death; but because of the difficulty of not being able even to exhale, he slowly became aware of the pressure of the air building up in his chest and felt as though his eyeballs would burst.

■ ■ ■

If you wish to know what was to become of Baoyu, please listen to the explanation in the following chapter.

Chapter Twenty

Where to find those who still abide by the law?

A letter arrives suddenly from a distant place

WE WERE speaking of Baoyu, who was being crushed to the point of suffocation and eventually lost consciousness. He could feel his body lightly floating, as if flying, and was troubled only by the fact that he could neither hear nor see and couldn't even ascertain whether he was alive or dead. As he drifted in this state of hazy confusion, he suddenly heard someone calling his name as if from a great distance. He attempted to reply and ask who was there, but the words caught in his mouth, and, as if mute, he could not get them out. Gradually the voice calling out to him seemed to grow nearer and nearer, yet he was still unable to respond. With a jolt, he felt a rush of warm air surge down his windpipe and all the way into his abdomen. He heard the voice again, this time startlingly close to his ear. When he opened his eyes, he saw Bohui kneeling beside him, with the jailer to his side, along with two or three other men who were all bustling around him. But he could not tell what it was that occupied them.

Looking around him, Baoyu saw that he now lay upon a bed. He thought, "Just now, they had clearly put me on the floor—how is it that I am now on a bed? They obviously intended to suffocate me, so how is it that I find myself here instead? And how was Bohui tipped off so that he was able to rush over and rescue me on the very same night? For surely it was he who saved me." While Baoyu's thoughts careened about distractedly in his mind, he was still unable to speak a word. After Bohui fed him a couple of mouthfuls of ginseng broth, Baoyu slowly began to recover his breath and murmured faintly to Bohui, "I've caused you such trouble."

"It's all right. How are you feeling now?"

"Fine, I'm just having a little difficulty breathing."

As Bohui was about to reply, someone burst in from outside and asked, "Has he come to?"

"He has," Bohui answered.

"Then I should go report back," replied the other, as he rushed from the room.

As Baoyu observed this new arrival, he felt that he seemed very familiar. Silently searching his memory, he suddenly realized that it was none other than the student who had been staying in the same inn as themselves. Baoyu was exceedingly puzzled and could not understand why he had come. He wished to ask, but again his jaw wouldn't move to get the words out.

Bohui uttered a few words of comfort, and once again fed him some ginseng broth, of which Baoyu weakly sipped another two mouthfuls. A short while later Beiming entered with a lantern.

"It's already after one in the morning," said Bohui. "I must be getting back, I'll leave Beiming here to look after you. You'll be able to leave after it's light out; until then, you should rest." Baoyu nodded his assent, after which Bohui left.

■ ■ ■

Baoyu rested for a good long while, then slowly drew himself up to a seated position. By this time all of the others had gone, leaving only Beiming at his side. Baoyu stood and attempted to take a couple of steps but found his energies weak and his breathing labored. Every joint in his body ached intensely. He also had the impression that he was treading on large quantities of coarse grit on the floor underfoot. When he had once again sat down, he asked Beiming to find out what was all over the floor. Beiming took up a candle and had a look: "Yi! Where did all of this rice come from?"

Baoyu inspected his own person and noticed that his clothes were covered with a layer of fine white dust. Only then did he understand: "It must have been bags of rice that the jailer used to crush me," he thought. "But if he'd wanted to kill me, why would he then help save me? And more important, that student who was just in here—how is it that he came to be here at all? It's really all too incomprehensible." He then asked Beiming, "Do you know what Master Wu has been doing these past few days, or with whom he has been communicating?"

"When Master Wu goes out each day, I either come here to deliver master's food, or else I stay in the inn. I don't know anything of his comings and goings. All I know is that yesterday the man who was previously in the inn with us—the one in the short jacket and the straw hat—came and talked with Master Wu at length about some 'Sir Liang' or 'Sir Jiang,'[1] as well as something about you having to go to pay your respects to a door or to a window.[2] Your servant didn't understand any of it."

As Baoyu listened, he felt even more confused. His body was still in great discomfort as well, and so he lay back down, still fully clothed. His mind was spinning like a whirligig, thinking over everything that had just happened and still not able to understand it all. It was only when a faint light began to spread across the morning sky that he finally drifted off to sleep. As he slumbered, he once again felt that his body was light and buoyant, floating along with the wind. Just as he entered a state of dreamy haziness, he suddenly heard someone speaking beside him and he awoke with a start. Opening his eyes, he saw that Bohui was once again standing at his side. Baoyu hurriedly sat up.

"Congratulations! This whole affair is over!" announced Bohui. "Let's go." He then instructed Beiming to gather up Baoyu's bedding, slipped some liquor money to the jailer, and led Baoyu out. Two sedan chairs were already waiting for them at the entrance and each man climbed into a chair to be transported back to the inn.

For the entire length of the trip back, Baoyu gazed at the sunlight in the sky, feeling unencumbered at last. The scene around him seemed completely different from before. When they arrived at the inn, he immediately bathed and changed his clothes. Bohui then poured him a drink to calm him after his ordeal. "This whole affair has been such a farce!" cried Baoyu. "I was rattling around in there for nearly a fortnight, and I still feel as though I am trapped in some kind of dream. Even now, I still don't understand it all. All I know is that I have imposed upon you terribly and caused you to expend great efforts on my behalf."

Bohui sighed. "Truly, this case has been like navigating a labyrinth of brambles. You came within a hair's breadth of losing that life of yours! Had I been delayed by even two or three minutes, I'm afraid that at this moment I would instead be purchasing a coffin and arranging to have you laid out. I've already told you a little bit about how you caused offense, so there's no need to go back over that. Ever since I heard that they had labeled you a 'remnant Boxer,' I have been extremely anxious and have left no stone unturned in seeking a solution. On the day that the jailer said he'd been told to report that you had 'fallen ill,' I became even more distressed. As you will be aware, in this evil practice, once the higher-ups have instructed that someone should be reported 'ill,' well, that person hasn't got long left. In a matter of a few days they would have further instructed the jailer to act to 'resolve' your situation, and he would eventually report that you'd died of your 'illness.' Where could you have gone to seek justice? So I hurriedly sent someone to make introductions and to track down that student in order to have him act as a go-between. After three days of negotiations they were able to reach an agreement, and my agent was told that the act was to take place yesterday. And so, when yesterday came around, I went to see the student three or four times, but he was never at home. After that I did my best to find out his whereabouts and learned that he had crossed the river to go drinking at a brothel in Hankou the previous night and hadn't yet returned. I hastily made my way across the river, found him, and dragged him back. By then it was already sometime between nine and eleven at night. I then made him spend the rest of the evening dealing with the task at hand and even accompanied him to the superintendent's residence. He went in to consult with the superintendent while I waited outside. After a little while he rushed back out, saying, 'I'm afraid we're too late: as per what you were told a few days ago, tonight was the night they were to kill him. And as no one has gone in to intercede on his behalf all day today, I don't know what state he'll be in now.' Immediately he and I raced to the prison, where I was frightened half to death by what we encountered. The jailer adamantly refused to let us see you, which I took as a sign that the situation must be dire, indeed. The student first pulled the jailer to one side and spoke with him briefly, then went off to discuss the matter personally with the prison officials. Only then was I permitted to go in to you. You were stretched out stiffly on the floor and had already ceased breathing. We scrambled to get you breathing again, with some difficulty. In the wee hours of this morning I was able to put together a bail letter and had it stamped by a local broker. I had to lay out a great number of taels of silver, which I had delivered immediately. Only after it was all deemed to be in order was I finally able to get you out of there."

Baoyu commented, "Now that you've gone on at such length, I feel like I have a somewhat better understanding of the superintendent's tactics and the perverse nature of officialdom here. But please—you must tell me as well what methods of negotiation were used on my behalf."

Bohui laughed. "You may find this bit a little humiliating. As you know, the superintendent hates nothing more than being mocked; and the kind of man who hates being mocked almost certainly takes pleasure in flattery and praise. But he also has another peculiarity: he is most pleased when others pledge themselves to him as disciples. After I had looked all over and finally managed to meet with the student, I promised to reward him in exchange for speaking with the superintendent on your behalf. He told the superintendent that your previous insults were spoken in a moment of thoughtlessness and that you had later come to regret having spoken so rashly. He also said that you had heard of the vastness and rectitude of the superintendent's learning and as a result wished to become his disciple. Even once he had talked the superintendent around, the superintendent still insisted that you must send around the gifts and note of introduction that would be appropriate to establishing a master-disciple relationship; only then would he be willing to have you freed. I spent most of last night arranging for the gifts and the note of introduction. Now that you are out, you'll have to go pay him your respects in person!"

Baoyu sat in silence for a moment. "How can I accept that? Why should I go and offer my respects to such a person?"

Bohui laughed. "Because that promise saved your life! It's not as though you're actually going to take him as your teacher."

"You have already sent the gifts and the card—what's done is done. But surely there is no need for me to go call on him in person! We must at least come up with some way to avoid my having to do this."

"If you truly are unwilling to go, then I shall have to go in your stead. Since he's never actually seen you in person, and neither has he seen me, I might as well assume your identity and go see him myself."

"It's beneath you to go see him as well! And besides, he may not recognize us, but that student of his would."

"Why are you being so stubborn? You must know the old saying: 'When walking under another's eaves, one dare not but bow his head.' You bore the misfortune of being imprisoned for over ten days; how can you care so much about a simple meeting?"

"When you came here originally, it was to help your friend out of his predicament. Is your friend free yet, or not?"

"He's been free for a little while now and has already left to study in Japan."

"So you have no further business here?"

"Correct."

"Then it's easy enough to settle! Let's cross the river immediately and catch a steamship for Shanghai. Then it'll all be over and done with. Or are you afraid the superintendent will come to Shanghai to hunt us down?"

"That course of action would be inappropriate. It's still best to go see him."

Baoyu was steadfast in his refusal to go. "You've said it's not right to leave—but there is another way. We can write him a letter saying that after being imprisoned for some days, I have fallen ill and can't come to see him just now. Once we've arranged with him to delay our visit by a few days, we'll have more time to come up with a way to avoid seeing him. But you'll have to write the letter—I can't bring myself to write a letter of supplication to the 'Great Master.'"

Bohui laughed again. "That is one way to deal with it!" Thereupon, he took out a brush and inkstone and wrote the letter on Baoyu's behalf, then handed it over to Huang Fu for delivery. The two men then sat opposite each other drinking and chatting about how human nature could be so deceitful and wily, and about the difficulties of being involved in human affairs.

Huang Fu returned after they'd eaten, proffering the letter the superintendent had sent in response, along with two books. Baoyu had no interest whatsoever in reading the letter, so this fell to Bohui. The letter contained a great deal of musty condescension. As for the two books, one was some anthology or other, while the second was a manuscript of poetry and prose. These were both considered the superintendent's master works, which he regularly bestowed upon new disciples. Bohui flipped through a couple of pages, then handed the texts to Baoyu. Baoyu distractedly tossed them to one side.

Now, can you guess why Baoyu was so distracted all of a sudden? As it happened, he had begun to think back on his time sitting beneath Greenridge Peak on the Great Barren Mountain. He thought, "I spent so many years in self-purification, but because I lacked the means to fulfill my original purpose of mending the heavens, I decided to leave. Not even to speak of encountering the Boxer bandits when I made my way to the capital; in coming here, I became embroiled in this mess. I can't blame anyone who would call this a 'barbaric country'—nor could I blame them if they called this a 'benighted world'! Thinking back on my original purpose, I'm afraid that in the end, it will be difficult to fulfill. If I were to return to Greenridge Peak without having done so, seeing all of the trees, stones, deer, and boars would bring me shame; but even if I don't return, the question remains: How am I ever to fulfill my purpose?" Having arrived at this point in his thoughts, it was as if he had lost control of his six souls, and his heart was mired in confusion. He sat in dazed silence, his ears unhearing, his eyes unseeing.

Just then Beiming began to pour tea and served Baoyu a cup. He called out twice to his master, but Baoyu gave no response.

"Just swell!" said Beiming. "What's happened now? He must have relapsed into his old malady."

At first, Bohui had paid no heed, but when he heard Beiming say this, he hurriedly looked at Baoyu and indeed saw that his eyes were fixed and his mouth silent. Bohui assumed that Baoyu must have suffered some injury on the previous evening that was now making him feel unwell, and so he urged Baoyu to rest.

Hearing Bohui's voice, Baoyu's spirits returned, and he replied, "I'm fine, I was just lost in thought and wound up in a bit of a daze."

"What were you thinking about?" asked Bohui.

"I was thinking that it would really be for the best to return to Shanghai, and soon. Now that we've sent off that letter, he knows that I won't be able to go see him for a couple of days. If we seize the opportunity to leave today, what could he possibly do about it?"

"Actually, that would work fine—it's just a bit hasty."

"We haven't got much luggage, so if we want to leave, we can leave. What's 'hasty' about that?"

"Rest for one more day first. If we leave tomorrow, that will still give us plenty of time."

And so it was agreed. On the following day they tallied up and paid the bill for their lodgings. As twilight fell, they hired a man to carry their luggage from the inn. Exiting through Hanyang Gate, they then hired a boat which rowed them out to the side of the waiting steamship. They boarded the steamship, selected a room, and were soon riding the wind and waves toward Shanghai once more. The superintendent, having received the gifts and note of introduction and sent two of his master works to return the honor, never did lay eyes on Baoyu in the end. Whether or not he ever attempted to search for Baoyu is not related in this story.

But let us speak instead of how upon the arrival of the party in Shanghai, Bohui inveighed upon Baoyu to no longer live in an inn but to move into Bohui's own home instead. Baoyu consented to this. When the steamship had finally moored at the wharf, the two men disembarked and made their way to Bohui's home. (All of luggage they had brought with them on the steamship, they naturally left in the care of Huang Fu and Beiming.) By the time Bohui and Baoyu arrived at Bohui's home, they couldn't help but need a little rest after their journey. Servants brought Bohui a number of letters that had arrived for him since he'd gone. Bohui read through them one at a time. Among them, however, was one letter that had been sent to Baoyu care of Bohui, which Bohui quickly handed over. Baoyu took the letter and looked it over: it was in Xue Pan's handwriting. Baoyu tore the letter open and read it. There, half in literary style and half in coarser language, Xue Pan had written:

Brother Bao,

Ever since we parted in Beijing, I fled to the Changxin Inn and waited, still hoping every day that the Heavenly Soldiers would be victorious. Who could have known that in the end, things would transpire just as you, my wise brother, had predicted?

Someone came to tell me that the emperor had already fled, and so I knew that your advice was not in error. I was afraid that I was no longer safe there, and wished to go to Freedom Village, but I did not know the way. I asked around, and nobody else knew either. Luckily I happened upon a friend named Liu Xuesheng, who also goes by Maoming.[3] *He knew the way, and so I traveled with him. We have since arrived in Freedom Village and are staying in Liu Xuesheng's home.*

This place is wonderful—it truly is free and unrestrained. It is worlds apart from Shanghai, and many times better. Why not come visit for a spell? Then you will know that I am not deceiving you. If you intend to come, could you please bring the valuables I left behind? If not, there would be no harm if my sage younger brother should make use of them himself. Etc.

After reading the letter, Baoyu handed it to Bohui.

"I don't know where this 'Freedom Village' place is," said Bohui. "It must be extremely remote."

"You are almost certainly right. But I don't know how it could be 'many times better' than Shanghai. I will stay here and rest for some time first, but after that, I definitely intend to venture out to see it."

▪ ▪ ▪

If you wish to know whether Baoyu ultimately went or not, please listen to the explanation in the following chapter.

Chapter Twenty-One

After firing a gun, Baoyu captures the thieves

Struck by a stealthy arrow, Beiming returns to his original form

WE WERE speaking of how Baoyu had received Xue Pan's letter and was now thinking of making a trip to Freedom Village.

"It's not as though there's anything you need to do now," said Bohui. "Why go to the trouble of rushing back off to the north?"

"It's precisely because I've got nothing to do that I can take some time to roam around—I'd like to do a little sightseeing," replied Baoyu.

"I've only heard of people going 'sightseeing' abroad. I've never heard of anyone 'sightseeing' in a village!"

"It's that very thing that makes me so uncomfortable. I hear people constantly talking about going sightseeing abroad—but I have no idea what benefit there is to it! The most bizarre part of all is that every sightseer keeps his own sightseeing journal. Regardless of which country he goes to, the first page of the journal will assuredly be a sketch of the globe. And the things recorded in these journals!—there's no mention of the politics, customs, behavior, or local products of the sites they visit. What little they do write of these is so muddled that it couldn't possibly be of any practical use! They write about things like how much they walked on a given day, or how on such-and-such day they encountered such-and-such person, and whatever it was they chatted about. Or they write about how on such-and-such day, they toured such-and-such factory, and saw whatever goods being produced there. They also monotonously exaggerate how prosperous foreign countries are, and how beautiful! Reading such journals as these is completely useless. They've put the effort into drawing a globe—why not instead draw the strategic topography of the land they are visiting? If they can make the effort to roam around, why not investigate the local customs and products? If they can make the effort to go visit and chat with people, why not make inquiries about their government or their customs? If they can make the effort to tour a factory, why not inquire as to the means of manufacturing the goods they see? To make a trip such as this one must spend money, time, and energy—but what benefit can it actually be said to have?

"And moreover, anyone who has traveled to foreign countries should really have a thorough understanding of conditions in China first. Perhaps we might ask this group of travelers how many places they've been to *within China*, or in how many of our different regional languages they are conversant? That's why I say that it is more important to go sightseeing within China than to go sightseeing abroad. We only need send a few students—let them each determine which province they are willing to travel to and send them there. The method of sightseeing should be thus: they must be sure to visit every seat of government, every department, every prefecture, every county. In each location they must closely examine customs and behaviors, any hardships suffered by the people, the region's strengths and shortcomings, and agricultural and mineral production. Each of these should be recorded in a journal, and the student must be permitted to provide commentary and submit recommendations on each item. This year we send one student, next year another. After several students have gone, their journals will all be compared: whoever has provided the clearest examination, and who has submitted the best recommendations, shall be dispatched to serve as an official in that place. Could there still exist a barrier between officials and the public then? If it were so done, is there any place that would not be well governed?"

"Your insightful comments are not wrong, of course!" replied Bohui. "However, for now, you are neither planning to become an official, nor are you setting out to visit every seat of government, every department, every prefecture, or every county—you just want to go to some 'Freedom Village.' The north experienced such great chaos last year, and killing was widespread. The foul stench of the decaying dead will surely have lingered, meaning that this year there will be a great many outbreaks of disease. Furthermore, the weather will only keep growing slowly hotter from now on, so by the time it gets really hot, the air of pestilence will have grown that much more intense. Since the trip isn't urgent, why risk encountering such unpleasantness?"

"Why should I be afraid of disease? After all, the majority of those who die from disease are the poor, or else otherwise hygienic people who live without restraint and eat and drink according to whim rather than according to a proper schedule. Those who live fastidiously very rarely become ill."

"Since you put it like that, I suppose you insist on going."

"Of course, I want to keep traveling all over, but I may as well go there first for a spell, and at the same time return Xue Pan's money. Can you please have it converted into the form of remittance notes, since it is once again possible to send remittances?"

"I can have it sent, but I've never heard of any 'Freedom Village'—so where should I have it sent *to*?"

Hearing this, Baoyu was silent for a moment. The men dropped the subject and did not raise it again.

■ ■ ■

Several days later Baoyu said to Bohui, "I think Cousin Xue's money must be returned to him. Since a normal remittance won't work, I've thought of what we can do. Now, if we were to take it all out as silver, it would be extremely heavy and burdensome to carry. It's better to have it exchanged for gold. That way I can bring it to him, since, fortunately, gold is readily exchangeable everywhere for silver."

"So you're really planning to go?"

"If he were anywhere else, I would be fine with not going. But since he's in 'Freedom Village,' I simply can't resist. Recently I've heard people talking about how there are so many benefits to 'freedom,' so I intend to go and see what the 'freedom' in 'Freedom Village' is like. I just want to have a look around, and then I'll return straight back to the south, as I also want to explore Guangdong, Fujian, and their environs."

"When do you intend to depart?"

"I plan to leave within the next few days. Because it is the warm season I can travel fairly lightly. A few unlined jackets and summer clothing will suffice, so I won't even need to bring a trunk—I'll just need to buy a large foreign suitcase made of leather. I'll return after a month or two at most."

Bohui knew that he would be unable to keep Baoyu from going, and so, as requested, he helped convert all of Xue Pan's money into gold, which he then turned over entirely to Baoyu. Baoyu then purchased a suitcase and packed his clothes in preparation for his voyage. As it happened, the steamship *Taishun* was scheduled to depart around this time. Bohui had once served as the accountant aboard this very ship and still had two former shipmates on board. When he escorted Baoyu on board, he tasked them with taking care of Baoyu's every need. Only then did Bohui say goodbye and depart.

After sailing for two days the *Taishun* reached Yantai, where it dropped anchor—there was a great deal of cargo to lade and unlade, so the ship was held up for a long time with no sign of departing. Baoyu suddenly became excited, thinking, "This is Shandong! Why don't I go ashore and have a look around? Perhaps I could take an inland route into Beijing from here—there wouldn't be any harm in it. Otherwise I can just visit here for a few days and wait for another ship to come through and take that to Tianjin instead." He then hurriedly instructed Beiming to repack the luggage, and they took their leave of the people aboard the ship. Baoyu then hailed a sampan, which carried them directly ashore. They roomed at an inn for several days, and at some point Baoyu thought, "Since I'm in Shandong, why not take the opportunity to climb Mount Tai?" Having made up his mind, he tasked an employee of the inn with hiring a long-distance cart for him. Baoyu and Beiming, master and servant, then climbed into the cart and set off toward the west. After eight or nine days on the road they reached Tai'an, where they then ventured up Mount Tai to admire the views. They ran their hands along the Five-Bureaucrat Pine, amused themselves searching for the Stele of Tranquility, paid their respects at the Temple of the Green Emperor, and visited the Palace of the Goddess Bixia; they gazed westward toward the ancient Qin capital of Chang'an and southward toward the ancient Yue capital of Kuaiji. They spent two nights on the mountain before eventually making their way back down.

They then hired two horses to carry them to Qufu, where they dropped off their bags before setting off again for a visit to the Tomb of Confucius. Here they admired the ancient pistachio trees before making their way to the Apricot Temple. More than a day was spent wandering about in this fashion. As far as Baoyu was concerned, each place they visited was deeply satisfying. He then wished to proceed from here to the capital, taking the road through Jinan, so that he might visit Mount Li along the way. He spoke with the proprietor of the inn in which they were staying and said that he wished to hire either two long-distance mounts or a cart to take them there. The proprietor replied, "It's too late to set out now, better to leave bright and early tomorrow morning!" Baoyu assented to this.

The proprietor followed Baoyu back to his room and said, "This room is no good. Please allow me to move sir into a different one."

"We're only staying for one night. We can make do just fine here. What need is there to move?"

"You gentlemen have come up from the south and are accustomed to comfort. Please let me move you." The proprietor was particularly solicitous and carried Baoyu's suitcase and bedding to another room. This room was indeed cleaner than the previous one and had recently been repapered with white paper decorated with silver flowers. Once the proprietor had got them settled, he took his leave.

Baoyu looked around the room and noticed that while the décor had not departed from the simple, rustic style of the area, the four walls had been hung with works of calligraphy. In one corner there had been hung what was obviously meant to be centerpiece scroll for a focal wall, painted with a colorful peony. Baoyu laughed to himself, "Even a village shouldn't be so . . . *rustic* as this! How is it that they've put up a centerpiece scroll in a corner?" He sat and rested for a while, then had his dinner. After eating he lit the lamp, while Beiming laid out the bedding. Baoyu happened to glance at the scroll hanging in the corner and noticed that there was a scorpion creeping up it. He instructed Beiming: "Kill it!—and don't let it sting you!" Beiming dared not try to strike it with his hand, so he picked up a small piece of broken tile, took aim, and hurled it at the scorpion. Beiming's aim was true, but the scorpion was neither killed nor indeed even injured—it just skittered off, *huala!* They searched for it for a while without locating it and finally gave up.

Now, Baoyu was the kind of person who considered all things carefully. He thought, "He clearly aimed right at it—how could it not have died? Nor even been injured? The piece of tile hit the scroll—and with quite a lot of force behind it—but barely made a sound. There must be a hollow behind the scroll. What could the reason for that be?" He pulled back the scroll and saw that indeed behind it was not a wall, but rather a small doorway with a wooden door that evidently opened out into another room. There was a tiny gap in the planks of the door, and as Baoyu drew up close and peered through it, he could see some very dim lamplight but couldn't make out any of the objects on the other side. He dropped the scroll back into place, now feeling extremely perplexed. A square table had been placed below the scroll, and when Baoyu peered underneath it, he saw that there was solid wall behind it. "Could that door then actually be a window?" he thought. He pulled the scroll back again and estimated that the window was five or six feet in length from top to bottom. He thought, "Since when has there ever been such a long window? I have often heard that in the north, there is a type of shady establishment that specializes in hiding bandits and thieves so that they may rob the guests and traveling merchants of their wealth and goods. I have certainly run up against just such a place today! This can't be good." He lowered his head and thought in silence for some moments when suddenly he remembered the six-shot revolver he had bought in Shanghai and had been carrying for some time. When he was in Beijing, staying in the association hall, he had taken it out and fired some practice shots to hone his aim and his technique, but he had never used it to shoot a person. Today he would need to rely heavily on it. He very quietly informed Beiming of the situation and instructed him not to fall asleep that night, but to stay on his guard. He then took out the gun, loaded it, and placed it beside his pillow. He thought, "If there are only one or two of them, that would be all right. But if there are more than that, then we may be in trouble. If that's the case, there's nothing we can do about it but fight with our backs to the wall. Otherwise, it's already late, so where could we possibly run to now?" He instructed Beiming to shut the door, then turned up the lamp. He sat for some time, until it was already the second watch, then climbed into bed—still fully clothed—and pretended to be asleep. Beiming lay down as well, careful not to make a sound.

Sometime after the third watch had passed and the sound of voices throughout the inn had quieted, Baoyu could hear the scroll moving almost imperceptibly. When he stealthily opened an eye to take look, he saw a young man sidle out from behind the scroll, a large, glinting knife held aloft in his hand. Slowly he stepped out onto the table. Baoyu, still lying in bed, observed the young man carefully, then pulled out his gun, leveled it, and pulled the trigger. Thick smoke erupted suddenly from the spring mechanism, and with a loud crack, a lead bullet as big as a chicken heart lodged itself in the burglar's thigh. Unable to keep his footing, he fell from the table; the knife he'd been holding fell to the ground as well. Beiming cried out "Hua!" and Baoyu hurriedly sat up and shouted for him to apprehend the burglar. The burglar was attempting to pull himself up to flee, but Beiming gave him a mighty shove and sent him sprawling backward. Baoyu himself then came to hold him down and instructed Beiming to tie him up with the cord from the bedding.

By this time someone had arrived outside the door and was pounding on it thunderously, shouting all the while, "Spare him! Spare him!" Baoyu ignored this and instructed Beiming to tie the man up before discussing it further. Beiming was unable to immobilize the man by himself, so Baoyu assisted him in binding the man's hands and feet together like a trussed pig. Outside the door the thunderous pounding continued unabated. Baoyu grasped the gun firmly in his hand, then ordered Beiming to open the door. The owner of the inn came stumbling in. Upon seeing Baoyu, he fell to his knees and began to kowtow, still pleading, "Spare him! Spare him!"

"This is a fine establishment you run, concealing brigands who would seize travelers' money and possessions! I've managed to get the best of one of them, and you beg me to spare his life. But pray tell, what would have happened if you lot had managed to get the best of me?"

The innkeeper continued knocking his head against the floor and replied, "Honorable master, take pity on your servant, who only has this one son. Please spare him. If you do, I'll bless ten thousand generations of your lordship's offspring."

Beiming snorted and said with a laugh, "You have the ability to grant blessings, do you? If that's really true, then why not first impart your blessings upon your son instead, so that he might have avoided being struck by the thunder that my Master shot out from the palm of his hand?"

When the innkeeper had rushed in, he was in such a state of anxiety that he did not notice the gun Baoyu held in his hand.

Now hearing what Beiming said, he took it to be true that Baoyu had magic powers and grew so terrified that he rushed again to knock his head against the floor, saying, "Heavenly Master, if you struck him with a blast of your palm-thunder, my son shall surely die. Master, please spare him!"

Baoyu thought, "Ignorant people like this take ignorance to the point of absurdity! How on earth could there by such a thing as 'palm-thunder'?" As he was thinking this, he discreetly tucked away the gun and decided to take advantage of the situation to frighten the innkeeper a bit, when the innkeeper's son—the now-restrained burglar—suddenly piped up from the floor, "It was a foreign gun that struck me. It wasn't any 'palm-thunder.'"

"If I had used my 'palm-thunder,'" Baoyu replied, "it would have brought the whole building down."

By now the entire inn had been startled awake by the commotion. The innkeeper's wife had gotten up, and now she too came to kneel in front of Baoyu to beg him to spare the burglar's life. The innkeeper kept rushing in and out of the room, ordering his employees to make tea, fetch water, and make snacks for his guests. Baoyu no longer dared try to go back to sleep, so he thought he might as well keep talking to the innkeeper. "What possessed you to try to rob me?" he asked.

"We usually only target those who travel with a lot of luggage," came the reply. "When you came and I carried that leather suitcase for you, I could feel that one end of it was much heavier than the other, and so I knew that you must be carrying a great deal of silver. That's when I got the idea. If you had been traveling in a larger party, we would have made arrangements to have more men on hand. But we saw there were only two of you gentlemen, so my son didn't arrange for anyone else to come help. He thought he could do it alone. But who could have known that he'd be struck down by you?"

As the conversation went on, dawn was gradually approaching. There came a knock at the door, and the innkeeper went out to see what it was about. When he returned he said, "Your mounts have arrived. You have a long distance to cover before you reach the first waystation, so you had better set off early—I recommend you depart immediately." Baoyu instructed Beiming to start collecting their things; Beiming set about gathering their bedding and packing it on the horses' backs before hoisting the suitcase onto his own back. Then they freed the bound thief, exited the inn, mounted their horses, and set off.

They had been traveling for some four or five li, and still day had not broken. Dense forest lined both sides of their path. Beiming rode out in front, with Baoyu behind. As they traveled along, they suddenly heard a whooshing sound: an arrow had come flying from out of nowhere and found its mark in the leg of Baoyu's horse. Rearing in pain, the horse flung Baoyu to the ground, slipped its reins, and ran off. As he tumbled to the ground, Baoyu hurriedly pulled the concealed gun from his breast. Because of what had transpired that evening, Baoyu had thought it prudent to take further precautions and so had decided to conceal the gun under his jacket. As he had anticipated, they had only traveled a short distance and already had need of it.

He had only just pulled out the gun when he saw Beiming—still in front of him—go tumbling from his horse as well.

Beiming's horse, too, fled; the grooms, it goes without saying, ran off in pursuit of their respective horses. Beiming stood there in the road, rigid and stock-still. Not knowing how many brigands there were, Baoyu decided to lie on the ground and observe the situation rather than give himself away. He saw four or five torches simultaneously approach from both sides, then rush upon Beiming. Beiming, for his part, continued to stand completely still. Baoyu suddenly heard one of the brigands blurt out, "Ya! How did we manage to hit a statue of a bodhisattva?"

With a jolt, Baoyu recalled that on the day he had stumbled upon Beiming in the Jade Cloud Temple, his appearance had originally been rather spectral. Was it possible that he had once again undergone some kind of transformation? Casting his glance over to Beiming, he could see by the torchlight that an arrow had pierced Beiming's shoulder. Surrounding him were four or five brigands, staring at him in stupefaction. Still another had knelt in front of the petrified Beiming and was now kowtowing at his feet. Baoyu thought, "This lot seems to be of the superstitious sort that believes in ghosts and spirits. I'll use that to my advantage to give them a fright!" And so, he jumped up and ran over to the brigands. The group of thieves was startled speechless. They make no effort to stop him, and in fact seemed terrified of him.

"You curs!" he bellowed. "You have wounded my kin with that arrow, and yet you still stare!" As he looked at Beiming, it became clear that it was no longer possible to say it *was* Beiming—it was in fact a statue of a child-immortal, sculpted from wood, whose painted-on facial features were in an unfortunate state of flaking and peeling. Baoyu found this exceedingly strange, but since he was still face-to-face with the bandits, he could not let his feelings show. Instead he turned to the statue and sighed, "I told you that your practice of the Dao was not yet deep enough, so it is unsurprising that you met with this misfortune."

The bandits were so frightened that they didn't know how to respond and could only conclude that Baoyu must be some kind of immortal, so they all turned and began kowtowing to him. Baoyu acted as though he had taken no notice of this and concerned himself with unfastening the leather suitcase from the sculpture before taking it upon his own back. He then addressed the brigands: "What do you have to say for yourselves?"

The brigands continued kowtowing and pleaded, "We beg the Venerable Master Immortal to spare our lives!"

"The likes of you aren't even worth killing," Baoyu replied. "My companion the child-immortal has been grievously wounded by your arrow. You should know that his flight from here is only temporary. He will return in due time. You would do well to carry him back with you and surround him with incense, flowers, candles, and lanterns. From now on you must atone for your evil ways and return to the path of righteousness. Then I shall spare you all." The bandits hurriedly agreed to do this and knocked their heads against the ground again in thanks. Then, hoisting the statue aloft, they departed.

By now a faint light had begun to appear in the sky. Seeing that the brigands had all left, Baoyu secretly found the whole thing quite amusing. However, the fact that his fine companion Beiming had been turned into a wooden statue caused him a great deal of bemusement. He thought, "I've never been one to believe in evil spirits, fox fairies, ghosts, and monsters—but now I myself have seen such a bizarre occurrence!" Thinking this to himself, he continued along the path aimlessly without paying attention to how much distance he had covered. Suddenly, raising his head, he saw the sun rising in front of him. He couldn't help but be startled and said aloud, "The road toward Jinan should lead north, so how is it that I am now walking toward the east?" Upon closer inspection, however, he realized that what he was actually seeing was the distant gleam of myriad rays of auspicious radiance and a thousand tendrils of propitious aura. In the midst of the auspicious radiance and propitious aura, the dim outline of a tall ceremonial arch appeared.

■ ■ ■

If you wish to know whither this archway led, please listen to the explanation in the following chapter.

Chapter Twenty-Two

Jia Baoyu enters for the first time the Realm of Civilization

Lao Shaonian expounds upon the remaking of Heaven

WE HAD been speaking, in the previous chapter, of how Beiming had been struck by an arrow and was suddenly transformed into a wooden statue. Now, in such an enlightened and advanced age as ours, that I, the author of this book, should suddenly start speaking of such ridiculous things—well, how can this not be a case of reveling in barbarity? How could I not be berated by my readers for this? But you may not be aware that there is a logic at play in all of it, which is that it was my own secret intention to deliberately leave this episode in the text, in order that I might cause my readers to take this idea as a prompt for deep reflection. Who could have predicted that, the manuscript of my book as yet unfinished, a certain Mr. Mirror-Me would see the previous installment and reveal my intention in a single remark! He even said that once the entire manuscript is completed, he would be willing to append a commentary to it. Dear readers, if you are unable to work out what my secret intention was, just wait and read Mr. Mirror-Me's comments.

But let us not speak of idle things. Let us speak instead of how Baoyu had lost not only his horse but Beiming as well. Though he had successfully scared off the group of brigands, he was now left with no choice but to carry the leather suitcase himself and continue onward. Off in the distance he had spied an archway, with auspicious radiance and propitious aura streaming out above it. And so he continued steadfastly forward. By the time he reached the arch, it had already been light out for some time. Looking up at it, he read inscribed there the words, "Realm of Civilization." He thought, "No wonder everyone is always talking nonstop about 'civilization' and 'barbarity' of late! So, as it happens, there is actually a 'Realm of Civilization'! But I wonder just what kind of 'civilization' exists in this Realm. Though I have only happened upon this place by coincidence, I must go inside and have a look!" Having thus decided, he stepped through the archway. Turning to look at the reverse face of the arch as he moved past it, he saw the characters *kongdao*—which could mean either 'the path' or 'The Way of Confucius'—carved thereupon. "*Kongdao* probably just means 'main road' here," he thought. Before he had finished his musings, he saw that a man had appeared at his side. The man had a squarish face and large ears, black mustaches in the shape of an inverted V, a jolly bearing, and a spirited, bold demeanor. The man greeted Baoyu with a bow and said, "Our honored guest has traveled a long way, it can't have been easy for you."

Baoyu hurriedly returned the man's bow and said, "I am lost and found my way here quite by chance. I wonder whether I might be permitted to have a look around and admire your honorable Realm?"

"Our humble Realm is quite open-minded: as long as visitors are able to respect our civilized rules, they are not turned away. Now that you have arrived here, I invite you to first repair to one of our humble lodgings, where you may rest." So saying, he led Baoyu onward.

They had not gone very far when they arrived in front of a large building. On the door lintel there hung a horizontal plaque that read "Arrival Hotel No. 1." The man bade Baoyu proceed to a guest reception room inside. Baoyu set down his suitcase, and guest and host both seated themselves, each asking the other his name. It was then that Baoyu learned that the man's surname was Lao, meaning "Old," and his courtesy name was Shaonian, meaning "Youth." A serving boy then served tea; but as Baoyu took the cup in his hand and looked at it, the cup seemed to be full of clear water. However, when he put it to his lips and took a sip, he found the tea to be richly fragrant. To himself, he thought this very peculiar. Raising his eyes to glance round the reception room, he noticed that it had been tidied into a state of exceptional cleanliness.

Once they had finished their tea, Lao Shaonian led Baoyu into yet another room to take a seat. This room was quite distinct from the reception room: while the four walls had been freshly whitewashed, giving the room a very clean appearance, it was completely empty save for a few chairs in the very center. They had been sitting here for a little while, when suddenly a small side door opened and a person emerged therefrom. This person, an elderly man with a gray beard, addressed Lao Shaonian: "The honorable guest's quality of character is crystal-clear; however, there are some impurities in his digestive tract.

This is the result of his not being sufficiently discerning in his eating and drinking habits. Once he has lived here for several days, this issue will resolve itself." Lao Shaonian was delighted by this and led Baoyu back into the reception room.

Baoyu inquired, "Who was that elderly man?"

"That was one of our doctors. The room in which we were just sitting is our Character Examination Room. I bring every new arrival from outside the Realm here, then take them into the Character Examination Room, where a doctor in the adjoining room uses a 'character-analyzing lens' to examine them. If they are found to be of civilized character, they are allowed to remain within the Realm; but if their character is found to contain some traces of barbarism, they are sent to the Character Reformation office. Once a doctor there has reformed their character, they are welcome here once again. But among our would-be visitors there are also those who are barbaric to their core—who cannot be reformed. Such persons are ejected from the Realm. Just now, the doctor examined you and found that your character was 'crystal-clear': such a character is rarely seen in even one out of ten thousand guests from the outside! That is sufficient to show us that you are one of the 'civilized'—such persons are always the most exceptional of those from the outside."

"I must admit to being ignorant of such things," said Baoyu. "What is it about me that is sufficient to be called 'civilized'? Besides, I've always heard that character is a formless thing, so if you wanted to examine someone's character, you would need to look at his intentions and his actions in daily life and evaluate carefully from there. How can it be analyzed with a lens? Moreover, how can character be reformed? What special techniques do you have for that? And if your honorable Realm already has the technology, why not go out around the world and reform everyone?"

Lao Shaonian sighed. "That's easier said than done! Right now, the character of most people in the world is barbaric through-and-through and cannot be reformed. Although we do have marvelous techniques, there is nothing even we can do about such people but wait for them to die out. As for those who are still capable of being reformed, it's currently not necessary that we should go out and try to reform them, for they will eventually make their way here and seek reformation on their own. So there is no need for us to overexert ourselves in the way you suggest."

Baoyu continued to push. "But character is a formless thing, so how can it be analyzed? I still request your instruction on this."

"Once science has flourished, it is possible to analyze everything! For example, if we closely analyze the air, we find it to be composed of all kinds of different elements. There are those barbaric, half-enlightened peoples, who readily believe that 'air' is simply a homogenous, all-encompassing substance—but how could that be so? If it's as you say, that things without form cannot be analyzed, then how is it that European and American scholars of acoustics are able to measure soundwaves? However, while those scholars have been able to measure the waves, the drawings they have been able to produce of them are mere representations of their own imaginations. Whereas each time *our* scientists analyze something, they actually simultaneously create a method to render it *visible to the human eye*! So, let's say we wished to analyze a person's character: we would use a lens. Our lenses pass through a process, overseen by high-level medical scientists, of first using advanced chemistry to create the glass, then applying several rounds of specialized sera in order to perfect it. Standing on one side of this lens and looking through it at the body of a person on the other side, the person's flesh, blood, sinew, and bones all disappear, and all that can be seen is his character. If his character is civilized it appears as crystalline and clear as ice or snow; if it is barbaric it appears murky and turbulent, like smoke or fog. Depending on just how thick or attenuated the smoke or fog is, we can determine the true depth of his barbarism. Those whose characters appear as dense and black as ink are the ones who are incapable of being reformed."

"Such a lens is indeed a marvelous creation! Not only have I never seen one, I've never so much as heard of one."

"It ultimately emerged out of an ideal. The stories of the ancients were largely about gods and ghosts, and whenever they touched on the subject of good or evil, they described moral exemplars as having beams of red light several feet in length shining out from over their heads; meanwhile, evildoers had coiling black auras over theirs. They also said that there were such things as 'flourishing auras' and 'waning auras,' which humans could not see—these could be seen only by ghosts and spirits. The people who wrote these stories had certainly never been ghosts or spirits themselves, so how could they have known? It was just an ideal they were expressing. But once the ideal existed, it became possible to put it into practice. That is why the scientists of our humble Realm have exhausted their energies in order to create this lens."

Baoyu couldn't help but nod his head, sighing in awe.

As they were talking, they suddenly heard someone call out in a loud voice: "One-quarter past *chen* proper!"[1] When Baoyu raised his head to look, he saw a person standing up at the corner of the high wall. The man was wearing the robe and cap of an ancient era, and in his hands he held out a wooden plaque that read "One-quarter past *chen* proper." The man seemed to be observing Baoyu with an expression of something like subtle amusement. Baoyu was surprised, and thought, "I didn't pay him much notice at all earlier." He was about to stand to greet the man, when he noticed that the man seemed frozen in place, about to move, yet not moving. This caused Baoyu to continue staring up at him somewhat discomfited. A short while later, beneath the characters reading "One-quarter past *chen* proper" there now appeared more small characters: "one minute past." Baoyu once again marveled at this in silence.

Lao Shaonian had noticed his surprise and laughed. "This is a 'timekeeping automaton.' It is similar to the clocks of the Europeans and Americans—it reports the time."

"Clocks are already such a clever creation. But this! This isn't even on the same scale!"

"Although clocks are indeed clever, they use different units than we do. We break the day and night into twelve two-hour periods from *zi* to *hai*, whereas they break it into twenty-four hours.[2] The faces of their clocks only have twelve numbers on them, which means that when one wants to make a note of the time, one must always add 'a.m.' or 'p.m.'—isn't that cumbersome? For example, right now it is a quarter past *chen* proper; but if you wanted to put it in their terms, it would be 8:15 a.m. Now, if you were just asking someone the time, of course that would be quite clear. But if you were trying to keep a record of the day's happenings, you would have to add 'a.m.,' otherwise your record might be misunderstood to mean 8:15 *in the evening!*

Not only is their system troublesome, but why must we be expected to give up our own way of keeping the time to follow that of others?" Saying this, he pulled out a watch, which he extended to Baoyu. Baoyu took it in his hand and saw that it was no larger than a copper coin, with the character *chen* displayed prominently in the center. To the left were displayed the characters "proper; one quarter past"; to the right, the words "three minutes past." Baoyu looked once again at the timekeeping automaton, and found that its plaque, too, now bore the characters "three minutes past." When he had finished, he handed the watch back to Lao Shaonian and sighed once more in admiration.

A serving boy now emerged to invite them to take breakfast, at which point Lao Shaonian let Baoyu lead the way. By now, Baoyu was starving, so he did not demur, and together they arrived at the dining room. A serving boy served them each a cup of tea—again, as Baoyu looked at it, he noted that it was as clear as water, but slightly more viscous. He watched as Lao Shaonian drank, then took a sip himself. The flavor was indescribable, beyond words like "sour," "salty," "bitter," or "spicy"—indeed, it was a uniquely gentle, pleasant flavor. Without really noticing, he sipped away until the cup was empty. Strangely enough, after having drunk just a single cup of this substance, he no longer felt any hunger.

The serving boy now came to ask Lao Shaonian for instructions as to which quarters were to be allocated to the newly arrived guest.

"He'll stay in Dormitory Room No. 1," was the reply. Hearing this, the serving boy departed. Lao Shaonian then led Baoyu to Dormitory Room No. 1, where Baoyu's leather suitcase had already been deposited. The décor was refined and elegant, without any airs of ostentation or grandeur, yet similarly without with any feeling of rustic crudeness. The room had been outfitted completely, with ready-made bed curtains and comforter on the bed and the four treasures of the scholar's study—ink, inkstone, paper, and brush—laid out on the desk. To one side, there was also a bookcase filled with books, beside which there was a reclining chair; near this, stood a row of ordinary chairs. In the corner, there was another timekeeping automaton, this one in the shape of a boy, gently plump with snow-white skin, smiling brightly. With both hands he held aloft over his head a sign similar to the one Baoyu had seen outside, but this time in the shape of a scroll. As it happened, it was just now half past *chen* proper, which the automaton announced, just as if it were a real human speaking.

"That voice," said Baoyu, "must be produced by something similar to a phonograph?"

Lao Shaonian shook his head. "No, not at all. How could a phonograph ever produce such a clear, crisp sound? The phonograph uses friction to create sound, whereas our system mimics the flow of the breath through the organs and tubes of the human respiratory system. The system is crafted out of soft leather, then inserted into the automaton and fitted with a small fan to create air flow. When the time comes for the automaton to speak, the fan turns on, causing inflation of the leather tubes, which creates the sound. Now, if, when you try to sleep tonight, you find it disagreeable for him to keep making his announcements, there is a small knob in his left ear—if you turn it, he will stop speaking. Tomorrow, if you wish for him to start speaking again, just turn the knob back again, and you're all set." Saying this, he turned the knob by way of demonstration.

"The workmanship is indeed exceedingly clever!" remarked Baoyu.

As they were speaking, Baoyu was suddenly assailed by a burst of clean, fresh fragrance. He turned to look and saw that a dish of green-stemmed plum blossoms had been set out on a small round table in the room. He was surprised by this, and said, "It's already the fifth month, where did you manage to get plum blossoms?"

"That's nothing so special. Our humble Realm has four different types of seasonal park, each dedicated to spring, summer, fall, or winter. In addition to being allowed to stroll through and enjoy the scenery, people are also permitted to buy the flowers that are grown there. In this way, one can go and admire the flowers and trees of each season at any time of year."

"But the weather is wrong—how do you get the flowers to bloom out of season?"

"The chemists in our Realm are able to control the weather. For example, it is now early summer, so the weather in the spring, fall, and winter parks is necessarily artificially controlled. Once summer is over and fall begins, then they will begin to control the weather in the summer park again."

Baoyu gasped. "It goes without saying that this ability to control the weather is a marvel, but back before it had ever been done—why, just the ability to imagine this marvelous idea is truly admirable!"

"The technology was left to us over a hundred years ago. It was because back then our scientific development was still in a state of immaturity, and most of our people lived in poverty. One year, we suffered a terrible loss of the cotton harvest. When the winter came—an exceptionally cold one—there were charities and philanthropists who prepared aid to get the people through the winter, but it was unfortunately still impossible to buy cotton anywhere, so the aid was useless. At the time, a chemist named Hua Xing—whose courtesy name was Bizhen—made a suggestion: 'Rather than try to supply aid to each individual, surely it would be better to find a way to make it so that the weather is not so cold. Wouldn't that be more effective?'[3] At the time, everyone sniggered and thought that his suggestion was absurd. Who would have guessed that once he had articulated the idea, he would set about making it happen? He dispatched people riding tens of thousands of balloons into the skies, firing things like sulfur and nitrate into the clouds, hoping to drive off the cold air. He also used tens of thousands of enormous furnaces that could put out large quantities of steam and distributed them in all directions. Eventually he was able to brew up weather just like that of late spring. Even the grasses and trees began to put out shoots! The local poor were greatly relieved. While it was unsustainable to extend to the entire Realm, within that area of three hundred li square, you would never know there had been a winter that year. The scientist Hua Bizhen, who had been the one to organize it all, had, however, spent the entirety of his sizeable family wealth on the project. Afterward, when the government realized that he was possessed of such a unique skillset, they decided to cover his expenses and asked him to continue his specialized research. Over time he developed technologies for artificially creating all four seasons, and the cost gradually decreased.

"Nowadays the people of our humble Realm have plenty, and the government is wealthy, so there is no real need for this technology anymore. But, loath to let his great contributions be forgotten by time, we decided to make use of the techniques he passed down: each district in the Realm has established four parks of its own, dedicated to each of the four seasons; and in each of these parks, a stone statue of Hua Bizhen was erected. Whenever you would like, I can take you to go explore and see for yourself."[4]

"This can truly be called 'vying with the achievements of Heaven itself'!" said Baoyu.

"The people of Hua Bizhen's era created a dignified title for him: 'The Remaker of Heaven.'[5] Now, whenever men and women go to the parks, they look on the memorial statues with reverence, but none dares to call him by his name out of respect. They all call the statues 'The memorials to the Remaker of Heaven.'"

"Mr. Hua is certainly deserving of the title! I had originally intended to travel to Freedom Village but was struck with the desire to climb Mount Tai and visit the Tomb of Confucius. Without any intention on my part, I ended up stumbling upon this place, which has opened my eyes immeasurably! Truly, I have been most fortunate. But I wonder: how large an area does your honorable Realm occupy? I simply must travel around and see it all for myself."

"Our humble Realm consists of two million districts altogether, and each district is a hundred square li. These districts are divided into five sectors: East, West, South, North, and Central. Each sector comprises four named regions, and each region in turn comprises 100,000 districts, which means that each sector contains and has jurisdiction over 400,000 districts. Each district takes the name of its region and then is additionally assigned a number from 1 to 100,000. In the Central Sector the names of the four regions are Ritual, Music, Cultivation, and Literature. In the East the four regions are Benevolence, Righteousness, Ritual, and Wisdom. In the South they are Amity, Compassion, Respect, and Trust. In the West they are Unbending, Strong, Courageous, and Resolute. In the North they are Loyal, Filial, Honest, and Upright. Right now, we are in the Hundredth District of the Strong Region, which we shorten to 'Strong No. 100.' Just now, you mentioned wanting to travel to Freedom Village—Freedom Village is the name of one of the villages here."[6]

"When my cousin arrived in Freedom Village, he said that it was not far from the Changxin Inn in Beijing. How could it in fact be here?"

Lao Shaonian was startled by this. "How could there be any Freedom Village but ours?"

Baoyu retrieved Xue Pan's letter from his suitcase and handed it to Lao Shaonian to read. Upon reading it, Lao Shaonian became even more shocked.

■ ■ ■

If you wish to know what so shocked him, please listen to the explanation in the following chapter.

Chapter Twenty-Three

Medical research has led to the refinement of food and drink

The sciences flourish as a result of efforts to create marvelous machines

WE WERE speaking of how Lao Shaonian had read the letter that Xue Pan had sent to Baoyu. He was greatly shocked and remarked, "It is fortunate that you never managed to reach the place of which he speaks. There's no need to speak of all of the details for now, but this Liu Xuesheng he mentions came to our Realm three times. Upon going through medical examination the first time he arrived, his character was found to be murky, so he was sent back. After some time had passed he returned, and I thought that he must have reformed his character and had thus decided to try again. Who would have guessed that upon examination the doctors would declare that his character had grown even murkier than before! When he came for the third time, it was no longer even necessary to examine him; his barbaric essence was practically written all over his face. How could you possibly go to a place that someone like him would recommend?"

"Perhaps this is just a coincidental case of someone with a similar name and surname. It's hard to say," said Baoyu.

"His courtesy name was Maoming—I remember him very clearly. How could there be someone with the same name and courtesy name? It goes without saying that this 'Freedom Village' of his is built upon a barbaric sort of 'freedom.'"

"Can freedom be differentiated into 'civilized' and 'barbaric' types?"

"There is a huge distinction between the two! In general, the more civilized freedom is, the more ordered and disciplined it is; the more barbaric freedom is, the more order breaks down. The people who fall somewhere between civilized and barbaric believe that once they have achieved freedom, it is like stepping into Heaven. They don't know that for the citizenry to truly be able to live in freedom, each person must have the capacity for self-discipline, must be capable of obeying the rules of society, and must understand the limits of the law. Only then can one speak of freedom. Proponents of barbaric freedom constantly speak of 'domestic revolution'; they want first and foremost to completely dispense with longstanding social hierarchies, and they decry as 'barbaric' the teachings bequeathed to them by the sages and philosophers of antiquity! This is a class of person that we here in this humble Realm certainly dare not admire. Whatever 'Freedom Village' he may live in—how could you go there?"[1]

"What is the situation in your own Freedom Village?"

"The lower-level units of our Realm are given names quite casually—there is no greater systemic meaning to them. But this Freedom Village is the birthplace of our Master Dongfang.

As a young man in his thirties he frequently engaged in debates, expounding upon the reasons for establishing a 'Freedom Village.' That's why the village was given the name."

"And who is this 'Master Dongfang'?"

"Dongfang is a double surname; his given name is Qiang, and his courtesy name is Wenming. He has three sons and a daughter: the oldest son is Dongfang Ying, the next oldest is Dongfang De, the youngest is Dongfang Fa, and the daughter is called Dongfang Mei. This family of five all possess both incomparable talent and the will to establish a secure and peaceful state. That our humble Realm is now at peace and flourishing is due entirely to the Dongfangs, father and children. The daughter went on to marry a man by the name of Hua Zili, a descendant of the 'Remaker of Heaven.'[2] Since Hua came from a prominent family of scientists, this new son-in-law proved to be of great assistance, and our Realm made even more rapid progress. In order to commemorate the great merit performed by Master Dongfang, we took his courtesy name, Wenming—Civilization—to name this place. That way we could show that we would never forget his contributions. Nowadays Master Dongfang is of advanced age and has retired to the Benevolence No. 1 District in the Eastern Sector, where he lives in seclusion. His three sons, daughter, and son-in-law are still active in the running of the Realm."

"Your honorable Realm is certainly named appropriately. I would very much like to take a tour through it; my only regret is that I haven't got a guide to lead me."

"If you wish to go on a tour, that is simple enough. I can accompany you."

"But your job is to meet travelers coming from outside—how can you possibly leave your post?"

"I am not the only one who greets visitors; I also have colleagues. All I need to do is request time off, then there will be no impediment to taking some time to travel and explore. Now I have a few small things to which I must attend, so I must take my leave for the moment. On the desk, you'll find a bell for summoning a serving boy. If you want tea or water, press the bell and you will be attended to." So saying, he took his leave.

Now on his own, Baoyu spent a little while admiring the plum blossoms, then examining once again the timekeeping automaton. The little boy automaton had been crafted to look just like a living person, and Baoyu could not cease marveling to himself. He then sat at the desk and casually pulled a couple of books from the bookcase to read. He read for a little while but felt somewhat bored, so he took up the "four treasures" from the desk and began to toy with them. He unintentionally pressed the bell for summoning a serving boy, but it made no sound. Picking it up, he looked inside but was unable to make out any kind of mechanism there. Just as he was puzzling it over, a serving boy entered the room and asked, "How may I be of service?" Baoyu was unprepared for this and simply requested some tea. The boy turned and left, then returned with a cup of tea. Once again the tea was as clear as water, but when Baoyu drank it, he found the flavor to be rich and deep. He asked, "What tea leaves do you use here? How is it that the tea is colorless?"

"It's just normal tea—but we steep the leaves in aerated water, which is why the tea is colorless." When Baoyu had finished drinking the tea, the boy removed the cup and left.

Baoyu now pushed open the side window and looked out. As it happened, there was a garden just outside. Directly opposite the window stood a small pavilion, beside which grew a pomegranate tree. The tree was all abloom with bright red blossoms. Baoyu leaned against the window frame and continued gazing idly out into the garden. From behind him, the timekeeping automaton announced that it was noon, whereupon a serving boy promptly arrived to invite Baoyu to lunch. Arriving once more at the dining room, he found Lao Shaonian already there, so the two men could eat together. There were no bowls or chopsticks upon the table; a serving boy simply brought each man a cup, filled once more with clear liquid. Upon drinking it, Baoyu found the liquid inside to be fragrant and delicious as before. When they had drained these cups, the boy took them away and brought out another round. In this manner, they were served six or seven different cups; the contents of some were like steeped lotus root powder, while that of others were akin to almond tea. No two cups tasted alike.

Baoyu could bear his curiosity no longer. "What is it that we're drinking?"

"Why, it's just chicken, goose, fish, duck, beef, lamb—that sort of thing. They are the products of refinements to food and beverages invented by our humble Realm's great medical scientist Dongfang De. He experimented with rice, grains, and meat and found that while they can nourish a person, when the remains make their way into the intestines, they are not always fully digested, which can lead to illness. So he tried a new method, using chemistry to extract the essences from various foodstuffs. Now all we consume are these essences, so naturally there's no need to worry about anything not being digested.

"He also experimented with using flame to cook various foodstuffs but found that the overabundance of heat in the food became unhealthy. Now, the things Chinese people eat are largely fine in this regard, since there are many things that are cooked by steaming and are therefore not in close contact with flame. But as for the diets of Americans and Europeans, if it's not fried it's roasted, so the overabundance of heat is especially severe. I don't understand why they insist on it, but they are stubbornly unwilling to change. Moreover, it's not that they are unaware of the fact that the foods they fry and roast are unhealthy in this way. That's why they invented beer. Beer is made from hops and is very cooling in nature. Their intention is to use the cooling effect of the beer to dispel the harmful effects of the intense heat of their food. Little do they realize that if they've swallowed something hot, then drink something cold straight after in order to dispel those effects, they have actually turned their stomach and intestines into a battlefield upon which hot and cold wage war! And yet somehow they still claim to be advanced in the medical sciences!

"There are also those Chinese who have studied Western medicine—and who even knows how long they've studied it for?—the first thing they do is turn around and say that the Chinese medicine with which they grew up is completely worthless and that it will eventually become obsolete. Isn't that ridiculous? According to them, the way of Chinese medicine is unsustainable—but if that were so, the entirety of the Chinese population should have died out thousands of years ago! How could they have made it to the present day? If Western medicine is as good as they say, then Westerners should be stronger than Chinese in all areas; so why is it that the Chinese birthrate is so much higher than theirs? When it comes to life expectancy, they can't compete with the Chinese either.

"When he was quite young, our Master Dongfang De focused entirely on studying Chinese medicine; only after he had mastered it did he begin researching Western medicine. He then made use of the strengths of both disciplines—rejecting their respective weaknesses—and combining them impressively into a single doctrine. He also incorporated chemistry, so there is now no depth that cannot be plumbed. His first priority was to refine our food and beverages. He often says that a man who can cure an individual's illness is not a doctor but merely a servant attending upon the ill. A real doctor is engaged in curing the entire population of the country of its illnesses; only then may he be considered a skilled practitioner. Master Dongfang De's efforts in reforming our food were precisely because he hoped to prevent illness in the entire population."

Baoyu replied, "You've already explained the reasoning behind improving the food. But if you don't use fire to cook your food, how do you cook it?"

"How could we not use fire? We just boil water into steam, then use that to steam our food until cooked."

"If it's as you say, then it must be very difficult to feed one's family! Normally one only needs a cook and a stove; but to do it in the way you say must mean not only constructing a steam furnace in the kitchen but hiring a chemist!"

Lao Shaonian laughed. "The houses in our humble Realm have never had their own kitchens. Every district has a central kitchen, from which food-distribution pipes run in all directions. When it is time to eat, food is delivered through the pipes, as rich or as plain as people wish. These food-distribution pipes function the same way as the pipes that deliver running water. Not just the food we eat, but even the tea we drink, is all supplied by the central kitchens."

As he was speaking, a serving boy placed a tiny cup in front of each of the men. Lao Shaonian explained, "The fruit on today's menu is apple."

Baoyu looked at the cup, and again, it seemed to be filled with clear water. But when he sniffed it, it gave off a strong fragrance of apples. He sipped it down in one go; when they had finished this course, they left.

Lao Shaonian then took Baoyu for a stroll through the garden. As one would expect, the strange flowers and unfamiliar grasses were appropriately ornamental; the towers and pavilions were of exquisite construction. Lao Shaonian told Baoyu, "It goes without saying that the accommodations in Chinese inns are somewhat slipshod; whereas in European and American inns, the decorations are quite ostentatious, giving the impression that they are trying to appeal to a somewhat crass clientele. How do the accommodations here compare?"

Baoyu nodded and expressed his admiration of the beautiful environs, then asked, "I've heard that foreign buildings often have over ten stories—do you have any buildings like that here?"

"It is only those island nations where land is scarce and the population large that have such buildings. Those nearsighted myopes who perhaps see or hear about such buildings but don't bother to inquire as to the reason for them and simply declare them to be 'civilized buildings' are ridiculous! It's truly enough to make someone feel nauseated. In actuality, our land is quite sufficient to fit our population, so why should we need tall buildings?" As he spoke, the two meandered their way through the garden. When they finally emerged from it, Lao Shaonian pointed to a door and said, "That's the kitchen. You must want to go take a look."

When Baoyu entered and looked round, he saw a row of spigots on each wall, numbering no fewer than two or three hundred, all made of glass.

"I know those are what are commonly called 'faucets,'" said Baoyu. "But the ones I've seen previously have all been made of copper. Why is it that these are all made of glass?"

"Metals like copper and iron inevitably contain impurities. That's why we've chosen to use glass. And it's not just the faucets—the entire length of the pipes that run from here are all made of glass as well. It's only for the washing water and gas lighting that we use iron pipes." As he spoke, he and Baoyu exited the kitchen and went together to the reception room.

A serving boy once again served tea, and Baoyu asked, "How is it that all of the tea here is colorless? What is the purpose of removing the color from tea?"

Lao Shaonian replied, "One need take in only a small amount of the fragrant flavor of tea to stimulate the stomach and digest one's food. The color is not only useless but in fact hinders this process. Try observing sometime: when you've poured regular tea into a cup and left it to sit a long while, the tea will leave stains. From this we can deduce that when you take that same tea into your stomach, it also leaves stains there. Although the stomach can digest away such stains, why would you ask your stomach to exert its useful digestive efforts in the digestion of useless tea stains? That is why all of the tea here is made by steaming tea leaves into aerated water, thereby preserving only the fragrance and flavor, but without any of the color."

"And just now you spoke of 'gas lighting,' " continued Baoyu. "I wonder: from where is this 'gas' obtained?"

"Gas is nothing special. In Sichuan, they already use it in the process of evaporating saltwater to harvest the salt left behind. It's just that we have expanded its uses. We drill into the ground until we strike gas, then lay a series of iron pipelines running in all directions. The pipes then provide us with gas for the evening lamplight. The central kitchens, and even the manufacturing plants, all use gas as well."

"If it's as you say, then you have no use for coal here. So there must not be any coal mines either?"

"We have a great many coal mines! Once it is mined, it is transported overseas where we sell it to foreigners. We ourselves don't use it here, so the air is very clean. We are not like those barbarian countries, where even in their major city centers every home has a flue for letting out the smoke from their furnaces—not to mention the smokestacks from the factories that are mixed in as well, creating a world where smoke constantly fills the sky. And yet they praise themselves as 'civilized'!" And there are still those who admire their 'civilization'!"

"Since the state of science is so developed here, I imagine that you must have many factories."

"Our factories are all located in the Eastern Wisdom districts; nearly all 100,000 districts of the Wisdom Region are completely full of factories. Tomorrow when we begin our tour, we can go there and have a look."

"Aren't there any factories here?"

"There are a few, but they're quite small and not much to look at. However, this region is near the maritime frontier, so there is instead a naval academy—that would be worth seeing. The lecture hall there is big enough to fit fifty thousand people at once."

Baoyu furrowed his brow. "It's not strange that the lecture hall is so large; but how can those seated far from the speaker hear what is being said?"

"Hua Zili, the man who came from a long line of scientists, invented a new device called a 'listening aid.' Some type of metal is shaped into a very small tube, no more than half an inch in length, which is inserted into the ear. Regardless of how far away you are from the speaker, as long as there is no obstruction between you, even the faintest of voices can be heard clearly."

"Yet another marvelous contraption," said Baoyu. "Might I be able to see one?"

"Tomorrow we'll go together to the academy. On the one hand you'll be able to look around the academy itself, and on the other you'll be able to see one of those devices."

Baoyu was thrilled. Lao Shaonian wrote out a message requesting an appointment to visit the Naval Academy the following day, then called a serving boy to deliver it to the academy.

Baoyu then returned to his quarters alone. To his surprise he noticed that the plum flowers that had been on the table had disappeared and had been replaced with a dish of white chrysanthemums. He unconsciously sighed. "I have often read in fiction how in the lands of immortals flowers bloom year-round without fading, and the grasses of spring thrive throughout the changing of the seasons. They also say that one who is skilled in the technique can grow flowers and plants out of sync with the seasons. Quite to my surprise, I have today seen it all with my own eyes and have myself arrived in just such a place." He pushed open the window. Viewed together, the contrast of the fresh, red pomegranate blooming outside with the white chrysanthemums inside made for a striking scene. He stood admiring them a short while, then went back to reading to pass the time.

After taking his evening meal in the dining room, he returned once again to his room. As the night began to grow dark, he saw that the lights hanging on the wall suddenly illuminated with a brightness far exceeding that of electric lights. He thought, "So, this gas light is indeed very bright! If those who make electric lights were to see it, they couldn't help but acknowledge that they have fallen behind."

Lao Shaonian then walked in and said, "I have already been granted my time off—it is all settled. Tomorrow I shall accompany you on your tour."

Baoyu thanked him. Lao Shaonian glanced up at the lights, then pointed to a gauge on the wall. "That's the brightness gauge. If the light is too bright for you, just push the needle down; but if it's too dim you can push it up."

Baoyu looked at the mechanism. It was very much like a thermometer, except in the center, there was no glass tube, but rather a copper strip. Lines drawn across the strip divided it into fractional units, which were labeled with text. In front of this a silver needle was suspended horizontally. As Baoyu tried pushing the needle downward with his finger, the lights did indeed grow dimmer; and when he pushed the needle back toward the top, the lights returned to their original brightness. He was delighted by this and said, "These are much more versatile than electric lights!"

Lao Shaonian then took his leave. Baoyu sat for a short while, adjusted the light level to be on par with that of an oil lamp, then went to bed in preparation for the following day's excursion.

■ ■ ■

If you wish to know what sorts of things he saw while touring through the Realm of Civilization, please listen to the explanation in the following chapter.

Chapter Twenty-Four

In the hospital's examination room, a disquisition on medical science

Riding in a flying car, they speedily arrive at the Naval Academy

WE HAD been speaking of Baoyu, who had lain down to rest for the night. On the following morning, he washed his face and had some breakfast; shortly thereafter, Lao Shaonian came to arrange a time for them to proceed together to the Naval Academy. He explained, "It's early yet. The letter I wrote yesterday to the superintendent of the academy requested an appointment for one o'clock in the afternoon. Why don't we first head over to a hospital so you can take a look?"

"Excellent!" replied Baoyu. "I definitely want to examine all of your medical inventions!"

And so the two men set off together.

The path the entire way to the hospital was lined on both sides with weeping willows. The roadway was some hundred feet wide, and as smooth and level as the palm of one's hand.[1] The two men strolled along at a leisurely pace. Suddenly they saw something fly through the air above their heads.

"Where did that enormous bird come from?" asked Baoyu.

Lao Shaonian laughed. "That's a flying car. Ever since we invented them in recent years, it has been forbidden for carriages to drive along the main roads so as to prevent collisions with pedestrians. At the time the order was passed the intention was simply for the protection of pedestrians, but we didn't realize that once carriages were banned from the roads, it would have the additional effect of saving a substantial sum on road repairs each year!"

"How high can a car fly?"

"It can fly as high or as low as the driver chooses. Cars traveling a farther distance will fly at a slightly higher altitude, roughly a hundred feet off the ground. The one we just saw just flies back and forth within the city, so it flies at an altitude of only about fifty feet. The cars traveling longer distances can travel out across the sky in any direction. As for the intracity cars, even though they are flying in the air, they are required to follow the paths of the roads—were the cars permitted to fly over people's homes, we worried that if there were too many flying back and forth, the constant flickering and shimmering of their shadows passing overhead could damage the residents' eyesight."

"There must not be very many such cars," mused Baoyu. "We've been walking for quite a while and only seen this one."

"This is a fairly isolated area, that's why there relatively few here. In the busier areas, there are many more."

As they conversed, they soon came to see, far off in the distance, a large building over which fluttered a flag. The flag consisted of alternating fields of black and white, which made for a somewhat busy visual effect. Glancing at it quickly, it was difficult to make out the design, but studying it more carefully, one could see that it was a large black character reading "Medicine" set against a white field.

"That place with the flag must be a hospital," commented Baoyu.

"Precisely so."

"The flag was very well thought out."

"That was another brainchild of Hua Zili. In our humble Realm, with the exception of the Yellow Dragon flag[2] and the various international flags required by diplomacy, all other flags are of our own making and usage. They come from careful thought, and as a result take on novel forms. It is detestable that there are those who so wish to curry favor with foreigners that they mimic the foreigners in everything they do. For example, that a red flag should mean 'danger,' while a yellow flag means 'illness,' and a red cross means 'medicine'—those are all universal European and American symbols. Those who would ingratiate themselves to foreigners saw them and wanted to make them into universal symbols around the world, so they internalized them and now would rather die than forget them. At the time we first created this flag, when two people from outside the Realm saw it for the first time, they criticized it most forcefully, saying it couldn't be universally understood and that all hospitals should of course have a flag with a red cross! Hua Zili is a naturally blunt man, so when he heard this, he gave the two outsiders quite a lecture! They then felt so ashamed and intimidated that they couldn't bear to show their faces and scurried right out of the Realm."

While they spoke, they arrived at the entrance to the hospital. Lao Shaonian pulled out a calling card and handed it to the man minding the entry gate. The gateman brought the card inside and returned a short while later, saying, "Please go ahead." Lao Shaonian and Baoyu entered the building. The first thing they saw upon entering was an elderly man with a gray beard who came out to greet them. Lao Shaonian then introduced the two men: "This is the Director of Medicine for our humble district, the Honorable Qin Chaohe." He also then presented Baoyu to the director.

Chaohe asked Baoyu, "You must be newly arrived from outside the Realm?"

"I am."

Lao Shaonian added, "When Doctor Huang Yuehuan examined his character at the hotel, he said it was clear and crystalline as a looking glass. That's never before happened with someone from outside!"

"One can tell straightaway with just one look at his demeanor," said Chaohe. "Why did you need to examine him at all?"

"When I first arrived in your honorable Realm," began Baoyu, "I heard that your medical sciences were truly enlightened. So we've come especially to pay our respects. At the same time we hoped to admire your fine hospital."

"Then I wholeheartedly invite you to come look around. Fortunately, in recent years everyone has come to understand hygiene, so very few people suffer illness. As a result, things are extremely quiet at the hospital and there are very few patients in the ward."

Lao Shaonian queried, "The number of patients last year must have fallen from the year before?"

"Substantially so. Last year, we only saw thirty patients for the entire year."

"How large an area is this hospital responsible for?" asked Baoyu.

"Each district has only one hospital," replied Lao Shaonian. "This hospital is responsible for an area of a hundred li square."

Baoyu thought, "Within an area of a hundred li square there was only a total of thirty sick people in an entire year! I've never heard of such a thing!" He let out an involuntary sigh of admiration and said aloud, "I have finally met someone who merits the title of 'National Treasure'!" Chaohe modestly refused the compliment.

After a serving boy had proffered tea, Chaohe led the two men to go look around the hospital. Exiting the reception hall, they walked to another area, where a plaque hung outside a door. On the plaque were written the three words "Patient Examination Room." Upon entering the room, they saw that it was extraordinarily open and bright, with glass windows on three sides. Outside the windows one could see a variety of flowers, grasses, and trees, neatly arrayed as in a garden. Chaohe ordered a serving boy to retrieve the bone-examining lens; the boy returned shortly thereafter carrying a box that appeared to be much like a camera. It stood upon a tripod and was wrapped in a white silk cover. Chaohe himself removed the cover, then instructed the boy to stand in a particular spot. He then invited Baoyu to come take a look. When Baoyu peered through the lens, he was so startled that his soul very nearly left his body. He hastily stepped back from the lens and looked up to observe the boy once more.

Chaohe laughed. "There's no need to be afraid. This lens is designed specifically for the diagnosis of bone and joint disorders. Please, take another look."

When Baoyu had first looked through the lens, he had seen a figure of roughly the same height and size as the boy, but how could it be called a person? It was in fact a snow-white skeleton! This was what had so alarmed him that he had involuntarily retreated from the lens. Having heard what Chaohe said, he went to take another look, and as expected, he saw clearly before him a complete set of human bones. Even the joints where the bones met one another could be seen with total clarity. When Baoyu had finished his observations, Chaohe pulled out another glass lens and slid it in front of the device's aperture, explaining "This one is for examining the bone marrow." When Baoyu looked again, the white bones had vanished, and he now saw tracks of pinkish marrow positioned precisely where the bones had been. Looking at the marrow, he noticed that it constituted a highly organized system, circulating throughout the body like fine silk threads.

When they had finished this examination, Chaohe called for the lens to be traded out for yet another: "This one is for examining the blood," he explained. Once again, he instructed the boy to stand still. When Baoyu looked through the device once more, he saw that the lad had been replaced by a figure composed solely of bright red blood. The blood circulated through his body at a much faster pace than had the marrow. When Baoyu had finished, Chaohe also had a look through the lens, then asked the boy, "What kind of mischief have you been getting into, that you've managed to stumble and injure your right knee?"

Hearing this, Baoyu hurried to take another look through the lens. He could indeed see that on the right knee, a clot of blood as big around as the mouth of a tea bowl had formed and turned a faint purple color. All around the clot, the blood still flowed freely; but when it reached the clot, the circulation slowed. The boy replied, "Last night on my way back from the garden, I took a tumble. I certainly haven't been getting up to any 'mischief'!"

Chaohe called for the lens to be changed out once again, and the boy came and did so. "This one," explained Chaohe, "is for examining the muscles." When Baoyu looked, he saw, as anticipated, the entire musculature of the boy's body and tendons, all arrayed neatly and clearly. He could see the muscles, both large and fine, tensing and relaxing—almost as if they were breathing. He thought, "There was an injury to the circulatory system at the right knee—I wonder how the muscles there will look?" Looking carefully, he noted that there was a section of muscle at the right knee that was slightly swollen compared to its counterpart on the left. He then said to Chaohe, "It seems as though the muscles of the right knee have sustained an injury, too?"

Chaohe came and looked. "How could they not have?"

Thereupon yet another lens, for the examination of the organs, was fitted. Baoyu could clearly make out all of the serving boy's internal organs: the red one was the heart, the white was the intestine, the pale yellow was the stomach, the purple was the liver, green was the gallbladder, the light pink were the lungs. He could also see the heart contracting and relaxing, and the lungs filling and emptying. When he had had his fill of looking, Baoyu sighed and said, "This is miraculous. It is an accomplishment on par with the act of Creation itself."

They then took a seat, and a serving boy came with more tea. Chaohe mused, "How absurd it is that the people of the world are so myopic that as soon as they see Western medicine they immediately proclaim it to be marvelous and miraculous; they then change their entire outlook based on witnessing a different way of doing things. They don't know that Western medicine is so ignorant and clumsy that it still hasn't reached the sophistication of China's ancient medical practices; much less has it ever even dreamed of these types of new inventions. Chinese medicine never relied on the dissection of corpses and yet was still able to distinguish each of the twelve major conduits of *qi* with such great clarity. The Westerners need to be able to dissect a body and look inside and arrogantly believe that this is the best way to obtain the 'objective truth.' They don't understand that once a body has died, the blood begins to congeal, and the breath has ceased to flow. If one conducts one's examinations based on dissection, all that can be determined is the relative position of things. It goes without saying that not only do they not see the body in a state of activity, but even the color of everything inside will have changed—so how can they truly examine it? That, of course, is in the case of dissecting a corpse; but even if one were to capture a living person, kill him, and examine him immediately, one must still understand that his breathing has stopped, and the internal mechanisms of the body have all been arrested—so what does one even examine? Western doctors all mock Chinese medicine for relying solely on feeling the pulse in order to determine a prescription, claiming that this method is unreliable. And yet their stethoscopes are somehow reliable?

"These lenses of ours were all created through the exhaustive efforts of Dongfang De and Hua Zili. At the moment they are researching two more novel devices: one is a breath-examining lens, which will specifically examine the circulation of the breath throughout the entire body; and the other is a tool for the measuring of intelligence and a means for increasing it. In the future, when this new technology has been developed, it is to be hoped that there will not be a single person of low intelligence in the Realm."

Baoyu replied, "Those are singularly fantastic ideas! They make me feel such admiration I scarcely know what to say. By using these kinds of lenses to examine a patient, you can see everything clearly with a single glance! But I wonder: Is the medicine that you prescribe Chinese or Western?"

"Most of it is Chinese, though we have entirely changed the mode of administration. There are some Western medicines that we use as well, but only very rarely—and these, too, we administer differently."

"Can you please tell me how they are administered?"

"The digestive tract of the average person is very sensitive. Ever since Dongfang De reformed our foods and beverages, the residents of the Realm are, as a rule, not permitted to consume anything but clear water and the essences of meat and grains. As a result, they don't take medicine orally, either. Patients are taken into special medicine administration chambers—those with mild illnesses are seated, while those with severe illnesses lie down. These chambers are only six feet by six feet cubed. Once the patient has entered, the door is closed. The hospital has a special medicine-compounding room whence the medicine is issued. We take the medicine that is to be administered and steam it into a vapor; it is then vented into the chamber via a vapor duct. As the patient breathes and takes in the medicinal vapor, his illness is cured. Thus, the patient never has to 'take' medicine—except in cases where the illness is situated within the digestive tract itself, in which case a patient may occasionally be instructed to take medicine orally."

"And what means do you have for healing external ailments or wounds?" Baoyu asked.

"External ailments are treatable with washing and application of salves. As for healing wounds, we Chinese have long had an ancient recipe for very effective medicine that regrows muscle, reknits bone, and eases pain. Recently, we have even made some improvements to it. We are not like those cruel barbarians who, seeing that a man has partially severed a hand or a foot, and knowing that they have no way to save it, simply amputate it. The patient has already suffered so much, yet they put him through a second round of suffering, and the result? Not the healing of the limb, but instead the patient's permanent disability. That such a cruel and unfeeling person should still call himself a doctor is bizarre, indeed! And others even admire his 'civilization'—isn't that even more strange? Moreover, traumatic wounds can be unpredictable, so in treating them one must not only have adequate equipment, but must also use nuanced, sophisticated techniques. One must also be able to think quickly and alter one's approach to fit the circumstances—only then can one successfully treat traumatic wounds. How can a mere paper diploma guarantee all of this?"

Baoyu replied, "Western doctors all place great emphasis on the brain—do you also possess a brain-examining lens?"

Chaohe answered, "All of the lenses you saw just now were holistic lenses—they examine the entire body. But we do also have more targeted, specialized lenses. Why should we limit ourselves to just examining the brain? We also have lenses that examine the ears, eyes, nose, tongue, and each of the internal organs. But that all takes place in another room: when performing targeted examinations, certain patients will need to sit, while others will need to lie down. As a result, it wouldn't be very convenient to perform those examinations in the same room. But we can go over and take a look."

Baoyu wished to follow him at once, but Lao Shaonian interrupted, "We've already tarried here for too long! If we were to go on to see those rooms as well, we would end up staying quite a bit longer. We do still have an appointment to go see the Naval Academy today—we can come back here another time. For now, let us just take a quick trip through the medicinal garden. I do so like to smell the fragrance of all of the herbs."

Chaohe did not insist and agreed, "Yes, it would be fine to come back on another day."

And so, he led the two men out of the examination room and around to the back, where they exited through a moon gate emblazoned with the words "Medicinal Garden." Upon entering they could see that the grounds were filled with a range of interesting flowers and unique grasses. There were also old trees reaching up into the heavens and tiny shoots growing along trellises. There were plants with intertwining branches and winding tendrils of vine. Everywhere one looked the garden was ablaze with splendid color; one couldn't quite take it all in.

As they walked past an iron pen, Lao Shaonian pointed to it and explained to Baoyu, "That's where they raise the various animals that are used in the concoction of medicine." They had taken another few steps when they encountered an enormous bird cage surrounded with mesh made of iron wire; this was there the birds with medicinal uses were raised. Beside the cage was a large pond, where the aquatic creatures with medicinal uses were raised.

Baoyu sighed in admiration. "There's nothing you haven't provided for. But I wonder: do you grow the full complement of necessary plants here?"

"Those plants that are out of season are grown in the four seasonal gardens instead," explained Chaohe. "Here we primarily grow fresh herbs for the purpose of extracting from them their extraordinarily potent fresh flavor."

"Western medicine focuses only on efficacy, but not on taste. Why is that?"

Chaohe replied, "This is a mistake that they persist in making. Since they pay no attention to the usefulness of flavor, how could they understand, for example, that sour things serve to open the digestive tract?"

As they were speaking, they had managed to wend their way through the whole garden and back to the front of the hospital. Baoyu and Lao Shaonian then took their leave of Chaohe and departed. Lao Shaonian smiled, "It's already noon, let's go have some lunch." They proceeded to a restaurant, chatting all the while, and chose seats. A serving boy immediately emerged to wait on them. Lao Shaonian announced, "Lunch for two guests from Hotel No. 1." The boy nodded in agreement and went off. A short while later he began delivering dishes to the table, one after another. When they had finished their meal, they rinsed their faces; Lao Shaonian then paid two hundred cash, and they departed.

"Since the food here has been refined to be so exceptional, how is it that it's so inexpensive?"

"The things we ate here were rightfully ours, since they were produced in our central kitchen; we just imposed upon the staff here to phone over to the central kitchen and have our order sent here. The two hundred cash were just to compensate them for the effort they put into their service."

Only then did Baoyu understand. "If it's as you say, then they have only opened this restaurant in the hopes of earning a little money here and there based on their service."

"Actually, this restaurant is more like a branch location of the central kitchen. One was built every three to five li throughout the Realm, for the convenience of diners."

"That really is extremely convenient," agreed Baoyu.

At this point Lao Shaonian indicated that he wished to hire a vehicle to take them to their next destination.

"It would be better to walk," argued Baoyu. "That way we can take in the scenery on the way."

"We are currently in the western part of this district; the Naval Academy is situated right on the sea, which is on the eastern side. It's a hundred li between here and there—how could we possibly walk that far?"

Baoyu was startled by this. "If that's true, then not even a carriage will get us there in time."

"It's only just half-past noon. There's plenty of time." Lao Shaonian proceeded to a rental company and arranged to hire a flying car. The two men then seated themselves in the vehicle. The pilot started it up, and the car quickly rose into the sky, delighting Baoyu to the point of speechlessness.

■ ■ ■

If you wish to know how long it took them to reach their destination, please listen to the explanation in the following chapter.

Chapter Twenty-Five

Burrowing through the belly of a whale, a warship exercises vigorous force

In testing electronic weaponry, strange lights are emitted across the ocean's surface

WE WERE speaking of the flying car, whose form had originally been inspired by that of a bird, rather than relying on the use of wheels. In the early stages of development, flying cars had been outfitted with two wings, one on either side of the chassis. The motor was located within the body of the car and ran on electricity. The two wings would then carry the car up into the wind, allowing it to glide about freely. Later on it was determined that the outstretched wings made the cars too wide, which might lead to accidents or collisions. The form of the car was then improved by expert scientists, so that the two wings could be done away with. Instead a vertical propulsion drive rotor was now fitted to the top of the car, and at the rear, forward and reverse propellers.[1] The car was additionally outfitted with spring-loaded mechanisms on all other external surfaces, so that in the event that two cars should collide, they would simply brush past each other, obviating any concerns about accidents. The passengers could thus ride in safety and stability.

As their flying car was climbing into the sky, Baoyu was both startled and delighted. "I once read a novel called *Flowers in the Mirror*, in which the Zhourao people were able to manufacture flying cars.[2] I thought it was only aspirational, something that could be imagined but never put into practice. Who would have guessed that it would be a reality today! I wonder: is it like train service, where a private company has cars running according to a set schedule?"

Lao Shaonian replied, "We don't have such barbaric practices here. People leave their homes at all different times, rather than according to a set schedule—they want to leave whenever they decide to leave. If a car leaves only at only a specific time, that means it will depart even when people haven't yet left their homes; or perhaps something comes up suddenly and someone has to go out unexpectedly—the car might already have left, and they might have to wait ages for another to depart! Think about it: How could such a method possibly be convenient for travelers? That's why the flying cars here can be hired at any time—and one can even choose a large car or a small one, depending upon his need."

"How far can one travel in a day?"

"A fast car can travel six hundred li per hour. Right now, we're in a slow car, which can travel at only four hundred li per hour. We should be able to travel the hundred li to the Naval Academy in about fifteen minutes."

As they were speaking, the car had already begun to move forward through the sky. Baoyu, sitting beside a glass window, looked out and watched the scenery as it passed by. He saw numerous other flying cars, of a variety of different sizes, passing to and fro, flying as freely as birds across the vast sky. He was so enraptured he could hardly sit still. He declared, "This is a creation the likes of which has never been seen before, nor shall ever be seen again!"

"It is fine to say that its like has never been seen before; but I dare not claim that none will come after it. Even now, they are researching ways to improve upon and refine it. After we've seen the Naval Academy today, tomorrow we'll go exploring elsewhere and take a hunting car. That way we can have some fun hunting as we travel along."

Baoyu was greatly surprised. "One can hunt in the sky?"

"In this area there are very few birds to hunt; but in the Courageous Region and Resolute Region to the west there are a great many hawks and falcons."

"Your foodstuffs have already been refined, so what use have you for hunting fowl?"

"What makes you think we necessarily want them for eating? One goes hunting merely for the sport of it, that's all. Of the birds that we catch, we select those that can be used medicinally and send them to the hospital; those that can be turned into food, we send to the central kitchen. What would we do with them ourselves?"

As they continued talking, the flying car gradually began to lose altitude. A short while later, they had alighted on the ground. When the car landed there wasn't even the slightest jolting or jostling—rather, it seemed as though the car had been silently affixed to the ground. As the two men climbed out of the car, they saw that they were already outside the main entryway of the Naval Academy—an imposing structure with carved walls, magnificent to behold. Lao Shaonian entered to present his calling card to the gatekeeper. Seeing that these men had made an appointment to meet with the superintendent, the gatekeeper invited them inside to sit in the superintendent's reception room. Only then did he take the calling card and go into the superintendent's office. They sat for a little while before the superintendent came out to greet them. The superintendent's surname was Wu, his courtesy name Shuqi. Lao Shaonian once again made introductions. Once the men had finished their salutations, Lao Shaonian requested that Shuqi lead them into the academy so that they might admire the facilities.

Shuqi then led them on a route past the students' barracks and through the mess hall before eventually arriving at a lecture hall. Outside the lecture hall were the training grounds, so massive that they could not be viewed in their entirety in a single glance. Baoyu took a short stroll across the grounds and, observing just how enormous they were, repeatedly sighed in admiration. Shuqi then led the men to the instructors' guest-reception room so that they might meet with Sun Shengwu, the dean. Shengwu knew that the guests had come especially to tour the academy and was very pleased. He said, "Have you seen the whole place yet?"

"Yes, we have," replied Lao Shaonian.

"The lecture doesn't start until two o'clock," Shengwu went on. "In the lecture hall, we have erected a special seating area for guest auditors; would you be so kind as to sit there and join us?"

"The guest seats are too close to the dais," answered Lao Shaonian. "We'd like to sit a bit further away, as we've come not only to hear the lecture, but also to learn about your listening aids."

"That's easy enough!" As he said this, Shengwu pressed a bell to summon someone. A moment later someone did indeed come. Shengwu told him, "Go tell whoever's on duty in the lecture hall that a block of seats near the door is to be reserved for guest seating; the first-year students who usually sit by the door are to sit in the seats normally reserved for guests instead." The man assented and left.

Lao Shaonian spoke up. "Why go to the effort of moving the students around?"

"The seats in the lecture hall are all assigned. The academy has fifty thousand students, and the hall has exactly fifty thousand seats. If we don't tell the students to move their seats, wouldn't we have to rudely leave our guests to stand?"

They continued chatting for a while, then heard the *dang dang dang* of a bell being rung outside. It rang for some time before quieting. Shengwu then produced two listening aids and offered them to the two guests, saying, "The students will all be in the lecture hall now, let's go in."

Lao Shaonian showed Baoyu how to use the listening aid, after which the group of four men made their way into the lecture hall. The master of ceremonies rang an iron bell three times, and on cue the students all rose to stand as a single body. Shengwu took his leave of the others and proceeded directly to the dais at the front of the lecture hall.

Shuqi sat with the two guests in a row of chairs beside the exit. The lecture hall was, of course, broad and deep. The entire room was densely packed with people, and yet nary a peep was heard. Baoyu inserted the listening aid into his ear as instructed just as Shengwu began his lecture. Baoyu could hear him just as clearly as if Shengwu were seated beside him, and he couldn't help but be amazed. As Shengwu lectured on the navy's offensive and defensive strategies, Baoyu couldn't quite understand what he was saying; but when Shengwu expounded upon the topic of specialized learning, into which he injected a good deal of talk of "preserving the national character" and discourses on "unity and patriotism," Baoyu found it quite inspiring. Shengwu lectured from two o'clock until three, and only then did he descend from the dais and come to make his apologies to Baoyu. The students once again rose together, lined up according to class, and left the hall.

"Now they're off to the coast for drills," explained Shengwu. "You can go watch if you'd like."

Baoyu was pleased, and said, "Wonderful, this is such a rare opportunity! But how far it is from here to the coast?"

"It's in the No. 110 District of the Strong Region, only fifty li from here. A flying car will get us there in no time." So saying, he led them back out to the training ground.

There they saw countless flying cars parked in neat rows, into which the assembled students were piling. Shengwu then prompted Baoyu and Lao Shaonian to climb into one as well; Shengwu himself and Shuqi then followed them in. This car was naturally vastly different from the one that Lao Shaonian had hired to bring them here: there was no roof on it, and there were railings around all four sides. Standing upright in the center of the car was the vertical propulsion drive rotor, which looked much like the screw blades on a steamship. To one side there stood a flagpole, and this too was surrounded by railings on all sides. The car could accommodate upward of twenty or thirty people.

"What happens when it rains?" Baoyu asked.

"There's a canopy for when it rains, of course," replied Lao Shaonian.

Seeing that all of the students had since mounted their cars, Shengwu declared that the order to take flight should be given. A crewman immediately hoisted a green command flag up the flagpole. Rotors whirling fast as the wind itself, the innumerable flying cars rose into the sky in unison. Once the cars had reached their desired altitude the rotors ceased spinning. The massive fleet of flying cars then set out for the east.

Baoyu watched the fleet of cars arrayed before him: although they were flying through the air, they had still maintained their neat, orderly ranks as on the ground. He approached one of the railings and looked out toward the ground below. The mountains, rivers, and trees beneath his feet rushed past as swiftly as flowing water. Baoyu laughed. "In fiction, when people speak of 'mounting the clouds and riding the mists,' they must have been thinking of something just like this."

Shuqi answered, "When these cars were first created, it was precisely because the ancients had had such ideas that we began to think about ways to test them out. It's ridiculous to think that those Europeans and Americans could only come up with hot-air balloons—which are both clumsy and dangerous—and yet they still brag about it as a great achievement. How could their balloons achieve this kind of stability and agility? Even when fiction spoke of 'mounting the clouds and riding the mists,' it only ever referred to the ability of an individual; in truly 'miraculous' cases one might carry a mere one or two people under his arms! How can that compare to something like this which can be shared with everyone?"

As they chatted, the rotor started up once again, and the car slowly descended and came to a stop on the ground. Raising his eyes to look out, Baoyu could see that they had landed atop a coastal mountain looking out over the sea, while the students had landed on the level ground at the foot of the mountain and were disembarking. Upon the mountaintop there was a martial arts training hall. The four men climbed out of the car and, each insisting that the others go before him, made their way into the hall. As it happened, this hall had been constructed at the top of a steep precipice. In front of the hall, toward the cliff's edge, a flat empty area had been chiseled out of the rock, and this area was then enclosed by railings on three sides. Two signal cannons had been installed, one at either side; between these stood a flagpole. Within the hall itself a reviewing dais had been erected. Shuqi and Shengwu made their apologies to the others, and each took a seat upon the dais, while Baoyu and Lao Shaonian stood in the flat area in front of the hall and looked out over the vista. The ocean, its surface as smooth as a mirror, seemed to stretch out endlessly. Along the coast, waves of students had already boarded sampans and waited in readiness for the next command to be given. Suddenly the boom of a cannon was heard, and a command flag was raised on the pole in front of the hall. However, the students in the sampans remained motionless. Baoyu wondered to himself: "Why aren't they following the command?"

How could he have anticipated that in the blink of an eye, a countless number of vessels would rise to the surface of the water? Lao Shaonian pointed them out to Baoyu and explained, "Those are this district's defensive warships."

"But where did they come from? How did they manage to emerge simultaneously all at once? How many are there altogether?" Baoyu was full of questions.

"There are a thousand altogether. They are normally lying in readiness on the ocean floor."

"But they don't have any air pipes that run up to the water's surface—so how do they have enough air to survive on board?"

"Without air, it's not just a question of whether the men would survive—the ships wouldn't be able to rise to the surface, either. The ships each possess an electric machine that simultaneously creates fresh air and filters out carbon dioxide."

"So even air can be created! Will wonders never cease! But I wonder—just how big are these ships?"

"When barbarians build military ships, they're always concerned about how big they can make them. Those out there certainly aren't very big—they are each fifty feet in length, and each is crafted out of a single piece of iron. With the exception of the hatch, the windows, and the doorways, there is not a single seam or join in any of them."

Baoyu watched the ships intently. They were shaped like olives, lacking even masts and smokestacks. The students now set out en masse in the sampans, and upon reaching the ships they went aboard. At this time, the command flag in front of the hall was changed, and the entire fleet of ships began moving out across the ocean.

At this point Shengwu and Shuqi stepped down from the platform and joined the others outside, handing a pair of eyeglasses each to Baoyu and Lao Shaonian. "What kind of lenses are these?" Baoyu asked.

"Everyone calls them 'Thousand-li lenses' or 'telescopes,'" said Shengwu. "They were invented by Ms. Dongfang Mei. Their real name is 'clarity-aiding lenses.' "

As Baoyu looked them over, he observed that the inner face of the lens was only about as big as the tip of a finger, while the outer face was the size of a copper coin. Obviously, there were two separate glass lenses, each only a little more than a quarter of an inch thick. When Baoyu donned the glasses he could see the ships out on the sea as clearly as if they were immediately before him. He could also see a small deserted island some way out in the distance. When the first wave of ten ships approached the island, they fanned out in front of it, with each of their prows pointing toward the island. Baoyu saw that each of the ships fired something—something dazzlingly white—at the island before submerging. When the second wave of ten ships neared, they followed suit.

"They're firing silent electronic cannons," explained Shengwu. "Today, they are being drilled on target practice."

"But I didn't see any cannons mounted on the ships," said Baoyu. "Where were they being fired from?"

"These ships are different from those of the Europeans and Americans. One ship has only two cannons, one at the bow and one at the stern. But the body of the ship itself serves as the bore of the cannon. At each end, where the ship comes to a point, is the muzzle of the cannon. So while one may call those things out there 'ships,' it would not necessarily be unreasonable to call them 'cannons' as well."

"If it's as you say, then the cannons are fired from *inside* the ships themselves. But then how can they see to take aim?"

"Each ship is outfitted with a metal-penetrating lens that allows the men to see through the hull. When they look through the lens, it's as if there is no barrier between themselves and the outside."

As they were speaking, attendants came and set up a tripod at each side of the enclosure. Mounted upon these tripods were three-foot-long single-barrel telescopes. Shengwu gave instructions that two more of these should be set up; the attendants assented, and soon each of the four men had his own telescope.

"These are water-penetrating lenses," said Shengwu. "If you look through them you can see the bottom of the ocean, even from here!"

Baoyu sighed with wonder. "It's no use calling these things 'marvelous' or 'divine' anymore! I'm afraid that even immortals and demons would be overawed by the science of your Realm!"

Shengwu replied, "Unfortunately, this lens has not yet been fully perfected. It would be even better if it could be worn over the eyes like the clarity-aiding lenses."

Baoyu removed his pair of clarity-aiding lenses and took a look through the water-penetrating lens.

"You might as well keep the clarity-aiding lenses on at the same time," Lao Shaonian advised him. "Then you'll be able to see under the water and at great distance simultaneously."

Baoyu did as Lao Shaonian recommended and put the glasses back on. It was as he had been told: he could see the bottom of the ocean as clearly as if it were directly beneath his own feet. Looking closely, he saw that the entire ocean floor was made up of craggy outcroppings littered with stones, upon which lived a great many shellfish and sea snails. By now the first wave of warships had already returned to the shore and come to rest there. Baoyu could only stare in dumbfounded amazement as wave upon wave of ships—six of them already—returned from the island.

Suddenly he saw a massive whale, more than double the size of the warships, crossing the ocean toward the fleet. At that moment the seventh wave of ships was in the process of returning, and the whale was now blocking their return path. One of the ships proceeded straight ahead, striking the whale directly in its belly. Another ship then made its way around the whale's head, while still another passed around the whale's tail. Baoyu became very anxious for the one ship at the whale's belly, which he thought to be in danger: for who would have expected that upon being struck the whale would start thrashing about? However, the ship continued on as if nothing had changed and continued driving itself into the whale's stomach, eventually piercing through the side of the animal. The ocean's surface had grown rough with waves, but beneath the surface the ship continued on placidly in its task. Baoyu was stunned by all this. Suddenly, he saw the ship's bow poking through the opposite side of the whale's stomach—it had already successfully bored a path *through* the whale! After a little while longer, the entire ship emerged from the hole and made its way back to the other ships. The whale gave a shudder, then floated to the surface. Baoyu was extremely impressed. Lao Shaonian laughed and said, "Perhaps it's also one of those hunting ships—it made such easy work of its prey!"

By now, target practice had ended, and the ships had all returned. It was already rather late in the day. Shuqi and

Shengwu invited them to stay in the mountaintop training hall to take their dinner. They said, "We might as well watch them practice with their electric lights before leaving." Then, they gave the order that dinner be served. The four men sat together to eat, and when they had finished, sat a bit more casually.

A little while later, a bright moon rose in the east. Baoyu asked, "With such bright moonlight, how will they test electric lights?"

Shengwu replied, "A bright moonlit night is the best time to test them out—only then is it possible to see just how powerful the lights are!"

They waited until 9:00 p.m., at which time they let off three successive shots from the signal cannons. Before the echoes and reverberations from the surrounding mountains and valleys had ceased, they suddenly saw before them on the surface of the ocean myriad streams of electric light, illuminating the scene so that it was as bright as day. As they looked down more closely, they could even make out the brow and mustache hairs of the crew manning the sampans. Baoyu hurriedly looked through the water-penetrating lens and saw that the entire body of each of the warships was glowing, as if each were a ball of white flame. Raising his head to look at the moon, he noticed that in the presence of these bright white electric lights the moonlight had been reduced to a dusky red color. Baoyu involuntarily shook his head and sighed with admiration.

■ ■ ■

If you wish to know what events followed, please listen to the explanation in the following chapter.

Chapter Twenty-Six

Host and guest have a leisurely lamplit conversation about forms of governance

Riding in a hunting car, mankind does battle with giant bird

WE HAD been speaking of how Baoyu, looking through the water-penetrating lens, had watched the entire fleet of warships, each giving off such a brilliant light from the length of its entire body that the ocean was filled with white light and the moon, by contrast, appeared a dim red in the sky. He was sighing in appreciation when suddenly, in the blink of an eye, the white light that filled the ocean turned a brilliant red, like ten thousand gleaming sunset rays—truly a captivating sight to behold. Baoyu was startled and was just about to ask the meaning of it when suddenly the red light turned to green, making the ocean's water look like that of Lake Taihu. Just as suddenly the green light gave way to yellow, and at once ten thousand rays of golden radiance gleamed upon the ocean's surface. This, too, then unexpectedly gave way to a multicolored array of lights all appearing simultaneously, glimmering and changing color so quickly that it made the observer feel a bit dizzy. Suddenly,

Baoyu noticed that the fleet had divided itself into five flotillas, each of which was giving off one of five colors of light. The flotillas were moving around one another, gliding back and forth, advancing and retreating. By now, the light they gave off was so overwhelming that the moon appeared dark and colorless. The gleaming flotillas circled round one another for some time, when all of a sudden, all of their lights, in unison, went dark. Looking out, it was now as though one were enveloped in inky blackness. Only after the lights had been out for some little while did one gradually begin to see the glow of the moon once again.

Soon another signal cannon was fired and all of the ships, still underwater, surfaced simultaneously; each ship had electric lights installed at the bow and at each side of the hull. In the mountaintop training hall, Shengwu's attendants took out two electric lamps and waved them in the air. Upon this signal, the captains of the sampans sailed out together to the warships. In droves, the students debarked from the warships and climbed into the sampans, which then carried them back to shore.

At Shengwu's suggestion, the party got back into their flying car. The car's electric light, situated on the flagpole, was already gleaming brightly. The rotor of the party's car began whirling and the vehicle rose into the sky, then stopped and hovered in place. They watched as the students' cars once again rose into the sky in unison; only then did the party depart. The lights on the students' cars were like ten thousand twinkling stars. Baoyu sighed. "Today, I have witnessed one of the finest spectacles this world has to offer! But I am curious: the multicolored lights that the ships were projecting—what is their function?"

"The white light is used for exploring the ocean. The multicolored lights are used for signaling," explained Shengwu.

"And what do they use for signaling during the daytime?"

"It's very dark under the ocean's surface, so they still use the lights. When they are on the surface, they erect iron flagpoles and send signals using flags. But of course, if they need to communicate in more detail, they use wireless telephones."

"I've only heard of wireless telegraphs," Baoyu pressed him. "I wouldn't have expected that they could also make wireless telephones! But I've heard that when a wireless telegraph machine transmits a message, that message can be picked up by any other machine—no matter where—so long as it can receive the electromagnetic signals created by the first. So with wireless telegraphs, one must use secret codes to prevent the leaking of messages. When you use a wireless telephone, aren't you afraid that your conversations will be picked up by others?"

Shengwu smiled. "The wireless telegraph depends on such codes because they haven't yet perfected the technology of wireless transmission. But we *have* perfected it, so our messages go directly to their intended recipient. The bells we use to summon people, for example, are simply wireless electric bells." Only then did Baoyu understand why that summoning bell in his room had made no sound when pressed yet had still successfully summoned someone.

As they spoke, the flying car carried them back to the Naval Academy and landed once again upon the training grounds. Because it was already three-quarters past midnight, Shuqi insisted that his two guests stay the night and arranged for sleeping quarters for them, outfitted simply with light summer bedding. Baoyu was concerned that Shuqi must have other matters to which to attend, and so he encouraged Lao Shaonian to retire with him to the sleeping quarters.

Once inside, Baoyu asked Lao Shaonian, "These flying cars can truly be called miracles of high-speed travel! But that's only one side of it. Supposing a thief were to ride in a flying car, drop out of the sky, steal things, then flee back into the heavens? How ever could one ever hope to apprehend him? But I suppose that the bailiffs here must also have marvelous techniques of their own."

"Not only do our bailiffs not possess any marvelous techniques—why, we haven't even got a single bailiff! If you hadn't brought it up, I would have forgotten that title altogether."

"What is the reason for that?"

"For nearly fifty years in our Realm the people have been healthy and there is no scarcity. 'At night, no one locks their doors,' and 'no one keeps for themselves items lost by others along the roadside.'[1] This means that some time ago we did away with two things in our Realm: the first is that when we compiled a 'civilized dictionary,' we omitted such words as 'bandit,' 'schemer,' and 'thief.' The other is that the *yamen* of the Bureau of Punishments in the capital, and all the way down to the various district-level correctional and police officials, have all been abolished. The former *yamen* buildings have been converted into storehouses. If even the *yamen* have been done away with, how could we possibly still have bailiffs?"

Baoyu sighed. "'And the courtyards of the halls of justice shall with grasses o'ergrow,'" he quoted. "That was already a noble aspiration. That you have done away with the correctional *yamen* shows that your advanced system of governance is unparalleled throughout the ages. But I wonder—how is your system of government structured?"

"There are currently three forms of government in the world: authoritarianism, constitutionalism, and republicanism.[2] Currently there are debates about these forms all over the world. There are those who support constitutionalism, and those who support republicanism; and while no one advocates for authoritarianism, that is the very form that we have chosen in our humble Realm. Our current way of thinking is that republicanism is the most barbaric form of government, since the government is divided among an infinite number of parties, all in conflict with one another. Such a government is like a ghost without a body—whichever party happens to thrive controls the administration of the country. But should the fortunes of that party ever wane, the direction of the government changes with it. It's like a faithless wife taking a new husband—ridiculous! Constitutional governments also can't avoid having parties. And although they have established upper and lower chambers, the restrictions they have placed on voting rights and eligibility to run for office mean that they have merely changed what was a government of the hereditary aristocracy into a government of the wealthy. The common people protested that the wealthy were growing wealthier and the poor growing poorer. And so they formed a new party that seeks equality between the classes, and this they call 'socialism.' Ultimately, this is not a state of affairs that can remain at peace for very long. If you don't believe me, you just watch—there will come a day when it all collapses.

"We once believed ourselves that authoritarianism was no good and so reformed our government into a constitutional one. At that time a great hero emerged in the Realm. His surname was Wan, his given name Lü, and his style-name Zhouxiang. He issued a law requiring compulsory education. Out of the entire governmental infrastructure of the country, education was the only thing he cared about. And in the field of education, he cared most about 'moral education.'"

Baoyu clapped his hands. "So *that's* how you achieved a state where 'at night, no one locks their doors' and 'no one keeps for themselves items lost by others along the roadside.'"

"Mr. Wan oversaw the educational system for over fifty years before he passed away. In his final moments, the last words he spoke were: 'If moral education is widespread, then the constitution can be dissolved.' It was not many years later that we started to hear of the wave of 'egalitarian' parties sweeping other countries. Our citizenry convened two large meetings to discuss and look into this issue. They all agreed that government by the wealthy was at the root of the problem. And so all members of parliament relinquished to the emperor the power to govern, and we returned once again to having an authoritarian government."

Baoyu asked, "But how can an authoritarian government actually be good? I truly do not understand this."

"Looking at it from outside, it seems difficult to understand; but in fact, it is extremely simple to grasp. The emperor and the officials under him have merely put into practice two sentences from *The Great Learning*, and that has been sufficient."

"Though *The Great Learning* is a text on governance and pacification, how could its wisdom possibly be completely encompassed in only two of its sentences? Indeed, I must ask your instruction on which two sentences they were."

Lao Shaonian quoted: "That which the people cherish, you must cherish; that which the people revile, you must revile."

Baoyu thought for a moment, then laughed. "As you said, it is just two sentences, yet they contain everything that matters! As long as the officials and the emperor take those two sentences to heart and put them into practice, then all will be well."

"That is why it is necessary to speak of widespread moral education! What official doesn't emerge from among the common people? If he received moral education while he was still a commoner, then when he becomes an official, how could he govern with poor principles? When the commoners have such a good government, they are peaceful in their lives and content in their work, and everyone is free to pursue his own specialized field of learning. What need is there for the bother of having people constantly rushing off to parliament to debate things?"

"So as it turns out, authoritarianism has such benefits as these!"

"Of course, it's not a one-size-fits-all sort of thing. Those countries that don't have moral education, where violent and corrupt officials are widespread throughout, must instead strive to establish a constitution."

"But it's hard to say what might happen if they don't have moral education," replied Baoyu, sighing. "After establishing a constitution, they may not even reach the point of government by the wealthy and may simply be left with a government of evil officials. How many of them would take advantage of having earned the tiniest bit of merit to then visit their vicious tyrannical tendencies upon the entire area under their domain? Their sole area of expertise is petty disputation and abusing villagers the sole object of their study. If a constitution were established, and this kind of person were elected to serve as an official, I'm afraid it would be even worse than the most barbarous version of authoritarianism."

"That is indeed a deeper level of consideration. But it does seem to be the case that when a country has not yet reached civilization, a constitution is a slight improvement over authoritarianism. Although there may be evil officials in some places, it's not necessarily the case that all officials will be evil. And since the parliament is composed of more than a single person, it is to be hoped that it will at least create benefit and detriment in equal measure, and that it will gradually improve itself over time. As for authoritarianism, there is but a single government, reigning above all on high, weightily oppressing those beneath it. Though local officials may wish to be upstanding, they are unable to do so. That is why barbaric forms of authoritarianism bring a hundred detriments without even a single benefit; while civilized authoritarianism brings a hundred benefits and not a single detriment. Yet if you were to discuss this sort of thing with the half-civilized, you could talk yourself to death and they still wouldn't believe you!"

"Just now I heard Dean Sun say that the whole body of the warships is the barrel of a cannon and that there are muzzles at both ends of the ship. Can you please explain something? When the ship submerges itself, don't the muzzles fill with water?

"This kind of electronic gun is extremely responsive. When a shell is fired, another is instantly loaded into the barrel behind it and moved to the muzzle. This second shell serves to block up the muzzle so no water can get in."

"Does that mean that they can even fire shells when the ship is underwater?"

"Of course they can! Otherwise what would be the point of hiding themselves underwater?"

"I have already seen the tools of naval warfare, but regrettably, I have yet to see a single artillery emplacement."

"There are no artillery emplacements here! They are clumsy, useless things. Other people still believe that they are beneficial to the guarding of ports, but here even small children laugh as soon as you mention them! Wouldn't you say that those warships were more powerful than any artillery emplacement?"

"I wonder: where is the military academy?"

"There is one each in the Eastern Sector and Northern Sector."

"Given that your honorable Realm has been divided into five sectors, why is it that only these two sectors possess military academies? Doesn't that create an imbalance, with the army all concentrated in these sectors?"

"In our Realm, only the naval defenses near the sea make use of the navy, and only the territorial defenses near our land borders make use of the army. Not a single soldier is deployed within our borders."

"What is the reason for that?" asked Baoyu.

"Wouldn't the only purpose of deploying soldiers within the Realm be to defend against our own people? You must know that the adage 'drilling the soldiers in public to deter would-be thieves' is something only animals living in barbarism would say. Anyone with even the slightest bit of humanity would be unwilling to say such a thing. Besides, there is not even a single petty swindler in our Realm, so why should we need to defend ourselves against robbers or renegades?"

It was already the fifth month and the nights were short, so as the men chatted, dawn snuck up on them. Someone came in to wait upon them, helping them get washed up and change their clothes. Shuqi had also gotten up, and invited Sun Shengwu to come have breakfast. Lao Shaonian indicated that he wished to take his leave.

"Where are you going?" Shuqi inquired.

"Nowhere in particular. My plan is simply to accompany Mr. Jia to do a bit of exploring here and there. I thought we might as well hire a hunting car so we can do some hunting as we fly, for bit of fun."

"Why hire one?" replied Shengwu. "We have here one of the newest models, sent over by Miss Dongfang Mei just last month. I have been preoccupied with official business since then, so have not yet had the opportunity to take it out. This car doesn't even need a driver—you just take a seat and operate it yourself. The ignition and controls are all in the passenger area, and the controls come with instructions that explain their function and use. Additionally, all of the necessary hunting equipment is already loaded on board. I would be glad to allow you to borrow it."

Lao Shaonian was greatly pleased and thanked his host.

Shengwu then led his two guests to the training ground, where they saw a hunting car quite dissimilar to the two cars they had ridden in previously. The bottom level was flat like a table, with four table legs protruding from underneath. The rotor and propellers were all situated beneath this "table." The motor was located in the rear half of the middle level, while the front half of this level was an enclosed space for the holding of birds captured on the hunt. On the front wall of this enclosed space was a small round door, behind which there was a mechanism that ensured that any birds that entered through the door could not escape back out through it. The top level was surrounded on all four sides with railings—this was where the travelers were to sit. The front half was open, while a small cabin housing all of the car's operational apparatuses stood to the rear. Tables, chairs, and benches had been neatly laid out in this cabin, and upon the walls hung four electronic guns. In the drawers they found bullets, clarity-aiding lenses, and other supplies—anything they might need had been completely provided for. A roll of some kind of gleaming material, which even Lao Shaonian did not recognize, had been installed upon the front railing of this level. Shengwu explained: "This is a protective soft glass barrier created by Hua Zili. If we unfurl it and cover the ship with it, nothing outside the ship can see in, while those on the inside can still see everything outside quite clearly." Baoyu found this marvelous, indeed. Shengwu then instructed a servant to unfurl the glass. The top of the car was already outfitted with a frame; the servant then used a rope to hoist the soft glass to cover the frame. Half of the glass was now hanging over the front, and Baoyu saw, as he looked through the glass, his view of the outside was still very clear. He then hurried out of the car and around to the front to look, and found that it was indeed as though the entire car had vanished! All he could see was an expanse of crystalline blue, just like the sky itself. The only part of the car that was still visible was the small round door for the collection of birds: this was because when the sheet of glass was manufactured, a hole had been left intentionally so that the door would still be accessible.

"The glass can even change color!" Shengwu called out. "Right now, the weather is fine, so it's a crystalline blue. But when the weather is poor, it turns a dark, cloudy color. It is constantly changing to stay in keeping with the weather. Last month when Miss Dongfang Mei came to deliver the car, she went off to inquire as to the dimensions of our warships—I hear she wants to fabricate some glass barriers for them, to submit to the government for testing and eventual purchase." Having said this, he escorted his two guests into the car.

When Baoyu and Lao Shaonian were seated in the car, each respectfully clasped his hands together as a parting gesture to their hosts. Lao Shaonian then entered the cabin and activated the vertical propulsion drive, causing the car to rise up into the air. Using the compass to navigate, Lao Shaonian brought them to a landing in front of a hotel, where he instructed one of the serving boys employed there to go help him purchase a great many cans of food. He also made an appeal to the manager of the hotel, requesting to borrow two of his older serving boys to accompany himself and Baoyu on the journey. Once they had everything they needed onboard, he said to Baoyu, "I have already purchased food enough to last us over a fortnight. Let's go spend a few days in the skies!" Saying this, he brought the car once again into the air and steered them off toward the east. He instructed one of the serving boys to open a can of food, and lunch was served on board.

When they reached the Courageous Region, Lao Shaonian selected a thickly wooded area in which to put down. When they were a mere forty or fifty feet from the ground, a startling confusion of birdsong was suddenly emitted from within the car. Baoyu thought this very peculiar, and when he hurried to take a look he saw that Lao Shaonian had turned on some kind of mechanism that was labeled "Bird-Luring Machine." Lao Shaonian explained, "I'm as surprised as you are! I saw the label and thought I would turn it on to see what it did. I didn't expect that all of these noises would come out. Where are they coming from?" The two men then began searching all over the car for the source of the birdcalls. As they were peering out over the sides, they suddenly heard thudding sounds from somewhere around the middle level. Lifting their heads to look to the front of the car, they saw a dozen or so hawks swooping back and forth on either side; but as soon as the birds flew alongside the car, where the glass barrier no longer covered, they could see that there were people inside, and they darted off. The men were about to run back to the cabin to grab guns when they heard the two serving boys call out from the front of the car, "Here comes another one!" When Baoyu and Lao Shaonian rushed to look, they saw a hawk appear in front of the car; the hawk suddenly flew straight at the car, seeming to dash itself against the front of the middle level but then vanishing. Only then did they understand: the sound of birdsong was being emitted through the small round door on the front of the car, so that birds of prey would be lured into hurling themselves right through the small door on their own!

"This type of hunting is certainly comfortable!" commented Baoyu. "What need is there for using guns?"

As he said this, one of the serving boys pointed: "Look! There's another hawk coming from over there."

Lao Shaonian raised his head to look. He saw flying toward them a bird that appeared to be of roughly the same size as the hawks they had just seen; yet it was still far off in the distance, near the horizon. "It's so far away, and yet still appears from here to be the size of a hawk; how could it actually be one?" He and Baoyu hurriedly put on their clarity-aiding lenses and looked again. It was an incomparably large bird, flying from the north toward the south. "Let's shoot it and bring it back with us," said Lao Shaonian. "As you can see, it's flying from the north toward the south—let's intercept its path." He then steered the car off toward the west to meet it.

They were still in pursuit after dinner, and by the time the moon rose it seemed they were close to catching it. At this point they could see that the bird was terrifyingly large. Their hunting car was about twenty-four feet in length and ten feet in width; a single wing of this bird could span four such cars. Lao Shaonian urgently called for the others to take up guns, at which time the four men took up arms together, took aim at the tremendous bird, and fired. Who would have guessed that the bird wouldn't so much as notice the bullets as they struck its body?

"Its feathers are thick," said Baoyu. "I'm afraid we can't penetrate them. Let's aim for its feet—or better still, for its eyes." In less time than it took him to say this, Baoyu had leveled his gun at the bird's talons and fired. The wounded bird gave a great shriek, then turned in its path and began flying toward the car. The four guns were now firing together but were unable to slow it. As it drew closer, they saw that its enormous wings were big enough to blot out the moonlight, which instantly threw the car into darkness. Luckily, the car was equipped with two electric spotlights, so the men were still able to see their target. With a sudden jolt, the car began to pitch to and fro—as it happened, the bird had used its talons to grasp the frame on top of the car. The talons themselves were broader than a man's thigh. The bird craned its head forward to inspect the car, then opened its beak and let out another bizarre cry. The span of its gaping beak was somewhat over ten feet. Baoyu cried out, "Aim for the mouth! Aim for the mouth!" The electronic guns had a hundred bullets per ammunition belt; at this point each of the men loaded a fresh belt and fired at the bird's open mouth, raining bullets upon it.

■ ■ ■

If you wish to know whether man or bird was to be the victor, please listen to the explanation in the following chapter.

Chapter Twenty-Seven

Over Central Africa, they capture the great peng

In the archives, they peruse ancient texts

WE HAD been speaking of how the hunting car had been seized in the great bird's talons. When the bird opened its enormous beak in preparation to peck at the men, they took aim at its mouth and began firing. In this truly perilous moment one of the serving boys managed to strike the bird in the eye. The bird once again gave its strange cry, then loosened its grasp on the car, spread wide its wings, and flew off.

The hunting car pitched wildly, and Lao Shaonian rushed to take control of the helm. Though he was able to bring it back under control, the entire car was listing to one side. When he went to the front of the car to inspect the car's stabilizer, he found that it had been jostled askew when the bird had seized the car. After he hurriedly figured out how to set it aright, the car once again regained its balance.

Baoyu announced, "If that bird manages to give us the slip after we've suffered such a fright and spent seven or eight hundred bullets, it would be a great waste indeed. We have to catch up to it!"

Lao Shaonian glanced at the compass and noted that the car was now flying due north. "When it seized us, it altered our flight path," he remarked. "It's quite a powerful opponent. Luckily all of our machinery is on the deck below, so nothing was damaged." As he raised his head to look out at the retreating bird, he noted that it was still flying southward, so he turned the car in that direction in pursuit. The bird was flying higher and higher in the air, so the car, too, climbed higher as it gave chase. The bird was now four or five li off in the distance; the men pursued it all through the night until the sky began to grow light again but were still unable to catch up to it.

When the sun had been up for some time, they looked at the timekeeping automaton and saw that it was still only 2:30 a.m.

"We obviously must be really high up," remarked Baoyu.

Having seen the sun, Lao Shaonian checked the altimeter, which reported that they had exceeded 3,800 feet in altitude. The two serving boys had long since gone to bed. Baoyu and Lao Shaonian had a quick, light meal, then went back to observing their quarry.

Suddenly Baoyu thought of something. "Even if we were to shoot it, we could never fit it in the car to carry back! We shouldn't waste our efforts."

"Let's shoot it first, then talk about transporting it," said Lao Shaonian. "We can always think of something." He then increased the speed of the car, surging forward in pursuit. They raced along until 7:00 a.m., at which time they noticed that they were closing in on their prey. By now, the two serving boys had roused themselves, and the group once again took up their guns.

"We mustn't waste bullets this time," said Baoyu. "Its feathers are abundant and both thick and slick, so hitting the plumage is no use. You should fire only at its talons."

"That is very reasonable," replied Lao Shaonian. "Let's aim only for its feet." Saying this, he fired off a shot, after which Baoyu and the two serving boys each fired as well. All of them hit their mark. The bird shook its wings as if in great pain, then soared off further into the distance. Donning his clarity-aiding lenses, Baoyu could see that blood was flowing from wounds on the bird's feet.

Lao Shaonian opened up the throttle and chased the bird for another two hours before they were able to close in once again. "This time we must try something else," said Baoyu. "We mustn't keep shooting in vain." He disappeared into the cabin and had a rummage around. In his search he dug up a tiny box upon which were carved characters that read "Hunting Net." When he opened the box to examine its contents, his eyes were dazzled by a brilliant white light. A sheet of white paper had been pasted on the inside of the box's lid. It read: "*This is a platinum thread hunting net; it measures one hundred feet square.*" As he further examined the net, he noted that the platinum threads were as fine as hairs. He handed the net to Lao Shaonian for his appraisal.

Lao Shaonian smiled. "I've got it—after we've shot the bird, we'll transport it in this net. If we hang it off the car, it won't take up any space *in* the car. Isn't that a tidy solution?"

"I was just having a look around," said Baoyu, "to see if we might have something on board that could be used to subdue the bird; I turned this up quite by accident." Saying this, he resumed his search.

He then heard Lao Shaonian cry out, "I've got it! I've got it!" Baoyu quickly turned to look and saw that Lao Shaonian had turned up a small glass bottle, upon which was pasted a paper label reading "Merciless." On the other side was another bit of paper that read: *"Anytime you should encounter a monstrous or uncontrollable beast, apply this Merciless Tonic to the tip of a bullet. Should the bullet find its mark, the beast will be poisoned and die; should the bullet miss, you must recover it, to avoid others' being harmed by it."*

Baoyu laughed. "Then merciless we must be! We have to give it a try. But the note makes it very clear that if we miss we must search for the bullet. If we were to miss, what a lot of effort we'd have to take!"

"Don't worry," replied Lao Shaonian. "We'll get closer to it before we fire on it again. And if we aim for its ankles rather than its talons, that will make it much easier to strike." He then took out four bullets, applied the tonic to each, then exhorted the two serving boys to handle them with extreme caution.

In no time at all the car drew increasingly close to its target and was now within a hundred or so feet. Each man raised his gun and took aim, then all four fired in unison. Fortunately, each of them hit their mark; unfortunately, upon being struck, the great bird gave two cries, then increased its speed and darted off ahead. Lao Shaonian watched it, somewhat dumbstruck: "It's too bad I prepared so few bullets; if we had fired off a few more rounds in succession, I think we might have fared better."

By now it was already noon. Once everyone had had their lunch, they went back out to watch the bird. Though it had started flying more quickly upon first being hit by their bullets, it had now slowed to its normal speed. The men also noticed that the temperature had increased quite suddenly. They continued in their pursuit until evening but were still unable to catch back up to the bird. Lao Shaonian then proposed an arrangement with Baoyu: the two of them would sleep in shifts and would not give up until they had caught the beast. Baoyu agreed.

Their chase continued into the following day, by which time the heat had become unbearable. The men were now only wearing unlined clothes, but still the sweat poured off them like rain. By nightfall, it was so stiflingly hot that they could hardly breathe. The chase wore on, and by early evening on the third day they could see that the bird, still out ahead of them, was beginning to lose altitude. They, too, dropped lower to continue their pursuit. As they drew nearer, they saw the bird suddenly fold back its wings, turn a somersault midair, then start plummeting toward the ground headfirst. Lao Shaonian was delighted by this and hurriedly steered the car toward the ground. Upon landing they found themselves in a vast open desert, stretching out endlessly in all directions. In surprise, Lao Shaonian asked, "Where have we got ourselves to?" Looking up, he then saw that the great bird had fallen at about a distance of one li from where they had landed. It was still flailing and writhing, stirring up great quantities of sand.

"I think the poison must have taken effect," said Baoyu. "Let's wait a little longer for it to die, then we can go collect it." He then loosened his clothes to enjoy the cooling evening air. It was not until quarter past eleven that the bird finally ceased thrashing about. Lao Shaonian located a world map in the cabin, then, glancing up at the stars, consulting the compass, and making a note of where the moon had appeared on the horizon, uttered in surprise, "We've come all the way to Africa. This is one of the most famous deserts in the world. But we'll have to be careful of savages."

"Our guns are already loaded, so there's no need to worry about them. The real question is: How are we going to deal with that great hulk of a thing out there?"

"Let's wait until daylight—we can discuss it then."

■ ■ ■

That evening no one dared sleep; they all stayed awake until the sky grew light once again. Lao Shaonian then hastily took out the platinum thread net, and the four men shook it open. Gathering ropes the thickness of a little finger, made up of strands of platinum thread, ran around the edges of the net. The four men pulled at the net to spread it out across the sand before attempting to move the body of the great bird. They struggled until they were half-covered in sweat but were eventually able to drag the bird onto the net. Then, pulling on the gathering ropes, they drew the net closed, knotted it shut, and tied the ends of each of the ropes to one of the four railings on the flying car. Once the ropes had been secured they boarded the car, and Lao Shaonian started it up, setting the desired altitude on the vertical propulsion drive to one thousand feet. However, they had climbed only about thirty or forty feet when the car stopped rising; the weight of the bird dangling beneath them was preventing them from rising any further. Lao Shaonian increased the drive setting to two thousand feet, but all the same the car did not move. He tried three thousand feet, and still the car hovered in place.

"What can we do?" asked Baoyu.

"We can't just abandon it," replied Lao Shaonian. "For better or for worse, we must bring it back with us so we can present it to the museum." He then continued to increase the power to the drive. It was only when the drive was set to an altitude of eight thousand feet that the car finally began to rise a little—though even so, its movements were slow and awkward. When Lao Shaonian increased the altitude to ten thousand feet, the car finally became somewhat nimbler again. Looking at the compass, he set a northeasterly course. He then glanced at the altimeter and saw that they were only three hundred feet off the ground. After flying for three days and three nights, they finally reached the Realm of Civilization once again and proceeded to make their way toward the No. 1 District of the Cultivation Region in the Central Sector.

Lao Shaonian donned his pair of clarity-aiding lenses and selected an empty mountaintop over which he began their descent. When the dangling body of the bird had settled on the ground, he said, "We can't land on the bird, after all—and since this mountain is very steep, we'll just leave the bird here for the time being and find another more level surface upon which we can land." The four men then each went to one of the railings and in unison, released the platinum ropes holding the net in place. Who would have expected that as soon as the ropes had been released, the car would go careening wildly upward into the sky, startling them all? The car had been so weighed down by the massive bird that despite the drive's being set to an altitude of ten thousand feet, they had been able to hover only at three hundred. Now, to lower the car to deposit the bird on the ground, the drive had still needed to be set to over seven thousand feet of altitude. The result was that when their burdensome cargo was released, the car shot upward. Moreover, under normal circumstances, gaining altitude was a gradual process: with one turn of the dial, the car would rise fifty feet; with another turn, the car would rise another fifty feet, and so on. In this way, one normally rose quite slowly. But in this instance, the drive had been set at a whopping seven thousand–plus feet, which was why the car was now hurtling recklessly into the sky. Alarmed, Lao Shaonian frantically tried to rein in the drive. He could only adjust the altitude setting by fifty feet per turn of the dial, but by hurriedly turning it over and over he was able to reduce the altitude setting by a thousand feet. Baoyu noticed that the altimeter was indicating that they had already reached a height of 6,500 feet. As he leaned out over the railing to look down, all he could see was a vast expanse of white—he could not make out a single object below. It was as if the entire sky was now below his feet.

Lao Shaonian continued reducing the altitude until they were finally back to a height of fifty feet. He then put his clarity-aiding lenses back on and began to look for the mountain upon which they had deposited the bird. Luckily they had not moved far from it, and so he flew them nearby once again before landing. Seeking out a local resident, he asked what this place was called, and only then did he learn that it was "Ritual Deference Village." The mountain did not have a proper name of its own, but because it stood at the front of the village, the locals called it "Front Mountain." Lao Shaonian asked for a few more details before taking the car back up into the air and flying to the museum in the No. 1 District of the Cultivation Region. Upon landing in front of the museum, he had his calling card sent in and requested to meet with the museum's director.

The museum director's surname was Duo; his given name was Wen, and his style name was Jianshi.[1] Upon hearing that guests had arrived from afar, he hurried out to invite them in for a chat. Lao Shaonian explained that they had come to deliver the bird to the museum, then added, "The bird is currently on top of Front Mountain in Ritual Deference Village. I hope that you, Mr. Duo, might dispatch some people to go collect it."

Jianshi was delighted by this. "Such a strange creature will certainly be enough to add some luster to our collections! But how are we to transport something so large? I must impose upon you one more time to use your hunting car to carry it here by air. We have a large open space here where it will fit satisfactorily. I'll send a few people to assist you." Lao Shaonian promptly agreed. Duo Jianshi then dispatched eight museum employees to accompany them.

The party of twelve men boarded the car and arrived at their destination shortly thereafter. From aboard the car, Lao Shaonian scanned the area all round, but there was nowhere on the mountain to safely set the car down; and he worried that if he were to land on the flat land below the mountain and instruct the men to drag the bird down to the car, the dragging might damage the platinum thread net. He turned it over and over in his mind but was unable to come up with a solution.

Baoyu proposed, "Why not hover the car one or two feet off the ground over the mountain and have the men jump out and pass the ropes back up to the car?"

Lao Shaonian followed this suggestion and lowered the car; the eight men from the museum then leapt out. Unfortunately, however, with the car still hovering over the ground, the men were unable to reach high enough to pass the ropes up. After some discussion it was decided that one of the men should be sent to Ritual Deference Village to borrow a bamboo pole. Using the pole, they were finally then able to pass the ends of the ropes up to the men in the car. And while the eight men had been able to jump down out of the car, they were not able to jump back up into the car, so they had no choice but to walk all the way back to the museum.

By this time the residents of Ritual Deference Village had been stirred up by news that a tremendous bird had been caught, and so they had all come out to see it. Lao Shaonian then cranked the vertical propulsion drive into high gear, lifting the bird off the ground, and flew off toward the museum. The villagers all raised their heads to watch and dispersed only when the bird and car could no longer be seen.

Upon returning to the museum, Lao Shaonian deposited the bird in the open space Duo Jianshi had mentioned. This time, however, he was very attentive to how he proceeded: although he had placed the bird on the ground, he did not yet dare call for the ropes to be released until he had adjusted the altitude setting to only about fifty feet or so—only then were the ropes untied. He then steered the car to the side and set it down.

Duo Jianshi had already emerged and led his guests to a reception room, where he offered them tea. He instructed his men to untie the platinum net and pack it back up for the party. Lao Shaonian then called for the hawks and kites that had been caught up in the central deck of the car to be brought out for examination, but they were all found to be quite common, worthless for eating or for any other purpose, and so the order was given that they were all to be released. Duo Jianshi asked in detail about the circumstances under which they had caught the great bird, and Lao Shaonian gave him a complete account. He then added, "Although we did manage to catch it in the end, I still don't know what kind of bird it is!"

"Why, it's the *peng* bird that Zhuangzi spoke of!" replied Duo Jianshi.[2] "It is the transformation of the great *kun* fish. If you don't believe me, just look at its claws: it still has scales there. Our avian creatures exhibit was missing only this single specimen. How lucky that the two of you, at such great risk, were able to catch it and bring it here—truly, cause for admiration! A few moments ago, I instructed someone to send a telegram informing the government. At the same time, I wrote a message to the newspaper offices, so that they can publish a story on these events."

As they were speaking, the museum's secretary, having finished transcribing the telegram, came out and gave it to the director so that he might look over it. Jianshi asked for the names of the two serving boys, told the secretary to add them to the report, then ordered the telegram to be sent out immediately. "You two gentlemen have just returned after having endured the hardships of a journey spanning many thousands of li; please stay here for a few days and wait for the government to send a response before you go."

"It was no great feat," said Baoyu. "Why should we await a response from the government?"

Lao Shaonian replied, "We should be grateful for the director's kindness—now that he has made a report to the government, we may yet hope to receive some sort of a reward."

"I dare not hope for any kind of reward," said Baoyu. "Being here and seeing all sorts of new things—broadening my perspective and expanding my horizons—is enough."

Thereupon, Jianshi invited the two men to go view the various objects on display. As it happened, the articles held by the museum were all divided into different categories. First they went to the book repository: upon entering, they saw four walls all lined with books. The ten central rooms housed Chinese books, both ancient and contemporary; in five rooms on either side were books from the myriad countries around the world. Baoyu remarked, "It is commonly said in China, 'With twenty-four dynastic histories to choose from, it is difficult to know where to start reading!' But only after coming here do I finally know what it is to 'not know where to start reading'!"

Jianshi pointed to a glass case. "You should start with this."

When Baoyu looked, he saw standing in the center of the building an exquisitely carved table of red sandalwood on top of which lay a colorful brocade cloth. Upon this had been placed a red sandalwood box whose four sides were all set with clear glass panes. Inside the box was a piece of rope. Baoyu asked, "What rope is that?"

"It is the knotted rope that was used in ancient times to keep records of governance. Since it is an ancestor of the written character, we have displayed it in the book repository." Baoyu took a moment to admire it. Jianshi then called his attention to a small recess, over which hung a yellow curtain. Pulling the curtain aside revealed boxes crafted of glass and cedar in which rested a number of books. Jianshi pointed out one by one: "This is the very *Classic of Poetry* edited and compiled by Confucius; this is the *Book of Documents* he edited and compiled; these are his finalized *Classic of Ritual* and *Classic of Music*. The one displayed over here is the original manuscript of the *Spring and Autumn Annals*; the story as transmitted generation to generation is that Confucius did not write it with his own hand, but rather, it was transcribed by two of his disciples, Ziyou and Zixia."[3]

When they had finished looking these over, Jianshi pointed out a bookcase full of extremely old, tattered books, and said, "These are the books that escaped the all but complete destruction of first Qin emperor's literary inquisition. The story that has been passed down is that before Xiao He had achieved renown, he retrieved these remnants from the ashes. These are all extremely ancient items."

"Extremely ancient things, I have seen before," said Baoyu. "I wonder whether you have anything extremely new?"

Jianshi led him to another area and pointed out two books. "These are the newest," he said.

■ ■ ■

If you wish to know what the newest books were, please listen to the explanation in the following chapter.

Chapter Twenty-Eight

Having caught the great peng bird, they all receive commemorative plaques

To catch the kun fish, they ride swiftly in a hunting boat

WE WERE speaking of how, after seeing the collection's most ancient books, Baoyu had expressed a desire to see the newest books. Following Duo Jianshi's direction, he went to look: what he saw was a collection entitled *Civilized Laws and Regulations*, and one entitled *Scientific Inventions.* Jianshi explained, "*Civilized Laws and Regulations* was recently revised and finalized; it was only just published yesterday. *Scientific Inventions* is a recent work by Hua Zili that came out today and has only just been sent over. These are our newest books."

Baoyu flipped through them, but there wasn't time to read them carefully. He then looked into the rooms along the sides of the building before the party left the book repository. Arriving at their next destination, they saw the two characters "Treasure Vault" inscribed upon the door lintel. Upon entering the building, the first room they encountered was the Pearl Storeroom. Baoyu was stunned and asked, "How many pearls have you got, that you needed to build a storeroom for them?" Jianshi led the party inside, where they saw large cases and small boxes, all filled with pearls, lining both sides of the room. The largest ones were the size of fragrant Guangdong oranges; the smallest were roughly the size of a human eye. Baoyu was dazzled by it all. "It must have been extremely difficult to amass such a collection of pearls!" he remarked.

"Naturally occurring items such as these aren't anything special," said Jianshi. "It is rather ridiculous that ordinary people treat them as such treasures. It would cost a tremendous sum of money to buy just one! But really these things are produced in nature and require almost no human effort at all, so why should they be so valuable? What is really difficult is to collect them all in one place. So the residents of our humble Realm who possessed pearls sent them all here. Once they were all gathered together, we could then distinguish the different origins of each." When he had finished speaking, he pulled out a tiny placard from one of the pearl boxes. Upon the sign were written the characters "Hepu." "These pearls were produced in Hepu County," he continued. Baoyu examined the pearls case by case and box by box. Each had a similar placard indicating the pearls' provenance.

After the Pearl Storeroom came the Coral Forest. In an open-air chamber, there stood rows of corals planted in the ground, the tallest reaching over a hundred feet, the shortest as small as five or six feet. In addition to the more common varieties of red and white corals, there were also corals of yellow, blue, and green—a dazzling multihued display glimmering in the sunlight, its precious aura filling the sky. "These multicolored corals are truly a sight to behold," said Baoyu.

"There are all sorts of marvels at the bottom of the sea," said Jianshi. "These were all acquired during undersea hunting trips. Since they were determined to have no practical use, they were brought here for the edification of the masses."

Once they had crossed through the Coral Forest, they met with a building that positively glittered with an ostentatious rainbow of radiant color, the sight of which dazzled Baoyu's eyes.

"I've been to the museum before," Lao Shaonian began, "but I've never seen this building. When was it constructed? How is it that I've heard no announcement of it?"

"Construction hasn't quite finished yet," replied Jianshi. "Previously, all of the precious stones that were delivered to us were housed in a room and put on display for all to see. But as time went on we received too many, and we nearly ran out of space for them all, so we came up with the idea to cut them all into blocks and to build this structure using them instead of bricks. We've decided to name it the Hall of Collected Treasures. They only just finished building it yesterday. Today will be spent in cleaning it up, after which everything inside will need to be set up, but within another day or two, we'll be able to announce its completion." As he spoke, the party turned toward the building's main entrance. Over the door lintel was a sign bearing the characters "Hall of Collected Treasures," which had itself been constructed out of precious stones. Jianshi led his two guests inside, saying, "A great deal of consideration has gone into the construction of this building. Although the four walls are all built out of precious stones, the stones were arranged according to their place of origin: the east wall is made up of stones from the Eastern Sector; the west wall is made up of stones from the Western Sector; the stones used as roof tiles are all from the Central Sector; and the stones that make up the flooring are all from overseas. It's nothing too impressive, really, it's just that a good deal of time went into laying them out thus." As he listened to this explanation, Baoyu contemplated the building in admiration. It was truly spectacular, almost overwhelming in its opulence.

When they emerged from the Hall of Collected Treasures, they wandered through still more areas, each of which contained all sorts of rare and precious items; however, this text is unable to relate the details in full. Having wandered through the entirety of the Treasure Vault, they made their way thence to the Hall of Engineering. The items arrayed in the center of the hall were all creations native to the Realm, while foreign products were displayed along the two sides. Baoyu only cared to examine those in the center, most of which were newly invented things, and none of which he had ever laid eyes upon before. He wanted to ask about them, but scarcely knew how to. Among these were the Mountain-Opening Borer and River-Controlling Excavator that Dongfang Wenming had invented back in the day. Most of them were mechanically operated. Now that the wilderness had been tamed and the machines had served their purpose, they had been sent to the museum to be put on display. The party looked over them all, at which point a serving boy came and bade them come eat. Jianshi then invited his two guests into the dining room.

After they had eaten, the government's reply telegram arrived. It read: "Lao Shaonian and the others, braving great danger, hunted and captured the Great Peng bird, in order to broaden the knowledge of our citizenry. Their bravery is to be commended. Each man will receive a commemorative plaque recognizing him as a 'Valiant of the Highest Degree.' Once the plaques have been crafted, they will be issued forthwith by flying car," and so on. Jianshi shared the news with his guests. Lao Shaonian was naturally extremely pleased, while Baoyu was more or less indifferent. That the two serving boys, who would likewise be receiving award, were delighted goes without saying.

After this, Baoyu and the rest resided at the museum for three days. They visited the various buildings housing the avian and aquatic animals, as well terrestrial and aquatic plants. They viewed exhibits of metals and nonmetallic ores. They also pored over one by one all of the marvelous devices previously used by Dongfang Wenming in his explorations. The *peng* had already been treated with a preservative fluid and mounted in the center of the avian exhibit. After a clerk took its measurements, it was found to measure fifty-two feet from head to tail and thirty feet across at its widest point. The diameter of its eye sockets measured three feet, while the diameter of its shins and claws measured one foot two inches and eight inches, respectively. All of this information was written down on a small placard. The placard, which also made note of the names of the hunting party as well as the dates upon which the bird had been captured and delivered, was then hung beside the specimen. It was only at this point, thinking back on it all, that Baoyu realized the perils of the hunt and said to Lao Shaonian, "If we hadn't been able to best it that day, the four of us wouldn't even have been enough to give it a single good meal!"

Lao Shaonian laughed. "The measly four of us might possibly have been just enough for a snack!"

As they joked with each other, it was suddenly announced that the government envoy had arrived to deliver their award plaques. Jianshi led Lao Shaonian, Baoyu, and the two serving boys to meet with the official and graciously receive the award. The official then went to have a look at the *peng*, and he couldn't help but tut-tut a few times in wonder. He stayed to socialize for a little while, then took his leave.

On the following day, Duo Jianshi had the completion of the Hall of Collected Treasures and the installation of the *peng* bird announced in every newspaper. In very little time this caused a great commotion, and throngs of people came to see. After seeing the *peng*, they requested to see the people who had captured it. Baoyu eventually found this tiresome and tried to make his excuses, so Jianshi suggested that Lao Shaonian, Baoyu, and the two serving boys take a photo together to be displayed instead. Thereupon he led the foursome into a brightly lit room, set up a lens, and bade Lao Shaonian and Baoyu to take seats opposite each other, while the two serving boys stood beside them in attendance. The photographer then uncovered the lens. Beside the lens was a small handle that the photographer raised and lowered three or four times before covering the lens again. When he opened the apparatus to pull out the photograph, he pulled out twenty identical photos all at once! The images had been printed directly onto sheets of paper, which meant that not only were their likenesses captured perfectly, but even the color of their clothing and their faces were captured as well.

Baoyu said, "In previous photos I've seen, none of them have come out in color. And moreover, they're always printed on glass slides, which are then projected onto paper to make the image. It's quite a laborious process! This technique is new to me."

Duo Jianshi gave a slight smile and replied, "We stopped using such clumsy methods over ten years ago." Each person then received a copy of the photo, and the remainders were hung up around the museum.

A short while later the foursome took their leave of Duo Jianshi, climbed back into their hunting car, and flew back to their hotel. Lao Shaonian then instructed the serving-boys to deliver the car back into the care of Sun Shengwu. With nothing else to do, Lao Shaonian brought Baoyu to a lively part of the city so that they might wander about and amuse themselves. Everywhere around them were people bustling to and fro, always considerately making way for others as they went—truly a civilized scene. And fortunately, everyone who had somewhere to go was riding in flying cars, so there was no need to fear collision with horses or carts in the roads. The roads themselves were flat as mirrors and bore not a speck of dust.

After two days of exploring the city, Baoyu asked, "We've wandered around the city for two days, and simply put, it is kept extremely clean and has a very civilized air about it. Even the people walking the streets all make way for others in accordance with good manners. All of these things, I have observed with admiration. But amid all of this, there are only three types of things that I have not yet seen."

"What three types of things?" asked Lao Shaonian.

"First, there aren't any temples; second, there are no churches; and third, there are no beggars."

Lao Shaonian laughed. "Since all superstitions have been done away with, why should we have any temples? We did open wide our doors and allow outsiders to proselytize, and they came and established churches. But when they started talking about the 'Old Testament' and the 'New Testament' in their absurdly elaborate language, no one bothered to go listen to them. The result was that the foreigner would stand there talking to himself and had no choice but to leave. Naturally, from then on, none has ever come again. As for the question of beggars, that requires even less explanation. We did previously have such a thing as a poorhouse, where we took care of orphans and the needy. But in the last ten years even the poorhouses have stood empty and have been converted into schools. Almost all of the people within the Realm—whether male or female—can support themselves by their own labor. And speaking of that, I'm afraid you won't believe me when I tell you that in our humble Realm we haven't even got a single charity. If we did have one, there'd be no use for it."

"That is because the people have plenty and the state is wealthy—it goes without saying. But if there aren't any temples, and if there aren't any churches, I wonder whether you have any Confucian temples?"

"There is a portrait of Confucius in each of the schools; however, there are no Confucian temples."

"But if there are no Confucian temples, then what religion does the Realm observe? How can there be a country in this world that does not have a religion?"

Here Lao Shaonian gave a great laugh. "You should add a word to the sentence you just uttered: 'How can there be a *barbarian* country in this world that does not have a religion?' I would reply by asking, 'How can there be a *civilized* country in this world that *does* have a religion?' You should know that 'religion' is only used to transmit teachings to the ignorant masses. If the people are already enlightened with regard to the most important principles, then what religion could they possibly need? But if you wish to ask what *teachings* our humble Realm observes, then I must say that we observe the teachings of Confucius.[1] The people of our Realm start receiving 'familial education' at a young age. They are taught the correct social relationships and everyday principles at home by their mothers; once they have entered school, the first subject they study is self-cultivation. So no matter whether wealthy or poor, old or young, there is not a single person here who does not act in accordance with principle. Ideals of filiality, respect, loyalty, and honor are fully developed within the breast of every person here. That's the only reason we dared to use the word 'Civilization' in naming this place. Did you not see the sign on the archway upon entering that reads 'The Way of Confucius'? It means that within the Realm of Civilization all things are done according to the way of Confucius. As for what is called 'civilization' in the outside world these days, why, it's precisely the opposite of civilized! They praise one another as 'civilized countries,' and want to deceive the whole world; but they have no idea that we mock them so! I would ask for your opinion here: imagine there are two people walking along a road. One of them is a martial warrior and the other has tuberculosis. The warrior sets about intimidating and terrifying the sick man in a hundred different ways, even striking and kicking him, to the point that the sick man is now half-dead. Would you say that the warrior is acting with principle? Are those the actions of a civilized person? I'm afraid that the *yamen* of Punishments would seize him and charge him with a crime. But the warrior himself might claim that his actions were indeed extremely civilized. Do you agree or not? Right now, of all the countries out there that claim to be civilized, which of them does not behave just like this? They see other countries' weaknesses, then intentionally bully and abuse them, even going so far as seizing their territory and interfering in their governance, all while claiming to be protecting them. To speak of it almost makes one want to laugh and fly into a rage simultaneously, and yet neither of these brings satisfaction. According to what they say, thieves and robbers must be the most civilized men in the world! So how is it that within their own countries, they have laws for dealing with robbers? If all of the countries of the world were to establish a joint international *yamen*, so that when two countries had a conflict they could go there to bring suit against one another, I'm afraid that those 'civilized countries' would be convicted as thieves!"

"It's only because such a *yamen* does not exist that they are able to wreak their havoc so widely with no fear of consequences," mused Baoyu.

"By their reckoning, the tiger must be the most civilized animal in the world," continued Lao Shaonian. "It capriciously eats animals and people, and the laws of the land have no means of controlling it. Is that not indeed the most civilized?"

Baoyu laughed. "Now, if one day you were to summon a hunter to kill the tiger, then the hunter should surely be considered 'civilized,' too."

"Just so. But this is actually despotism—how can it ever be civilized? Because they are accustomed to despotism, I'm afraid that the people who live within such a country become of despotic character themselves, so they also think that the only way to behave toward other countries is despotically. But if the people of the country begin to behave despotically toward one another, then all will be thrown into chaos. That is why they established religion, spouting all this nonsense about Heaven and Hell, and proselytizing everywhere, even as they constantly talk of 'enlightening the people.' As I see it, this proselytizing is in fact leading their people to ignorance. Think about it: they are urging their people to believe in a bunch of absurd talk—which even a three-year-old here would know not to be credible. The person who believes it, why, isn't his wisdom beneath that of a child? However, if these despotic people *didn't* believe in this, then they would wreak havoc with no respect for any law. But what need would a person from a *civilized* country have for it? That is why I say that there is no barbaric country in this world that lacks religion, while there is no civilized country in this world that practices it."

"If that's the case, then I suppose China can't be considered civilized, either?" Baoyu asked.

"How could China be *uncivilized*? China has only ever had Confucius but has never had any religion. And Confucius never appointed himself the head of a religion. It's just regrettable that later generations were never able to broadly propagate the virtues of Confucius's teachings—that is why China cannot yet be considered to have achieved true civilization. As for Zhang Daoling, he was just a practitioner of the occult from a later generation, but he certainly didn't create a religion.[2] It's only because those who came after him persisted in passing down their own misconceptions that people started saying it was the

Daoist *religion*. And the Buddhist religion came in from India, it is not something native to China. A group of lazy idlers who wish to eat without doing the work of plowing, to wear clothes without doing the work of weaving, and simply become monks—that cannot be considered a religion, either. If these are religions, then why has there never been any Daoist urging others to become Daoists or monks urging others to become monks? China doesn't have this practice of religious proselytizing. It would be fairly simple for China to become a civilized country. As for other countries, I dare not say."

As they were speaking, a serving boy entered bearing a calling card and announced that a visitor had arrived. Lao Shaonian accepted the card and looked at it—as it happened, their visitor was Wu Shuqi. Lao Shaonian hurriedly instructed that their guest be invited in. Once Shuqi had come in and they had all greeted one another, Shuqi said, "Today is my day off, so I have some free time. I have come here, first of all, to thank you for your previous visit to the academy; and second, I have come to congratulate you."

"What is there to congratulate us for?" asked Lao Shaonian.

"You received the highest level of award, are you not pleased?"

Lao Shaonian and Baoyu humbly demurred.

"Third," Shuqi continued, "I have come to offer you an opportunity."

"And what opportunity would that be?" Lao Shaonian inquired.

"Your reputations have already spread throughout the Realm for the feat of having hunted down the great *peng*. Yesterday Mr. Dongfang Fa had an underwater hunting ship delivered to the academy, originally intending to select several of the students to take it out and test their mettle; but the summer break begins in just a few days, and the students will have a month off. I discussed the matter with Shengwu this morning, and we thought that given the skill the two of you displayed in hunting the *peng*, why not invite you to take to the seas to see if you can catch and bring back a *kun* fish as well?[3] Thus, I have specially come here to inform you that we are willing to lend this ship out to you. I don't know whether the two of you are interested?"

Before Lao Shaonian had time to respond, Baoyu cut in with great enthusiasm, "Since I have been able to see your underwater warships in action but have never been able to set foot on one to see what it's like on board, I should be happy just to expand my knowledge of underwater travel, regardless of whether we are able to catch a *kun* fish or not."

Lao Shaonian also agreed with pleasure. And so the three men rode together in Shuqi's flying car, stopping first at the academy. After they had met with Shengwu, they took with them a water-penetrating scope, got back into the car, and headed for the coast.

■ ■ ■

If you wish to know whether or not they were able to capture a *kun* fish, please listen to the explanation in the following chapter.

Chapter Twenty-Nine

Coming upon a deserted isle, a noisy gun is fired at a sea hippo

Sinking beneath the waves, they use electricity to wage war against the qiu fish

WE WERE speaking of the four men, who had taken a flying car to the coast. They then instructed the crew to set up the water-penetrating scope so that they might look out and see the hunting submarine as it lay underwater. They saw that the submarine had the elegant, streamlined form of a whale, complete with fins and scaled armor. From its two "eyes" shone the bright light of electric lamps. In comparison with the coastal defense warships they had seen previously, the submarine was at least four or five times larger. Shengwu said, "The captains, helmsmen, crewmen, and various workers—the whole complement—were sent over from the academy. Once you two gentlemen are on board, feel free to give orders as you wish—there is no need to be polite." He then pulled out a wireless telephone receiver from inside his coat and gave it a quick flick with his wrist. There came a ringing sound from inside the receiver, after which Shengwu spoke into it and gave the command that the submarine should be brought to the surface. It was not long before they saw the submarine slowly float up to the surface of the water, revealing the top half of its whale-like body. The four men then climbed down into a sampan, which carried them out to the hunting vessel's side. Baoyu observed the sampan carefully and noticed that it too relied upon an electric motor rather than the rowing of oars to propel itself.

As they approached, one of the whale's scales opened suddenly before them—as it happened, this was a hatch, through which the four men then entered. Once inside, they saw one long corridor circling the circumference of the ship; in the middle of this stood separate rooms for machinery, helm, a reception hall, mess hall, and sleeping quarters, all outfitted immaculately. They inspected this area, then took the stairs down to the lower level. Here too was a corridor, running straight down the center of the space for the entire length of the ship. The rooms that flanked either side of the hall were all labeled with the names of the various pieces of hunting equipment and general-use items that were stored inside.

When the men descended yet another level, they found themselves in an empty, cavernous space. Toward the bow of the ship there was a small door—in terms of its position, this door could have been considered the whale's "throat." Crossing through this door, one would then find himself inside the whale's "head." When a diver wished to go out into the sea from aboard the ship, he would open this small door and enter the "head." Once inside, he would put on a diving suit and close the small door behind himself. Only then would he open the door at the whale's "mouth"—which let the room fill with seawater—before swimming out the "mouth" and into the open sea. With the small door at the "throat" closed, no water could enter the rest of the ship. Upon returning to the vessel, the diver would once again enter the whale's "mouth," close that door behind himself, and press an electric bell. This would signal the captain to turn on a water-removal pump; once the water had been drained away, the diver could open the small door at the "throat" and reenter the ship proper.

To the stern on this level was a large tank full of seawater, waiting in readiness for the holding of any fish captured alive during the hunt. This, too, the men inspected before returning to the top level. Shuqi then requested that the captains and helmsmen come to introduce themselves. Four men made up the command crew: Tan Ying, Hai Dao, Jiang Yin, and She Jin. There were likewise four helmsmen: Wang Zuoji, Li Ji, You Long, and Fang Zhinan. When all of the men had made their introductions, Shuqi and Shengwu bade the group goodbye and boarded the sampan back to the flying car, so that they could return to the academy. But of them, let us say no more.

Let us speak instead of how after Lao Shaonian and Baoyu had seen off the others, they began to discuss with the captains and helmsmen the question of where they should go to hunt. Hai Dao volunteered, "We should choose somewhere where we know we can catch lots of fish."

"But we've already seen all of the fish that can be caught nearby," replied Lao Shaonian. "It would be better if we could go a little further out, catch a few that no one has ever seen before, and bring them back. We can send the living ones to the zoo and the dead ones to the museum!"

Baoyu laughed. “One award isn’t enough for you, so now you’re angling for a second?” Lao Shaonian laughed at this. Baoyu then went on, asking, “How fast this can this ship go?”

“With the motor at full throttle, it can travel a little over a thousand li in a two-hour period. In a full day and night, it can travel more than twelve thousand li!” answered Wang Zuoji.

“If that’s the case, why don’t we try to travel around the whole globe underwater?” asked Baoyu. “We can set off from the Pacific Ocean and come back via the Atlantic. Wouldn’t that be wonderful?”

When the men had finished their discussions and settled on a decision, they all parted and went about tending to their own duties. But first they instructed the crewmen to close the hatch, submerge the ship, and set out toward the east.

■ ■ ■

As Baoyu closely inspected the ship, he noticed that there were electric lights installed on every wall. The reception hall was outfitted with extraordinarily refined taste. There was even a library, its four walls covered with shelves of books. On the library desk, the “four treasures” of the scholar’s study had been set out carefully. As he approached the external wall of the corridor, he noticed that innumerable glass windows were arrayed along it, allowing one to clearly make out the ocean scenery outside. He was delighted and said, “So it turns out that there is light under the sea! If that’s the case, then why is it that we must still use electric lights within the ship? Don’t these windows allow the light to come in from outside?”

Lao Shaonian replied, "You're looking through a special water-penetrating glass made for use underwater. It allows us to look out from inside, but those looking from outside can't see in. If the windows were set with regular glass, the sea would be so pitch-dark that you wouldn't be able to make anything out."

Baoyu then made his way to the machinery room. Here, he saw the propulsion system, the lighting system controls, the oxygen generator, the carbon dioxide filter, and the illumination system controls, each of which had their names etched into them.

"There is already a 'lighting system,'" said Baoyu, "so why do we also need an 'illumination system'?"

Tan Ying answered, "The illumination system is for hunting at night. The entire exterior of the ship illuminates to light up the sea so we can see to hunt."

"And the illumination is electrical, naturally? Can you please tell me: When the whole exterior of the ship is lit up with electricity, is there any need for those inside the ship to be worried about electrocution?"

"The interior steel hull of the ship has been plastered over with soft ceramic to insulate us from the electricity. So the people inside the ship are not affected by it at all."

"Ceramic makes sense, sure. But why would you need *soft* ceramic?"

"In the event that we suffer some kind of collision, normal ceramic would shatter with the impact. That's why we use soft ceramic."

"So is the steel used on the exterior soft, too?"

At this Lao Shaonian laughed and interjected: "Liu Yueshi wrote in a poem: 'Who would have thought that the steel refired a hundred times over becomes supple enough to bend round a finger?'[1] As you can see, the ancients already had this knowledge. It's really not all that strange."

Baoyu then made his way to the helm. A fixed compass was set in the center of the room; Li Ji was currently on duty. Baoyu noticed that on the wall in front of him there hung a large, round glass lens. When he looked into it, all he could see was the vast expanse of the sea. Startled, he asked, "That's not an external wall—how is it that I can see outside?"

"That is a metal-penetrating lens. It allows us to see through the hull. All of our underwater travels are completely dependent upon it. Without it we'd just have to go along blindly and risk knocking into things. Wouldn't that be unacceptable?"

Baoyu continued looking for a moment, then returned to the library. In a drawer he found a notebook in which was recorded a list of all the rooms below-deck, what each room contained, and the uses of each item, all laid out in clear detail. He and Lao Shaonian then proceeded to read it carefully, one entry at a time. Eventually an attendant came and requested that the men come to eat. After they had eaten, She Jin came and asked, "There is no natural night or day aboard this ship; as aboard warships, the policy is that 'day' and 'night' are established based on the time reported by the timekeeping automatons. When it is nighttime, the lighting system is turned off and is only turned back on when it should start to get light again. What do you two gentlemen think?"

Looking at the timekeeping automaton, Baoyu realized that it was already 7:00 p.m.

"Let's turn out the lights at ten," said Lao Shaonian. She Jin agreed to this and departed.

Baoyu and Lao Shaonian then resumed their reading of the notebook, learning everything about the ship's outfitting and fish-hunting techniques, after which they went back to the exterior windows and looked out. They could see that the ship's hull was already illuminated with an electric glow, lighting the whole of the sea before them so clearly that they could count the fish swimming by. The algae and kelp were a beautiful scallion-green. There were also a countless number of small underwater reefs; as the ship passed over or alongside them, Baoyu saw that they were inhabited by a multitude of strange creatures, none of which he had ever before beheld.

At ten o'clock, everyone repaired to their sleeping quarters. The lights were turned out, and everyone went to bed. Of course, the eight captains and helmsmen stayed up and performed their duties in rotating shifts, but we need not go into detail here. Of that night we have nothing else to report.

On the following day the ship reached the middle of the Pacific Ocean. Hai Dao was on duty and brought the ship to the surface, then invited Baoyu and Lao Shaonian to follow him up a flight of stairs. They suddenly emerged into a wide open space—as it turned out, what had previously looked like the whale's "back" was actually a retractable hull. A section in the middle of the hull had now been opened, revealing a deck area much like that of an ordinary ship—encircled on all sides by railings, and with a telescope mounted on it. Hai Dao looked out through this and took some measurements, then pronounced, "We've already reached 158.9° E longitude and 5.4° N latitude. In a little while longer, we'll have crossed into the Western Hemisphere."

As he was speaking, a small deserted island suddenly appeared on the horizon. All of the men put on their clarity-aiding glasses to observe it and saw that it was quite barren, with nothing growing on it. But on one coast of the island there crouched a wild beast that appeared to be a tiger. Lao Shaonian hurriedly ordered that guns be brought out and that attendants should go down and instruct the helmsmen to change course toward the island. Watching as the ship approached, Lao Shaonian laughed: "It is truly impossible to anticipate the things that might happen in this world! We set out originally planning to hunt fish, who could have known that we'd end up hunting a beast instead?" As he finished speaking, he leveled a gun at the beast and fired off a shot. However, he hadn't realized that this was not one of the silent guns, and it gave off a loud bang. Before the bullet could reach its mark, the startled beast gave a great roar and plunged into the sea.

Lao Shaonian had a sudden realization: "That's a sea hippo! One of the fiercest beasts there is! It can live both on land and in water."[2] Hurriedly, he called for the hull to be sealed, and once everyone had descended back into the ship proper, he gave the order that the ship submerge so that they could go in pursuit of the sea hippo. Looking through the windows in the hull, Lao Shaonian was surprised to see nothing but a sheet of pitch-blackness, as if the ship had encountered a thick swathe of smoke. He pulled out a tiny pair of metal-penetrating glasses and looked through them, but the results were the same. He then called out to Hai Dao, instructing him to turn on the illumination system, and the sea around them was instantly suffused with light. Lao Shaonian saw that the sea hippo had seized an enormous cuttlefish and was in the middle of devouring it, opening wide its tremendous, bloody jaws. The sea hippo saw the submarine approaching and, taking it for a whale, became afraid. Still carrying the cuttlefish along with it, the sea hippo fled desperately. As it turned out, the black substance that had created the effect of smoke was the ink that the cuttlefish had spurted out in self-defense.

By this time, Baoyu had also put on a pair of metal-penetrating glasses. He and Lao Shaonian each took control of an electronic cannon, and, watching very closely, both fired at the same moment and struck the beast. Having been struck by their shells, the sea hippo released the cuttlefish and shot upward. Baoyu thought the sea hippo would flee all the way to the surface and was about to give the command for the submarine to surface as well so that they could better give chase, when he saw the sea hippo slowly sinking back into the deep, its four feet pointed toward the sky. It was already dead. The cuttlefish, too, was dead, having been gnawed to death by the sea hippo. By now the ink that had been sprayed out by the cuttlefish had already been completely dispersed by the ocean currents.

Lao Shaonian, referring to the headings in the inventory notebook, called for one of the rooms in the middle level to be opened and two sets of diving clothes obtained therefrom. These were given to two crewmen, who put them on and went out to recover the bodies of the sea hippo and the cuttlefish. As Baoyu looked at the suits, he noticed that they were designed to cover the body from head to foot, and that each was fitted with several small mechanisms. The eyeholes were set with two underwater water-penetrating lenses; beneath the ribcage on either side were fins fashioned from thin sheets of copper; over the left breast was a set of electronic controls that operated the fins; over the right breast was another mechanism that when activated, would blow air into the suit sufficient for the diver to breathe.[3] The entire suit was fabricated from soft leather, and once a diver had put it on only his two hands remained exposed, with buttons sealing the sleeves off tightly at his wrist.

Once the two divers were appropriately outfitted, they gathered ropes and ties and made their way to the lower level. Here they opened the small door, and once they had passed through into the "head" of the ship, the door was of course closed behind them. The divers then opened the other door at the whale's "mouth" and swam out.

Within the main cabin, Baoyu watched through the windows. Once in the water, the two men activated their fins and glided forward with ease. They approached the dead sea hippo and tied it up, then did the same to the cuttlefish, before dragging them back to the ship, where they reentered the small door according to procedure. Only then did they set down their trophies and remove the diving suits.

Lao Shaonian ordered someone to produce a bottle of preservative fluid, which was then administered to the body of the sea hippo to prevent decomposition. Because the cuttlefish had already been chewed up by the sea hippo and was no longer a complete specimen, he said, "There's no need to keep this one. The next time the door is opened, throw it back into the sea."

"This creature is over twenty feet long," observed Baoyu. "Even if we don't want to keep its flesh, we simply must save its bone. If we bring that back, there will surely be a clever use for it."

"What kind of clever use?"

"If you slice it in half and hollow out the center, couldn't you make a couple of sampans out of it?"

As they were speaking, an attendant entered in haste and said, "Helmsman Wang has summoned the two gentlemen. Something urgent has come up."

At this the two men hurried upstairs. There, they saw Hai Dao, Jiang Yin, She Jin, and the four helmsmen all standing around the helm. Only Tan Ying was absent, as he was currently on duty. All of the men were observing something through the metal-penetrating lens, so Baoyu and Lao Shaonian joined them. They saw something long threading its way toward them through the water but couldn't tell how big or how long it was. Some among the group asserted that it must be one or another kind of dragon; Lao Shaonian put on his clarity-aiding glasses and declared, "I'm afraid not—it's a *qiu* fish. According to the *Classic of Water*, 'The *qiu* is several thousand li long and makes its lair at the bottom of the sea. When it enters its lair the tide surges; when it leaves the tide recedes.' It seems probable that the entry in the *Classic of Water* is somewhat exaggerated; however, it is certain that this thing is not small. Even if it's not several thousand li long, it appears to be at least five or six hundred feet, more than twice the size of our ship. We will have to take thorough precautions against it."

Baoyu, who was watching closely, saw that the *qiu* was much like an eel, with a yellowish-black body that appeared not to have any scales. Its two eyes, each the size of a basket, were fixed on the ship as it wriggled its way forward. At this point, each of the men took up metal-penetrating glasses, stationed himself at one of the electronic cannons, and prepared to meet the enemy so as to prevent it from coming any nearer. Once the *qiu* had come within range of the cannons, they fired together. Who would have known that because the *qiu*'s body was round, their shells would simply glance off? But having taken several hits, the *qiu* grew increasingly enraged and now surged forward through the waves, seemingly oblivious to the continuing cannon fire.

When it had gotten quite close to the ship, the *qiu* turned its body and coiled itself around the middle of the hunting vessel, shaking it so violently that the entire boat quaked. The crew paled with fear. As it happened, the port in front of Baoyu's cannon was now blocked by the body of the *qiu*. Cranking up the firing mechanism, Baoyu got off four or five shots in rapid succession. You should know that before, when they had been firing upon the *qiu* from a distance, its round body had prevented the shells from striking directly; but now that its body was clinging to the torpedo port, there was nowhere for the shells to ricochet off to, so each one exploded against its flesh, tearing through its skin and bone. The *qiu*, having sustained such grievous injury, writhed in agony, releasing the ship.

At this point the ship attempted to flee, but the *qiu* would not give up and chased closely behind. Looking through their metal-penetrating lenses, the men saw that the sea around it bore traces of blood and realized that the *qiu* had been injured; but unfortunately, this just meant that it was now pursuing them all the more fiercely. Baoyu went to the bridge to discuss the matter with Tan Ying: "Why don't we let off a burst of electricity from the hull of the ship and electrocute it to death?"

"There is a layer of soft glass surrounding the outside of the ship. Otherwise, if the current just made contact with the air, how could it create light?"

Baoyu was silent for a moment, then asked, "Then what can we do?"

"I've already brought the ship to the surface, so only one thing matters now: I'm afraid that if the *qiu* destroys the propeller, we'll really be in for it!"

"Then there's nothing else to be done. For now we need to break the soft glass to save ourselves. We can consider anything else later."

"Perhaps there's a way we can remove the glass—let me look it up quickly." Saying this, Tan Ying pulled out a notebook and leafed through it, then announced happily, "Since this is my first time piloting this ship, there are still a lot of technical aspects I am not familiar with. The glass is removable!" He then summoned Hai Dao to come take over the controls. At the same time, he handed Hai Dao the notebook, and said, "Read this. When you hear the bell, activate this apparatus following the instructions in the manual," before leading a group of crewmen up to the top level. Baoyu looked out through one of the windows and saw that the *qiu* was still about two or three li off. He then followed Tan Ying up to the top level. When he arrived, he saw that the center part of the hull had already been opened, and a number of crewmen were all pitching in, climbing up beside the hatchway to undo the fasteners that held the soft glass in place. Once they had loosened all of the fastenings, Tan Ying pressed an electric bell. Hai Dao turned on the machine according to the instructions, and the soft glass was slowly rolled up beneath the ship.

"Won't it fall off and be lost if it's all gathered beneath the ship?" asked Baoyu.

"Once it's all gathered underneath, there is of course a mechanism that will secure it in place," answered Tan Ying. The two men then hurried back below decks and once again closed the hull.

As they descended, they heard Wang Zuoji cry out, "This one's even bigger than the other! What are we to do?" It so happened that as they had closed the hull and the ship had once again submerged, Wang Zuoji had been looking through a metal-penetrating lens and saw another *qiu* approaching from the south. He had been watching as it approached, and now gave this involuntary cry.

■ ■ ■

If wish to know whether or not the crew will ultimately be able to vanquish the *qiu*-fish in battle, please listen to the explanation in the following chapter.

Chapter Thirty

Courageous sailors plunge into the sea and do battle with man-fish

The clever "Spirit Jade" braves the cold to capture a sable

WE HAD been speaking of how the group had seen yet another *qiu* coming toward them. They watched it approach as the injured *qiu* pursued closely from behind.

"There's nothing else for it now," said Baoyu. "We have to turn and attack the injured one first. After that, we can discuss what to do next. Moreover, if we turn to face it, then even if it wraps itself around us again, hopefully it won't be able to damage our propeller; whereas if it catches up to us from behind, the propeller will be the first thing it strikes."

Wang Zuoji felt that this was reasonable and so turned the helm. By the time the ship had completed its turn, the injured *qiu* was no more than a li away. The hunting vessel made directly for the *qiu*, which in turn hurled itself toward the ship, and in no time at all, the two bodies collided. The *qiu* did its utmost to coil its tail and wrap itself once again around the body of the ship. Tan Ying quickly turned on the illumination apparatus, which instantly sent electric current coursing across the ship's iron hull, immediately shocking the *qiu* so that its entire body went slack. After a few moments, Tan Ying turned the illumination apparatus off, and the *qiu* slid limply off the hull of the ship, slowly sinking straight toward the seafloor. When the *qiu* that had been approaching from the south saw the lifeless body of the other, it turned and fled back toward the south, evidently afraid.

The crew aboard the vessel did not give chase; rather, they stopped the motor and discussed what to do with the body of the dead *qiu*. They decided to bring the ship down to the seabed, and as before, order two sailors to put on diving suits, secure the body with ropes, and bring it back. Suddenly, they realized that this creature was much too large and could never fit within the body of the ship; moreover, it seemed doubtful that just two men would be able to recover the body on their own. Lao Shaonian then suggested that they send ten sailors, all in diving suits, and equipped with guns and knives as well as platinum chains and locks. Once they had locked the chains around the *qiu*, they would then secure the other ends of the chains around the tail of the vessel. A group of sailors set off to complete these instructions. They arrived beside the *qiu*'s body and were about to chain it up when they found to their surprise that the *qiu*'s entire body was smooth, leaving them nowhere to get a purchase on it. Eventually one of the sailors came up with an idea: he used his gun to prop the *qiu*'s mouth open, then used a knife to pry open one of the *qiu*'s gills, leaving this, too, propped open. He instructed another sailor to take the platinum chain and feed it in through the gill and out through the mouth before finally affixing a lock to hold the chain in place. Together they dragged the *qiu* to the rear of the ship and secured it there before going back on board.

The ship set out toward the east once more. As dusk was approaching, Tan Ying remembered that the soft glass casing on the external hull ought to be replaced, so that they could use the illumination system by night. The ship was thus brought to the surface and the retractable hull opened, to enable the crew to return the soft glass to its correct position. Who could have expected that the furled glass would get stuck partway? Fearing a malfunction in the spooling mechanism, they went to make a closer inspection of it; but as it happened, there was nothing wrong with it. They then used metal-penetrating lenses to look all around the circumference of the ship and saw that on all sides the glass had unfurled to cover only about half of it; the only part of the ship they could not observe was the rear portion containing the crew's quarters, which had been built out of wooden planks, and through which the metal-penetrating lenses could not see. As a result, they were unable to determine whether there was some sort of hindrance there.

Baoyu suddenly had a thought. "Of course! The *qiu* is fettered to the rear of the ship—how could the platinum chain not create some kind of impediment?"

Tan Ying immediately understood, so he closed the hatch once more and had the ship resubmerge. He then ordered two crewmen to put on diving clothes, giving them each an electronic gun for self-defense. After releasing the *qiu*, the two crewmen would then need to wait for the others to bring the ship back to the surface and replace the soft glass cover before resubmerging to allow them back inside; so it was necessary that they should have weapons for protection in the meantime to prevent any kind of unforeseen mishap. The two crewmen followed their orders and took to the water, releasing the *qiu*, after which the ship rose to the surface. By now, it was already growing dark, so the crewmen on board hurriedly replaced the glass covering and sealed the hull. The ship submerged once more, and the illumination system was turned on. This time, strangely enough, the lighting failed to come on. Tan Ying was perplexed by this and was forced to pore over the manual once again. He finally discovered a line that read: "*If the soft glass is removed and replaced, it is unavoidable that some air will become trapped inside, preventing the ignition of the electricity. You must, following the schemata provided here, turn on the vacuum pump mechanism to draw the air out. Once all of the air has been removed, you may start the illumination process . . .*" and so on. Tan Ying used the schemata to identify the switch for the vacuum pump and turned it on. As he pumped the air out, Tan Ying was simultaneously listening for the electric bell from the front of the ship that would indicate a request for the pumping of water from the diving chamber, thus signaling the divers' return; however, the bell had still not been rung.

"Perhaps because it's dark, they can't see to find their way back?" he thought. "But there must be some light coming out from the portholes on both sides!" He was extremely worried. He turned the vacuum pump up to its highest setting, and had to run it for quite some time before all of the air was finally removed. He then attempted to activate the illumination system again, and as he had hoped, it now emitted its wonted brilliance. Quickly using his metal-penetrating lens to scan all round outside the ship, he saw the body of the *qiu* drifting to one side. The two crewmen were nowhere to be seen. With some exasperation, he declared, "To senselessly waste two human lives—how could that not diminish the dignity of civilization?" He immediately transmitted orders to a group of crewmen to begin searching all around.

Lao Shaonian was also extremely anxious and had put on a pair of clarity-aiding lenses so that he could help search at further distances. Suddenly, to the northwest he saw what appeared to be a swarm of people engaged in a struggle. He rushed into the helm cabin and instructed the helmsman to change their course. Looking through the metal-penetrating lens, it turned out that what he had seen before was a swarm of man-fish, who had pinned down the captured sailors and were attempting to eat them.[1] Lao Shaonian grew pale with shock. At this moment Fang Zhinan was on duty at the helm, so he seized it and steered straight for the group of man-fish. Suddenly, they saw the man-fish fling the sailors aside and scatter in all directions. The two divers pulled themselves up and swam to meet the ship. As they approached the vessel, it came to a stop; however, the sailors did not attempt to board and swam off toward the east instead. Fang Zhinan was confounded for a moment and didn't understand what the divers were doing, and so could only turn the helm toward the east, slowly following them along. As it happened, the two sailors were returning to gather the remains of the *qiu*, and only after they had once again chained it to the rear of the vessel did they proceed to the front, enter the diving chamber according to procedure, and take off their diving clothes. Other crewmembers gathered around them and asked what had happened.

One explained, "We were given our orders and went down to release the *qiu*. When the ship surfaced, a group of man-fish suddenly appeared, wanting to steal the *qiu* from us. We thought of how everyone had faced such peril and gone to such great lengths to catch it. If we were to bring it back and deliver it to a museum, it would be a feather in our cap, too. How could we let it go? So we fought them. Luckily, we had brought electronic guns with us and were able to shoot down two of them straight away; the others fled. We stood guard over the *qiu*, but they came back, so we had no choice but go out to meet them, firing our guns at them, which caused them to flee again. We pressed toward them, firing all the while. But who could have known that our guns would run out of ammunition? We didn't even get off a hundred shots—we probably only fired about thirty—and we were already out of bullets. When they saw that we were no longer firing at them they rushed toward us again, and we tried to fend them off with our guns. In the end, we were vastly outnumbered, and they managed to overpower us. That's when they opened their mouths to start biting us. Luckily the diving suits are sturdy and filled with plenty of air, so that they never actually got through to our flesh, and we were able to abide their gnawing without coming to any harm. Even the diving suits were undamaged! All we had to do was contrive a way to protect our exposed hands. Just as we were down to our last bit of strength, the ship arrived, and when the man-fish saw it, they scattered."

Lao Shaonian spoke a few words of comfort and praise, then told the two men to go rest. By now, with everything that had happened, it was already 10:00 p.m., so everyone stood around talking for a little longer, then went to bed.

On the following day the ship changed course and set out toward the south. Along the way Baoyu observed that amid the passing scenery of the ocean floor were more rare and precious treasures than one could possibly describe; however, these were all things that he had already seen at the museum, so he paid them no mind. After seeing several odd types of fish, he declared that he wished to catch them, but Lao Shaonian said that all of these were also already on display at the zoo, so Baoyu had to give up the idea.

They had been traveling in this way for two days when Lao Shaonian, having taken up a position at the helm, spotted a school of fish far off in the distance. When he put on his clarity-aiding lenses and took a closer look, he let out an involuntary cry of delight: "Since we have the rare opportunity of encountering such creatures today, we absolutely mustn't miss our chance!" He hurriedly gave the order to raise the ship by forty or fifty feet and went with Baoyu to the middle level, where they each donned diving suits.

"I still can't clearly see what kind of fish those are," said Baoyu. "Why are we going into the water ourselves?"

"We're certainly not going out into the sea," replied Lao Shaonian. "We're just going to spread nets from the diving chamber."

"But what fish *are* they?"

"It is recorded in the *Classic of Mountains and Seas* that 'Near Mount Dai, there is a river called the Peng, which flows west into Lake Pi, and in which are many *shu* fish. Their form is like that of a chicken, but with red feathers; it has three tails, six fins, and four eyes. Their call is like that of a magpie.'[2] I have long suspected that the words of the *Classic of Mountains and Seas* are unreliable; but this group of fish now approaching fit that description exactly—except that we haven't heard their cries yet. You and I have never tried out these diving suits, and luckily we now have the opportunity to try them out while staying on board. It's possible that we'll encounter some other marvelous things in the sea over the next few days; this way we'll be ready to go out into the water and take part in the action ourselves." So saying, he finished putting on his diving suit, picked up a platinum thread net, then opened the small door to the diving chamber and went in. Only when both were inside, with the first door closed safely behind them, did they open the door in front of them, allowing seawater to come rushing in. As the two men had not quite prepared themselves for this, they were nearly thrown off their feet by the surging water; fortunately, however, they were able to stand firm. They hurriedly spread wide the net, and soon the school of *shu* fish had reached the ship and began swimming past in a path directly underneath it. It was not long before the two men felt resistance in the net and quickly worked together to haul it back in. After closing the front door they pressed the electric signal button, and after about five minutes the chamber had been completely drained. The small door was then opened by someone on the other side, and the two men then reentered the body of the ship, where they removed their diving clothes. The air was filled with chaotic chirping—*jiji chacha*—the sound of the *shu* fish crying out from the nets. Lao Shaonian was greatly pleased and called for the fish to be placed in the holding tank. He also instructed someone to notify the kitchen that the dregs of any enhanced-essence foodstuffs were to be sent to the tank to feed the fish. He then returned with Baoyu to the upper level.

When everyone heard that they had caught *shu* fish, they descended to the middle level to go look. They marveled at them and commented on how strange they were. Lao Shaonian remarked, "What I hate the most are those people who declare that they understand current affairs, and who are constantly speaking of the five continents and the myriad countries. They claim to know everything about astronomy and geography, and yet have not *experienced* anything personally—they've just read about it from a couple of translated foreign books. Meanwhile, they insist on universally rejecting the ancient texts and records of their own ancestral homeland, claiming that they contain nothing but absurd nonsense. Today my catching of the *shu* fish has disproven such unjust criticism of the *Classic of Mountains and Seas*—it will surely stop the mouths of those who claim to understand current affairs!"

"It's just that the *Classic of Mountains and Seas* speaks of 'Mount Dai,' 'the Peng River,' and 'Lake Pi,'" Baoyu interjected. "While we are where, exactly?"

Fang Zhinan replied, "We arrived in the Southern Pacific Ocean some time ago now."

"What need is there to ask him where we are?" retorted Lao Shaonian. "Do you mean to suggest that fish can't move about? Besides, there are many places whose names have changed between ancient times and today!"

While they were speaking, Jiang Yin had dispatched someone to deliver them the following message: "The ship has surfaced. Please, everyone, put on your winter clothing and come to the top level to see the scenery of the Pacific Ocean."

"Why do we need to put on winter clothes?" asked Baoyu.

Lao Shaonian explained, "The weather in the Southern Hemisphere is the opposite of that in the Northern Hemisphere. Right now, though it's the sixth month in our Northern Hemisphere, it's like the twelfth month in the Southern Hemisphere!"

"But I didn't bring my winter clothes," Baoyu protested.

"Neither did I," added Lao Shaonian.

"There's no need to worry," said Fang Zhinan. "We have plenty. Just take some and put them on, you'll be fine." Thereupon, everyone changed into winter clothing and walked up to the top level, where the retractable hull had already been opened. As anticipated, the cold was fierce and biting, just as in the deepest winter. Suddenly a frigid gale blasted them in the face.

One of the crew called out, "How strange! The wind is so cold—how can it be coming from the south?"

Lao Shaonian replied, "In the Northern Hemisphere, our northerly winds blow from the Arctic Ocean in the north—that is why they are so cold. Here, these cold winds are being blown from the Antarctic Ocean in the south!"

These words animated Baoyu, who asked, "Where are we headed now?"

"Right now we are on a southeasterly course," answered Fang Zhinan. "We'll soon come upon South America; after that, if we keep heading east, we will reach the Atlantic."

"Why not plot a course directly south, so we can explore the Antarctic?" Baoyu asked.

"It's all ice down there," replied Lao Shaonian. "How could the ship move?"

"By my reckoning," Baoyu mused, "it won't necessarily be ice all the way down. Just now when we put out the nets to catch the *shu* fish, the water didn't feel cold, even though the air up above must have been as cold as this. So you see, it must be warmer under the water. If we were able to find a route through, wouldn't that be splendid? And on the off chance that it is indeed frozen all the way down, we'll turn around. Luckily, this ship is so fast that it wouldn't delay us by that much."

Everyone approved of this idea and went back below, after which the hull was then closed, and the ship returned to the depths. After setting a new course they set out directly south. But who could have known that as soon as the hull had been opened, frigid air would rush in, filling the ship? At once, it had become so cold throughout the ship that not only were those who had just been outside unable to remove their winter clothes—even those who had not gone out at all felt that it was too cold and put on more layers. Tan Ying opened the heating vents, which had to put out warm air for quite a while before the ship once again achieved a normal temperature. By now the party had no interest in watching the passing ocean scenery, so intent were they on reaching the Antarctic. The captain kicked up the throttle past its usual setting, and the ship sped along southward day and night.

One day, just as evening had fallen, they turned on the ship's illumination system; and when it was supposed to grow light again the following morning, they turned it back off. But who would have guessed that upon turning the system off all around them would remain in pitch darkness, for it had not yet grown light outside! They had no choice but to turn the illumination system back on—and from that point on, it did not grow light out again.

"Perhaps we've already reached the South Pole," mused Baoyu. "We must observe everything attentively!" He then went to look out one of the porthole windows. He could see that off to the side there were a number of small seamounts; the rocks that lay upon the mounts were a uniform white. Continuing his careful observations, Baoyu suddenly noticed that upon one of the mounts was growing a spire of multicolored coral of such crystalline transparency that it was as though it had been made of multihued glass. He pointed this out to Lao Shaonian, and said, "The museum's coral forest also has some multicolored specimens, but they don't have one of such crystalline clarity! We must go and take a few branches to bring back!"

Lao Shaonian agreed and issued instructions that the ship should be steered over toward the mount, then lowered to the bottom. He further instructed four crewmen to don diving suits, and to proceed through the small door of the diving chamber and thence out into the sea. No sooner had the small door been closed than the desperate ringing of the electric alarm bell, signaling the need for the water to be pumped back out of the chamber, could be heard by those on the upper level. They rushed to turn on the mechanism and pumped the water out; the bell was then pressed again to signal that the door could now be opened. The four crewmen came staggering back through the doorway. Removing their diving suits, they exclaimed, shivering all the while, "It's unbearable! The cold is much too intense—you could freeze to death out there!"

"Can you describe what happened?" Lao Shaonian inquired.

"We opened the outer door, and the seawater came pouring in. It was like ice! The cold was so intense, it immediately spread from our hands through our whole bodies."

"There's no need to worry," Lao Shaonian replied. "I've got a solution." Thereupon, he opened the door to one of the rooms in the middle level, retrieved a few pairs of gloves, and instructed the crewmen to put these on first before putting their diving suits back on. He also took four lengths of leather tubing, connecting one end of each to the heating system and the other to the breasts of the diving suits, filling the suits with warm air.

"Given how cold it is, we have certainly reached the South Pole," said Baoyu. "We absolutely must go down and have a look."

"It's fine for us to go look," replied Lao Shaonian, "But we must bring some extra men with us, so that if we encounter any kind of marvelous thing it will be easier to bring it back."

"We will need to bring guns, too. And this time, we must verify how much ammunition we have. We don't want to get caught out in a dangerous situation."

"In a place as cold as this, I'm afraid there won't be any wildlife."

"We'll just bring them along as a precautionary measure."

"If we're planning to bring guns, then we might as well bring some nets, just in case we catch anything to bring back."

When Lao Shaonian had finished saying this, he called up twenty-six crewmen, in addition to the four who had attempted to go out previously, for a total crew of thirty. Together they made all of the necessary preparations and filled their suits with warm air. They then proceeded out through the small door into the diving chamber, which was closed behind them. The outer door was opened, and the entire complement of thirty-two men swam out into the sea.

Baoyu activated the fins on his suit and, making his way onto the seamount, felt that this was an extremely untaxing method of travel. In a short time they had all arrived on the mount. Of the thirty crewmen, twenty had brought chisels and other such tools, while the remaining ten held guns. Those with the chisels began to chop away at the coral; those with the guns followed Baoyu and Lao Shaonian around to the rear of the mount to explore. Suddenly the group spied a tiny ocher-hued creature darting back and forth beneath Baoyu's feet. As Baoyu fixed his gaze on it, he realized that it was a sable, and it was not at all afraid of humans. Seeing that it was not afraid, Baoyu grabbed hold of it.

■ ■ ■

If you wish to know what kind of misadventure awaited our party after the catching of the sable, please listen to the explanation in the following chapter.

Chapter Thirty-One

While exploring the alien scenery of the South Pole, they see a whirlpool

Pursuing the gargantuan qiu, they accidentally discover an undersea tunnel

WE WERE speaking of how Baoyu had picked up the sable, which he handed to Lao Shaonian. Because they were both wearing diving suits they were unable to converse: even if they were to speak, their voices could not be heard through their suits, so the one would be unable to hear what the other said. As such, all they could do was look at each other to try to understand each other's meaning. Upon taking hold of the sable, Lao Shaonian scanned the area in all directions, and noticed that in front of him, at the base of the seamount, was a large group of sables numbering somewhere around two or three hundred. He gestured for the ten crewmen with guns to join him and Baoyu in pursuit. The twelve men activated the fins on their suits and propelled themselves forward. One of the crewmen fired off a shot, striking one of the sables; the group of sables then darted away toward the surface. Fins still flapping, the men made for the surface as well. Who could have known that having raced a hundred-some feet upward toward the surface, they would now see before them a profusion of sheer crystalline spines, jutting downward, preventing them from rising any further? Reaching out and stroking them with his hand, Baoyu found these outcroppings to be smooth and nearly frictionless. Raising the butt of his gun, he struck one of them, breaking off a piece. To his surprise, instead of sinking, the broken piece floated upward toward the surface. At this point, Baoyu became convinced that they had indeed arrived underneath the frozen Antarctic Ocean. "The water at the South Pole doesn't freeze all the way down," he thought, "so we have been traveling beneath the ice." The group of sables had fled into these icy outcroppings and by now had all vanished.

The icy spikes hung down in a confusion of crisscrossing points and sharp edges, like so many swords or blades, so the party dared not approach too closely. Lao Shaonian fired his gun at them and was able to dislodge several pieces; at this, Baoyu and the others also began to fire at will. Suddenly they saw the sables reemerge from their hiding places among the ice and hie back downward into the water. The party once again gave chase, following them all the way to the bottom, only for the sables to flee back to the surface, whither the party followed them once again. When they had pursued the sables back to within a short distance from the ice, Lao Shaonian suddenly turned off his fins and signaled to the rest of the party to do the same. He pulled out the bag containing the net, extracted the net, and passed it to a group of five crewmen. Using hand signals, he indicated that four of them were to spread the net open, while the fifth was to be in charge of the gathering rope.

He then gestured to them to hold their positions and remain motionless. This settled, Lao Shaonian and Baoyu led the other group of five crewmen to a spot just beyond the icy outcroppings, from which all seven began firing their guns at random toward the ice. As expected, the sables once again came surging out, swimming straight toward the depths. But how could they have known that this time they would be caught up in the net that had been stretched out across their path? When the sables hit the net, the men at the corners let go, allowing the man in charge of the rope to quickly draw the net closed so that not a single sable was able to escape. Lao Shaonian was most pleased by this and waved his hands to signal that the sables should be brought back to the ship straight away. The crewmen understood and departed.

Baoyu suddenly felt something strike his foot, and when he looked down to see, he discovered that it was a piece of coral—so big around that he could probably have just fit his arms around it—drifting upward toward the surface. Baoyu hurriedly seized hold of it, then straddled it to keep it from floating away. However, the piece of coral continued floating upward, so Baoyu had to quickly activate his fins and apply downward force to keep it from rising further. Making his way over to the seamount, he saw a number of crewmen also grappling with pieces of coral, looking helplessly at one another for guidance. When they saw how Baoyu had managed to straddle his piece of coral, they all happily followed his example and in this manner guided the pieces of coral back to the ship. Altogether, twenty-one such pieces of coral were gathered, but in the end only two were brought into the ship since the others were either too long or their branches forked too widely to fit on board. Baoyu gestured to a crewman to come hold onto his piece of coral for him. After entering through the outer door of the ship, he closed it behind himself; then he pressed the electric button, and in a short while, the water had all been drained away. From beside the small inner door, he took up two bundles of platinum-thread ropes, then went back out into the sea, handing one bundle to a group of crewmen, and making hand gestures to indicate that they should use the ropes to tie the large pieces of coral to the rear of the vessel. He then pointed back to the mount and gestured that they should return there once the corals had been secured.

Baoyu returned to the mount with his own bundle of ropes under his arm. The remaining eleven men of his own party—including Lao Shaonian—were still there, hacking away at the corals. Baoyu pulled out a few strands of rope and signed to the others that they should tie the ropes around their corals, then gestured toward the rear of the ship to communicate his intention. He himself set to work pulling up a number of small corals and tying them into several bundles before towing them back to the ship. He brought these smaller corals in through the front doorway as per normal procedure, then had them piled into an empty storeroom. Just as he was about to go back out the front door opened, and Lao Shaonian and the group of crewmen accompanying him returned. They, too, carried with them a number of bunches of small corals and brought these on board. As each man hurriedly divested himself of his diving clothes, he found himself shivering. They all commented, "How strange! We weren't cold at all while in the sea, how is it that we're so cold now that we've returned to the ship?" The men who had remained on board reported that a swell of frigid air had suddenly pervaded the ship at just that moment. As they spoke, the air grew colder still, and the group hastened to go upstairs and put on more clothes. Lao Shaonian and Baoyu borrowed some clothing from Fang Zhinan and put it on.

"Everything we collected today is some kind of marvelous object," remarked Baoyu. "I had only ever heard of the sea hippo, the sea tiger, the sea otter, and the sea dragon; I'd never before heard of a sea sable, but there is no way that the creature we caught today can be called anything but a 'sea sable.' And corals that are so brilliant all the way through—not only had I never seen such a thing, but they even float in water! Song-era neo-Confucians believed that anything they hadn't seen with their own eyes simply didn't exist; I wonder what today's scholars of neo-Confucianism would do if they heard about this?"

"This kind of sable has never appeared before. As it makes its nest among the icy cliffs, it might just as easily be called an 'ice sable.' And as for the floating corals, once we've brought them back with us, they will put the 'floating stones' of the South Seas to shame!" replied Lao Shaonian.[1]

By now Tan Ying had turned on the heating system, but the men still felt cold. Suddenly a messenger sent by helmsman You Long appeared and announced, "Please come to the helm to observe a strange phenomenon."

The two men hastened off to the helm, and, positioning themselves in front of the metal-penetrating lens, looked out. There in the middle of the ocean they saw a stream of water rising vertically from the sea floor, as straight as the handle of a brush. The water on all sides of this stream whirled and flowed round it. The men all immediately commented on how bizarre this was, and Baoyu asked, "Did you notice this while we were stopped?"

"No," replied You Long. "We'd already been moving for quite a while again before we saw it."

Baoyu was lost in thought for a moment, then looked back out and carefully reexamined the stream of water before he came to a sudden realization: "Of course! That column of water must mark the center of the South Pole. The Earth rotates toward the east, and if you look, you'll see that the water flowing all round that column is flowing toward the west. That is because the Earth is spinning quickly: the water, which just sits on top of the actual Earth itself, must necessarily rotate in the opposite direction. As the Earth spins more rapidly toward the east, the water, spinning toward the west, flows more quickly, as well. When the flow becomes quite strong, it turns into a whirlpool. What we're seeing is the lower part of the vortex."

Lao Shaonian nodded. "That's in line with my understanding as well."

The others all agreed that Baoyu's conclusion seemed correct. After a short while the ship had passed the vortex, and it was no longer possible to see the stream of water from the helm. By now it had become extraordinarily cold aboard the ship, but no one could quite understand why. They all assumed that it must be because the South Pole was so extremely cold that the ship's hull was unable to prevent the cold from penetrating it, and so they didn't really pay it much mind.

Recalling the ice sables, Lao Shaonian decided to go down to the lower level to have a look at them. He saw the sables swimming and playing about freely in the ship's holding tanks. However, he also noticed that some thirty or forty of the sables had died, so he asked the guard, "How did they die?"

The guard replied, "Within a short time of coming on board, they started dying one after the other; and those that didn't die seemed stunned. But now that it's gotten so cold, they seem to have come back to life. Look—a layer of ice has even formed on the surface of the water!"

Lao Shaonian looked closely, and indeed, a layer of ice had formed there. He then gave instructions for the ice to be broken up and for the bodies of the dead sables to be fished out from the tank. The guard began to do as instructed. Lao Shaonian took one of the dead sables from him and looked it over. Though the sable had just come out of the water, its fur was completely dry. Lao Shaonian thought, "It would be wonderful indeed to make a fur coat from their pelts." By now the cold had penetrated into his bones, and he felt he couldn't bear to stay down there much longer. Wanting to see the corals, he walked toward the front of the ship to have a look—but who would have guessed that all that cold air was being given off by the corals themselves? As he made his way closer and closer to them, the air became so cold that he could scarcely breathe and was forced to retreat.

Upon returning to the upper level, he gave instructions that ample food for the sables and *shu* fish should be deposited in the tanks, thus obviating the need for guards. The lower-deck personnel all came up into the middle level, and the lower level was tightly sealed off. After some time had passed the upper two levels finally began to grow warmer again.

The ship traveled on for another two days, still beneath the icy surface of the Antarctic Ocean. "We should have been able to cross into the Indian Ocean from here," commented Lao Shaonian. "But how is it that after traveling for so many days, we are still in the Antarctic?"

Wang Zuoji answered him, "Under the Antarctic the current is very strong, so the ship travels quite a bit more slowly. We should be able to get out of here by tomorrow."

As the group stood chatting around the helm, they suddenly noticed a towering seamount, scallion-green in color, in front of them.

"How is it that algae can still grow in such a cold place?" asked Baoyu. But when he put on his clarity-aiding lenses and looked again, he saw that it was not green with algae but was in fact a mountain of natural green stone. He was delighted and announced, "We must gather some of these stones to bring back with us. Take a look—it's simply breathtaking!"

"We must prepare well before going out to collect it," said Lao Shaonian. "Last time after bringing back a few branches of coral, we nearly froze the entire crew solid! If these stones were to be the same, it would be terrible. We should bring some ropes with us and tie any samples we collect to the rear of the boat."

"Ropes won't work!" Baoyu disagreed. "The stones are extremely craggy. If we were to use ropes we wouldn't be able to secure very many. We'd better use a net!"

They discussed it for a while before settling on a suitable approach, and finally, as before, they instructed forty sailors to outfit themselves appropriately and fill their suits with warm air. Even those sailors who were tasked with staying in the lower level to man the diving chamber doors were instructed to do the same. By the time the procession of sailors entered the sea, the ship had already navigated to a position in front of the mountain and stopped. As the divers made their way to the front of the mountain, Baoyu swam out in front and selected a piece. Luckily the stones were plentiful and not at all difficult to dig out. Baoyu was afraid that the stones would float away like the corals, so he gingerly took his hands off the piece he had collected; however, it didn't move. Only then was he reassured and placed the stone in the net. The group of divers all pitched in to fill the large net before finally bearing it back to the rear of the ship and fastening it there. They then reboarded the ship and removed their diving suits, and the ship proceeded on its way.

After another day of travel they finally emerged from under the frozen Antarctic Ocean, which put the entire crew in a jubilant mood. The natural cycle of day and night was also restored, albeit with short days and long nights. Of course, electric lighting had always been available on board the ship at any time, but it would no longer be necessary to use the underwater illumination system during the day: looking out through a porthole, one could see clearly enough without making use of any artificial lighting.

Around noon they decided to surface the ship and investigate their surroundings. Just as they were about to start the ascent, there suddenly appeared a *qiu*, writhing and coiling in an adversarial stance. It was clear that it intended to strike the ship. Hai Dao cried out, "Oh no! There are so many things tied to the rear of the ship, we would have to cut them all loose before we can roll up the soft glass barrier again! What can we do?" Just as everyone went back and forth over the best way to confront the *qiu*, they saw that the *qiu* suddenly turned tail and fled. Lao Shaonian clapped his hands. "Well, since it's decided to flee, we might as well go after it!" Thereupon they opened the throttle, and the ship pressed full speed ahead in pursuit. The *qiu* swam at great speed, and the ship gave chase for an entire day and night. As they finally drew nearer their quarry, they knew they needed to guard against it turning round to attack the ship, so every man—from the highest ranking to the lowest—focused his sights wholly and intently on the figure of the *qiu*. As they watched, the *qiu* darted away along the side of a great mountain. Since they themselves were following in great haste, they were unable to determine just how large the mountain was, but it appeared large enough to be part of a continental coastline. The men felt that now that the *qiu* had run itself into a dead end at the coast, it would likely turn and lash out at them like a cornered beast, and so they watched with ever greater vigilance. They saw the *qiu* approach the foot of the mountain, when suddenly, with a twist of its body, it vanished. The crew were shocked and continued observing closely. It so happened that there was an enormous cave at the base of the mountain, into which the *qiu* had plunged. Lao Shaonian called for the illumination system to be turned on, so that light could be shone into the depths of the cave. The light was shone into the cave for a little while, but they found that they were unable to determine just how deep the cave went. Lao Shaonian and Baoyu cried out in unison: "'How can you catch the tiger if you don't go into its lair?' Since it's fleeing from us, it must be afraid. How can we let it go now? We simply must go in after it!"

Baoyu added, "Perhaps it's the same one that previously saw us kill the other *qiu*, which is why it became afraid as soon as it saw us."

"You're right!" replied Lao Shaonian. "That one swam off toward the south, and just now, we are ourselves returning to the north from the south, which is why we have encountered it on the way. Go after it!"

At this command, the ship was maneuvered to the mouth of the cave. The electric lights of the illumination system were turned up to full brightness, and the ship was steered in.

Inside the cave, a number of tunnels led off in different directions, but they simply decided to follow the widest one. The *qiu* had long since disappeared from view ahead of them. As they moved through the cave the way grew narrower and narrower, but Lao Shaonian was concerned only with pressing onward. After four hours of pursuit, the ship suddenly emerged from the other end of the cave; but there was no trace of the *qiu*. The crew all commented on how surprising this was before turning off the illumination system and bringing the ship to the surface. Opening the hull and looking out in all directions—strange indeed!—they found that they had arrived at the northern coast of Australia. Lao Shaonian looked back to contemplate the cave and realized that the cave was in fact an ocean tunnel running under Australia. In their pursuit of the *qiu*, they had unintentionally discovered this new route. When they had finished looking around, they once again closed the hatch, resubmerged the ship, and set off toward the north.

They had not been traveling for long when they suddenly spied another vessel. It, too, was traveling underwater, but at quite a shallow depth, nowhere near the bottom. Lao Shaonian pointed it out to Baoyu: "Look—that is an undersea warship belonging to one of the current 'civilized countries.'" Baoyu noted that the hull of the other vessel was infested with clinging snails and mollusks and was covered with a green mat of algae.

"How is it that our ship isn't covered in snails and algae like theirs is?" Baoyu asked.

"Our soft glass is coated with a particular fluid," replied Lao Shaonian, "which inhibits the growth of these things. And look—even though their ship is submerged, the smokestack still has to stick out of the water! Watch, I'll give them a fright!" He then instructed Tan Ying to turn on the illumination system. After a moment, they turned it off, then on again. The other vessel immediately surfaced.

Baoyu asked, "Why did they do that?"

"They don't have water-penetrating lenses or metal-penetrating lenses," replied Lao Shaonian. "So when they look out, all they see is vast murkiness. Even if they can see a bit of a shadow, it is incredibly blurry. When we gave off those sudden flashes of light just now, they will have been able to see the flashes, but not make out our true form. This will have put them on alert, so they have chosen to surface. Now, when they return to their home country, they will make a report to the government, causing much ado among who knows how many scientists, PhDs, and scholars, who will come to research the source of this underwater illumination!"

Tan Ying, watching Lao Shaonian speaking with such glee, smiled, brought the ship close to the surface, and gave a couple more flashes of light before hurriedly diving into the depths once again and speeding off toward the north. He said, "I just know that when they go back to make their report to their scientists, PhDs, and scholars, they will say that they have discovered an enormous electric fish in their explorations off the northern coast of Australia!" At this the whole group laughed.

"Indeed, they will certainly think we were some kind of animal," Baoyu commented.

"Not *us*!" retorted Tan Ying. "It is the ship that is the animal—*we* are but the contents of its stomach!"

As they were joking, they suddenly heard the thundering of a cannon. Rushing to look out the windows, they saw a shell sinking through the water, straight toward the bottom, having been fired at the location near the surface where their own vessel had last flashed the illumination system. As it turned out, the other ship was pursuing them. Lao Shaonian snorted, "A ship like that can't travel even half as far as we can in an hour—yet they would try to give chase! It's both pitiful and ridiculous!"

"There's no reason to let them blunder after us vainly in blind pursuit," added Tan Ying, giving another flash of the illumination system. After about fifteen minutes had passed he gave another flash, explaining, "This way, they can see just how fast we travel. Of course, they'll give up the chase now."

■ ■ ■

If you wish to know whether the warship continued its pursuit or not, please listen to the explanation in the following chapter.

Chapter Thirty-Two

Collected treasures change warm to cool in an instant

Partaking of fine liquor at a feast, they discuss civilization and barbarity

WE HAD been speaking of how Tan Ying had let off two further bursts of illumination, after which, as anticipated, the other vessel abandoned its pursuit. Baoyu commented, "You could say they have 'retreated in the face of difficulty'!"

Lao Shaonian replied, "Though they may have 'retreated in the face of difficulty,' I dare say we still managed to unsettle them a bit!" Everyone chatted and laughed together for a little while before the group broke up and each man found a spot at the side of the ship from which to watch the passing ocean scenery.

Not much later the ship crossed the equator. Baoyu noted, "We've already been to a place of extreme cold; but it is too bad that we were only able to travel beneath the ice there and never got to surface. Now that we have arrived in an extremely hot place, I'd like to go to the surface to see what the weather's like."

Hai Dao heard this and brought the ship to the surface. After opening the hull, the group made its way to the topmost level so they could look out. As expected, it was swelteringly hot. Lao

Shaonian suddenly recalled that the coral that was being stored in the lower level gave off cold air—so why not bring a stalk of it up here and see what happened when exposed to such a hot environment? He instructed a crewmember to go fetch a branch of coral. The crewmember was gone for a short time, then returned with the coral. He said, "It's strange—up here it feels like summer, but down in the lower level it feels like winter!" He then set down the coral, and the group instantly felt a burst of coolness, which they found thoroughly refreshing—though they all agreed that it was strange.

Baoyu asked Lao Shaonian, "How did you know it could be used like this?"

Lao Shaonian then explained in detail what he had discovered previously on the lower level.

"Ah, so that's how it is," replied Baoyu. "This coral will be quite the treasure in summertime!"

They continued gazing out for some time before finally going back below decks and closing the hull. By this time, the cabins had all filled with hot air from outside, so Hai Dao was about to turn on the cooling system when Lao Shaonian stopped him, saying, "Don't turn it on yet—let's test out this coral first." As hoped, in very little time, the air inside grew cooler. Lao Shaonian then instructed someone to bring the coral back down to the lower level. Baoyu wished to go along to see the situation down there for himself. The crewman informed him, "If you gentlemen wish to go down there, you should first put on some winter clothes—it's freezing down there!" The rest of the group, hearing this, also put on winter clothes and accompanied him down to the lower level, where, just as the man had said, it was extraordinarily cold.

"How has it gotten so cold?" Baoyu asked.

"Just think about it," replied Lao Shaonian. "One stem of coral gave off so much cool air while outside under the blazing sun. Down here we've amassed some hundred-plus corals, and there's nowhere for the cold air to escape to—how could it not be cold?"

The group gathered round the corals to look for a little while, until their hands and feet started to grow numb and stiffen with the cold. Turning his head, Baoyu noticed the heap of dead sables and asked how they had died; Lao Shaonian repeated what the guard had told him previously. Baoyu picked up one of the dead sables and, observing that its coat was glossy and smooth—quite lovely—couldn't help but repeatedly stroke the fur. After a few moments, he noticed that his hands had begun to warm back up. He suddenly realized that this was a creature that lived in an extremely cold place, so naturally it was possessed of an extremely warm pelt, which was how it was able to protect itself from the cold. The dead sables had obviously died of overheating after being brought onboard the ship. Looking back over at the holding tank, upon which a layer of ice two or three feet thick had already formed, he saw that the sables and the *shu* fish were swimming about freely beneath the ice. He thought, "It's lucky that we brought those corals on board, so that they could give off all that cold air. Otherwise we wouldn't have been able to keep these animals alive." He then said as much to Lao Shaonian.

Lao Shaonian took the dead sable from Baoyu and stroked it for a few moments—as expected, his hands grew warmer, too. He nodded: "You were right, of course!" The rest of the group observed the scene for a little while longer before returning to the upper level and sealing off the lower level. By now the upper level had filled with cold air from below, such that Hai Dao had to run the heating system for some time before the temperature was back to normal.

As it happened, all of the air that circulated through the ship's cabins was man-made and so was insulated from the external weather. The ship also had both cooling and heating systems, so the crew could control the internal climate as they desired and create a climate that was comfortably temperate—neither too hot nor too cold. It was only when the hull was retracted or the hatch opened that they would be affected by the seasonal climate outside.

But let us speak no more of idle things. Let us speak instead of how within another two days of travel, our underwater hunting vessel finally reached the Realm of Civilization once more and pulled into the harbor of the No. 2 District of the Strong Region. They brought the vessel to the surface, retracted the hull, and threw open all of the hatches and portholes. Fang Zhinan picked up the wireless telephone and notified Wu Shuqi of their return. A short while later, Shuqi arrived at the coast in a flying car, boarded a sampan, and came out to greet them. Lao Shaonian and Baoyu recounted to him in brief everything they had encountered on the journey. Shuqi was delighted and said, "You've brought back so many unique items! The learning of our people will benefit greatly from your efforts. The two of you endured a great deal of hardship on your journey, please go back to the Naval Academy for now and have a rest."

"First we must devise a way to deal with the things we brought back with us," Lao Shaonian protested. "The *qiu* is enormous—it must be about four or five hundred feet long. How will we get it onto shore?"

Shuqi replied, "You've managed to bring it back all the way from the South Pole, and yet you're afraid we lack the means to get it onto shore? Please come ashore first, and we can talk about it at greater length then."

Having heard him say this, Lao Shaonian and Baoyu took their leave of the crew and rode a sampan back to shore, where they boarded Shuqi's flying car and flew back to the academy. Once both host and guests had sat down together, a serving boy came and served tea.

"The two of you faced great perils on this trip," mused Shuqi. "And not only did you obtain all of those rare specimens, but you discovered that there is a vortex at the South Pole. The merit you have earned is truly to be celebrated." Lao Shaonian and Baoyu both modestly refused the compliment.

"I would ask that we first come up with a means of securing the *qiu*," replied Baoyu. "Otherwise, in this sweltering summer weather, won't it start rotting?"

"Let's send a telegram to Duo Jianshi and explain it to him. We can ask him what to do about it," said Shuqi.

"Excellent! Excellent!" Lao Shaonian agreed. "And as for those sables, if they are removed from the ice, they will die. Please send another telegram to the zoo and ask them to devise a solution. However, I don't know who is currently director of the zoo."

"Why, it's Duo Jianshi's older brother Duo Zhi, whose style name is Nengshi."[1]

"The names of these two brothers were chosen aptly!" declared Baoyu. "And it almost seems a self-fulfilling prophecy that men with names like theirs should end up in charge of such institutions."

"There is also a younger brother," added Shuqi, "whose name is Duo Cai, and whose style name is Duo Yishi. His scientific abilities are even more formidable! Right now, in the No. 1 District of the Wisdom Region of the Eastern Sector, he and Dongfang Fa have worked together to open an enormous factory complex. Within the district, there are no residential areas—the entire district is dedicated to their factories."

"That is even more formidable!" Baoyu breathed.

"That being the case," said Lao Shaonian, "why don't we first send out those telegrams, then we can have a more leisurely chat."

At this, Shuqi instructed his secretary to send off the two telegrams.

Lao Shaonian started again: "The *qiu* and the sables are the only things that need to be dealt with carefully. As for all of the other specimens, why not just have them brought here first?"

"How many other things are there?" asked Shuqi. Lao Shaonian gave him a rough estimate, after which Shuqi dispatched forty workmen in five flying cars to go collect the specimens from the ship. The three men then resumed their leisurely conversation.

Baoyu asked why Shengwu had not made an appearance. Shuqi answered, "The academy has let out for summer break recently—all of the instructors have left to escape the heat."

"How many instructors does your academy have?" Baoyu continued.

"Altogether there are five hundred different instructors. But Shengwu is the only dean."

"Since your academy has fifty thousand students, I wonder: How do you teach them all? Five hundred faculty to teach fifty thousand students seems adequate, but what I mean is, how do you *accommodate* them all?"

"The day that you went to listen to Shengwu's lecture, you were in the main lecture hall. We have fifty other separate lecture halls, each of which can accommodate a thousand students attending a lecture." When he had finished speaking, Shuqi led Lao Shaonian and Baoyu to go look at two of the separate lecture halls, which had all been built near the student residences. After examining two of these halls they meandered back out to the training grounds, where they encountered a cohort of students, numbering somewhere over a thousand, engaged in physical training.

"How is it that this group of students hasn't left for the summer break?" inquired Baoyu.

"These are the students who were unwilling to leave and instead chose to remain here to hone their skills."

The students, seeing that the superintendent had brought guests with him, all bowed in respectful greeting. Shuqi returned the courtesy, while Lao Shaonian and Baoyu bowed to them as well.

Suddenly they were buffeted by a blast of cool wind, and saw five flying cars descending through the air. The large pieces of coral and the stones were suspended beneath the cars, while the smaller corals, the sea hippo, and the dead sables had all been carried within. The forty laborers transporting these items were so cold that they were shivering, and one of them remarked, "The weather sure is strange this year! I'm afraid we're due for a summer snow!"

Lao Shaonian gave a self-reproaching stamp of his foot and replied, "That's my fault! In a lapse of caution, I neglected to tell you to put on winter clothes before you went! Hurry up and get out of there—once you've gotten away from these things, you won't feel so cold." The forty laborers then hurriedly dispersed.

By this time the entire training ground had grown chilly, as if it were already deep autumn. Shuqi ordered some men to carry the sea hippo and the dead sables into the reception hall. Lao Shaonian further instructed them to take a small piece of coral and one of the stones to the reception hall as well, as gifts for Shuqi. He likewise selected one of each of these to leave as a gift for Shengwu, saying, "By rights, having collected all of these samples, we shouldn't give them to people as private gifts; rather, we should be sending them all to the museum. But these are to express our thanks for letting us make use of your hunting ship."

Shuqi accepted the gifts with his thanks, and the men returned together to the reception hall. Once the coral and stone had been set out, the entire hall was filled with fresh, cool air. Lao Shaonian gave the order that the coral should be relocated to another room, leaving only the stone, as an experiment. They soon discovered to their great delight that the stone, too, emitted cold air.

"This stone must have been formed by the congelation of cold air over who-knows-how-many eons," remarked Shuqi. "It is natural that it should possess such properties and must be considered a rare treasure!"

"Since such a stone has never before been discovered," mused Lao Shaonian, "I don't know what it is called. Perhaps it is best to call it 'Precious Stone.'"

"How could anything in nature have its own name?" Shuqi corrected him. "Everything with a name is named by people. Since it can give off chilly air, we must include the word 'chill' in its name: let's call it 'Precious Chillstone.'"

Baoyu protested, "But we found it ourselves, how can we possibly be so self-aggrandizing as to pronounce it 'precious'? Its vibrant emerald color is extremely captivating, it would be better to call it 'Emerald Chillstone.'"

"'Emerald Chillstone'—wonderful!" Shuqi exclaimed. "Very elegant indeed."

As they were discussing this, Sun Shengwu suddenly arrived, followed by Duo Jianshi and two serving boys, each carrying a leather sack on his back. The three men hurried to their feet to greet the new arrivals. Shuqi asked, "How is it that you come to be here so opportunely?"

Shengwu replied, "I just happened to have gone to the museum to see the *peng* that these two gentlemen had captured. When your telegram arrived there, Jianshi was concerned that the *qiu* would begin to rot; and I, hearing that you had obtained all kinds of marvelous treasures, was keen to come inspect them. So I caught a lift in Jianshi's flying car."

"But how did you get here so quickly?" Shuqi pressed.

"We couldn't have if we'd come in a normal fast car. Luckily Jianshi's younger brother Duo Yishi built this extra-fast car, which can travel 2,500 li in two hours. That's how we were able to get here so quickly." As he continued speaking, the men politely urged each other to sit.

Duo Jianshi thanked Lao Shaonian and Baoyu for their efforts, then asked them to estimate the length of the *qiu*.

"We haven't measured it," replied Lao Shaonian.

"Once we've measured it, we'll be better able to devise a way to transport it."

Shuqi added, "These two were just worrying that there might not be a good way to move it."

"Oh, that's easy!" said Duo Jianshi. "Once we know its length, we'll craft a leather bag to fit it in and transport it by tunnel car."

Shuqi picked up the wireless telephone and called the ship. He instructed them to send someone down into the water to measure the length of the *qiu*. A short while later the report came back through the line: "From head to tail, 550 feet in length; at the widest point of its torso, the circumference is 180 feet; at the narrowest point, the circumference is 80 feet. The widest segment starts 100 feet from the head and ends 350 feet from the tail."

Having heard this, Duo Jianshi sent a telegram to his younger brother Duo Cai, instructing him to quickly fabricate a leather sack corresponding to these specifications and asking how many days it would take to complete the work.

Not long after that Jianshi's older brother Duo Nengshi arrived from the zoo, having come in an extra-fast car as well. After they had all completed all the social niceties, Nengshi pulled a large crate out of the car and asked Lao Shaonian, "Would the sables fit in a crate of this size?"

"I'm afraid it's much too small," Lao Shaonian replied.

Nengshi was taken aback. "Just how many did you bring back?"

"We caught them with a net, so I only know that we caught a great many—we didn't count them. But I'd estimate that it's no fewer than five or six hundred."

"And how large is each one?"

Lao Shaonian pulled out one of the dead sables to show him. Nengshi looked at it and laughed: "If there are indeed six hundred of them, they should fit just fine! That leaves the *shu* fish, but since they can withstand either hot or cold temperatures, we can transport them in any kind of container."

Shuqi and Shengwu then immediately called for liquor to be poured so that they could serve a welcome dinner for Lao Shaonian and Baoyu. The two Duo brothers were invited to stay as well. A flying car was also dispatched to go retrieve the eight members of the bridge crew from the hunting ship. Two tables were laid out, and once guests and hosts had all taken their seats, a serving boy entered and began pouring liquor. Up until this point Baoyu had not yet drunk any of the Realm's spirits, nor had he participated in any kind of toast. He thought, "They've made improvements on everything here—I honestly don't know how they will have improved on liquor, but I certainly must give it a try!" When the boy set the liquor in front of him, its fragrance immediately filled his nose. In addition to his cup of liquor, each man was served a cup of fruit nectar. Shuqi raised his glass, encouraging his guests to drink first; so Baoyu took a sip and found the liquor to be rich and flavorful. He then used a spoon to taste a mouthful of the fruit nectar and determined it to have the fragrant savor of tangerines. He then asked Lao Shaonian, "All of the refinements you make to food and beverages here are naturally made with an eye to making them healthier. But I've heard that liquor is a substance that is completely without any health benefit, so I wonder how you have refined it?"

"We have simply eliminated the liquor's fiery quality while at the same time enriching it with fortifying substances. We have also made it so that the flavor of the liquor is extremely rich and deep, so that people might better enjoy drinking it. But none of this is anything special—the most remarkable improvement we've made is that you can drink it and not get drunk! No matter who, once they have drunk to the point where they would normally be greatly inebriated, they simply become joyful and uninhibited and feel as if there is a new realm of happiness within their hearts—like when someone unexpectedly receives joyful news. It goes without saying that neither do they get into drunken mischief, nor do they give off the wafting stench of alcohol."

Shuqi added, "Originally, the purpose of drinking liquor was to aid the flow of conversation, where drinking could be taken as a topic of discussion. Why should anyone decide they needed to turn it into some kind of crazy drug that induces madness in those who imbibe it? What is achieved by that?"

"I wouldn't say that," said Shengwu. "The ancients liked to use liquor as a means of observing man's true morality: once a person is drunk, he will necessarily expose his true nature. That is how alcohol enables observation of morality; so if they'd only had liquor like ours, how could they do it? I have previously seen people from barbaric countries proudly and arrogantly refer to themselves as 'civilized'; but when they become drunk they become violent and cruel, running amok and causing trouble. If they're not refusing to pay their rickshaw fare, they are randomly barging into people's homes or even stealing things as they walk down the street—they wreak havoc until eventually, they lie down to sleep in the street wherever the fancy strikes them. Does this not completely expose their uncivilized nature?"

"Indeed." Baoyu agreed. "I lived for a time in Shanghai, and when I read about the various court cases in the newspaper, there were almost never cases of drunken Chinese causing trouble. But the police did often report cases where someone had gotten drunk and caused trouble—and it was always a high-ranking person from a 'civilized' country. That's what I'd call strange."

"There's a reason for this," said Lao Shaonian. "Chinese society became enlightened a long time ago. As far back as the times of the three sovereigns and the five patriarchs, culture had already taken form, so that by the time of emperors Wen and Wu, ritual and music were already largely complete. It is only to be lamented that the Chinese continued to hold onto the accomplishments of their forebears and did not change, and so they were much delayed in evolving beyond that; whereas those countries that now call themselves 'civilized,' though much delayed in achieving enlightenment, have in fact been able to evolve quickly. China became enlightened early on, so before a Chinese person ever even emerges from the womb, his nervous system already contains an innate understanding of social mores and respect for ritual and law. So although their evolution has been slow, their original, innate character has not been extinguished, which is why even after they get drunk they do not create havoc. Even if one or two among a group does tend to become wild when drunk, among his drinking companions there will always those who remain orderly and go to help steady their disorderly friends. That is why it never reaches the point of causing chaos.

"As for the people who have only belatedly become enlightened, the character that runs through their entire being is still precariously built upon a foundation of barbarity. Although they have evolved quickly, this has merely compelled them to restrict their behaviors to those defined by 'righteousness and morality.' Try as they might to obey these externally imposed restrictions, their entire being chafes against them. So as soon as they become drunk, how can they not but expose their original character? That is why when any one of them becomes drunk, he necessarily becomes wild. When a hundred of them become drunk, then that hundred all become wild. If there ever came a day when the entire country were to get drunk, then the entire country would go wild!"

The rest of the group, hearing this, all laughed.

■ ■ ■

If you wish to know what other commentaries would be made, please listen to the explanation in the following chapter.

Chapter Thirty-Three

A secretary embarks on a trip to present regional rarities to the emperor

Strolling through a park, they admire the summer snow

WE WERE speaking of how, at the end of his discourse on alcohol, Lao Shaonian had unexpectedly thrown in the joke, "If there ever came a day when the entire country were to get drunk, then the entire country would go wild!" getting a laugh from the rest of the group.

Lao Shaonian went on, "That's not entirely a joke—as I recall, they have a particular day of commemoration, and every year on that day, the entire country's students, craftsmen, soldiers and sailors, as well as all of the administrators, are given a holiday. The entire country ceases working. Everyone drinks, and not a single person fails to get drunk. Once they've gotten drunk, they jostle and shove this way and that through the streets, committing all kinds of misdeeds, while law enforcement turns a blind eye, as if there were no laws at all."

"But—" Shengwu cut in, "if they were to drink our own civilized liquor, how could anyone ever be able to see their true barbaric selves? Wouldn't they then just be able to deceive the entire world with their false facade of civilization?"

Shuqi laughed. "Among themselves, of course, they may not be able to do without alcohol to expose their true selves; but using liquor as a means of observing man's true morality is no more than a crude method that the ancients relied upon. We here have our special lens for examining a man's quality, so we can ascertain it with a single glance. Why should we need to rely on alcohol?"

Three rounds of drinks were served while they chatted. Every time a new round was presented, a new type of fruit nectar was brought out as well, which, upon trying, all proved to be different. The nectars were sweet, fragrant, and crisp, and as they rinsed over one's palate, their flavors surged to one's head just as did the fragrance of the liquor. As promised, the more they drank, the more enlivened their spirits became, but without even a trace of drunkenness. They all continued speaking of overseas affairs, all praising and commending one another in turn, merrily and expansively. Once they had finished eating and drinking, they each stood up from their tables. The eight bridge crew presently took their leave, while the others retired to their rooms at the academy. We have no further details of the evening's events.

On the following day Nengshi arrived with an iron crate and appointed a group of men to proceed with him to the hunting ship to retrieve the ice sables. They were transported to the coast immediately in flying cars, then ferried over to the ship in sampans. When they reached the lower level of the hunting ship, they discovered that the ice that had formed within the tank had already almost completely melted. Nengshi remarked, "Luckily we've arrived as quickly as we have—if the ice had melted completely, they all would have died!" He then took out a small electronic box and ran two leads from it onto the ice. He activated the electronic mechanism, and in the blink of an eye, the sables and the *shu* fish that had just been swimming about so energetically in the tank were all simultaneously stunned into a state of paralysis. Nengshi instructed four crewmen to don electricity-proof diving suits and insulated gloves, then to go into the tank to gather the sables one by one. At the same time he opened the iron crate so that all of the collected sables could be placed within it. When Baoyu approached the crate to get a better look, he saw that a shallow layer of water filled half the crate and felt a burst of cool air coming from within. As each sable was placed in the crate, it became animated once again—however, the crate was too small to permit them to swim about as they had been before. After a little while, all of the sables had been transferred to the crate, and a count was made: it turned out that there were only 450, so the crate was not completely full. Nengshi gave orders for the crate to be filled the rest of the way with water. The sables were so tightly packed within the crate that they could only just turn themselves around. Nengshi then sealed the crate and cranked a small lever that was mounted on its side.

"What kind of mechanism is that?" asked Baoyu.

"An ice-making machine has been installed between the double walls of the crate," Nengshi replied. "With just a few cranks of the lever, half of the space inside the crate will have turned into ice, leaving liquid water in the other half, so that the sables can breathe. That way they'll survive transport." He proceeded to take out two soft leather bags and had the *shu* fish placed in them. The bags, too, were then filled with water before being tied shut. Nengshi instructed some sailors to lade these and the crate onto the sampans; he then took his leave of the group and headed back to shore, where he boarded a flying car and returned with his specimens to the zoo.

Jianshi subsequently ordered some of the remaining crew-members to go down into the water to untether the *qiu* from the ship and bring the end of the platinum chain onto shore. After this had been done, the group rode sampans back ashore, where a system of winches and cranes were activated to haul the tremendous *qiu* up onto land. Upon closer inspection, the *qiu* was actually of terrifyingly large proportions. Nengshi furrowed his brow and commented, "Now where can we lay this out to preserve it? Not only that, but the machines we've brought are all too small, and we didn't bring enough preservative. It's a bit of a conundrum."

"There is a place where we can preserve it," said Shuqi. "The training grounds at the academy would suffice, but as for the machinery and the preservative—those issues will be difficult to resolve."

"Let's not worry about those for now," replied Jianshi. "Let's get it to the training grounds first, and then we can discuss further. But how shall we transport it?"

Baoyu suggested, "Last time, when we caught the *peng*, we fastened it under the flying car—why not do that again?"

"The *qiu* is too big," said Lao Shaonian. "I'm afraid we'll have to use multiple flying cars for it to work."

Shuqi pulled out his telephone and ordered the academy to send over ten flying cars. When the cars arrived a short time later, Shuqi directed the laborers to begin tying ropes around the *qiu* and fastening these to the cars one section at a time. They worked at this for a long time before it was finally ready. Baoyu made sure to tell everyone about their previous experience with the *peng*—how releasing it too suddenly had caused the flying car to go careening upward into the sky—and cautioned them to lower their altitude settings completely before releasing the *qiu*. Everyone indicated that they understood these instructions. Thereupon, they boarded the flying cars, activated the vertical propulsion drives, and, working together, transported the massive *qiu* to the training grounds where they deposited it. Baoyu saw that the sun was beating down on the field and feared that the *qiu* would start to decompose, so he ordered some men to bring pieces of the floating corals as well as pieces of Emerald Chillstone and to distribute them all over the enormous body of the *qiu*. He then had all of the platinum thread ropes and nets and other hunting supplies returned to the ship. Jianshi, seeing that there was no way to resolve his current predicament, climbed into a flying car and went off to find his brother Duo Yishi.

Lao Shaonian was engaged in discussion with Shuqi and opined that since they had determined that the pelt of the sables could ward off cold, a furrier should be summoned to skin the dead sables, cure the pelts, and sew them into a sable coat. They should also take ten branches of small corals and ten pieces of Emerald Chillstone and present them to the emperor. He continued, "These items were difficult to obtain, and the emperor is already advanced in age; if he were to possess these items in winter and summer, they would help to preserve his health." Shuqi, hearing this idea, approved wholeheartedly; naturally, Shengwu and Baoyu were in agreement as well. And so a furrier was immediately summoned and was told to work out how many sables he would need to make a fur coat, then to take that number and start curing the pelts. The group also picked out ten branches of corals and ten pieces of Emerald Chillstone, instructing a craftsman to set about building cases for them out of red sandalwood.

We previously mentioned that Jianshi had left. He was gone for more than a day before finally returning with his brother Yishi. After everyone had made the appropriate salutations, Yishi gave instructions that the collection of various machines aboard his car be unloaded and moved over to the training grounds. Once these had all been laid out to his satisfaction, he turned on a dehydrator, which removed all of the moisture from the *qiu*'s body. He then used another machine to fill the body with preservative. After two days' efforts this work was finally completed, and Yishi took his leave.

After another day had passed a flying car arrived, delivering some leather bags; a carpenter had also been instructed to build a number of wooden crates. The corals, the Emerald Chillstone, the unused sables, and the sea hippo were then packed up. Baoyu asked, "We're awfully far from the Cultivation Region—how will we transport everything?"

"For such heavy items as these, it will be best to use a tunnel car," replied Shuqi.

"What is a tunnel car?"

"We have carved out underground tunnels," explained Shuqi, "through which electric cars run, so we call them 'tunnel cars' for short."

"I've heard of foreign countries having underground trains," Baoyu mused, "but I've never seen one."

Shuqi laughed. "But those run on fixed rail lines and come and go according to strict schedules. Such a nuisance! Our humble Realm doesn't use rails in the tunnels—our tunnels are over five hundred feet wide, extremely open, and paved with flat iron plates—no rails at all. Along both sides of the tunnel we have set up tunnel car companies so that travelers may use the cars whenever they wish."

"But without rails," ventured Baoyu, "aren't you afraid of collisions?"

"The tunnel cars are completely fabricated out of iron plates, too. There is enough electric current running through the plates that the cars become electromagnets with great repulsive power. When two cars come within five feet of each other, they will begin to repel each other and will not be able to come any closer. How could there ever be any collisions?" Shuqi then promptly dispatched one of the laborers to the tunnel car office to request a company employee come over. Once he had assessed their cargo and set a price for transport, the employee then instructed some of his men to carry the boxes over. Only the *qiu* was too big to move and would still have to be carried by flying car to the tunnel car company, after which it would be up to the employees of the company to devise a way to get it down into the tunnels and wrangle it onto a car underground. At this point Jianshi rose and made his farewells before getting into a flying car of his own and departing.

Shuqi waited until after he had supervised the furrier in his curing of the sable pelts, and after the completion of display stands, before instructing his secretary to write a draft of a letter of presentation to the emperor.

"How is it that you're just using a letter rather than a more official form of communication in presenting these to the emperor?" asked Baoyu.

"Only reports on public matters require the use of memorials," said Shuqi. "Reports that detail governmental affairs use memoranda. For making a presentation of this kind, we need only submit a letter."

"Why not write an encomium?"

"Encomia as a form are too full of praise and exaggeration. We stopped using them a long time ago—ever since we began to revere realism and eschew ornamentation."

And so the secretary proceeded to draft a letter in the names of Shuqi, Shengwu, Baoyu, and Lao Shaonian. Only after showing it to the four men did he then make a fair copy. Once everything had been completed, Shuqi dispatched the secretary, who, bearing with him the various items, set out in a flying car toward the Ritual Region of the Central Sector to present them.

By this time, Baoyu and Lao Shaonian had been back at the hotel for some time, and upon discussion, decided that they wanted to go back out and do some more exploring. Lao Shaonian asked Baoyu where he wanted to go, and Baoyu replied, "Anywhere is fine with me—all I want is to take a ride in a tunnel car!"

"Riding in a tunnel car is simple enough to arrange, but we must have a direction in mind before we set out! Otherwise wouldn't we just be riding about aimlessly?"

"It's been scorching hot these past couple of days, it would be great if we can find somewhere a bit cooler to go."

"If you're uncomfortable in the heat, then the choice is easy! We'll go have a stroll in the nearby Winterscape Park."

"Where is this Winterscape Park? How far is it?"

"It's no more than ten li from here, we could get there in no time in a flying car."

"But the weather is already so hot, and it would be even hotter riding so high up in a flying car."

"For such a short trip, the heat is easily borne. Let us first go to the park to have a stroll, and while we are there, we can discuss where we should go next. We can hire a tunnel car from there. What do you think? There is a major tunnel-car rental company very close to the park."

"That would be very convenient," agreed Baoyu.

When they had agreed on this course of action, they instructed a serving boy to call them a flying car. The two men then proceeded into the car and the driver started it up. As usual for this type of car, it flew at a relatively low elevation, and following along the gridlines of the city streets below, they soon arrived at their destination. Lao Shaonian got out of the car, but rather than proceed directly into the park, he first led Baoyu to a clothing stall just opposite the park's entrance. There they picked out two long sheepskin coats. The proprietor said, "They're generating snow in the park today, I imagine you two gentlemen were not aware of that. Sheepskin coats likely won't be warm enough!"

"Then let's trade these for sable coats!" said Lao Shaonian.

The proprietor took out two sable coats as requested and bundled them up. Lao Shaonian took the bundles, and he and

Baoyu proceeded to the park. As soon as Baoyu stepped inside, he could feel the soft caress of a cool wind—the summer heat had completely dissipated. After taking a few dozen steps further into the park, it began to feel like late autumn. There was a great variety of different trees, and the path that curled through them was winding and circuitous. As they wound their way through an area of pine forest, Baoyu could feel the north wind buffeting him in the face. He shivered and hurriedly put on the sable coat. Upon exiting the pine forest, he saw a number of strange stones rising precipitously in front of him, having been piled up to create a mountainscape. Passing through a cavelike tunnel in the rocks, the men emerged on the other side and found themselves amid a myriad of blossoming plum trees, whose cold fragrance pervaded this secluded, austere formation. Baoyu shook his head and sighed: "Indeed, you have been able to create a world that is far beyond our own! When the ancients spoke of 'skill that surpasses that of Heaven,' I never anticipated that I should be able to experience such a place for myself today!" Sighing, he continued to advance steadily forward. As they moved along the path, they found that it became more crowded with other visitors, all of whom had come to escape the summer heat. Lao Shaonian and Baoyu had explored several of the nearby towers and walked through a number of pavilions when suddenly they noticed snowflakes drifting down gently around them. Looking up, they saw that the sky had been obscured by thick, dark clouds, and it was clear that it would soon be snowing in earnest. Baoyu pointed toward a pavilion and said, "Let's go rest there for a little while."

Lao Shaonian replied, "Up ahead in that bamboo grove, I can see a banner for a liquor shop hung out—why not go and buy a few drinks and admire the snow from there? Look, the snow has already begun to fall."

Baoyu fell in with this suggestion, and they crossed over to the bamboo grove. Standing just outside the grove was a three-room thatched cottage from above the doorway of which hung a banner reading "liquor." Upon entering the cottage they made their way round to some seats at the rear; Baoyu found it to be quite unlike the average reception hall. In front of it there ran a winding course of flowing water, parallel to which had been erected a long, wide covered walkway. Curving railings had also been installed, following the meandering undulations of the walkway itself. All had been ornamented in exceedingly refined style.

The two men took up seats opposite each other. The proprietor of the shop brought them two cups of warmed liquor, as well as two cups of fruit nectar.

"The sky just now is filled with such thick clouds," commented Baoyu. "How is it that they couldn't be seen when we were outside the park just now? Can snow begin to fall immediately after the clouds have formed?"

"All clouds are simply mist that has risen up from the ground. Naturally occurring clouds rise up higher, which is why you can see them from farther away. The snow-generating clouds here only rise up about a hundred feet. Outside the park the sun is still shining bright, which is why you didn't see them."

"It is also truly marvelous to me that snow can be generated," Baoyu continued.

"We can generate rain, too! Every time rain is generated, it can be extended to cover a span of five hundred li square, which is why our humble Realm never suffers from disasters like flood or drought."

"If you are able to prevent disasters like flood and drought, then surely you must be able to generate fine weather as well?"

"Fine weather cannot be *generated*, exactly," Lao Shaonian corrected him. "But it can still be achieved. If it is the case that it has been pouring rain for a long time, they will send a flying car up into the sky to fire off some gunpowder made of saltpeter and sulfur. This dissipates the mist, and the sky becomes clear."

"When we first entered the park, while we were in the pine forest, I felt a burst of northerly wind—it was quite bracing. I imagine you can create the wind, too?"

"That wasn't actually wind—it was just a blast of cold air. We had just come in from a hot place, and suddenly encountered cold air—that's why it felt like wind to you. In reality there is no need to create wind, since the wind changes according to the climate, and is highly variable. The wind that blows from a snowy plain is cold, just like that which blows from a great furnace is hot. No matter what its origins, by the time a wind blows through here, it will always be cold."

"To be able to generate rain in times of extreme drought, or to make the sky clear in times of excessive rain—why, it can't be inexpensive! Who is responsible for paying for it?"

"Originally each district established its own charities, specifically to administer relief funds. But eventually, as the common people grew wealthier, there was no longer any use for the charities. Instead they took on the function of simply banking these funds. Each district was able to save up a substantial amount, but to no purpose. They tried to give the funds over to the government, but the government felt that it was not right to accept them—indeed, they already had sufficient operating funds, and so they refused to accept the money. The districts then thought they could use the money toward projects in furtherance of the public good, but any project of this kind was already being suitably administered by the government—not the least thing had been overlooked. The districts then thought of simply returning the money to the donors, but everyone agreed that they had already given over the money, and there was absolutely no reason to take it back. So for a while, the funds just sat there, serving no purpose, continuing to grow over time. As it happened, when it became necessary to generate rain one year, the people met to discuss the matter and debated making a report to the government and requesting funding. Later they remembered that they had funds of their own and drew on them instead to avoid burdening the government. It has been the established practice here ever since."

"What a government! And what a populace! How could they be considered anything but civilized?" Baoyu sighed.

"We've already had three rounds of drinks," said Lao Shaonian. "Where shall we go next? Once we've decided, we should go hire a tunnel car."

"How about we go see the factories?"

"All right, let's see the factories first! I still have not seen the factory complex that Duo Yishi recently opened. According to what I've heard, he and Dongfang Fa have been giving it their all and have made a great many improvements."

As the two men continued chatting, the snow fell ever heavier outside, and in no time at all a blanket of over three inches had accumulated on the ground. Baoyu suddenly called another place to mind, so he said, "Let's not rush off to observe the industrial arts just yet—let's go somewhere else first." Lao Shaonian then asked where they should go.

■ ■ ■

If you wish to know where Baoyu said he'd like to go, please listen to the explanation in the following chapter.

Chapter Thirty-Four

Along the tunnelway, they travel through strange realms

While perusing the factories, they quickly obtain a grand perspective

WE HAD been speaking of Baoyu, who, as a result of having strolled through Winterscape Park and seen the snow, had suddenly thought of the floating corals and the Emerald Chillstones, which by now would have been assembled together in a building at the museum. He wondered just how cold the air given off by this collection of objects would be. He thought, "Aboard the ship, just a few bundles of coral were sufficient to cause a layer of ice to form in the tank; and even placed out in the open air at the training grounds, they caused the whole of the grounds to feel like deepest winter. Enclosed within a building, so that the cold air they give off will be stopped up and collect therein—why, I can't imagine what it must be like! Why not go have a look?" He shared these thoughts with Lao Shaonian.

"It would be fine for us to go," Lao Shaonian replied. "But there's no need for us to go just now. Let us first go for a stroll alongside the park and see whether there are any notices in the newspapers. If we go later, there'll still be plenty of time." The two men agreed on this course of action, rose from their seats, paid their tab, and found their path out of the park.

"This park has so many hills and dells," Baoyu commented. "The composition of it is extremely pleasing. What's funny is that when I was in Shanghai, I saw a place called Weichun Garden, which was just a flat field of grass with a building erected upon it; and yet, they considered it a garden!"

Lao Shaonian laughed. "That's the style of 'civilized' countries—do you dare make fun of it?"

As they spoke, they passed back into the pine forest, and within a few dozen steps they began to feel the temperature growing warmer. Lao Shaonian led Baoyu into a pavilion where they sat and undid the fastenings on their sable coats. They sat here for a little while longer before finally heading toward the exit. Another few dozen steps from where they had just been sitting, there stood yet another pavilion, which the two men entered. Here, they divested themselves of their coats and paced back and forth briefly, noting that the temperature was now like that of the first chill of autumn. After quitting this pavilion, they continued their leisurely stroll out of the park. Lao Shaonian explained, "These two pavilions were specifically provided so that patrons exiting the park might rest and gradually acclimatize themselves to the change in temperature. Otherwise the risk is that were they to come visit the winter park while it's summertime outside and rush in one breath from this frigid setting back out into the summer heat, they might become ill!" Still chatting, they exited the park gate, and found that indeed, it was still blisteringly hot outside. Lao Shaonian strode over to the clothing stall where he returned their coats and worked out the rental fee.

"Lucky that this clothing stall is here," observed Baoyu. "Otherwise, how could we have gone in?"

"If this stall weren't here, then you would only be able to take a quick look inside before turning back. Or else you'd have to bring extra clothes from home."

The two men then proceeded immediately to a tunnel car company, where they explained that they wished to rent a car to take them to the No. 1 District in the Wisdom Region. The employee asked them, "You won't be able to get there today anymore—would you two gentlemen prefer to spend the night in the car and change to a fresh driver when it gets late? Or would you prefer to spend the night at a station?"

"We have no urgent business," Lao Shaonian replied. "We'll stay overnight at a station." Once a price had been agreed upon and paid, the tunnel car company employee wrote out a paper ticket, which he handed to Lao Shaonian. Opening a door to another room, he said, "Please go in." Lao Shaonian and Baoyu entered the room. As it happened, the policy in the tunnel car business was as follows: the office where guests were greeted was located above ground, and only after a price had been negotiated and paid were they allowed into the tunnels. Within the tunnels, there were also shops and staff to see to all of the travelers' needs.

As soon as the two men crossed through the doorway they were greeted by another man who bade them enter, then carried in two chairs, placed them in the middle of the room, and invited the guests to be seated. The man then left to activate a mechanism of some kind. Lao Shaonian and Baoyu felt a very slight vibration, and a moment later they had begun a slow descent. It turned out that this was the entrance to the tunnels, and they were in an elevator. As the two men continued to descend, Baoyu noticed that they were surrounded on all four sides by pitch darkness; but when he raised his head and looked up he could still see above him the square patch of light at the mouth of the shaft. He reckoned that they had traveled some fifty or sixty feet when suddenly the space was illuminated with gas light, as brilliant as the sun in daytime: the elevator had descended into a subterranean building. When the elevator had arrived on terra firma, a third company employee came out to wait on them. After looking over their ticket, he assigned them a two-person electric car. Lao Shaonian and Baoyu then exited the building and got into the car. The driver also got in, turned on the motor, set the four wheels in motion, and set out straight ahead.

Baoyu raised his eyes to look around: it wasn't at all like a tunnel! It had much of the atmosphere of a busy city center at night, filled with brightly gleaming lamplight. Along both sides of the tunnel were buildings, most of which were car stations and warehouses, but there were also some shops selling miscellaneous items. The bottom of the tunnel was paved entirely with iron plates, and railings along the two sides demarcated the space within which pedestrians could walk. Looming overpasses had been erected at intersections so that when traffic was heavy in both directions, pedestrians would still be able to cross to the other side without fear of being struck. If one lifted one's head to look at the ceiling, one saw that it consisted primarily of iron beams and trusses. Along the ceiling at roughly half-li intervals were large openings which ran all the way to the surface; these had been cut for ventilation, allowing the expulsion of carbon dioxide and the replenishment of oxygen. The cars traveling in both directions were lightning-fast, flying past in a swift stream, like the shuttle on a weaver's loom. Most of these were transporting merchandise. Baoyu remarked, "It's no wonder that the few times we've been out exploring your cities, everyone seems to be walking around empty-handed. It turns out that all of your commercial goods are transported underground! You've really created two different worlds out of one!"

"Most of the big businesses above ground have selected sites along the tunnel system, so that they can easily open their own tunnel entrances and build underground warehouses to store and distribute the goods they accumulate from cars traveling in either direction," replied Lao Shaonian.

"But if you've cut out such deep tunnels that run back and forth as densely as the weft on a loom, just like the official roads above ground, then where do your wastewater pipes run?"

"Our wastewater pipes run in two locations: those for the aboveground area run above the tunnel, while those for the tunnel run beneath it."

The two men continued chatting in the car, and before they knew it, it was already 7:00 p.m., and the car came to a stop. The driver alighted from the car and invited the two men to go into a car station to have dinner and rest. Upon entering the station, Baoyu saw that it was an unremarkable sort of large hall.

They thereupon selected a room for the night, and after they had eaten their dinner, Lao Shaonian and Baoyu left the station to have a stroll. Behind the car station there was a small garden, which, though not terribly large, contained winding corridors along curving pathways and was immaculate in its layout. Beside the trees at the center of the garden, a number of gaslight lamps had been lit, which were so brilliant as to make it appear that the trees were aflame and the flowers gleaming silver. When they had finished admiring the garden, they returned to the station and retired for the night. Of the rest of the evening's events we have nothing to say.

Early the following morning, after eating their breakfast, they got back into the car and set off. By noon they had arrived in the No. 1 District of the Wisdom Region. The two men had lunch at a car station, after which they seated themselves in the elevator and ascended once more to the surface. Upon exiting the station, they hired a small flying car and departed for the factories. When they arrived, they first presented their calling cards, at which time Duo Yishi invited them to come in and meet with him. As Lao Shaonian and Baoyu explained that they wished to admire his fine factories, Yishi humbly replied, "I am ashamed to say that I myself am unable to invent anything scientific—everything has been created under the direction of Mr. Dongfang Fa. If you two gentlemen wish to see our machinery, I should first introduce you to him." He thereupon sent someone to invite Dongfang Fa to come out to meet with the guests. Once they had made their introductions, Baoyu expressed his deep admiration for Dongfang Fa's work, which, naturally, Dongfang Fa modestly refused. Requisite niceties now complete, Dongfang Fa then invited the two guests to join him on a tour of the factories. Yishi accompanied them as well.

Upon exiting the guest reception hall, they climbed into a flying car and traveled for somewhere around four or five li before setting down again. At the roadside stood an enormous factory building, over the doorway of which were written—quite large—the words "Clothing Factory." The four men walked in together. Baoyu looked around carefully and saw that the space was so vast that he was unable to estimate how large it was; there was, however, machinery spread about all over the place. Dongfang Fa pointed to one side and said, "On the other side of that wall is the raw cotton storeroom. There is a large iron chute in the wall itself; machinery set up within the storeroom sends the cotton out through the chute."

As Baoyu watched, he did indeed see raw cotton being churned out through the chute. Beside this was the cotton carding machine, which combed out the raw cotton as it emerged from the chute. After it had been combed out, the cotton was then shunted toward another set of machines, all without any human intervention. When the cotton arrived at this set of machines, it was first divided up and each load was sent through one of several spinning machines. Each spinning machine, which was overseen by a child worker, then spun the cotton into thread; once this was done, yet another mechanism delivered the thread to the dyeing machines. Each dyeing machine produced thread of a different color: blue, yellow, red, green, or black. After the dyeing process had been completed, another mechanism delivered the thread to the drying machines; having passed through these machines, the thread was now dry.

From here the thread was transported to the weaving machines—however, these machines didn't weave cloth: they wove the thread directly into clothes! After the item of clothing had been woven, it was again moved along, this time onto a frame made of bamboo slats. This frame was then turned over onto the folding machine, where the article of clothing was folded. From here it was turned out onto another machine, where it was wrapped in paper before being moved along and deposited in a cardboard box already waiting to receive it. This box was finally picked up by a worker standing beside the machine. The machine then pushed out another cardboard box, and in an instant, a second article of clothing, having already been wrapped, was immediately deposited into this new box. Baoyu observed that the entire process, from the cotton emerging from the storeroom and all the way through its being woven into clothes, wrapped, and packed, did not require the expenditure of any human effort; it was only after the clothing had been boxed that someone had to remove it from the boxing machine to place it in a crate. The machines created items of various sizes and lengths, but each box was stamped with the size of the item, so there was no risk of things getting mixed up.

Baoyu was extremely impressed by this and suddenly thought of something. Inspecting the clothes Lao Shaonian was wearing, he found that as expected they were woven perfectly and did not have any seams. So he said, "Since your Realm has this clothing factory, it seems that you must be able to do without skilled garment workers?"

Dongfang Fa replied, "At the moment, we still cannot, only because we have not yet come up with a way to mechanize the production of leather and fur garments. But we are in the process of researching it!" He then pointed to a row of machinery diagonally opposite them and said, "That's where the paper and cardboard is made. We start with things like bamboo, wood chips, and scrap cotton, and put them into a vat of chemicals to dissolve them into pulp. The second machine bleaches the pulp, the third turns it into cardboard, the fourth dries the cardboard, the fifth cuts it and applies glue, and the sixth turns it into boxes. The boxes are then labeled and delivered into the boxing queue by a seventh machine." He pointed to the machine wrapping the clothing in paper and added, "That paper is different—its pulp is separated from the rest after the second machine, and then a third machine turns it into thin paper, a fourth machine buffs it until glossy, a fifth cuts it down, a sixth creases it according to the correct dimensions. The creased paper is used by a seventh machine to wrap the clothes, after which the wrapped bundle gets sent over to the box-packing machine. The entire production line involves no human labor—and that's just the line for cotton clothes." He then led them to another part of the room to have a look; this area was dedicated to the making of silk clothes. Every kind of silken clothing, from long robes to short jackets, was being produced. Not only were the lengths and the sizes of item being produced by each machine different, but the machines were further divided by the weight of the fabric. The summer clothes were as thin as a cicada's wing, while the winter clothing was about quarter of an inch thick, with an inner layer that had been brushed out into a velvety softness. Dongfang Fa explained, "This can take the place of cotton clothing, but unfortunately, it isn't as warm as fur. The machines here are the same as the ones making cotton clothes, it's just that the spinning machines spin silk instead."

When they had finished looking around, they exited and got back into their flying car and went to go see the firearms factory. This factory was at least ten times larger than the clothing factory, with thousands of pieces of machinery arrayed throughout. Baoyu unconsciously sighed in admiration and said, "This is *truly* a grand prospect!"[1]

Dongfang Fa replied, "After my kinsman Hua Zili invented silent electronic guns and artillery, the government tested them out and decided from then on to entrust the production of the entire nation's weapons to him. My kinsman spends all of his time developing new technologies, so once he has invented something new, he turns it over to me to replicate, and so the responsibility for their production becomes mine. This factory must supply the guns and ammunition for the entire country, which is why it is so large. None of the machinery is particularly remarkable, but we do smelt our own steel, iron, copper, and lead here in the factory—the ore is sent here from the mines, turned into bullets, then shipped back out. As compared to foreigners' factories, it is a somewhat superior arrangement."

Baoyu toured through the factory and, finding that all of the machinery was unusually clever, inquired about each one in turn. Dongfang Fa was able to answer all of his questions, which pleased Baoyu greatly. After they had seen everything here, they proceeded to a much smaller factory building, where Dongfang Fa directed them to go in and seat themselves in the accountant's office, while he made a tour of the factory and put a number of queries to his craftsmen. Yishi said to Baoyu, "This is the test facility. Anything that hasn't quite been perfected is brought here to be tried out first; once we have run experiments on it here, then a new factory is built for its manufacture."

"What are they testing now?" asked Baoyu.

"They are testing many different types of things. For example, in the past few days, they have been testing water boots—I hope that the tests will be successful."

Baoyu was about to ask about the water boots when Dongfang Fa returned, having completed his inspection. He reported, "It's really a tough one! I'm afraid it still isn't useable just yet."

"Could you please explain," asked Baoyu, "what it is you're talking about?"

"My elder brother suddenly had an odd idea one day: he is a medical expert and wanted to research a way to artificially manufacture intelligence. He drew up plans for us to build a small set of machinery, but so far we've tried building five versions, and none of them are useable. Now they're working on a sixth, but I'm afraid it still doesn't work!"

"Before coming here, I also heard it said that one of the great scientists in your Realm wished to devise a way to manufacture intelligence. But how can it be done?"

Dongfang Fa laughed. "That shows the wiliness of my brother. He intentionally described it that way, in order to pique people's curiosity. Intelligence is a formless, abstract thing—so how can it be manufactured? Generally, a person's intelligence or stupidity depends upon the size of their brain. Through his research, he was able to discover the basic substance that makes up the brain. He collected some of this substance and ground it into a fine powder, then mixed in some medicinal components and a quantity of light, pure vapor. The idea was to instruct a test subject to take it and inhale it like snuff. Since the nostrils lead to the brain, this concoction would reach the brain and, upon contact with the heat of the brain tissue, be converted into brain tissue as well. The new tissue would grow right on top, and as a result, the subject's intellect would naturally be enriched."

"That truly is fantastical," replied Baoyu. "Has it ever been tested?"

"At first, because he had only created a small quantity, he instructed a serving boy to inhale it while under observation with a brain-examining lens. As he had hoped, when the basic substance reached the brain, it did indeed become a strand of brain tissue. Only then did he increase his efforts and resolve to try on a larger scale."

When he had finished speaking, Dongfang Fa led Baoyu and the others to go see the small machine. It turned out to be a small case only about two feet square, and within it, in addition to a series of gears, were numerous glass implements like bottles, tubes, cups, and boxes. Dongfang Fa pointed to them each and explained, "This box is filled with the medicinal components, this bottle holds the basic substance of the brain. The clear vapor is introduced through this tube here, while any impure vapors are drawn out through that tube there. When these gears here move, the medicine is mixed in; when those wheels move, the clear vapor is added to the basic brain substance." Baoyu could only click his tongue in amazement.

Yishi then pointed off to the side and said, "That's where the water boots are made."

Baoyu replied, "I wanted to ask before—what is the use of these water boots?"

Yishi answered, "While wearing these boots, you can walk on water—and what's more, you can walk very quickly."

As Baoyu looked, he saw not boots but two small flat-bottomed boats, roughly seven inches wide by two feet long. Their hulls had been crafted out of platinum, and a countless number of small gears were installed on the inside. At the very center was an empty space, just large enough for a foot. The top was outfitted with leather boot uppers.

"Wearing these," explained Yishi, "if you step down onto the water, you'll sink to only about a foot deep. The leather uppers go all the way up to the knee, so as long as you button them tightly at the top, no water will get in. When the gears start turning, there is no need for you to lift your feet to move yourself across the surface—you will automatically move forward. When we tested these previously, we found them to be somewhat less nimble than we'd like in making turns or turning around, so we had to make improvements."

Baoyu then noticed that over to one side, a flying car was being assembled. He asked, "Flying cars must have been tested successfully long ago—so why is there one being put together here?"

"That is a new, advanced model," replied Dongfang Fa. "It travels at tremendous speeds. We calculate that once it is airborne, it will be able to keep pace with the sun! For example, if you were to set out today at noon and follow the sun along its path toward the west, it would always be midday wherever you were flying over. Eventually, by noon on the following day, you would be back here."

Baoyu stuck out his tongue in amazement. "You mean to say that it can fly around the entire planet in one day?"

Lao Shaonian laughed. "Once the car has been completed, I shall bestow a fine name upon it."

"Please tell us—what is this 'fine name' you would bestow?" asked Dongfang Fa.

Lao Shaonian nonchalantly revealed the name he had thought of.

■ ■ ■

If you wish to know what name he had chosen, please listen to the explanation in the following chapter.

Chapter Thirty-Five

Debating the topic of competition, they casually discuss political factions

A request to visit farmland leads instead to the observation of military drills

WE WERE speaking of how Dongfang Fa had asked Lao Shaonian what name he would give the new flying car. Lao Shaonian replied, "According to the *Classic of Mountains and Seas*, 'Kuafu chases the sun.'[1] Since this flying car can keep up with the sun, we could call it the Kuafu Car."

"That would be taking the quote out of context," replied Dongfang Fa. "According to the text that follows that line, Kuafu can't actually keep pace with the sun at all, whereas our car actually does—so how could we call it a Kuafu Car?"

Lao Shaonian tried again. "A poem by Li Qiao says: 'the green dragon races the distant sun, the purple swallow chases the homeward wind.' So Green Dragon Car would also be suitable."

"But that is a poem in praise of horses," retorted Dongfang Fa. "How can we extend the quote to a car?"

Baoyu offered a suggestion: "Zhang Wencheng's poem 'Sakyamuni Stele' says: 'The fine charger follows a path from the east, to achieve its ambitions of racing the sun; the *peng* rises aloft over the north sea, frequently folding its cloud-brushing wings.' Why not call it the Eastern Charger?"

Dongfang Fa laughed. "It's not enough to have captured one *peng*, you still wish to hunt another?" The group continued laughing and chatting and were just about to depart to tour some other factories when suddenly they heard three peals of a bell ring out through the air and discovered that it was already 5:00 p.m.—the end of the workday. All of the craftsmen began filing out of the factory. Dongfang Fa then bade Baoyu and the others get back into their flying car, and the group returned to the reception hall where he invited them to stay for dinner and made overnight guest accommodations available to them, so that they could go back out to see the various other factories all the more easily the following morning. From this point Baoyu ended up staying at the factory complex for two or three days. He was able to get a broad overview of all different types of astounding manufacturing, ceaselessly clicking his tongue in admiration at each. He was delighted that he had been able to expand his knowledge so vastly. Truly, this outing had been most worthwhile.

Suddenly, one day, Duo Yishi appeared carrying a newspaper. Chuckling to himself, he approached the others and said, "I see that after you returned from your undersea hunting expedition, you presented tribute to the emperor."

"How is it that it's in the newspaper?" asked Lao Shaonian.

Yishi handed him the paper. Lao Shaonian and Baoyu looked it over together and saw the headline "To Memorialize the Virtues of Certain Gentlemen" at the top of the page. Below it read:

On such-and-such date, the cabinet records and presents this edict on behalf of the emperor: On this day, We have seen the letter written by so-and-so et al., as well as received from them one (1) ice-sable coat, ten (10) branches of floating corals, and ten (10) pieces of Emerald Chillstone. According to what We are told, these items were obtained from the South Pole; and the ice-sable fur, though coming from a cold place, in fact resists the cold and keeps one warm; while the corals and stones give off cool air even in humid summer heat. The corals and stones We examined did indeed live up to this description. Nevertheless, since these gentlemen risked myriad dangers in order to obtain these items, and then, in addition to having made donations of same to our museum and to our zoo, have chosen not to keep any of the remaining items for their own personal use and have instead made gifts of these items to Ourself, how can We accept them in good conscience? Now, if the gentlemen had captured hundreds of millions of sables, which could be sewn into coats to clothe the whole Realm, why should We not accept such a boon! Today, that We alone should receive this boon while Our subjects should not—is it because We alone are susceptible to the cold while Our subjects are not? If We were to accept and wear this coat, how could We bear to face Our ministers and subjects? The same applies to the coral and the stones. And yet, if We were to ultimately reject these offerings, we could not but fail to honor the sincere esteem which the gentlemen have shown Us. Thus, We have instructed a jade-worker to carve a corner piece from one Emerald Chillstone, to be kept upon Our desk, as a memento of the great

> merit the gentlemen have achieved; the remainder We respectfully send back with the gentlemen's messenger, so that these too might be displayed in a museum, for the edification of the entire populace. We are indeed honored by this. The emperor so declares.

Having read the edict, Baoyu couldn't help but silently sigh to himself and think, "With an emperor like this, no wonder they prefer authoritarianism here! Moreover, the language of the edict itself is so humble and restrained! With the exception of the royal 'We,' you could hardly tell it was an imperial edict at all. One can easily see from this that there is a flourishing system of government here, where a single moral code applies to both ruler and subject. Based on what I've seen here, it's obvious that no constitutional monarchy or republic could ever compare."

As Baoyu stood, distracted by these thoughts, he suddenly heard Lao Shaonian say, "The corals and the Emerald Chillstones have already been put on display at the museum. We can go have a look."

When Baoyu looked again at the newspaper, he saw that an announcement to that effect had been printed there, so he asked Lao Shaonian, "When shall we go?"

"We can go after we've seen everything here."

"Then let's go today."

Duo Yishi asked, "Are you planning to take a flying car again?"

"It's extremely hot out," replied Baoyu. "Taking a tunnel car would be a bit cooler."

"You won't be able to get there by tunnel car anymore today," Yishi informed him. "You'd have to stay overnight somewhere along the way, so you might as well set out tomorrow. If you leave early tomorrow morning, you'll be able to make it there."

Lao Shaonian and Baoyu both agreed that this made sense, and so they spent the rest of the day seeing a few other kinds of clever and ingenious machines.

That evening, having nothing to do, they sat in the garden taking the cool night air. Baoyu continued to praise all of the different machines he had seen, and Yishi told him, "We conduct research day and night, but have yielded only modest results. Since we are concerned that we might be outdone by others, each year we send people out to foreign countries to look into all of their mechanical developments. Luckily, we have never yet fallen behind."

"I have never been to a foreign country," Baoyu confessed. "But I have seen one or two of the products that the foreigners have imported into China. How could they possibly compare with your inventions?"

Lao Shaonian added, "It's funny, now that you mention it—last year a friend went to the Americas, and when he returned, he brought with him a photograph that showed one of their airships. The photograph could only capture a black shadow—you couldn't even tell what color it was!—but enough about that. The design of the airship was even more ridiculous! A gallbladder-shaped hydrogen balloon had been attached over the top of the actual vessel, lying horizontally over it; along the two sides they had installed four winglike sails. Built in such a way, the entire thing relied upon the balloon to ascend, and upon wind power to move. Yet I've heard that they have presented these things at fairground exhibitions!"[2]

Yishi sighed. "It's no wonder—the extent of their knowledge is still so limited! Say we had wanted to take to the air a hundred years ago, wouldn't we have used balloons too? And even the flying cars we made fifty years ago—though they didn't rely on balloons, we still made them in the shape of birds! If it hadn't been for that one car that crashed and caused such an uproar, I'm afraid to say we'd never have learned how to improve them!"

Baoyu asked, "I've often heard it said that without political parties or factions, there is no competition; and that if there is no competition, there is no progress. Your entire Realm from top to bottom is united in its thinking, so naturally there are no factions—just how is it that you are able to make such rapid progress?"

Dongfang Fa replied, "That is something said by irrelevant people who aren't motivated to improve themselves. In all things, it is only when there are others with whom to compare themselves that they are they willing to apply themselves; in the absence of competitors, they are unwilling to make the effort. So for them, progress necessarily requires competition. They don't understand that even in the absence of competition, as long as one is constantly vigilant against complacency, there will always be improvement. Besides, it can't be said that we've never been involved in political factionalism—just not among ourselves."

Baoyu was surprised by this. "If not among yourselves, then with whom?"

"Our entire populace has unified into a single faction; the 'other' factions are of course made up of foreigners. If we are going to compete, we will compete against the foreigners—how could there be no competition at all? What is funny is that currently, foreigners seem to be talking about their 'compatriots' whenever they open or close their mouths; yet their compatriots are splintered into who knows how many factions, attacking one another, even smearing one another. But when they encounter opposition that knows how to behave with self-respect, they won't go up against them fairly. Rather, when they see that the opposition doesn't acknowledge them, they will go so far as to attack the personal morality of the individuals, exposing their private affairs, crowing with satisfaction. This type of person is an exemplar of the petty man, a creature worse than a dog or a pig. In depending upon such political factions as these, because they require competition to make progress, the foreigners merely end up with a couple more petty men! What progress is made? We ourselves have unified our entire country and joined into a single faction, so when we compete with foreign countries, isn't our faction bigger than theirs? Aren't we the fiercer competitors? Isn't our progress swifter? As for the people of this country, how can it be said that we've never had ideas at odds with one another? But when we encounter an area of disagreement we all discuss it together, and everyone engages in earnest, sincere conversation; we must reach a consensus before the debate can rest. Never have we seen that someone's aims are out of alignment with our own and used that as a reason to engage in such barbaric and ruthless behaviors as wantonly attacking them."

Baoyu sighed. "So uniting the people from top to bottom with one mind, and thereby attaining a flourishing system of government, can be achieved within a collegial atmosphere!" He then continued, "Yesterday, while we were seeing all of the various machines that your factories have to offer, I noted that it was gas burning in all the furnaces. That suddenly reminded me of something I wanted to inquire about: the flying cars and the underwater vessels and even things like sampans—since none of them seemed to be burning coal, what do they burn?"

Dongfang Fa replied, "For all those machines, it is only necessary to burn fuel the first time they are used. This creates steam, which runs the machinery and also creates energy in the form of electricity. Afterward this electricity can then be used to generate the steam. This creates a cycle: when the electricity is used to generate steam, the steam runs the machinery as before, which creates still more electricity. When the cycle is completed, it begins again, repeating itself endlessly, so we can draw on and use this energy without ever depleting or exhausting it. Currently we are planning to implement reforms in our factories so that they too run on electricity."

"The gas used within the furnaces doesn't burn brightly—so how is it that that the gas lamps are so bright?"

"That is because certain chemical components have been added to the lamps' burners. Without those added chemicals, the lamps would be just as dim as the furnaces."

The men continued their conversation deep into the night before finally retiring. Of the rest of the evening's events, we have no further details.

Early the following morning, Lao Shaonian and Baoyu took their leave of Dongfang Fa and Duo Yishi, then hired a tunnel car and departed for the Cultivation Region of the Central Sector. As evening was falling, they emerged from the tunnel and proceeded to the museum, where Duo Jianshi greeted them. After they finished with the usual pleasantries, Jianshi asked, "Where have you two come from? Have you already been back to the Naval Academy?"

"We spent several days in the Wisdom Region looking at the factories there," answered Lao Shaonian. "Yesterday, we saw the announcement your museum placed in the paper, advertising that the coral and everything else had been put out on display, and so we made a special trip to see how your talented self had arranged everything. So no, we still haven't been back there!"

"You two gentlemen risked all kinds of perils to bring the specimens here, my own feeble attempts at arranging them are hardly worth mentioning! Anyway, the day before yesterday, a letter arrived for Shuqi, inquiring as to your whereabouts. It said that the government had once again bestowed upon you the highest award and requested that you go in person to receive it."

"Is the messenger tasked with delivering the award still waiting for us there?" asked Baoyu. "If he is, then we cannot afford to tarry here—rather, we must depart quickly to avoid making him wait too much longer."

"Shuqi has already accepted the award on your behalf," said Jianshi, "so there's no need to rush off. If the two of you wish to go see the corals, please go have a look—after that, I invite you to join me for dinner."

He then rose, leading his two guests out of the reception room and into the Treasure Vault. Here they saw that beside the Coral Forest a tremendous hall had been constructed in which all of the large trunks of multihued, transparent coral had been erected. Without getting particularly close, they could already feel the cold air billowing thickly around them. The *qiu* had been suspended above the corals, its supple body arranged in a series of undulating twists and bends, giving the appearance that it might start gliding away at any moment.

Baoyu commented, "This arrangement—to display these things together—is certainly unique. But surely the *qiu* doesn't really belong in the Treasure Vault."

"It was actually because of the *qiu* that we had to construct a hall to house them all—to keep it out of the rain. But that's just the preliminary stage. We are also going to build a wall around it and post a placard. Given the intense cold of the coral, when I had brought it all back here, I took a chunk from one of the small ones and had it filed into a piece one-inch square, then left it in the sun as an experiment; in no time at all, it had completely cooled an area of ten feet square! Wouldn't it be a problem to keep so many larger pieces in one place? Right now, if you were to get much closer and stand still for a bit, it would be too cold to bear! The cleaners already have to put on winter clothes to come clean every day—and won't it be even worse in winter? That's why we need to build a wall surrounding it—we'll line the wall with airtight wooden planks, which will prevent the cold air from seeping through."

The three men quickly looked over the exhibit, then returned to the reception hall. Jianshi added, "Our humble museum has kept all of the large pieces of coral, but only one of the Emerald Chillstones—the remaining Chillstones and the smaller pieces of coral have been distributed among the other regional museums. We also kept only one of the sables—the rest of those have been distributed as well. The sable cloak and the twenty specimens of coral and Chillstone which the emperor declined to accept are also here, as is the sea hippo. But it's getting late—let's wait until tomorrow to go see them."

"It's only because the *qiu* and the corals were so big that I was interested in seeing how they were exhibited," said Baoyu. "There's no point in seeing the other things."

After dinner had concluded, the two guests stayed the night at the museum.

On the following day they took their leave of Jianshi, then rode a tunnel car back to the Strong Region, where they made their way to the Naval Academy and met with Shuqi. Shuqi produced the imperial edict that his secretary had brought back with him, and, after giving it to the two men to read over, presented them with their award plaques. Upon receiving his award, Baoyu noticed that it was quite unlike the one he had received previously: the previous one was round, while this one was in the style of a small *dingsheng* cake roughly one inch long by seven or eight tenths of an inch wide. His name had been inlaid in the center with chips of precious stone, above which were inlaid the words "Peril-risking Valiant of the Highest Degree." On the bottom even more stones had been inlaid, forming figures as fine as spider-silk, so that it was impossible to tell whether they were words or flowers. Lao Shaonian, looking closely at his own award, asked Shuqi if he could borrow a magnifying lens. Shuqi produced the lens, and Lao Shaonian looked through it for a time before handing it to Baoyu. Looking at his own award through the lens, Baoyu found that the inlays formed a narrative account of their undersea hunting adventure, with commentary interspersed throughout, replete with enthusiastic praise. Seen through the lens, the characters became the size of mung beans, while the characters for his name were now as large as the mouth of a bowl. He asked Shuqi, "How many times does this lens magnify the object being observed?"

"This is an everyday lens, so it magnifies only ten thousand times."

Baoyu was astonished. "And what about the lenses that aren't for 'everyday' use?"

"There are some that can magnify objects twenty or thirty thousand times, and perhaps even some capable of fifty or sixty thousand times. I've never seen one that goes up to a hundred thousand times—I've heard that Dongfang Fa has such a lens, but I don't know whether that's true or not."

Baoyu stamped his foot. "It's a pity I'm only just learning this now! Otherwise I could have asked about it while we were there. If he does indeed have one, I could have expanded my horizons a little further." The men exchanged a few more words, then Lao Shaonian and Baoyu said goodbye to Shuqi, left the academy, and hired a flying car to return to their hotel.

By now Baoyu had become familiar with his surroundings, so whenever he had nothing to do he would make his way to the bustling city center for a stroll. Suddenly, it occurred to him: "I've only been focused on seeing urban areas but haven't seen any of the Realm's rural areas. Why not ask Lao Shaonian about it?" And so he sought out Lao Shaonian and asked where one might go to observe a more rural setting.

"What kind of rural setting?" asked Lao Shaonian.

"I'd just like to see some farmland or mulberry orchards."

"Those can be found anywhere, but they are at their most flourishing in the Compassion Region of the Southern Sector, or the Benevolence Region of the Eastern Sector. However, there's not much to see—it's the same as anywhere else, except that here we have no footpaths between fields."

"But with no footpaths, how can you distinguish whose fields are whose?"

"All of the landowning families have unified into companies, working together to grow and harvest their crops. When the grain is ripe, they divide the harvest as is commensurate to each family's land holdings."

"Why do it that way?"

"Here, all of the plowing, weeding, sowing, and harvesting is done by machine. If the fields were divided up by footpaths, it would be a case of the land being so narrow you can't even turn around in it!" This made Baoyu laugh.

"There's not much to see in the rural areas," Lao Shaonian continued. "But in the paper today, they published an announcement from the army, saying that they will be carrying out large-scale training exercises the day after tomorrow. Let's go see those instead."

Baoyu was delighted. "That's even better! Where will they be training?"

"In the Loyal Region of the Northern Sector. That is the most important area for our border defenses, so we have built a strategic stronghold there."

"Can anyone go watch?"

"When the exercises begin, a staff member is sent out especially to entertain any visiting guests. But if we want to go watch, there is no need for us to trouble their staff. The commander-in-chief of the army, Ximen Guan—whose style name is Zizhang—is a good friend of mine. We'd get a much better view if we go watch with him!"

Baoyu agreed happily, "Better still! Let's leave tomorrow. How long will it take us to get there?"

"If we take a flying car and leave early, we can be there by noon."

And so Baoyu began to make preparations to go watch the training exercises.

■ ■ ■

If you wish to know whether he ultimately went or not, please listen to the explanation in the following chapter.

Chapter Thirty-Six

An evaluation of local customs leads to the topic of prostitutes and actors

An item of benefit to the army is paradoxically "humane"

WE WERE speaking of how, on the following day, Baoyu and Lao Shaonian were to take a flying car to the Loyal Region. When they arrived at the main encampment, Lao Shaonian sent in one of his calling cards and Zizhang immediately invited them to enter, at which time the two men went in to meet with him. Lao Shaonian introduced Baoyu and Zizhang, and the requisite polite greetings were offered. Looking at Zizhang, Baoyu noted that he had a strong chin, paired with powerful shoulders; his bearing was upright and proper while at the same time warm, respectful, and refined. He received the men graciously. Lao Shaonian explained the reason they had come and added, "Since we are such good friends, I thought it best not to trouble your staff, which is why we have come directly to pay our respects to you, Commander. We beg your forgiveness for the having taken the liberty."

"You are very welcome to watch the exercises," replied Zizhang. "The only issue is that it is not convenient to install guest seating on the reviewing stand. What shall we do?"

"Since it is not convenient to install guest seating, why don't we dress up as two soldiers and stand beside you to watch?"

"How on Earth could I allow that? If the situation were different, I'd gladly invite the two of you to put on staff officer uniforms to come watch. However, since this is our one main ceremonial event of the year, how can we engage in such childish antics?"

"But there will already be too many visiting guests being entertained by your staff," said Lao Shaonian.

"I have another solution: I have my own private secretary who has no engagements tomorrow. I will ask him to accompany you to watch the drills."

"That would be wonderful," Lao Shaonian agreed.

As they were speaking, the camp's timekeeping automaton, holding a bugle, reported that it was noon. Zizhang then bade his two guests get into a flying car and travel to his private quarters to have lunch and meet with his private secretary. The secretary's name was Gao Pan, and his style name was Yutian. When the men met, they all introduced themselves. After they had eaten, Zizhang said, "Please, both of you, stay here—Yutian will keep you company. I have some official matters to which I must attend back at the camp. We can chat again in the evening."

Lao Shaonian replied, "If you have things to do, please go at your convenience."

Zizhang made his goodbyes and left, after which Yutian led the two visitors out to a pavilion overlooking the water in the rear garden, where they could sit and take the cool air.

Baoyu observed, "Just about everyone seems to have a garden here—why, even the underground tunnels have them. That's pretty rare to see."

"Gardens are something that one absolutely cannot do without," replied Lao Shaonian. "We are completely reliant upon them for the fostering of a contented temperament—so how could we do without them? Only a truly destitute family might lack one."

"But even that is rare," added Gao Yutian. "According to a new survey taken this year, starting at the new year, the number of people who lacked their own garden had decreased by two-thirds when compared with the number of people counted in last year's survey. In another two years' time, I reckon the entire country will have them—though the size of the gardens will vary, of course."

"Why is it that you conduct a survey about gardens?" Baoyu asked.

"Flowers, grasses, and trees are most intimately connected with human health, so the government is attentive to the issue," answered Lao Shaonian.

"Although you say that, it must also mean that your Realm has quite a lot of land," Baoyu mused.

Gao Yutian answered, "We have recently begun to cultivate a great deal of land along the northern and western frontiers, all of which was previously desolate and uninhabited. The first thing the government did was establish a large convention ground in that desolate area. People from different countries started coming to attend events there, and naturally, it goes without saying no small number of commonfolk from our own country started going as well, so things immediately grew livelier. The government then sold all of the publicly held land to our commonfolk at a low price and extended the tunnel system out to them. As a result, a great number of people moved out there, populating the area fairly evenly."

"If it's as you say, then with respect to your population, no place has more or fewer people than anywhere else," Baoyu said.

"You can't really say that," Gao Yutian corrected him. "The Compassion Region of the Southern Sector and the Benevolence Region of the Eastern Sector are thriving agricultural zones. Much of the land there is designated for farming, so the population is somewhat less dense."

"Meanwhile, the entirety of the Trust Region is a trading area," added Lao Shaonian, "so how could the population not be a bit denser there? But I think you could say it generally evens out."

As they were chatting, a serving boy came and offered them cooling watermelon nectar. Baoyu said, "I've been to so many places, and I see that everywhere uses serving boys. What is the reason behind that?"

"They are all children of poor families," answered Lao Shaonian. "They can't afford to be in school for a full day, so they only attend for half the day, then come and carry out tasks for others. Some work in the morning and attend classes in the afternoon; others work in the afternoon and attend classes in the morning."

Baoyu sighed. "That's what I'd call having a love of learning!"

"The custom in our humble Realm," Lao Shaonian continued, "is that illiteracy, ignorance of established principles, and lack of willingness to improve one's personal morality are all the most shameful traits that one can possess. How could one have children and not ensure that they go to school?"

"Do you have free community schools?"

"We used to, but not anymore. When we first met to discuss it, we spent quite a lot of time debating the issue because there were two camps, each with their own ideas. The first said that free schools were different from other kinds of charitable endeavor, since they related to the important issue of education, and therefore we must continue to maintain them as before, for the sake of our poorer citizens. The second said that while these schools were a charitable endeavor, they feared that if the children of the poor could attend without paying a cent, they might develop a dependent nature. If we were to establish community schools, it would teach these children to be dependent from a young age—so how could we ever hope to inculcate a self-reliant spirit in them? The two sides talked it over in great detail but were still unable to arrive at the truth of the matter or work out who was right and who was wrong. And so their only option was to submit a petition to the emperor and ask him to make a ruling. The emperor summoned a hundred officials to discuss the matter before him, but they too were unable to reach a conclusion. Finally, someone submitted a memorandum, saying that the community schools were built for the sake of the poor, but seeing as none of the hundred court officials were poor themselves, even if they did their best to reach a solution, there was no way of knowing whether that solution was in accordance with the wishes of the poor or not. It would be better to issue communiqués to each region calling upon the local poor to voice their own opinions as to whether the schools should be maintained or done away with and ask them to propose a recommendation. The government should then count how many people approved or disapproved and on that basis decide whether to follow the recommendation or not—that was the only logical choice. After deliberation, the government approved the ideas in the memorandum, then dispatched communiqués to each of the regions, asking those poor people who currently had children in school to share their opinions in the form of written notes to be collected by their region head, who would send them on to the government so that a decision might be made. When the responses were all collected and tabulated, it turned out that the vast majority advocated doing away with the community schools. However, the reason they advocated this was because when one pays tuition for school, the amount he pays is limited; whereas when the government established the community schools for the education of the masses, its expenditure was necessarily quite large. It would be better to allow the government to save that money by leaving it up to individuals to provide tuition fees once again. The government, having obtained this response, was worried that the poor had misunderstood their intentions in asking, and so wrote out the respective positions of the two sides in the debate and sent yet another round of communiqués, asking the poor to read them over and discuss them once again. Who would have expected that when the responses came back, they were now unanimously in favor of doing away with the community schools? And so the government acted in accordance with the people's wishes and did just that. The government, having saved this sum of money, now had nothing to spend it on, so they used it to establish a yearly examination prize in each primary school."

"It's obvious that the people in your Realm are all full of independent spirit! It's really quite admirable. But I wonder: are there girls' schools, too?"

Gao Yutian laughed. "If there were no girls' schools, then where would the girls go to study?"

Lao Shaonian added, "Among the people born into this world, for every man, there is a woman—male and female each make up half of the population. So for every boys' school there is a girls' school. What is to be gained from biasing ourselves in favor of one group?"

"And is the separation between men and women here strict?" Baoyu continued.

"What do you mean, 'separation between men and women'?" asked Gao Yutian.

Lao Shaonian laughed and said to Gao Yutian, "You were born and raised here, so of course you don't know what he means. I frequently receive guests from outside, and they often bring up this topic, so I know a little bit about it." Then, turning to Baoyu, he went on: "There is no 'separation between men and women' here. Though we do not engage in such vile practices as handholding, embracing, or kissing, women are not expected to adhere to the etiquette of making themselves scarce in male presence, either. A man and a woman may meet just as easily as two men or two women might."

"If that is the case, then why have separate boys' and girls' schools?"

"There's a different reason for that. We place great emphasis on moral education, and when it comes to moral education, it is only in the area of *public* morality that the obligations of men and women are the same. When it comes to *private* morality, women and men have slightly different obligations, so the books the boys and the girls read are different. And that is especially true when they then go on to more specialized learning—the women's studies will be completely different from the men's."

"Might I ask what the women specialize in?"

"Many different subjects! In addition to needlework, many of the light industrial arts are primarily studied by women. And recently, in the area of medicine, we have designated the two disciplines of pediatrics and women's health as female fields of specialization."

"According to what you say—that there is no separation between men and women—then can the ritual practices dictated by the *Classic of Ritual*, which states that 'by the age of seven, male and female must sit at separate mats' and that 'male and female may not directly hand items to one another,' be done away with?"

"There was another reason behind those proscriptions. Back before our civilization had evolved, certain licentious and impulsive behaviors were unavoidable, so the sages established ritual in order to prevent moral laxity. If you don't believe me, you need only read the 'Airs' from the *Classic of Poetry* to see that licentious poems about elopement make up seven or eight out of every ten! So you can imagine what I mean. But after civilization had evolved and everyone's hearts and bellies were filled with virtue and morality, what need had we for such practices? What's laughable is that those people who swallow everything the ancients said without really digesting it, and revere everything the ancients did, were always saying that the cultural glory of the reigns of Emperors Yao and Shun, and the Xia, Shang, and Zhou dynasties that followed, could never again be attained, because back in those days they had the leadership of Yao, Shun, and King Wen and King Wu of Zhou. Now, you must know that Yao and Shun were unique; likewise, there was only one King Wen and one King Wu. It was not necessarily the case that every commoner those days could have become a Yao, Shun, Wen, or Wu. Even leaving aside the topic of wanton behavior—for example, if all of the commoners were merely elderly people sitting and playing around in the dirt—what is the use of having such an ignorant populace?[1] In this day and age, if all of our commoners were like that, I'm afraid that the country would soon meet its demise. As I see it, it is the people from *before* the time of Yao and Shun who are most worthy of reverence."

"What do you mean by that?" asked Baoyu.

"Back then they invented clothing, housing, and writing; they experimented with eating a hundred types of grasses and taught themselves to grow crops; they learned to mine flint for starting fires; they invented the calendrical system and established the four seasons—they created all of these things out of nothing. How can we not revere them? These early ancients had already accomplished everything, so that by the reigns of Yao and Shun, the world was at peace without their so much as lifting a finger. But you should know that the peace was achieved by those who came before them. Why should we revere Yao, Shun, and the three dynasties that followed, while forgetting about the ancients who preceded them?"

"I have only ever detested those who revere foreigners—I've never said that the ancients are not to be revered," Baoyu replied.

Lao Shaonian corrected him: "You shouldn't think about it too simplistically: the ancients did have their admirable points, so why shouldn't we admire those? But one mustn't be too sycophantic, insisting left and right that we can never again achieve their greatness."

"All right, but for now let's not go on about the ancients. Let's talk about contemporary people instead. In your Realm everyone is independent, and families are sufficiently able to provide for themselves—so much so that there are no beggars here. But I wonder—are there prostitutes here?"

Lao Shaonian shook his head. "Whoever would be willing to engage in such a profession! Not only is there not any such person or occupation here, why, you won't even find the words 'courtesan,' 'prostitute,' or 'whoring' in our dictionaries. You may be aware of another country that considers itself to be 'civilized,' which is home to a certain brothel that contains a room all four walls of which are completely mirrored. When the clients arrive, they proffer a few coins, at which point the madam rings an electric bell. When the prostitutes hear the bell, they push open a mirrored door and emerge—twenty or thirty of them—completely nude, not wearing a stitch of clothing. They then all writhe about on the floor, embracing and cavorting with one another, taking up hundreds of grotesque positions. This is called 'Watching the Preview.' When the client spies a woman he likes, they go into a bedroom together, and they continue to carry on in this manner. A bed is positioned in the center of the room, while small peepholes have been drilled into the walls all around it, so that people outside the room can watch. The people who watch from outside are also charged some amount of money. Just think: a country like this still calls itself 'civilized'—why, I'm afraid that in all its history the word 'civilized' has never been so abused."

"If there are no brothels here, then I wonder: Are there theaters?"

Lao Shaonian laughed at this. "Our dictionaries do not contain the word 'actor,' either! Who would be willing to do something so shameless as performing! While someone might perform a few songs, it is only to commemorate the artistic achievements of our forebears. Sometimes, if several singers happen to be in a good mood, they might sing together, but this too is only to express their joyful feelings—no one has ever done it for money."

Gao Yutian asked Lao Shaonian, "What are you two talking about? I don't understand any of it!"

Lao Shaonian smiled at Baoyu and said, "How's that for proof? Mr. Gao doesn't even understand what we're talking about it, so you can see that I'm not lying to you." He then explained the phenomena of prostitution and acting to Gao Yutian.

Gao Yutian's face flushed, and his ears grew hot. "I have often seen these kinds of things mentioned in the records left by the ancients, but always assumed they were parables invented to mock their own eras. I have also seen that among compilations of the ancients' poetry are such titles as 'A Gift for the Chanteuse' and 'A Gift for the Prostitute.' I assumed that even if things might have existed once, they couldn't possibly still exist now. Who would have expected that there would still be such shameless people in the world? It really is horrifically absurd."

Hearing this comment, Baoyu found it quite strange, and thought, "Here I was, thinking that my knowledge was so limited; why, his is even more narrow!"

The men continued their conversation, and before they realized it the red sun was already sinking toward the west. Gao Yutian led his two guests into a study to sit down. At six, Zizhang returned to have dinner with them; he departed again immediately afterward and did not return again until after ten. Lao Shaonian greeted him: "So busy! Your military obligations must keep you at sixes and sevens!"

Zizhang laughed. "It's already past ten—nearly eleven. You say I am 'at sixes and sevens,' but if you think about it literally, it seems more apt to say that I am actually 'at tens and elevens'!" This gave the rest of the party a good laugh. Zizhang then continued, "Because of tomorrow's drills, I have needed to make a number of preparations, so I have been a bit busier than usual. Actually, normally, there is not much to do, and I have much more leisure, yet somehow you don't see fit to come chat with me when I *do* have free time!"

"How could it be that I have free time whenever you do?" Lao Shaonian retorted. "I have requested a few days' leave, which have just about run out. It just so happened that you were holding your drills here during this time, so I thought I might as well bring this friend of mine to come see."

"Have you worked out a good site from which to watch the exercises?"

"No, we haven't," answered Gao Yutian.

"Wouldn't it be all right if we were to ride in a flying car and fly slowly back and forth observing it all?" asked Lao Shaonian.

"No, not tomorrow," Zizhang replied. "Tomorrow, the mobile strike force is performing its exercises first, which will involve firing into the air. You don't want to be struck by accident—that would be no joke. I have already instructed someone to erect an awning on a high hillside to the east of the reviewing stand. A table and chairs have already been set out, so that you can go there to watch tomorrow."

"For how many days will the exercises go on this year?" asked Lao Shaonian.

"As usual, the drills will go on for three days, but this year we will practice troop deployment and munitions together on the second day. On the third day we will be drilling the newly trained flying-car unit."

"Since the foreigners don't even have flying cars yet, why bother training a unit of them? You surely aren't afraid that the foreigners will come and breach our borders in flying cars."

Zizhang replied, "Why must the foreigners have flying cars in order for our training with them to be worthwhile? Besides, perhaps the foreigners will develop their own flying cars someday—if we wait for them to invent theirs before we start training with our own, wouldn't it be too late? Moreover, once the unit is adequately trained, it will be prepared in the event that the foreigners start any kind of unreasonable trouble here, and we can easily dispatch it to go visit punitive damage upon them. And on top of that, the day after tomorrow, they will be testing out a new kind of chemical spray recently developed by Dongfang De. If his projection is accurate, this chemical will be even more powerful than the barbaric chlorine gas shells used by the foreigners, while at the same time being more humane—a true boon to our army."

"What kind of chemical is it that it is both powerful and humane? I don't understand!" said Lao Shaonian.

"I know putting it like that makes it seem difficult to understand, but in fact it's nothing more than a knockout drug. Dongfang De detests when doctors have to resort to using scalpels and needles; for this reason, he also disapproved of their anesthetics and decided to test them to see whether they were harmful to people or not. Who could have expected that after testing them, it turned out that while they *did* cause harm to people, they could be improved upon? And so, he made improvements. At first there seemed to be no use for such a thing, but he eventually thought that it would be a beneficial tool for our military, so he has increased the potency and sent it here for testing. Once we've tested it, you will know the results."

Lao Shaonian wished to follow up on this topic, but Zizhang had already made his excuses and retired to his inner rooms to rest.

■ ■ ■

If you wish to know just what this chemical is, please listen to the explanation in the following chapter.

Chapter Thirty-Seven

The flying cars put on a show, making formations high up in the clouds

In a strange new cannon, otherworldly electronic technology

WE WERE speaking of how Zizhang, on account of having much to do the following day, and given that it was already quite late, had not stuck around long to chat and had left the group to retire for the evening. Bright and early the following morning, Gao Yutian breakfasted with Lao Shaonian and Baoyu, after which they set out for the training ground, serving boy in tow. They found that a cloth awning had indeed been erected upon a tall hill to the east of the reviewing stand, and a table and chairs had been set up within. Although it was only a temporary installation, everything had been arranged very neatly. When Baoyu looked out, he noticed that the general's flag had been erected high over the reviewing stand and that Zizhang, garbed in military uniform, was already seated high upon the platform, looking grand and imposing. The staff officers, commanding officers, regional vice commanders, assistant regional commanders, brigade commanders, and assistant commanders flanking him were all uniformly outfitted in bright armor and bore swords at their waists.[1] In the camp the soldiers lined up in ranks and proceeded in order to the front of the training grounds, while soldiers at both sides of the reviewing stand played military music in unison. Once the lines of troops had come to a stop, the commanding officers took up their command flags, which fluttered in the breeze. An order was given, at which point several laborers carried out to the center of the training grounds a railing against which the soldiers could lean their guns. They also carried out two large baskets of stones. A company commander belted out an order, at which a row of five soldiers strode out from among the rest, marched over to the railing, and set their guns down against it. Then each took up a stone from the basket and hurled it into the sky. Having thrown his stone, each man took up his gun and fired at his respective stone, and with a *woosh* each man hit his target. This group of five soldiers then held their guns upright once again, and once they had wound their way back to their unit, another row of soldiers stepped up to the front and performed the same drill as the others. Baoyu watched in astonishment. By now, there were already more than ten flying cars, draped with prominent warning flags, patrolling in all directions to prevent any hapless driver from crossing into the space, thereby avoiding any accidental injuries.

"How do they train for such accuracy of aim?" asked Baoyu. "It is really admirable."

Lao Shaonian replied, "When it comes to aim, it's really about hand technique and using your hands as your eyes. If you were to rely on your eyes to take aim first, you could never strike the target in time."

"It's the same as throwing something," Gao Yutian added. "If you throw something into the air and want to catch it in your hand, you don't watch your hand—as long as you watch the object as it falls, your hand will catch it quite automatically. We follow this principle our whole lives without really thinking about it. So we extended the logic of throwing and catching an object to the problem of aim in order to achieve a deeper understanding of it and were thus able to drill this skill into our soldiers."

Baoyu continued watching, transfixed, as row after row of soldiers completed their drills, without a single one fumbling his weapon or missing his target. "How strange!" he muttered repeatedly. "How strange!"

Gao Yutian remarked, "Of course, this particular drill is one the soldiers have practiced extensively; but you should be aware that the skills required by the commander-in-chief to assess the drills is even greater than that required for their execution. In a row of five soldiers, even though they are all standing in a line, you can see that when they throw their stones, the stones are not thrown uniformly but rather at different heights. The bullets that are fired naturally follow their respective targets. With our eyes we are able to see only whether a given stone is struck by a bullet or not and thereby know whether the shooter has been successful. How could our eyes possibly have the power to watch the guns being fired and to distinguish which bullet was fired by whom? But the commander-in-chief can distinguish it all quite clearly, and if a soldier were ever to miss his target, the commander would immediately be able to identify who it was."

Upon hearing this, Baoyu turned his eyes to the soldiers, waiting for them to fire. He eagerly tried to follow the bullets with his eyes, but how could he track them quickly enough? He watched ten rows of soldiers fire in succession but was unsuccessful each time. He couldn't help but laugh and say, "You're right—it's very difficult to see."

The drills continued until noon, at which time the order was given that the exercises should temporarily cease while the soldiers returned to their respective units. Two serving boys then carried out baskets of food, and the three men sat and ate together. Looking up, Baoyu noticed that the red sun was beating down from overhead and realized that it was a particularly sweltering day. He asked, "Why is it that you've chosen such a hot day to start the drills?"

"Each year we hold two drill sessions, one in winter and one in summer," Gao Yutian replied. "We want our soldiers to have experience running exercises in both extreme cold and heat. This prepares them in the event that military conflict requires them to be sent somewhere outside of the Realm: there will be no need to worry about sending them into the cold of the Arctic or into the heat of the tropics, as neither climate will present any impediment to them."

Baoyu looked and noticed that while the soldiers had ceased their drills, they remained lined up in their units. Each man had taken up a small leather tube from which he was drinking. Baoyu asked, "What are they drinking?"

"They're eating," said Gao Yutian. "The leather pouch that each man carries on his person contains food. The leather tube runs from the pouch."

"How much food can the leather pouches hold?"

"Five days' worth."

Lao Shaonian interjected, "Seeing this calls to mind the fact that when the ancients went on military campaigns, their camps still needed to use stoves for cooking—how clumsy!"

"It's not just clumsy!" Baoyu replied. "If you look at what is written in works of fiction, the soldiers had to dig out cooking pits and build stoves in the camps to cook—and when they moved out they had to carry their woks with them!"

An hour passed as they conversed. At 1:00 p.m., the military music struck up once again in unison, and a commanding officer issued an order that the drills were to carry on as before. Only at 6:00 p.m. did they cease.

As the three men returned to Zizhang's apartment, Baoyu commented, "I was told that today's drills were for the mobile strike force, but it seems to me that the exercise we saw was more like a drill for hunters."

Gao Yutian told him, "The skill was originally taught to us by hunters. At the time, when we were just starting to discuss regularizing the military and standardizing our training, someone submitted a memorandum saying that when hunters fire their bird rifles they don't rely on their eyes, but rather upon their hands, which made their aim extremely accurate. They also said that we could summon all of the hunters and integrate them into a unit to serve as a mobile strike force. At the time some ridiculed this memorandum as absurd, but the honored father of our current commander-in-chief—whose name was Zhen, and whose style name was Jingbo—was the head official in charge of training the soldiers, and seeing the memorandum, he thought it to have great merit. But since the number of hunters was too few—not even enough to create a few battalions—he decided on a different method, and chose instead to summon the hunters to come train the soldiers. By now the program has gradually expanded and has resulted in the successful training of some thirty thousand men who have been dispatched to defend different strategic border areas. In the event of military conflict, when the main force of our military goes out to face the enemy, these specialized soldiers set out in teams of three or five and fan out, conducting reconnaissance of the enemy troops. When they discover a gap in the enemy's defenses, they attack. That is why they are called the 'mobile strike force.'"

Baoyu replied, "Altogether, how many participated in today's drills?"

Gao Yutian said, "All units were mobilized to come drill here, so there were thirty thousand people performing the exercises today. Now that the drills have concluded, they will all return to their respective defensive positions." After dinner the three men rested for a while in the cool night air before retiring for the night. Zizhang did not return to his apartment that night.

On the following day the army practiced battle formations and the use of artillery. Gao Yutian once again accompanied his two guests in their viewing. On the third day the flying car company was to perform their exercises. Baoyu awoke extremely early that morning and tried to rouse Lao Shaonian and Gao Yutian to go with him to watch the exercises.

"It's not even 6:00 a.m. yet," Gao Yutian protested. "It's too early."

"But I want to see the soldiers get into the cars," Baoyu insisted.

"How could you see that? The flying car company isn't stationed here, they will only come here once they've received the command. Let's have a little something to eat first and then go." Gao Yutian then ordered a serving boy to bring in a light meal.

After the three men had eaten they proceeded together to the training ground.

The general's reviewing stand was silent and empty. The men had been sitting for a time when suddenly they heard a burst of military music. Looking toward the source of the music, they saw that the general's flag had already been raised and was billowing in the breeze. Zizhang, leading several dozen staff officers and commanding officers, as well as other military men of various ranks, was climbing the steps leading up to the reviewing stand. When the music had ceased playing, two signal fireworks were passed down from the stand. Two signalmen each took one firework and then, in unison, lit the fuses. With a great boom, the two fireworks shot simultaneously into the sky. This was followed by the sound of a loud crack as the fireworks burst apart, each creating the image of a different flag: one a blue general's pennant emblazoned with a flying dragon, the other a striped tiger on a white field. Baoyu thought, "Those are Japanese fireworks, I saw them in Shanghai. If the goal is to drill the troops, why should they be playing about with these?" He was still ruminating on this when suddenly he saw that in the sky to the west, where one of the "flags" was waving, a fleet of flying cars had arrived. Another fleet had arrived to the east as well, and each fleet had lined itself up in battle formation. Only then did Baoyu realize that the fireworks were a signal. As he continued to watch the two companies of flying cars, he observed that they were flying some fifty feet off the ground, each squared off against the other in a straight line. The fronts of the cars had been layered with steel sheets forming protective armored plates. The two parties began to fire upon one another.

Baoyu was shocked. "Why are they actually *firing* on one another? Aren't you afraid that someone will get hurt?"

Gao Yutian told him, "The bullets in their guns are made of rubber—they won't hurt anyone if they hit. But the bullets have been plastered with white powder, so that if they do hit, they will leave a white mark. In cases where a real hit would have caused serious damage, if it's the pilot that is hit, he is considered 'dead'; and if it's the car that is hit, the car is considered 'wrecked.' In either case, the pilot or the car cannot rejoin the formation. That is how the winner and loser are ultimately determined." Hearing this, Baoyu raised his head to look again, and it was just as Gao Yutian had said—some cars already bore white marks upon their armored plates.

The cars of the two fleets circled round each other in the air, soaring and diving, all firing their guns, as if face-to-face with a great enemy. Each company comprised roughly fifty cars, all running through a multitude of various battle formations. Suddenly, the western fleet formed up once again into a line and withdrew; the eastern fleet drew itself into a V formation and gave chase. When the eastern fleet had almost caught up, the western fleet suddenly turned and attacked their pursuers, quickly outflanking them on both sides. As the eastern fleet had been rushing forward, they were unable to stop all at once and were soon completely surrounded. A short exchange of fire ensued, but the eastern fleet could not withstand their opponent and had to withdraw from the exercise en masse, lowering their cars to the ground and bringing them to rest there. Meanwhile, the western fleet continued to soar impressively through the sky, showing off their prowess. Suddenly a hail of bullets fell from somewhere in the sky above them. The western fleet was not fast enough to counter this onslaught, and as a result every one of their cars was "damaged," forcing them all down to the ground. As it happened, when the western fleet had surrounded the eastern, five cars from the eastern fleet had shrouded themselves in one-way mirrored glass and risen high above the field of battle, observing everything. When they saw that their own fleet had been defeated, they swooped down and, from a position above the western fleet, had shot downward at all of them. From this high vantage point their shots had all struck their targets, and thus were they able to snatch victory from the jaws of defeat. Having bested their opponents, these cars, too, came to a landing upon the training ground. The fleet commanders proceeded to the reviewing stand for orders, at which time Zizhang instructed them to return to their normal defensive positions. Each of the two fleet commanders bowed and withdrew, then got back into his flying car to coordinate the departure of his respective fleet.

Two more fireworks were passed down from the reviewing stand, which, when set off, created red and black flags in the sky. A few moments later two more fleets of flying cars arrived, one from the south and one from the north. The two fleets circled up facing each other and took aim with their weapons. Whirling here and turning there, they engaged in fierce battle for quite some time, with neither side willing to concede defeat. Zizhang eventually sent out an order that the battle should be halted and the cars grounded, so that the commanding officers could go out to inspect the number of white marks. The cars of the northern fleet had sustained more hits, while the southern fleet's cars had sustained fewer; however, more southern pilots had been hit than had northern pilots, so in the end it was considered a draw. As previously, the two fleet commanders each coordinated the departure of his fleet.

By now it was already noon, and Zizhang gave the order that all of the soldiers should eat and rest. Once Baoyu and his companions had likewise eaten, they rehashed the flying car exercises. Baoyu said, "In all those absurd novels that are always speaking of spirits and demons, they also talk about 'great wars extending to the farthest reaches of the clouds.' I didn't expect that today I should actually see it with my own eyes."

Lao Shaonian replied, "Though you've now seen that 'great war extending to the farthest reaches of the clouds' is a reality, we still lack the kinds of precious magical weapons the stories speak of—like flying knives or immortal-binding chains. But as I see it, we will also see weapons modeled on such ideals being experimented with in the future."

"But those are all just silly fantasies," protested Gao Yutian. "How could they serve as a basis for experimentation?"

"Wasn't 'ascending the clouds and riding on mist' once a silly fantasy? Yet as soon as flying cars were created, all of a sudden it actually became possible," Lao Shaonian retorted.

"That time when we set down the *peng* in Ritual Deference Village," Baoyu mused, "the car plunged helter-skelter upward into the sky, reaching an altitude of 6,500 feet before stopping. I reckon the 'farthest reaches of the clouds' must be just about there!"

Gao Yutian replied, "It's unfortunate that you didn't leave anyone on the ground to observe and find out whether you remained visible or not."

"According to what I've heard, there is no air above the clouds," said Baoyu. "Were we to bring along an air-creating machine, we could go up above the clouds to have a look. If we were lucky enough to reach a planet, we could study it and find out once and for all whether other planets are home to other worlds or not. Otherwise such thoughts are all speculation, just based on empty words without any real proof."

"Someone else had this idea a long time ago," said Lao Shaonian. "But it can't be done like that. Because once you've reached the space where there's no air, it's a true vacuum—and when electricity encounters a vacuum, it will ignite. Now, if you generate air, you can only seal up the doors and windows tightly and let the people inside breathe the air being generated; but there can be absolutely no opening to vent to the outside. Because the inner workings of the car all use electricity—if they were exposed to the vacuum of space, wouldn't the whole car just catch fire? That is why no one dares proceed recklessly with the idea. But for that, we would have sent someone up a long time ago."

"It would be great if you were able to come up with a way to send someone up—otherwise it will always remain a puzzle."

Gao Yutian interrupted: "Enough about that—we should go watch the drills!" They suddenly heard the strains of military music being played once again, though there was still no one to be seen on or in front of the reviewing stand. Gazing off in the distance toward the main camp, they saw five fireworks being set off over an open field. Each firework formed a flag of a different color, and a great fleet of flying cars soon emerged in response. At the center of this fleet was a car that had a yellow flying-dragon pennant hanging from its prow; from the flagpole in the center of the car fluttered the general's flag. As this fleet proceeded to the training ground, Baoyu realized that Zizhang himself was now in a flying car. In an instant, four additional fleets had arrived from the east, south, west, and north. The general's car raised a command flag: all of the assembled fleets took up battle formations and practiced with their weapons for a while.

Baoyu observed, "It's truly marvelous that your electronic guns don't make any sound. If that weren't so, one would go deaf from the noise!"

"But that's not the only good thing about them," said Lao Shaonian. "Fortunately, they don't give off any smoke, either. If they gave off smoke, after just a few rounds were fired, the sky would be filled with it! How would a pilot be able to see the other cars?"

"That," Baoyu replied, "would truly be ascending the clouds and riding on mist!"

Just as they were speaking, a burst of very fine vapor came wafting down from the general's car. Carried along by the southern wind, it drifted all the way to the main encampment. A car bearing a flag reading "Medical" emerged from the fleet, flew directly to the camp, and came to a landing there. Meanwhile the other cars shot off high into the air. As Baoyu and his companions raised their heads to watch, the cars flew higher and higher, growing smaller and smaller as they went—all while still maintaining their battle formations. In an instant they had gone so high that they were no longer visible, causing the civilians who had gathered around the training ground to watch the exercises to erupt simultaneously in thunderous applause. A long time passed, and the cars still had not returned to view. When the cars had been gone for over four hours, Baoyu finally asked, "Have they all gone up out of the atmosphere?"

"If they'd gone up into the vacuum of space, then their ships would all have been reduced to rubble," replied Gao Yutian.

Lao Shaonian, gazing blankly to the west, suddenly pointed and said, "Geese? At this time of year?"

Baoyu looked where Lao Shaonian had pointed and indeed saw two rows of flying geese. He watched them fixedly for a while and determined that they were flying toward the training ground.

"How could they be geese?" asked Gao Yutian. "It's the fleets of flying cars returning." As he spoke, the cars grew nearer, and in a short time they had all arrived. The general's car raised high a command flag, and each fleet departed at once, heading in separate directions. The fleet led by Zizhang came to a landing upon the training ground.

Zizhang led the various officers from their cars and back up onto the reviewing stand. He was just about to issue a new order when suddenly two flying cars came zooming in from the southeast with lightning speed and landed on the training ground. A person emerged from one of the cars, walked up beside the reviewing stand, and withdrew a letter from the breast of his jacket. He handed the letter to a signalman, who brought it up onto the reviewing stand and presented it to Zizhang. As Zizhang tore it open and read it, his face lit up. He then gave the order that the man should be brought up onto the stand to answer a few questions. After the man had answered Zizhang's queries, he left the stand.

Baoyu was watching all of this, somewhat confused. He thought, "They were drilling so intently, I can't think why this person has come to interrupt." He continued watching as the man departed from the reviewing stand, proceeded back to the cars, and instructed someone on board one of them to pass down a wooden box. Once the box had been produced from within the car, the man busily set about opening it, then extracted a few miscellaneous pieces of machinery from within, which he assembled at the foot of the reviewing stand. Once he had done this he withdrew a cannon from the box. This cannon not only stunned Baoyu and caused Lao Shaonian to remark on its strangeness, but upon seeing it, even Gao Yutian—who was often at the commander-in-chief's side, and was no stranger to military weaponry—was quite bewildered.

■ ■ ■

If you wish to know just what kind of cannon it was, please listen to the explanation in the following chapter.

Chapter Thirty-Eight

In the invention of marvelous weaponry, humaneness must still be a consideration

His grand adventure having led him far and wide, he plans to pay a call on Dongfang Wenming

AS IT happened, the cannon in question was a miraculous electronic cannon, in the development of which Dongfang Fa, Duo Yishi, and Hua Zili had all combined their energies and pushed their brainpower to the limit. With the sole exception of the various electrical components, which were made of metals like steel and iron, the entire body of the cannon itself was made of neither metal nor stone, but rather, of exceptionally pure, clear glass. Think about it: How could those who were seeing it for the first time help but be astonished over such a novelty?

Let us speak of how, once work on the cannon had been completed, the three learned gentlemen had composed a joint letter, which they sent to Zizhang, the commander-in-chief of the army. In the letter they detailed the cannon's use and explained that this kind of cannon was not only smokeless and silent but also didn't require shells. It was so powerful that, provided there were no impediments in the way, it could hit a target sitting as far away as the horizon line. The learned gentlemen then dispatched an engineer to deliver the cannon to Zizhang and to convey the letter as well; the engineer had also been instructed to assemble the cannon and perform a demonstration on site. Knowing that the army was undergoing training exercises during these three days, the gentlemen had hastened to send the cannon over on this particular day. Upon receiving the letter Zizhang was naturally quite pleased and hastily instructed the engineer to assemble the cannon. He then gave one order that his fleet of flying cars should return to the main encampment, and another that a tall flagpole should be erected at the edge of the training ground, with warning banners affixed to both sides. When the spectators saw the banners, they naturally backed away.

In no time, assembly of the cannon had been completed, and Zizhang gave the command that a pig should be trussed up and brought forth; its feet bound with rope, the pig was to be suspended from the top of the high flagpole. Zizhang then descended from his place on the stand to personally observe the demonstration of the cannon. He watched as the engineer aligned his aim, pointed the barrel of the cannon at the pig, grasped the firing mechanism with his hand, and gave it a pull. The cannon gave off neither sound nor the smell of smoke—indeed, the firing was undetectable not just by ear or nose but by eye as well. The engineer then called for someone to lower the pig from where it had been hung, and they saw that it was dead from electrocution. The assembled observers were all astonished. Among the group were a few skeptics who thought that perhaps the pig had merely been strangled by the ropes, for how could the pig have been killed thus, as if by magic? In his heart of hearts, Zizhang, too, was a little taken aback, so he called for an ox to be bound and hung from the flagpole, then instructed the engineer to fire upon it. The engineer took aim as the ox, having been suspended from the pole, lowed and thrashed. When the engineer pulled the firing mechanism, the ox instantly went rigid. Only upon seeing this did everyone watching believe in the efficacy of the weapon and burst into thunderous applause.

Next the engineer pulled a rod from the box and said, "This is an electricity-diverting rod." When Zizhang took the rod in his hands and examined it, he saw that it was much like the spears used by the ancients, crafted from wood—but this had a layer of pliable ceramic wrapped around the outside. An iron strip about a foot long had been fitted into the end of the rod, making the entire thing about ten feet long altogether. Zizhang asked how it was used. The engineer gave instructions for a second ox to be brought forth, but this time the rod was to be tied to its back. Then, after its hooves were bound, he called for the ox to be hung vertically from the tall pole. He explained: "Now, no matter how many times the cannon is fired, the ox will not be struck." Zizhang was incredulous, and so took aim with the cannon himself and fired it; but as predicted, he was unable to strike the ox and quickly gave the order that it be released.

"The tip of the rod is made of magnetic iron," the engineer told him. "When electrical energy like this is released, it is attracted by the iron's magnetism. It gets diverted from its original trajectory because it is drawn away to the rod instead. We developed these as defensive measures—in the event that other countries are able to replicate this cannon, we will be able to make these to avoid their attacks."

"And what is the farthest distance this cannon can fire?" asked Zizhang. "Have you investigated that?"

"We have attempted to calculate it but have been unable to. I suspect it can hit a target at any distance." As he said this, the engineer spun a wheel, raising the mouth of the cannon so that it was at a sixty-degree angle, and fired again. The crowd, having raised their heads and fixed their eyes intently on the sky, suddenly saw a streak of flame tear through space above them like lightning.

"The electricity has now traveled beyond the atmosphere," said the engineer. "That is why it has ignited. Mr. Hua says that the lightning we see in spring and summer is also a result of electricity igniting in the vacuum of space."

The engineer proceeded to fire off a few more shots. The crowd watched as shimmering electricity streaked through space like myriad golden snakes. Zizhang was delighted and led the assembled officials, as well as the engineer, back to the main camp. The engineer was given a letter to take back with him, after which he departed.

Gao Yutian, along with Lao Shaonian and Baoyu, returned to Zizhang's residence. By now the three men, still not knowing for what kinds of special uses the cannon was intended, began to guess among themselves. They were at this until 11:00 p.m., when Zizhang returned. The three men greeted him, then clamored to ask him questions about the cannon. As Zizhang gave them a detailed description of the cannon's uses, all three men clicked their tongues and commented on how marvelous it was.

"How can it be called a cannon?" asked Baoyu. "It's really an electricity-shooting tube."

"It does have its benefits," replied Zizhang, "but it is unfortunately a bit too inhumane. It would be fine to use during terrestrial warfare, but if it were to be used at sea, why, all battleships are made of steel and iron and are thus all conductive. As soon as a ship is hit, the electricity would course through the entire ship! What would happen to the people on board?"

"It is difficult to be fastidious about 'humaneness and humane techniques' in times of war," said Baoyu.

"Not true. When two countries come into conflict, they may become enemies; however, it is still a question of humans against humans. If all we cared about were satisfying our greed for glory and our desire to obtain victory, and as a result were willing to perpetrate the wanton slaughter of others, then on the battlefield, we would naturally forget that we and our enemy are of the same species, and would savage one another, lashing out violently with hearts of stone. I put it to you: as soon as you look at it from the perspective of a third party, it would become evident that it is a case of inflicting harm upon one's own kind because of a momentary fit of pique. How could that not be considered inhumane in the extreme?"

"But when your people are united by hatred for a shared enemy, the implementation of 'humane techniques' is surely a difficult issue."

"One 'humane technique' that we will certainly implement is the one recently developed by Mr. Dongfang De; but even without the invention of such a technique, battle should still be carried out in an aboveboard and proper manner. Even if there must be slaughter, it ought to be done in an honorable way. Recently, certain cruel countries have pushed the limits of their own wicked ingenuity and have created a kind of chlorine gas shell. The chlorine gas is contained within the shell, and after the shell is launched it explodes, killing who knows how many people. What is truly risible is that after creating these weapons, they adopt sanctimonious facades and declare that their use is to be prohibited.[1] But as soon as they find themselves at war and unable to secure a victory, they bring the shells back out and use them again, making all kinds of excuses, claiming that they'll use them *just this one time.* Having engaged in such cruel practices, they still claim to be civilized!"

"What is your newly developed humane technique?" asked Baoyu.

"It's the knockout drug I started telling you about the other day. I was finally able to test it out today: we sprayed a little into the main camp, and as we'd hoped, a slew of soldiers were all rendered unconscious. The doctor then followed along, and only after he'd applied an antidote did they waken. In the future, using just this substance, our troops will be able to capture an entire enemy army alive and bring them back without harming a single soul—isn't that a humane technique? However, it is still extremely difficult to use: one must account very carefully for the wind before attempting to administer it. Of course, when there is no wind, it can simply be sprayed straight down on top of them; but when there is wind, one must spray it downwind. However, because the strength of the wind, the altitude of the flying car, and the distance to the target can all vary, it is necessary to devise a means to accurately take the wind into account before this tool can be used. Currently we can make fairly confident calculations when the car is about fifty feet off the ground; but any higher than that and our calculations are no longer accurate."

Baoyu sighed. "I didn't realize that scientific inventions could have such clever uses. Why, you could pacify the entire world without firing a single arrow!"

"In fact, it wouldn't be an exaggeration to say that if our government wished to issue a command that the army swallow up every other country, we could pacify all of them in no time at all. Now, it is not the case that our government has never harbored the desire to do so—it is only that Mr. Dongfang Wenming was unwilling to allow it. After being in power here for fifty years, last year he resigned from office and took up a life of rural seclusion. His life's greatest wish was to create a country that was truly civilized, for the particular purpose of standing in opposition to those false, so-called 'civilized countries,' and to await the day that, looking at our example, those countries become ashamed of themselves and decide to learn the way of true civilization from us. For that way we can foster a civilized world without having to make use of weapons and soldiers."

"That the esteemed Mr. Dongfang should wish to make himself the teacher of the world is truly admirable," remarked Baoyu. "How can I meet him?"

"That's easy," answered Lao Shaonian. "He is an extremely kindly man who takes the utmost delight in entertaining guests and is, moreover, a skilled conversationalist. Since we've finished observing the drills, we can go see him tomorrow."

"Stay for a few more days," said Zizhang. "I've been so preoccupied with official matters these past few days, I haven't had a chance to chat with you properly. Now my duties have all been discharged—even my report to the emperor on the drills and the requisite documentation for the government have all been sent off. Why have I been working so busily? For the simple reason that once everything had been taken care of, we could spend a couple days enjoying each other's company—so why must you go rushing off so urgently? I need an early night tonight, but let's continue to discuss this tomorrow." He had said his goodnights and was about to walk into his room when suddenly he stopped and removed something from his pocket. Placing it on the table, he said, "See if you can guess what this is!" He then went into his room.

When the three men all drew closer to look, they saw that it was a small bundle of dried grasses bound together with thread. The grasses were similar to rushes, except that whereas rushes are hollow in the center, these had solid cores. None of the men understood what they were looking at, so they did not dwell on it and went to bed. Of this night we have nothing further to report.

On the following day Baoyu wished to depart, but Zizhang took great pains to detain them. That day Zizhang just needed to go to the camp to tend to some mundane tasks, after which he returned to his quarters and chatted with Lao Shaonian and Baoyu, discussing topics of military strategy. As evening drew near, the messenger who had been dispatched to the emperor on the previous day returned, bearing an imperial edict. Because Zizhang had been in charge of overseeing the drills of the flying car army, he was to be granted the additional title of "Flight General."

"The rank of Flight General must have been created specially for you," remarked Lao Shaonian.

Zizhang replied, "Although I did oversee the drills, it is not convenient for me to hold this new post concurrently. It is only right that I should resign it tomorrow and request that the government dispatch a new commander-in-chief for the flying car division."

"It only took the messenger one day and one night to go and return. With such flying cars as you have, there's no need for the mystic fast-travel of the sages," commented Baoyu.

"That's nothing!" answered Zizhang. "Yesterday when we were drilling the flying car fleets—do you know how far we went?"

"It took you roughly six hours to go there and back," mused Gao Yutian. "So it must have been three hours one-way. How far could you possibly have gotten?"

"Have you worked out yet what the bundle of grass I left you last night was?" asked Zizhang.

Gao Yutian pulled the bundle from a drawer. "In fact, none of us understands what it is."

"I was afraid you wouldn't believe me if I told you, so I took that as proof. That bundle of grasses is what the Arabs use to brush their teeth!"

Baoyu's jaw hung open in amazement. "You went to Arabia yesterday?"

"If you lay a course directly west of here, you end up in Turkey. But if you veer a little southward along the way, you end up in Arabia. I landed my car there, and as it happened, a group of natives there were selling these. Seeing me drop out of the sky like I did, they all took me to be a god and threw themselves to their knees. Since I wished to take some proof of our journey back with me, I gave them two tins of military rations and took this bundle of grass in exchange."

"Dropping out of the sky like that, you can hardly blame them for being startled and taking you for a god," said Baoyu.

Zizhang replied, "In barbarian cultures that have yet to become civilized, whenever the people encounter anything they haven't seen before, they always take it to be a god. Back when the Spanish began their conquest of Mexico, they needed only a calvary unit of ten or so horses—since there had never been horses in Mexico, the natives had never seen them before and didn't know they were merely seeing men riding horses. They thought they were seeing creatures that were half-man, half-beast and took them to be gods. And when they heard the Spaniards fire their guns, they thought that these gods could command the very thunder. Isn't that too ridiculous?" After he'd finished speaking, Zizhang ordered someone to go request that the camp secretary come over. When the secretary arrived, Zizhang had him take down a letter indicating that he wished to resign the position of Flight General and that another commander-in-chief for the flying car division should be selected. Baoyu and the others stayed with him for another two days, after which they said their goodbyes to Zizhang and departed.

Baoyu, having heard that the Trust Region in the Southern Sector was a trading area, implored Lao Shaonian to go with him there to explore. Lao Shaonian agreed, and the two men set out directly southward in a flying car. As the car flew along, Lao Shaonian suddenly called out for it to land. The pilot obeyed and slowly brought the car down, finally coming to a stop in an open field. From within the car Baoyu surveyed the scene and found that clouds of yellow covered the vast expanse of the field—they were surrounded by ripe wheat.

Lao Shaonian said, "The past couple of days, you've been saying you wished to see some rural scenery, so I've brought us down to have a look. This is the Compassion Region, the most thriving agricultural area in the Southern Sector."

Baoyu cast a glance all around. His entire field of vision, as far as he could see, was filled with boundless wheatfields. He asked, "But wheat would already have been harvested in the fourth month. How can there be wheat again now?"

"We have improved the quality of the soil in our humble Realm such that all of our crops, whether rice or wheat, mature once per season, for a total of four harvests per year."

After they'd looked around for a bit, the car rose back into the air to an altitude of about twenty feet. Flying now at a leisurely speed, they passed a number of forested areas. Baoyu watched it all with rapt attention: there were all kinds of fruit trees, as well as groves of mulberry, willow, and rubber trees. He asked, "Obviously, the mulberry orchards are for the rearing of silkworms, and the rubber trees are perhaps for the extraction of rubber; but for what purpose do you grow willow trees?"

"Those are both also for the rearing of silkworms."

Baoyu was shocked by this. "Silkworms also eat willow and rubber-tree leaves?"

"There are willow-silkworms that eat willow leaves and rubber-tree silkworms that eat rubber-tree leaves. But other people don't know that and simply call them all 'wild silkworms.' When people looking to make silken clothes for special occasions gathered these wild silkworm cocoons to spool into silk, it turned out that the silk was terribly coarse, so they declared it to be unfit to use. But they didn't know that this was because the silkworms had hatched and lived in a natural setting—up there in the trees, there was no one overseeing their production. Thus, when they spun their cocoons, they spun them onto the leaves of the trees, so naturally the cocoons were coarse. But we devised a way to gather them and rear them ourselves, just as we did with the silkworms that feed on mulberry trees—so isn't it exactly the same? It's just that the silk they produce is slightly less lustrous. It's a shame other people gave up on such a tremendous source of benefit."

"I don't know about rubber-tree silkworms, but when willow-silkworms become moths, aren't their wings quite large? Won't they fly away?"

"I'm afraid it is for this reason that others aren't willing to raise willow-silkworms. They worry that the moths will eventually fly away, leaving no eggs behind. They don't realize that in order to farm willow-silkworms, they need to construct a special moth house, paste up paper on all four interior walls, and then place all of the cocoons within. When the silkworm moths emerge from the cocoons they will be unable to fly out, and will thus lay all of their eggs on the paper."

Having taken in their fill of the scenes below as they chatted, they instructed the pilot to take the car up higher and start flying faster. They then proceeded directly to the Trust Region, where they landed once again.

The superintendent of the trading district was Dongfang Ying. All goods to be imported or exported first had to be registered with him. He was responsible for tracking profits and losses year to year and now employed a staff of one hundred investigators beneath himself whom he dispatched to different countries to investigate and report on the varied dispositions and predilections of each locale. After receiving these reports, Dongfang Ying would inform each of the factories in the Realm. Because of this, he was extremely busy with his work and was unwilling to meet with guests except on his days off. Thus, Lao Shaonian and Baoyu felt it was not convenient to go call on him, so they went instead to roam around heart of the district. Truly, this place was abustle with stores and treasures—transported both over land and by water—and myriad merchants gathering like clouds. The two men went into a shop in which various goods were arrayed; displayed in the center of the shop were domestically produced goods, with foreign goods along the sides. Baoyu looked everything over one by one and remarked that it was strange—back when he was in Shanghai and had gone into the foreign goods shop, he had felt that everything before him was tacky and bizarre, and his eyes had been incapable of taking it all in, as if he were walking through the overwhelming splendor of Shanyin. Here, however, he saw that every one of the locally manufactured products was simple and elegant; whereas looking at the tacky, bizarre foreign goods, he felt them to be unbearably vulgar. After he'd looked over the lot, they reemerged onto the street and strolled back and forth a couple of times before finally proceeding to a tunnel-car company. They hired a tunnel car, with the intention of going to pay a call on Dongfang Wenming.

■ ■ ■

If you wish to know how their visit to Dongfang Wenming went, please listen to the explanation in the following chapter.

Chapter Thirty-Nine

Old friends joyfully reunite over drinks

Thriving medical sciences ensure longer life and youthful appearance

WE WERE speaking of how since Baoyu's arrival in the Realm of Civilization, he had traveled exhaustively within it. He had heard of all manner of things that he had hitherto never heard of and had seen all manner of things he had hitherto never seen. Because he had long held the reputation of Dongfang Wenming in the highest regard, he arranged with Lao Shaonian to ride together in a tunnel car to the No. 1 District of the Benevolence Region in the Eastern Sector so that they might call on him. By the time their car had reached its destination, it was already late in the day. Baoyu recognized that Dongfang Wenming was an elderly man of high official status, as well as a man of virtue equal to his many years; this, coupled with the fact that this was to be his first-ever visit to him—and that it was already getting late—meant that calling on him tonight couldn't but be seen as disrespectful. And so he decided that they should stay the night at the tunnel-car station.

Bright and early the following day, he proceeded along with Lao Shaonian to Dongfang Wenming's home, where they proffered their calling cards. Dongfang Wenming quickly gave instructions that they should be invited in, and the two men made their way into a reception room. As Baoyu was about to join his hands in respectful greeting and bow, Dongfang Wenming rushed forward toward him, took him by the hands and asked, "I do hope that mine elder brother has been in good health since last we parted company?"

Baoyu was stunned. "Long have I held your reputation in high esteem, sir, which is why I have made the special effort to come call on you. I believed that this was to be the first time I would have the opportunity to pay my respects to your august person; however, I don't know on what other occasion I might have had the honor of serving you and benefitting from your tutelage?"

Dongfang Wenming, still holding him by the hands, urged Baoyu to sit, then began: "It is many years now since we parted. Perhaps mine elder brother is just having a momentary lapse of memory—but in time, you will recall."

Baoyu was filled with a sense of uncertainty, telling himself that never in his life had he numbered an elderly man among his friends. But upon closer inspection he saw that Dongfang Wenming had a beard and hair that gleamed like silver, long eyebrows, soft eyes, rosy lips, and white teeth—indeed, he appeared much like a youth. Baoyu racked his brain, but still could not recall having known him. Wenming added, "My old friend, you've traveled such a long way, and it can't have been easy on you! As it happens, I am at leisure today, and my sons and son-in-law are all coming to pay their respects. I shall instruct them to accompany us in a day of drinking, in recognition of our long separation." This rendered Baoyu even more speechless.

Lao Shaonian said, "Mr. Jia has come especially to call on you out of reverence for your fine reputation; but it appears he did not anticipate that you would in fact be an old acquaintance."

Baoyu added, "Recently, when we visited with Commander-in-Chief Ximen, he mentioned that you wished to establish the Realm as an exemplar of 'true civilization' so that the 'false civilized' countries should have a model to follow; and that you intended to use yourself as an example after which the behavior of other world leaders might be patterned. That is why I have come especially to show my admiration, hoping that I might listen attentively to your lofty ideas. I truly cannot think of when I would have had the opportunity to attend upon a man of such great learning as yourself."

Wenming sighed. "It is easier said than done. I wielded political power and served as master of this state for fifty years, overseeing it and encouraging innovation so that we might arrive where we are today. I still have so many ambitions that have not yet been realized, but I do not know to whom I can look to continue these endeavors. My heirs have all thrown themselves wholeheartedly into science and are too preoccupied to turn their attention to such things. Although I have discussed the matter with the various gentlemen who are currently in power, most of them fear that we would be drawn into military conflict as a result. Because of their hesitation, we have not yet been able to begin. However, if I were able to bring these ambitions to fruition, then perhaps there is hope that the world will become civilized."

"And what are the great ambitions that you have, sir?" asked Lao Shaonian.

"Of all the beings on earth that have hair and teeth, round skulls and square feet, none does not belong to the category of 'human'; it is just that occasionally, there are one or two places that education has not yet reached, so there are disparities in intellect. But considering this question from the perspective of most benevolent Heaven—can it be said that any of the races was not bestowed upon the earth by Heaven itself? Now, the red, black, and brown races have long been mired in calamity and have suffered such extreme abuse that they are on the verge of extinction. It makes me uneasy every time I think of them. They are humans just like us, so why should those groups alone encounter such misfortune? Whenever I try to think of ways to extricate them from their misery and lead them to a new livelihood, I am helpless to change the fact that the work would involve exerting tremendous effort, and across great distances. And so I have never yet been able to devise a good solution."

Lao Shaonian said, "I fear that as soon as you begin to interfere in these issues, you will not be able to avoid the calamities of war."

"I've heard it said," added Baoyu, "that in the Americas, after the black slaves were emancipated, the freed black people had no means by which to procure food, so they became wanderers and drifters, with many dying of hunger, one beside the next. They had been warmer and better-fed as slaves. Since they were born with an extremely ignorant nature, I'm afraid it won't be easy to lift them up and lead them."

Wenming replied, "It is precisely because of this that I have said the work would involve exerting tremendous effort across great distances. After extricating them from their misery, we must also devise a livelihood for them before we can consider the job complete. If we were only to save them from their immiseration, then wait for them to find their own livelihoods, they would not be able to do so and would necessarily sink back into calamity once more. If it were otherwise, and all we needed to do was use our military might to free them from their shackles, why shouldn't it be possible? But the fact remains that after freeing them from their shackles, we must also create a means of educating them, expanding their knowledge, and inculcating in them a self-reliant character; only then could we consider our great task to have been completed successfully."

"Put like that, the task sounds even more daunting," said Baoyu.

"When you look at people, the most important thing is to distinguish whether they are true or false. If our 'true civilization' here were not fully developed, then those 'false civilized' countries would still be able to deceive others with their facade of civilization. On the topic of emancipating black slaves in the Americas, if you only consider it from the surface, how could it not be considered a civilized act and a compassionate undertaking? How could you know that the man who undertook it had ulterior motives? All he wanted, and with all of his being, was to be president; but because those who would vote for him were in the minority he was forced to devise an unconventional stratagem, and so he advocated the emancipation of the slaves. He thought, 'Once this population has been freed, they will establish for themselves a position of equality and freedom and will necessarily feel gratitude for my having freed them. Moreover, they will be given the right to vote, and in the future, when it comes to electing a president, they will certainly vote for me.' Who could have predicted that the freed black people were as simple-minded as animals, so that upon their emancipation, they were unable to support themselves, and contrary to expectations, they were worse off than when they had been slaves? Not only did they not feel gratitude toward that man, but they positively resented him."[1]

As they were chatting, Dongfang Ying and his two brothers arrived one after the other to pay their respects. Hua Zili, bringing along his wife Dongfang Mei, had also come to call on his father-in-law. Dongfang Wenming said, "Today, we have a guest who has come to us from afar, you should all come to meet him. I have found solitude extremely tiresome of late, and it is rare that an old friend should come to see me. You must all accompany us in a day of drinking." His sons and son-in-law all agreed to this.

Wenming then instructed his sons and daughter to address Baoyu as "uncle," which made Baoyu feel even more uncomfortable. He thought, "This old man is so strange! When have I ever encountered him, that he insists on saying that I am an old acquaintance? And even his sons have lengthy beards, so why should they have to call me 'uncle'? When I ask him, he is unwilling to explain. It really is most bizarre!" However, he decided, "I'll put it out of my mind for now, for it certainly seems that he is well intentioned." As he thought this, he appraised the three brothers: Dongfang Fa, he had already met; but the other two were just as refined and charismatic as he. Dongfang

Mei was gentle, serene, and of a naturally dignified disposition. Only Hua Zili had a somewhat sallow complexion—though he did not look sickly, for from within the sallow complexion his expression radiated a certain brightness, and his strong brows and large eyes lent him a distinguished, imposing air. At the moment, Dongfang Ying and the others were smilingly attending to Dongfang Wenming while simultaneously entertaining the guests. Dongfang Mei was gracious and self-possessed; she did not appear to be a frivolous woman, nor was she a shrinking violet. She held forth in socializing and conversing just as the others did. Not only did she not appear to consider herself a woman—even her interlocutors seemed to forget that she was one.

Lao Shaonian and Baoyu discussed business and trade with Dongfang Ying; with Dongfang Fa and Hua Zili they discussed all kinds of technologies; with Dongfang De they first discussed medical practices, then casually asked whether he had any new inventions.

"In terms of new inventions in the medical field, only the intelligence-augmenting powder has already been completed. Currently I would like to research two other areas, but I don't know whether they are feasible or not, so all I can do is fully expend my energies and intellect in pursuing them. If by the end of my life I have been unable to produce any result, then I can only hope that my successors will be able to do so."

Baoyu asked him what areas he wished to research, and Dongfang De replied, "I believe that death is the most tragic part of human existence; but no one is able to escape it. So first I wish to research a method to prevent death. Meanwhile, the need to eat is the most burdensome part of human existence;

no matter what kind of great tasks one would seek to accomplish, they become impossible to do if one has not eaten one's fill. Moreover, eating wastes quite a lot of time—why, every meal takes at least a quarter of an hour. Though you might only eat twice per day, if you were to add it all up over the span of a year, you would have spent a hundred and eighty hours just in eating, at the expense of completing who knows how many other tasks! So I also intend to research a way to obviate eating."

"Neither eating nor dying," mused Baoyu. "Then wouldn't one become an immortal?"

Dongfang De replied, "It was precisely because of the legends of the Daoist practice of ingesting *qi* to sustain long life that I initially believed it to be a mere ideal, a fable—yet when I actually examined the texts of the ancients, it seemed not to be entirely fantastical, so I decided to initiate research on the topic. However, even if the ancients did ever possess such a technique, it was only perfected by individuals, who were unwilling to pass down their secrets. My intention is that once our research has yielded a result, we will share it with all."

Lao Shaonian asked, "But if your sole focus is to stop people from dying, won't you eventually have the problem of overcrowding?"

Dongfang De answered, "I believe that after we have mastered a technique to prevent death, we will cease to produce offspring. If you don't believe me, all you need do is read the books passed down from antiquity which tell of the immortals and Daoists—when do they ever tell of immortals or Daoists having children? Although the ancients did not necessarily consider this particular aspect of it, it is plain to see that this is a natural ideal."

"If that's the case," said Baoyu, "then it's less like being an immortal and more like being a Buddha."

"How is it like being a Buddha?" asked Lao Shaonian.

Baoyu laughed: "Neither being born nor being extinguished, neither adding to nor decreasing their number—isn't that something straight out of a Buddhist sutra?" He then added, "Just now, the old gentleman said that he planned to rescue the red, black, and brown races from calamity and ensure a livelihood for them all, but that the difficulty lies in the fact that those peoples are all so unintelligent that they might be difficult to educate. Since you already have a method for augmenting intelligence, why not use it to treat them?"

Dongfang De said, "It wouldn't work. My intelligence-augmenting powder works thus: when one inhales the powder like snuff, the substance of the brain itself increases. When one's brain matter increases, then naturally one's thinking is enriched. Its function is simply to aid in people's thinking; so one must first have subjects who are capable of thought if it is to produce any benefit. When it comes to those people who are utterly incapable of thought, though we might attempt to use it on them, it would not be successful. When civilized peoples use it, it can make them even more civilized; but when barbaric peoples use it, it may actually make them even more barbaric. The thinking of the red, black, and other races can be summed up in the word 'lazy.' If they were to use this formula, it would only increase their ability for thinking of new ways to be lazy." At this, all the others laughed.

Wenming sighed. "My desire to help save the red and black peoples is a matter of 'abandoning what is near to pursue what is distant; abandoning oneself to follow others,' for in actuality, the number of our own race mired in the calamities of barbarism is not small. That I, to this day, have still not been able to rectify this situation is a source of tremendous regret. Meanwhile, the next generation have all committed themselves to science without paying much attention to politics. I can only hope that this aspiration will be fulfilled by my grandchildren's generation."

It was only as the question arose in the course of this conversation that the guests learned that Dongfang Wenming already had a number of grandchildren and great-grandchildren. His sons' sons, Dongfang Wen, Dongfang Wu, Dongfang Tao, and Dongfang Qian, as well as his daughter's son, Hua Wuben, had all taken up positions in government. His great-grandsons, Dongfang Xin, Dongfang Sheng, Dongfang Zhen, Dongfang Xing, Dongfang Rui, Dongfang Yong, Dongfang Meng, and Dongfang Wei, as well as Hua Rijin and Hua Rixin, had already finished their general education and were each continuing their studies at specialized colleges. Wenming's great-great-grandsons, Dongfang Datong, Dongfang Dazhi, and Hua Fuyi, were currently receiving education in nursery school. As for the women of the family, they were all teachers in girls' schools. At the moment, it happened to be the summer holidays, so they had planned to return home to see to Wenming's needs; but in recognition of the fact that they had all been working so hard all year and only had this one month to rest, Wenming instead instructed them to travel off somewhere to avoid the summer heat, each making plans according to her own wishes, so as to avoid remaining stuck in the house. Moreover, the more elderly among them could enjoy the relative quiet. Among the women were a few daughters-in-law who still wished to fulfill their filial duties; however, Wenming had insisted that they travel to somewhere cooler, saying, "If you don't do as I say, you would be betraying the affection I have for you." The daughters-in-law had no choice but to depart, only returning to call on him every three to five days. Several of the great-grandsons were still at school, for although it was the summer holiday, they had chosen to remain to study independently and so had not returned home. But of this let us say no more.

Let us speak instead of how those present had already drunk more than ten cups of liquor, and fortunately, since the liquor here did not make one drunk, they had simply grown more ebullient the more they drank. The atmosphere was boisterous and unrestrained. And even though the liquor had been accompanied by fruit nectar, no matter how much one imbibed he never felt overfull. Wenming raised the question of where Baoyu had come from, so Baoyu told him about how he'd wanted to go to Freedom Village in search of Xue Pan, and how he had met with robbers along the road from Shandong. Wenming said, "The charms of a place in which Xue Pan is willing to live—and to which he was introduced by Liu Xuesheng—are sure to have been exaggerated.[2] How could you possibly go to such a place? And as for the robbers—before one can enter our humble Realm, he must first have successfully overcome an adversity—it is the law of evolution."

"Does the old gentleman also know Cousin Xue?" asked Baoyu.

"I've not met him face-to-face, but I have long heard of his . . . storied reputation."

Baoyu was once again bewildered by this, and thought, "The old boy speaks so evasively; it seems that I am to die of frustration today!" As he sat with this feeling of befuddlement, a burst of boozy vapor surged upon his heart, and he immediately felt cheerful once more, completely forgetting the frustration of a moment before.

Wenming added, "If you, elder brother, would insist upon going to Freedom Village, we have our own Freedom Village here, twenty li to the east; it was my old stomping grounds in years past. Tomorrow, you can go there and take a stroll around the place—I reckon it's a fair bit better than where Xue Pan is living." As he finished saying this, he once again earnestly urged his guests to continue drinking.

In this manner, they drank the whole day away. As dusk fell, Dongfang Ying and the others all took their leave one after the other. Wenming noted, "I have long grown accustomed to quiet, a day of activity like today is rare for me. If it hadn't been that an old friend had come from afar, I would simply have discussed a few household matters with my children during their visit before sending them on their way."

"I have been warmed by your liquor and sated by your virtue," said Baoyu. "For that, I am unable to express my gratitude. But where was it that I met you and benefitted from your tutelage? I honestly have not the foggiest idea, and hope that the venerable gentleman will elucidate."

Wenming laughed. "Elder brother, you must sleep here tonight and think it over carefully; if you are still unable to remember, I shall tell you tomorrow." He then instructed a serving boy to make up the guest quarters in preparation for the two guests to stay the night. It had only just grown dark enough for the lanterns to be lit, and Wenming said, "I am an old man, accustomed to going to bed early. You must forgive me for being unable to accompany you any longer. The two of you are welcome to continue your conversation before going to bed." He then said his goodnights and went into his own chamber.

Baoyu mused, "It's because I have long admired the old gentleman's august reputation that I came specially to call on him, so that I might hear his great teachings and enlighten myself. I didn't anticipate that two new points of confusion would emerge." When Lao Shaonian asked what the two points of confusion were, Baoyu continued, "First, how does he know me? Why is it I can't think of it?"

"Perhaps you've just forgotten and are just unable to think of it now. One can't be sure."

"It wouldn't matter if I'd forgotten anything else, but my whole life I've never had a friend old enough to have a beard—I would certainly remember that."

Lao Shaonian tugged at his mustache and gave a wry smile. "What about me?"

At this Baoyu smiled, too, and said, "You were the first!"

"And what is the other point of confusion?"

"His three sons appear to be no older than forty, and his daughter, not yet thirty—so how can he already have great-grandchildren? How old were they when they had their children?"

"Prescriptions for stopping the aging process have been passed down all over the world—a great many, in fact—why should that be so strange?"

"You're just saying that to tease me."

"What makes you say I'm teasing you? The ancients' anti-aging techniques relied on certain medical concoctions, and their use is widespread here. As a result, even our normal food and beverages have an anti-aging function. When this was first implemented, all of the elderly people of the Realm were transformed back into youths! If you don't believe me, give yourself a quick inspection. You've been in the Realm for several days now. How do you feel?"

Baoyu considered this carefully and realized that indeed he had felt spry and hale of late as he had traveled throughout the Realm, and he seemed to have gained quite a bit of strength. When they had been hunting the *peng* he had still felt somewhat vulnerable to weariness, but by the time of their underwater hunting adventure he had felt that his strength had increased as he used it. He said, "You're right that my health is somewhat improved, but how is it possible that one's face shows no signs of age? That is somewhat unbelievable."

"How old do you think I am?" asked Lao Shaonian.

"No more than forty, give or take."

Lao Shaonian broke into a hearty laugh and gave a response that caused Baoyu no small amount of shock.

■ ■ ■

If you wish to know what he said, please listen to the explanation in the following chapter.

Chapter Forty

In the realm of dreams, portents of civilization

Our New Story of the Stone reaches its conclusion

WE WERE speaking of how Baoyu, just looking at Lao Shaonian, had assessed his age to be forty-some years. At this, Lao Shaonian had given a great laugh and said, "You've guessed just a fraction of my true age!"

Baoyu was startled by this and asked, "What do you mean?"

"As of this year, I've been rattling around for one hundred and forty years." Baoyu shook his head in disbelief, prompting Lao Shaonian to laugh and continue: "I'm not trying to purchase a position or take the official examinations—so why should I lie?"

It was Baoyu's turn to laugh. "When men lie about their age for the official examinations, it's only older men pretending to be a few years younger—no one ever pretends to be older!"[1]

"In fact, it's nothing so strange. In the future, once other countries have studied our medical science, they too will be able to stave off aging and increase their longevity. An individual simply relies upon his own life force and vitality to survive, so all you have to do is find a way to protect his health so that his vitality doesn't wither and dry up and his life force is not depleted. It's as simple as that. You should know that a people's life expectancy is evidence of the sophistication or crudity of their medicine. Those countries whose life expectancies are the same as others yet would praise the 'sophistication' of their own medicine while criticizing the 'crudity' of others'—now *that* is ridiculous!" Baoyu, hearing that living to an age of over one hundred was nothing so remarkable, felt as though his spirits were soaring.

Lao Shaonian then said, "My time off will end tomorrow, so I must return to resume my duties. Where will you go next?"

"I want to go to Freedom Village so that I may admire venerable Mr. Wenming's old home."

"Then tomorrow, we must part company for the time being. You should get to bed early, the better to arise early tomorrow." At that, each man proceeded to his bed to rest for the evening.

Baoyu, however, tossed and turned, unable to fall asleep. He got out of bed and sat up for a while, then tried sleeping once again. Just as he was drifting toward slumber, he saw a serving boy enter with a letter, saying, "The courier is awaiting your response." Baoyu, looking at the envelope, saw that it had been addressed very clearly: *Mr. Jia, Dongfang Residence, Benevolence No. 1 District, Eastern Sector, Realm of Civilization*, and so on; but in Wu Bohui's handwriting! Baoyu thought, "How could he know that I am here?" Tearing open the envelope, he found that inside was a letter requesting that Baoyu hasten back to Shanghai, for there was an urgent matter afoot.

Baoyu asked the serving boy, "The courier?"

"He's outside."

Baoyu arose and went outside, where he discovered that the courier was Huang Fu. Upon seeing Baoyu, Huang Fu hurried forward a couple of steps and inquired after his health before continuing: "My master requests that the good gentleman return to Shanghai, as there is a matter of some urgency."

"Just wait for me to hire a flying car, and we'll set out."

"There's no need for a flying car, I've already readied a horse for you here."

When Baoyu looked, he saw that there were indeed two horses. He mounted one, while Huang Fu mounted the other and fell in behind him. When Baoyu gave the horse free rein, it took off as though it were chasing the wind or a bolt of lightning. They rode past several high mountains and through a great many tangled briars and thickets before finally reaching the coast, where Baoyu saw a steamship moored. He reined in his horse, intending to board the ship; but who could have guessed that Huang Fu's horse would refuse to be reined in and plunge straight into the sea? Baoyu was alarmed by this and was about to call for help when he saw Huang Fu looking back at him and gesturing for him to follow. As it turned out, the horse, treading on the very waves themselves, had continued racing ahead. Delighted, Baoyu loosed his reins to follow, and indeed his horse, too, began to run across the surface of the sea. He thought quietly to himself, "I've heard people say that a hundred-league horse can cross waters and scale mountains as if they were merely treading upon level ground, but I didn't believe it. It turns out to be true after all!"

The two horses raced on for quite some time before finally arriving in Shanghai. Wu Bohui greeted them cheerfully, regaling Baoyu with news of things that had happened since they had parted. When Baoyu asked him what the urgent matter was, Bohui laughed and said, "There's no urgent matter at all, it's just been so long since I've seen you that I asked you to come back to meet up and have a chat. I thought we could go off traveling, as well."

"From the moment I arrived in the Realm of Civilization," replied Baoyu, "everything was truly a marvel to behold. What else could there be to see?"

"You may not know it, but there has been quite a lot of news since you left. When the two royal households returned to the palace after the Boxer Rebellion, they began to implement new government policies one after another, almost all in keeping with the ideas laid out during the Hundred Days Reform. But whereas during the Hundred Days Reform they tried to rush everything through with lightning speed, this time, they were taking a more leisurely approach, which meant that it wasn't very effective. Then things suddenly came to a head because of the American treaty that had forbidden Chinese workers from entering the country. When it came time for the renegotiation of the treaty, the Chinese business and scholarly communities, recognizing that the treaty was ostensibly about the exclusion of laborers but was in fact about the exclusion of all Chinese, organized a boycott and prohibited everyone from using American products.[2] It started in Shanghai, but soon every province and every port had responded to the call, and were all holding meetings and staging talks. For several months there were letters and telegrams whizzing back and forth every day. When these efforts reached Beijing and those in the government heard the news, they knew that this outpouring of nationalist sentiment could be put to use. At the same time, someone had submitted a memorandum to the government saying that the kind of vague, noncommittal efforts being undertaken toward implementing the new policies could never be effective. It would first be necessary to establish a constitution—only then could they be made to work. Otherwise one need only look at the Russo-Japanese War: Japan was a small country yet was the victor; Russia was a large country yet was defeated. It certainly wasn't that the Japanese possessed any intrinsic skill that enabled the small to overcome the large—it was simply a question of a constitutional government versus an authoritarian one. The Russo-Japanese War thus shouldn't be considered a victory of small versus large, but rather a victory of constitutionalism versus authoritarianism.

"When this memorandum was submitted, the court came to their senses and considered establishing a constitution but didn't know where to begin. So they dispatched five high-ranking ministers to go abroad and investigate different constitutional governments. These five ministers set out separately and were gone for a long time, until they had investigated and understood the key features of each country. In the capital, a Bureau of Constitutional Government was created where each day the five ministers would meet, comparing the different constitutions they had studied. If a particular clause from the British constitution was good, they would adopt it; if a particular clause from the Japanese constitution was good, they would adopt that. Anything that wasn't appropriate for a Chinese constitution was discarded, and if there was anything that would be necessary in a Chinese constitution but which none of the other constitutions contained, they would add it themselves. They revised and discussed it until it was perfected, then promulgated their new constitutional government. As you'd expect, the benefits of establishing a constitution came rapidly: in very little time the entire country looked totally different.

"Do you think that Shanghai is the same as it used to be? It's completely changed. The foreigners' extraterritorial jurisdiction has been revoked, Shanghai's old city wall has been razed, and areas formerly within the wall, as well the whole of the southern city, have all set up commercial markets, extending as far as the Arsenal. The market at Wusong has become even more bustling, and in Pudong they've opened a convention ground—in fact, the World's Fair is being held there right now.[3] That's the main reason I asked you to come back: the opportunity to attend the World's Fair is very rare, so we simply have to go. The second reason I asked you back is to witness the World Peace Summit. It was decided via debate among all the countries that the current Peace Summit should take place in China, and the Chinese emperor was elected to preside over it. An enormous convention hall has already been erected outside the Yongding Gate in Beijing. Once the World's Fair has concluded here, the World Peace Summit will hold its inaugural meeting. After we've seen the fair, we'll go up to Beijing to have a look."

Baoyu replied abstractedly, "Can it be true that such a day has finally arrived in China?"

"Let's go see the fair!" said Bohui, pulling Baoyu with him. No sooner had they stepped out the door than they found the fairground standing immediately before them. The different countries' installations stood apart from one another, for each country had constructed its own exhibition building in which was arrayed all manner of goods. Each of China's provinces had also set up its own exhibition ground, and these were all extremely lively, with such a number of rare and marvelous manufactures on display that it was impossible to count them all. Baoyu was just in the process of poring over the new books from China's Official Publishing House when he suddenly spied Dongfang Wenming standing before him. Baoyu set the books to one side, intending to go speak with him, but in the instant it took Baoyu to raise his head, Dongfang Wenming had vanished, and Baoyu found himself on a steamboat—one that was traveling at great speed at that. Looking out over both riverbanks, Baoyu saw that they were filled with towering buildings; a veritable forest of smokestacks stretched out before him. Without thinking, he murmured to himself, "What is this place? I've never been here before."

Suddenly, he heard Bohui behind him, saying, "Why, this is the Yangzi River!"

Baoyu turned to face him and asked, "But since when have there been so many buildings along the banks of the Yangzi?"

"You didn't know? Currently the entire river from Wusong all the way to Hankou is lined on both sides with an endless row of Chinese factories!"

In the blink of an eye the steamship had already arrived in Hankou. Baoyu didn't know how it had happened, but he was now aboard a train, which was racing ahead like the wind. Mulberry groves, tea plantations, rice paddies, and wheat fields rushed past along both sides of the track, as if they themselves were flying backward. When everyone disembarked from the train in a flurry, Baoyu followed. Raising his head to look, he saw an enormous building standing at the side of the railway. In front of the building was an empty field; in the center of the field there stood a flagpole so tall it pierced the heavens; and upon the flagpole there hung the yellow flying-dragon flag, billowing in the breeze. A long rope ran between the top of the flagpole and the roof of the building, along which the national flags of all of the countries of the five continents had been suspended. When Baoyu looked to the entryway of the building, he saw that the words "World Peace Summit" had been carved above it and inlaid with gold leaf. Gleaming with the rays of the sun, it was a truly dazzling sight to behold. Striding inside, Baoyu found that a tremendous meeting hall had been constructed there and was now filled with innumerable attendees from both China and foreign countries. They sat for some time, remaining silent all the while.

Suddenly, the ringing of a bell could be heard, and someone whispered in Baoyu's ear, "The chairman has taken the dais—it's China's emperor." Baoyu turned his head to look and saw that it was Wu Bohui who had spoken. He was just about to reply when a sudden deafening burst of thunderous applause erupted. Baoyu hurriedly turned to look at the dais and discovered that standing at the podium was none other than Dongfang Wenming, who began: "Today marks the first day of the World Peace Summit, and the assembled countries have voted that I should preside over the meeting. Each country's representative—whether your emperor himself is in attendance, or whether a high official has been sent instead—is here to participate. In my role as meeting chairman I will first announce our objectives, then allow the assembled lords and officials to discuss among themselves how to implement them. As this meeting has been called a 'peace summit,' it is only appropriate that our objective should be peace. However, as we begin our proceedings, we must first make clear exactly what kind of peace it is that we seek. The World Peace Summit cannot simply seek to establish peace between *states*; if we seek only peace between states, it becomes a mere intergovernmental issue, and our scope would necessarily be too narrow. At most, such an approach might result in the prevention of bloodshed, but nothing more. This summit should strive to attain peace between all *peoples* of the world, and each government must undertake responsibility for protecting that peace. If the red, black, and brown races are to be treated as equals, then it will not be permitted to abuse their governments or their citizenry. This is a way that we human beings can protect one another and prevent forevermore such abuse or cruelty. If among those groups there are certain shortcomings in their level of achievement, then those of us in civilized countries—whether as individuals or as societies—all have a duty to lead and enlighten such benighted peoples."[14]

Having heard this much, Baoyu unwittingly began to applaud, and the entire assembly burst into thunderous applause as well. Dongfang Wenming continued, "It is not acceptable use our own strength and prosperity as a means to wantonly bully them for the simple reason that they belong to other ethnicities or other races! Thus, from today forward, we must extinguish the doctrine of might-makes-right and implement a doctrine of peace." The entire assembly broke out in applause once more.

Baoyu felt that just clapping was not sufficient, and wanted to stamp his feet in approbation, too. But who would have guessed that the moment he stamped his feet, his feet would strike nothingness, and he would plummet through a cavernous void? In a flash, everything around him went hazy and black, and he was so terrified that his entire body broke out in a cold sweat. Struggling to open his eyes, he discovered suddenly that he was still lying on the bed in the guest room of Dongfang Wenming's home. It had all been an elaborate dream.

Glancing at the timekeeping automaton, he saw that it was a quarter past four in the morning, and the sky outside was not yet fully light. Feeling hot and parched, he arose and went outside to enjoy the cool air. When he arrived outside, he was surprised to find that Dongfang Wenming had already risen and was gazing out over the lotus flowers in the courtyard pond. "You're up early," Baoyu greeted him.

"Ever since I became accustomed to this quiet life of mine, I have always gone to bed early and risen early. How is it that you, elder brother, have likewise come to rise so early?"

"I just happened to wake, so I decided to get up. It is rare that I wake so early as this." The two men continued their conversation, sitting together on ceramic garden seats in the courtyard.

Wenming asked, "Elder brother, last night were you able to think of where it was you met me?"

"I genuinely cannot recall. I must persist in asking you to elucidate."

Wenming sighed. "The year when your venerable grandmother Madame Shi passed into the realm of immortals, during the period of mourning—did you happen to receive any guests?"

Thinking it over for a moment, Baoyu answered, "No, we didn't."

"Think again—did any family or friends come to stay at to your family mansion?"

Baoyu racked his brain for a moment. "Only the Zhen family from Jinling."

"Exactly right. At that time your father was keeping vigil and sitting on a straw mat, so when we met, we sat on the floor as well, since it would have been disrespectful for us to do otherwise. Your father, understanding that we were still young and not wishing us to be bound by hierarchical etiquette in his presence, left us to ourselves, allowing us to chat freely. How could you have forgotten?"

Baoyu was greatly surprised by this and said, "Then you are my elder brother Zhen Baoyu! How is it that you have come to be an old man? And how is it that you have taken the double surname Dongfang?"[5]

"Dongfang is my original surname. Originally, because Lady Zhen had no heir, I was adopted into her line. Later Lady Zhen had a son of her own, so I was returned to my own household. That year when we met with each other, I spoke to you a bit about statecraft, and it appeared as though you were disappointed with me, which was when I knew that you were not of the same mind as myself. I never expected that after parting—and for so many years—we would once again have the opportunity to meet. However, you are still a carefree man, arriving here from a place of insensibility and nescience, so although you passed through a number of ages and calamities, your appearance is as it was before. Meanwhile, I have dedicated my life to the founding and oversight of this place, which is why my complexion is pallid and my hair white. That is why you didn't recognize me when we met each other again."

Hearing this, Baoyu felt as though he had just woken from a dream. He thought, "If he hadn't brought it up, I would have completely forgotten it all. I originally wished to fulfill the ambition of helping to mend the sky, and having only just reemerged into the world, I didn't expect to find that he had already snatched both the task and the glory completely away from me! Once again my aspirations have been in vain. It is better to go to Freedom Village for a little while and entrust myself to his aegis."

While Baoyu was thinking this, Lao Shaonian, too, had arisen. Having washed his face and dressed, Lao Shaonian indicated that he wished to return home so that he might report back to work. Baoyu also wished to depart for Freedom Village, so the two men each took their leave of Dongfang Wenming before hiring his own flying car. Baoyu clasped Lao Shaonian's hand and said, "'*We met as duckweed carried 'pon the water . . .*'[6] I am ever so indebted to you for your guidance and hospitality. Today we must part, and who knows when we may meet again? I have something for you, a token of my sincere esteem: although it is not terribly valuable, it is quite rare. It is neither jade nor stone, but I bore it in my mouth when I came into the world. You may keep it to amuse yourself or perhaps bequeath it to a museum—you have my blessing to do with it as you see fit." When he had finished speaking, he handed his precious jade amulet to Lao Shaonian, who accepted it with a stream of awe-struck comments and expressions of gratitude. Because Zhen

Baoyu had already fulfilled Jia Baoyu's goal of mending the sky, not only was there no use in keeping this item, but indeed, as he looked upon it, Baoyu couldn't help but feel distressed, and so it was better to be rid of it. Thus, he magnanimously bestowed it upon Lao Shaonian, then climbed into his flying car and departed for Freedom Village.

Having accepted the jade amulet from Baoyu, Lao Shaonian was overcome with a sense of wonder and surprise. After climbing into his own flying car, he toyed with the remarkable jade all along the way to his destination. Because the weather was stiflingly hot, Lao Shaonian opened one of the windows and leaned out to enjoy the breeze, continuing all the while to play with the precious jade in his hand. Unexpectedly, however, he lost his grip, and the jade plummeted straight down toward the ground. Lao Shaonian hurriedly called out for the car to be brought down to land, his eyes fixed intently on the falling jade. As it fell, the jade seemed to increase in size until it landed in the hollow of a mountain, where it could be seen quite clearly. The flying car came to rest at the foot of the mountain, which Lao Shaonian recognized as Mind and Spirit Mountain of the No. 100,000 District of the Benevolence Region in the Eastern Sector. As he walked up to the hollow, a cave appeared, above the entrance to which had been carved the words "Cave of Slanting Moonbeams and Three Stars"—this was also a place Lao Shaonian frequented.[7] He looked about for the jade—but how could he find it? There was not even a trace of it to be found. What he did find was a strange, towering stone standing at the mouth of the cave. It was delicate and translucent, with a network of pores and holes running through it. The entire face of the stone had been polished smooth and a great many characters carved thereon. When Lao Shaonian read them, he discovered an outstanding piece of marvelous writing, comprising a total of a 120,000 to 130,000 words or thereabouts. He thought, "For such a work of marvelous writing as this to lie hidden deep in the mountains where no one can see it is indeed a pity! Why don't I copy it out and present it to the world?" However, he had no paper or brush with him, so there was nothing for him to do but hurriedly climb back into his flying car, proceed to a market to buy some supplies, and return. When he examined the stone once more, he found that on its reverse side, behind the marvelous writing, the lyrics of a song had been added. They ran:

Within the mind, o!
  the "spirit platform" stands—
The mind, whose form, o!
  stars numb'ring three and moonlit beams aslant.
Therein an object, o!
  in which, the spark of sentience.
Sentience, o!
  the universe's accreted essence.

A human, I, with hair on head, o!
  and teeth in mouth
Uneasily beheld a nation troubled by the times, o!
  which in me earnest zeal ignited.
Woe, woe, o!
  these affairs of the world!

Alas, alas, o!
　　this helpless youth shortsighted!
I lacked the skill to mend the Heavens, o!
　　time waited not for me.
My vision fills with swarming rats, o!
　　by venal legion all the land now blighted.

Would that mine ears might deafen, o!
　　but alas, they hear all too keenly.
Would that mine sight might dim and blur, o!
　　but woe, I see all too clearly.
Unable to give voice to my sorrows, o!
　　'tis better to die in obscurity.
As a cry against the injustice of it all, o!
　　I bequeath now this poor history.

Lao Shaonian copied this out along with the rest and brought the text back with him. He thought of having it carved onto wooden printing blocks to disseminate it to the world, but he was afraid that this marvelous work was too abstruse, and that readers would not understand it completely. If it were to be seen by narrow-minded Confucian scholars, they would insist upon speculating as to its meaning, interpreting words and explicating sentences, making up all kinds of nonsense, and paradoxically losing the true meaning of it. And so, though he spent his days discharging his official duties, in the quiet of the night he would pull the strange manuscript back out and rework it into the form of a historical novel, retaining its meaning while using only the vernacular in the hope that readers of both refined and unrefined tastes could appreciate it. The title he chose for it was

New Story of the Stone. From this time on, the stone that had remained unused after Nüwa repaired the sky, which had started its journey at the foot of Greenridge Peak of the Great Barren Mountain, would forevermore remain in the Realm of Civilization, upon Mind and Spirit Mountain, outside the Cave of Slanting Moonbeams and Three Stars.

If you, dear readers, don't believe me, then please go there and have a look yourself—then you will know that your humble storyteller has not been telling you lies. However, one must be a man of substance who is passionate, sincere, and who loves his race and his country; one must be a true man who is willing to devote his energies to preserving the national essence—only such men will be able to reach the stone and to see what is written upon it. Even if a shit-eating flatterer of foreigners were to be permitted to reach the Cave of Slanting Moonbeams and Three Stars on Mind and Spirit Mountain, he would be completely unable to read the miraculous text written there. Why do you suppose that is? Because the text was meant to be read only by true men, not by slaves; it was meant to be read by men of substance, not by petty men. And so, if a shit-eating, foreigner-flattering slave or petty man were to reach the stone, upon its surface would instead appear several illusory lines of slanted, horizontal text, reading:

> All Foreigners thou shalt worship;
> Be always in sincere friendship.
> This the way to get bread to eat and money to spend.
> And upon this thy family's living will depend;
> There's one thing nobody can guess:
> Thy countrymen thou canst oppress.[8]

NOTES

NEW STORY OF THE STONE: AN INTRODUCTION TO THE TEXT

1. Wu's works have been published variously under the names Wu Jianren 吴趼人, Wu Woyao 吴沃尧, and his pen name, Wo Foshan Ren 我佛山人. The Qing dynasty spanned 1644 to 1911. The "late Qing" is usually considered to comprise the final decades of the dynasty.
2. Lu Xun, "Qingmo zhi qianze xiaoshuo" (Late Qing Exposé Fiction), in *Zhongguo xiaoshuo shilüe* (A Brief History of Chinese Fiction) (Guilin: Guangxi shifan daxue chubanshe, 2010), ch. 28.
3. The first eleven chapters of the present text were serialized in *Nanfang bao* (Southern Gazette) between September and December of 1905 under the pseudonym "Lao Shaonian." The integral forty-chapter version was later published in 1908 by the Shanghai Reform Fiction Press under Wu's pen name Wo Foshan Ren and included woodblock illustrations. See "Chuban shuoming" (Publication Note) in *Wu Jianren quanji: Shehui xiaoshuo* (The Complete Works of Wu Jianren: Social Novels), ed. Liu Jingqi (Harbin: Beifang wenyi chubanshe, 2019), vol. 1, front matter.
4. William T. Rowe, *The Great Qing: China's Last Empire* (Cambridge, MA: Belknap Press/Harvard University Press, 2009), ch. 6.
5. Theodore Huters, *Bringing the World Home: Appropriating the West in Late Qing and Early Republican China* (Honolulu: University of Hawai'i Press,

2005), ch. 1, 45. The historic Jiangnan Arsenal, established in 1865 and depicted in chapters 10–11 of the present text, was an important manifestation of the newfound emphasis on foreign technologies: in its early years, the arsenal was an important site of shipbuilding but by 1885 would pivot toward the production of munitions instead. It also housed a translation bureau that was instrumental in producing translations of European scientific and mathematical texts as well the Foreign Language School, in which students were trained both in Chinese classics and European scientific, industrial, and cultural knowledge. Benjamin A. Elman, *On Their Own Terms: Science in China, 1550–1900* (Cambridge, MA: Harvard University Press, 2005), 368–71.

6. Huters, *Bringing the World Home*, 46.
7. Hao Chang, *Chinese Intellectuals in Crisis: Search for Order and Meaning, 1890–1911*, (Berkeley: University of California Press, 1987), 110; James Reeve Pusey, *China and Charles Darwin* (Cambridge, MA: Council on East Asian Studies, Harvard University, 1983), 111.
8. The revolutionaries would eventually succeed in overthrowing the court in the 1911 Xinhai Revolution, establishing the Republic of China.
9. Hao Chang, *Liang Ch'i-ch'ao and Intellectual Transition in China, 1890–1907* (Cambridge, MA: Harvard University Press, 1971), 106, 201.
10. Liang Qichao, "Lun xinmin wei jinri Zhongguo diyi jiwu" (To Discuss the New Citizen Is China's Most Urgent Task) and "Lun guojia sixiang" (On National Thinking), in *Xinmin shuo: Shenwei jiedu ben* (On the New Citizen: A Deep Exegetical Reading), ed. Kang Xue (Beijing: Zhongguo wenshi chubanshe, 2013), 11–12, 43–44; Kang Xue, "Fabiao beijing" (Publication Background [to Liang Qichao's "Lun guojia sixiang"]), in *Xinmin shuo*, 41.
11. Liang Qichao, "On the Relationship Between Fiction and the Government of the People," trans. Gek Nai Cheng, in *Modern Chinese Literary Thought: Writings on Literature, 1893–1945*, ed. Kirk Denton (Stanford, CA: Stanford University Press, 1996), 74–81.
12. Huters, *Bringing the World Home*, 123–24.
13. The authorship of *Story of the Stone* is a matter of some contention, the elucidation of which is not in the purview of the current introduction. It is sufficient to note that there seems to be a general consensus that the bulk of the first eighty chapters (of an extant total of 120) were likely written by Cao Xueqin, while opinion on the provenance of the

latter forty is more divided. See Haun Saussy, "Authorship and *The Story of the Stone:* Open Questions," in *Approaches to Teaching The Story of the Stone*, ed. Andrew Schonebaum and Tina Lu (New York: MLA, 2012), 70–77.

14. We must concede, however, that this glowing depiction might partially reflect a fear of reprisal on Cao's part.
15. Tobie Meyer-Fong, "A Question of Taste: Material Culture, Connoisseurship, and Character in *The Story of the Stone*," in Schonebaum and Lu, eds., *Approaches*, 215–16.
16. While this is literally true within the novel itself, scholars generally accept the idea that in reality the Jia family's downfall is inspired by Cao's own family's precipitous fall from power as a result of shifts in the winds of imperial favor. See Saussy, "Authorship," 75.
17. Cao Xueqin, *Story of the Stone*, vol. 1, trans. David Hawkes (London: Penguin, 1973), ch. 6. All subsequent citations of Cao's *Story of the Stone* in the present introduction refer to the Penguin translation in five volumes by David Hawkes (chs. 1–80/vols. 1–3) and John Minford (chs. 81–120/vols. 4–5). Chapter numbers are provided where possible for the convenience of those using other editions.
18. Cao Xueqin, *Story of the Stone*, chs. 1–2. Translations of proper names from *Story* (The Land of Illusion, Lady Wang, and Tealeaf) provided in this introduction are David Hawkes's renderings, provided for readers familiar with that version.
19. He even characterizes, disparagingly, a chiming watch as "something a woman would use," which feels dramatically out of character for a young man who once so doted on and admired his female cousins.
20. Cao, *Story of the Stone*, ch. 4; chs. 85–86; ch. 120.
21. Cao, *Story of the Stone*, ch. 115 (vol. 5, p. 274, Minford trans.).
22. For a full-text translation see Tao Ch'ien, "The Peach Blossom Spring," translated by James R. Hightower, in *The Shorter Columbia Anthology of Traditional Chinese Literature*, ed. Victor Mair (New York: Columbia University Press, 2000), 364–66.
23. David Wang, *Fin-de-Siècle Splendor: Repressed Modernities of Late Qing Fiction, 1849–1911* (Stanford, CA: Stanford University Press, 1997), 272–73; Huters, *Bringing the World Home*, 107; Andrew Jones, "The Iron House of Narrative: Lu Xun and the Late Qing Fiction of Evolutionary Adventure," in *Developmental Fairy Tales* (Cambridge, MA: Harvard University Press, 2011), 31, 60.

24. Andrew Jones persuasively demonstrates that in his depictions of Baoyu's hunting voyages, Wu not only borrows from Jules Verne's science fiction novels, such as *Twenty Thousand Leagues Under the Sea*, but also reinscribes new layers of meaning onto them. Crucially, Jones argues that Captain Nemo's *Nautilus*, which intrepidly crosses national boundaries as a sort of renegade "stateless kingdom unto itself," is rewritten inversely by Wu as a *state-sanctioned* vessel whose boundary-crossing reinforces not the independence of its captain but rather the geopolitical "hegemony" of the Realm. ("The Iron House of Narrative," 47, 51.)
25. Nathaniel Isaacson, *Celestial Empire: The Emergence of Chinese Science Fiction* (Middletown, CT: Wesleyan University Press, 2017), 84.
26. Isaacson, *Celestial Empire*, 81. It bears noting that in certain scenes set in the Realm, even as Wu strains against Euro-American colonizing projects and attempts to envision an alternative thereto, he winds up reproducing rather than rejecting or fully reimagining those same fundamental colonial structures. We see, as Isaacson puts it, "a repetition of the European conquest and knowledge industry that Baoyu was so suspicious of, covered in the veil of a Confucian moral and social code" (79).
27. In the United States, for example, anti-Chinese racism resulted in brutal mob violence, the forcible "driving out" of Chinese populations from cities in the American West, and the passage of the 1882 Chinese Exclusion Act.
28. Jones, "The Iron House of Narrative," 60–62.
29. Wang, *Fin-de-Siècle Splendor*, 283; Huters, *Bringing the World Home*, 170.

CHAPTER 1

1. Jin Shengtan 金圣叹 (1608–1661) was a literary critic of the late Ming/early Qing.
2. I am indebted to Sterling Swallow's 2012 translation of chapter 1 in *Renditions* 77 & 78 (Spring–Autumn 2012) here for helping me catch a misapprehension in my own translation.
3. Jia Lan is Jia Baoyu's nephew. At the end of *Story*, Baoyu and Jia Lan have gone off together to take the imperial examinations; however, after the exams, Baoyu disappears dramatically, led by the monk and Daoist mentioned here to abandon the "dusty world" of wealth and familial drama and begin a life of religious asceticism.

4. For more on Baoyu's origins as a magical stone, see the introduction.
5. The queue was the normative male hairstyle of the Qing dynasty, in which the front of the scalp is shaved while the hair at the back of the scalp is allowed to grow long and is usually plaited.
6. Translated after Swallow 2012.
7. *Juren* examinations: provincial-level exams.
8. Jinling: an old administrative area that is now part of the territory of Nanjing. "On a lark": translated after Swallow 2012.
9. Li 里: a measure of distance, equal to roughly one-third of a mile.
10. The missing character is likely *bao* 报 (paper, journal). Baoyu is probably looking at a copy of *Xinwen bao* 新闻报, an influential Shanghai-based newspaper.
11. In the original text, the years on the newspaper are given as Guangxu 26/1901. Guangxu 26 spanned late January 1900 to mid-February 1901, so it is not inherently incorrect that Wu provides 1901 here; however, the besieging of the foreign legations in Beijing by Boxer rebels, which will be portrayed in chapters 14–16, broke out in 1900, which means that 1901 must be an inaccuracy here.

CHAPTER 2

1. The City of Stone referred to in the epigraph is Jinling.
2. Wuwei (无为): the Daoist principle of not-doing.
3. Rong Guo *fu* 荣国府: "Rong Guo mansion" is the name of Baoyu's family home. Because the double meaning of 府 *fu*, meaning "mansion" but also "government offices," leads to confusion in a conversation on the next page, I have left this word untranslated.
4. This is where the confusion begins: in this context, Baoyu is using the word *fu* to mean "mansion," but as mentioned in the previous note, it can also be interpreted as "government offices," which is how his interlocutor assumes he means it. Ning Guo *mansion* is the name of a second family home, owned by relatives of Baoyu's. He is excited to hear that the stranger can direct him to this landmark; however, the stranger is thinking of the Ning Guo *government offices* in Anhui, a good distance away.
5. Granny Liu is a rustic old woman who comes to visit the Jia family from the countryside. The name is translated after David Hawkes's rendering in his translation of Cao Xueqin's *Story of the Stone*.

CHAPTER 2

6. For more on the encounter between the two Baoyus in *Story*, see the introduction.

CHAPTER 3

1. As mentioned in the introduction, when Baoyu is born he has a piece of jade in his mouth. This is taken as a supernatural sign, and it is assumed that Baoyu and his jade share some otherworldly connection. In an episode in chapter 94 of *Stone*, when Baoyu's jade goes missing, he loses all of his faculties, throwing the family into desperation. Baoyu emerges from this state only when he is told, as a ruse, that he is to be married to his beloved Lin Daiyu.
2. The "mistress" ("Second Mistress" in the original, corresponding to Baoyu's title "Second Master") refers to Xue Baochai, Baoyu's wife, who was pregnant at the time Baoyu left home to take the imperial examinations.
3. A comprador (*maiban* 买办) was a Chinese trader who served as a go-between and negotiator for foreign trading companies. Compradors are often depicted in a negative light in contemporary fiction for the perception that they valued profit and loyalty to foreigners over loyalty to their own people and country.
4. Yihong courtyard is the name of Baoyu's personal residence in *Story*.
5. Bao Tuodang 包妥当: a pun for "preserve appropriateness" and a comment on the normalization of inappropriate behavior (sometimes exemplified by Bao himself) in this era.
6. Baoyu is surprised by a European-style shallow soup bowl.
7. The author uses the word for "fork," but since Baoyu obviously doesn't know what this object is, it seems wrong for him to identify it as a "fork." So I have taken some liberties.

CHAPTER 4

1. "Spirit Jade" (*shenying* 神瑛), mentioned in the epigraph, alludes to one of Baoyu's previous incarnations; here and in later chapter headings it simply points to Baoyu. "Oaf King" (*dai bawang* 呆霸王) is an old nickname for Xue Pan from *Story*. I have been unable to improve upon David Hawkes's apt rendering for the latter, so I use it here and elsewhere. Cao Xueqin, *Story of the Stone*, trans. David Hawkes, vol. 1 (London: Penguin, 1973).

2. Matches: literally, "foreign fire" (*yanghuo* 洋火).
3. Although China had its own native system of telling time, Bao Tuodang gives the time according to European convention, a sign of the colonial influence of foreign powers.
4. For more on Xue Pan, see the introduction.

CHAPTER 5

1. Wu actually gives the date here as "*Great Qing, Guangxu 27th year, 2nd month, 12th day*," which corresponds to March 31, 1901. However, as noted during Baoyu's previous encounter with a newspaper, Wu clearly intended the current action to be set during Guangxu 26/1900 rather than Guangxu 27/1901. As such, I have altered the year provided here as well. The revised date corresponds to March 12, 1900. See Fang Shiming and Fang Xiaofen, eds., *Zhongguoshi liri he Zhongxi liri duizhaobiao* (Shanghai: Renmin chubanshe, 2007), 698–716.
2. "Guest invitation slips" are written invitations that guests at a restaurant or brothel could have delivered by messenger to other people, inviting them to join the festivities.
3. Bai Yaolian 柏耀廉 is a pun for "shameless." I have been unable to find any historical record of the Meikai Company using the characters 梅开洋行, nor of a foreigner named 环梅 Huan Mei as given in the text; however, rather than leave the names in pinyin, I have decided to hazard a guess: it seems likely that Wu is referring to the Mackay family of telegraphy companies, founded by John Mackay. The Commercial Pacific Cable Company, a subsidiary of the Mackay Companies, would establish a telegraphic cable network linking San Francisco and Shanghai via the Philippines in the early years of the twentieth century, with work completed in 1906. Dwayne R. Wineck and Robert M. Pike, *Communication and Empire: Media, Markets, and Globalization, 1860–1930* (Durham, NC: Duke University Press, 2007), 169–71.

CHAPTER 6

1. *Mantou* 馒头: a small steamed bread roll. *Tuoshi* 拖士*:* toast. The character *shi* 士 can mean "scholar," which is the basis of Xue Pan's joke about restaurants favoring the educated—his gripe is that there is no such thing as *tuoshang* 拖商, where *shang* 商 means merchant. He is

essentially making the joke: "Why is toast transliterated as 'tuo-scholars' and not 'tuo-merchants?' Because restaurants don't respect merchants!" I have used Mandarin pinyin here for consistency, but *tuoshi* would be pronounced *tosi* in Southern Mandarin, which is a closer approximation to "toast." (Many thanks to Theodore Huters for this final point.)

2. The Han dynasty extended from 206 BCE to 220 CE.
3. Twenty-seventh year of Daoguang: 1847–1848, somewhere on the order of one hundred years after the events of *Story of the Stone*.
4. A style name was the name a young literatus took when he reached adulthood (usually around twenty years of age). This new name would then be used in social contexts instead of his given name, which was deemed too intimate for general use. The style name that Baoyu chooses for himself, Zhongying, shares the character *ying* 瑛 from his alternate appellation, Shenying 神瑛 (Spirit Jade).
5. Bai Jianren 柏建仁: "Bai Establishes Benevolence." This is Bai Yaolian's courtesy name, which Baoyu would find wholly unbefitting to Bai's character.
6. This is my attempt to express an authorial pun that is a play on different words pronounced *yun* (芸 weeding/云 clouds). Baoyu quotes a line from the canonical Confucian text the *Mencius*: 这才是'舍己芸人'呢, "This is 'ignoring one's own fields to *yun ren*' (pull weeds for another person). However, Xue Pan misunderstands this, (revealing his lack of scholarly learning), and glibly replies, 你别管他云人雨人 . . .: "Who cares whether he's a *yun ren* (a cloud-person) or a rain-person . . ."
7. The Birthday of the Flowers is a springtime celebration. "Flowers," in this context, is a euphemism for prostitutes.

CHAPTER 7

1. *Hutong*: a narrow alleyway connecting neighboring courtyards and homes.
2. Bai Yaoming 柏耀明 and Wu Bohui 吴伯惠: these names can be punned, respectively, as (negatively) "Reckless" and (positively) "Infallible" (literally, "Nothing he can't do").
3. Xue Pan is talking about invitation slips for summoning courtesans.
4. These are both reformist periodicals. *Shiwubao* 时务报 (The Chinese Progress) was a publication founded by Liang Qichao 梁启超, running out of Shanghai from 1896 to 1898. *Zhixinbao* 知新报 (The Reformer

China) was founded by Liang and his mentor Kang Youwei 康有为. Based in Macao, *The Reformer China* ran from 1896 to 1901.

5. The *Tuibei Illustrations* (*Tuibei tu* 推背图) and *Song of Shaobing* (*Shaobing ge* 烧饼歌) are two historic divination or augury books. See Zongli Lu, "Heaven's Mandate and Man's Destiny in Early Medieval China: The Role of Prophecy in Politics" (PhD diss., University of Wisconsin, Madison, 1995), 15–16.
6. *Qingyi bao* 清议报 (The China Discussion) was another influential journal created by Liang Qichao. Publication started in 1898 in Japan, whence Liang had fled after the failure of the Hundred Days Reform movement (see the introduction). *The China Discussion* published "political, scientific, and ideological articles" as well as translations of "Japanese political novels." See Keiko Kockum, "Liang Qichao: The Japanese Years," *Cina* 21 (1988): 195–203.

CHAPTER 8

1. This is a violation of *fengshui* principles.
2. Hundred Days Reform: see the introduction.
3. The word *tian* 天, which I translate as "nature"/"natural" throughout this passage, can also be translated as "Heaven" or "heavenly." The line that Xue Pan quotes, "天步艰难" (*tianbu jiannan*) is from the Minor Ode *Baihua* 白华 in the *Classic of Poetry*. In Arthur Waley's translation of this poem, he renders *tian* as "Heaven" ("Heaven is verging toward calamity"). See Arthur Waley, trans., *The Book of Songs: The Ancient Chinese Classic of Poetry*, ed. Joseph Allen (New York: Grove Press, 1996), 217. Notes in *Xinyi Shijing duben* indicate that *tian* here might be interpreted as "fate" or "fortune." *Xinyi Shijing duben* (The Classic of Poetry: A Reading Volume with Modern Translation) (Taipei: Sanmin shuju, 2016), 2:736. In either case, for Xue Pan's natural foot joke to work in English, I am forced to ignore the multiple possibilities for the meaning of *tian* and as a result to slightly alter the original meaning of the line of poetry he quotes.
4. This is a line Xue Pan produces during a poetic drinking contest in chapter 28 of *Story*. This translation is mine, but the structure and rhythm are indebted to Hawkes's translation of the same scene.
5. Six hundred mu 亩: roughly one hundred acres. *Daotai:* a high-ranking regional administrator responsible for overseeing a "circuit." The title is usually translated as "circuit intendant."

CHAPTER 9

1. In *Story*, Baoyu repeatedly comments that women are superior to men, whom he believes to be crude and brutish.

CHAPTER 10

1. Four liang: a little under half a pound of pressure.
2. Firearms factory: *yangqiang chang* 洋枪厂 (literally, "foreign gun factory").

CHAPTER 11

1. First year of Guangxu: ca. 1875.
2. This is an allusion to a passage in the *Mengzi* 孟子 about an archer (the servant of Duke Yu) who is sent to assassinate Master Zi Zhuoru, only to discover that Zi Zhuoru was his own instructor's teacher. Because this makes Zi Zhuoru his own teacher once removed, the archer refuses to use the skills that originated with Zi Zhuoru himself against him and lets him go. This is evidence of the servant's sense of righteousness. Baoyu is saying, "Do the foreigners expect us not to use their own weapons against them out of a sense of obligation?" *Mengzi, Lilou xia*, ch. 24, in *Sishu, huaying duizhao, xiangxi zhujie* (The Four Books with English Translation and Notes), trans. Chen Wei (Macao: Zhuwentang shuju, 1962), 322–24.
3. The Heaven-upending seal (*fantian yin* 翻天印) is a magical weapon from the Ming novel *Fengshen yanyi* 封神演义 (Investiture of the Gods). "Taking off the boots backward" (*dao tuoxue* 倒脱靴) is apparently a strategic move in Chinese chess. I am not sure of what kinds of deceptions these euphemistically refer to.

CHAPTER 12

1. I have made a slight alteration to Wang's dismissive retort here to make his insult work in English. In an earlier draft of the translation, I experimented with changing Yang's surname name to Cao to more closely capture the nature of the sheep/cow joke that Wang makes at his expense;

but, as explained in the following note, Yang's name is a pun and changing the surname would strip the character of that layer of meaning. So I have made do instead with an approximation.

2. I read the name Yang Shizi 杨势子 as a pun for "Foreign Influence" *yang shizi* 洋势子 and/or "Foreign Cross" *yang shizi* 洋十字 (in the Christian sense of "cross"). It is clearly Yang's association with foreigners—and Christians in particular—that empowers him to throw his weight around.

CHAPTER 13

1. *Wuju* 武举 is the title earned by someone who has passed the imperial military examination. Wang Ben is also a possible pun for "Lost the fundamentals" or "Lost the root."
2. The Militia of Righteous Harmony (Yihetuan 义和团, most commonly referred to in English as the "Boxers") was a group of xenophobic and specifically anti-Christian militants who engaged in widespread violence and destruction in northern China from 1899–1901. Empress Dowager Cixi 慈禧 initially downplayed the movement but eventually came to support and encourage its antiforeign activities. When the Boxers besieged the foreign legations in Beijing in summer 1900, an international military alliance swept in to put them down. The Boxer Protocol imposed on China by the foreign powers after the suppression of the Boxers forced the court to pay out exorbitant indemnities, as well as to execute or exile certain high-ranking supporters of the movement. See David C Wright, *The History of China* (Westport, CT: Greenwood Press, 2001), 115–18.

   As Wu satirizes so aptly in these chapters, the Boxer movement relied upon deceiving the poor and uneducated into believing that certain superstitious practices would make them invincible to foreign weaponry. As will be contrasted in later chapters, the Boxers are an example of what happens when native epistemologies and belief systems are seized upon by an uneducated, undisciplined, and, importantly, uncurious populace.
3. Princes (*wang* 王): note, these are not necessarily sons of the emperor. There are a large number (and different categories) of "princes," some of whom receive their titles by heredity; others might receive them by meritorious service to the empire.

CHAPTER 13

4. Wang Ming 王命: this name can be read as a pun for *wangming* 亡命, "to lose one's life."
5. One jin is half a kilogram, or a little over one pound.

CHAPTER 14

1. Sun Wukong 孙悟空: a mythical monkey deity from the famous Ming novel *Journey to the West* (*Xiyouji* 西游记). A beloved folk hero, he is mischievous and violent but has tremendous martial and magical skill. He is eventually "tamed" into moral behavior by Buddhist teachings.
2. Great Sage Equal to Heaven (*qitian dasheng* 齐天大圣): this is another name for Sun Wukong. One of his great powers is that he can chew up a piece of his hair and spit it out, with each tiny piece becoming a whole version of himself. In this way he can conjure up an army of monkeys like himself to fight his enemies. In total, he is capable of seventy-two different magical transformations. I borrow Anthony Yu's translation of the title here. Anthony C. Yu, ed. and trans., *Journey to the West* (Chicago: University of Chicago Press, 1983), 1:124.
3. Xue Rengui 薛仁贵 was a heroic Tang dynasty military figure with the same surname as Xue Pan. *Zhengdong zhuan* 征东传 (Account of the Eastern Campaign), also known as *Xue Rengui zhengdong zhuan* 薛仁贵征东传 (Xue Rengui Campaigns in the East), is a "military romance" that chronicles Xue Rengui's exploits. See Anne E. McLaren, "Ming Chantefable and the Early Chinese Novel: A Study of the Chenghua Period *Cihua*," PhD diss., Australian National University, 1981, 275.
4. For more on the Red Lanterns (*hongdeng zhao* 红灯照), see Ono Kazuko, *Chinese Women in a Century of Revolution, 1850–1950*, ed. Joshua Fogel (Stanford, CA: Stanford University Press, 1989), ch. 3.
5. Jiangning Association Hall (*Jiangning huiguan* 江宁会馆): a mutual-aid society geared toward helping people from Jiangning (today encompassed in modern Nanjing) while they were staying in Beijing. This type of mutual-aid society, where membership was based on native place, was quite common both within China and among Chinese communities overseas.
6. Wu is making a pun on names at Beiming's expense. Translation of the pun involved has been challenging without changing the name of the historical Grand Secretary Gang Yi, whose name, I felt, should be preserved.

Beiming has heard someone say the surname *Gang* 刚 (steel); however, he has erroneously understood it as a homonym, *gang* 缸 (clay pot). Later, in his confusion, he then further muddles it into *tan* 坛 (a word for another type of clay jar, and also the word for "altar"). Baoyu is confused, because he then understands Beiming's *tan* 坛 (clay jar) as *Tan* 谭 (a common surname) and insists that there is no such official. I have tried to thread the needle here by replacing the Gang/Tan pairing in Mandarin (both denoting clay vessels) with Gang/Goon in English (both denoting troublemakers) to attempt to approach the way that the slippage across meaning functions in the original; I have then introduced "Gun" as the intermediate term introduced by Baoyu (which is aurally similar to Goon but also related to violence) to replicate his aural confusion.

7. Grand General Li: Li Hongzhang 李鸿章 (1823–1901), governor-general of Guangdong and Guangxi (and former governor-general of Zhili).

CHAPTER 15

1. Tenth year of Xianfeng: 1860. Old Man Zhang is alluding to the ransacking of the Old Summer Palace (*Yuanming yuan* 圆明园) by the British and French armies during the Second Opium War in retaliation for the capture and horrific treatment of a group of foreign soldiers and diplomats. See W. Travis Hanes and Frank Sanello, *Opium Wars: The Addiction of One Empire and the Corruption of Another* (Naperville, IL: Sourcebooks, 2002), ch. 1.
2. Master Guo: Guo Songtao 郭嵩涛 (1818–1891), Chinese minister to the United Kingdom and France, 1877–1878. Master Zhang: points to Zhang Yinhuan 张荫桓 (1837–1900), Chinese ambassador to the United States, 1886–1889. I am indebted to Theodore Huters for making these references clear.

CHAPTER 16

1. Both royal households: this indicates Empress Dowager Cixi and the powerless Guangxu 光绪 emperor.
2. My attempt to capture the verbal confusion between the two men as a result of two different words, 洋/杨, that are both pronounced *yang*. Wang

says *Yang Daren* 洋大人 (Great Mr. Yang [Mr. Foreigner]). Baoyu misunderstands this appellation as 杨大人 (Great Mr. Yang, where Yang is simply a common surname).

3. A person's *hun* souls are associated with his or her spiritual essence, while the *po* souls are associated with the physical body.
4. This refers to an incident in chapter 77 of *Story*. Baoyu goes to visit his ailing young maid, Qingwen ("Skybright" in David Hawkes's rendering), in her family home; while he is there, Qingwen's cousin's wife awkwardly and inappropriately attempts to seduce him.

CHAPTER 17

1. The actual joke centers on horns rather than hooves: the surname of the *daotai* is Lu 陆, which is a homophone for "deer" 鹿. I have used the Cantonese surname Lam to make the joke, which is inconsistent with the Mandarin pinyin romanization used elsewhere.
2. "Three eastern provinces": Heilongjiang, Jilin, and Liaoning, generally referred to collectively in English as "Manchuria."
3. As mentioned previously, the queue was the normative hairstyle for male subjects of the Qing dynasty, where the back was grown long and the front part of the pate was clean-shaven. Besides certain religious practitioners, only men who were in mourning were permitted to be out of compliance. Baoyu initially believes this man to be in mourning; however, as he will soon realize, the man's choice to grow out his hair is a political one, marking him as Westernized at least, and a political agitator at most.
4. Shou Shan 寿山 (1860–1900) was a Qing general responsible for overseeing Heilongjiang. When the Boxer Rebellion broke out in 1900 and the Qing court declared war against the foreign powers present in China, the Russian army moved to seize and occupy territory in Heilongjiang. As the tides of the rebellion turned, the court's growing desire for rapprochement with the foreign powers hamstrung Shou Shan's efforts to push the Russians back. As a result, he was unable to prevent their advance, and he ultimately committed suicide. Qu Yongguang, "Shou Shan jiangjun he Cheng Deuquan yu gengzi zhi yi" (General Shou Shan, Cheng Dequan, and the *gengzi* campaigns), *Heilongjiang shizhi* (Historical Records of Heilongjiang) 24 (2012): 40–43.
5. The Heilong River was in the far northeast corner of Qing China's territory and marked, as it does now, China's territorial boundary with

Russia there. The Yangzi River, in addition to having tremendous cultural and civilizational significance, cuts across the center of China. The speaker is foreshadowing foreign occupation of China's territorial heartland and a key national symbol.

6. According to Theodore Huters, Wu Jianren participated in a public debate on this very topic in Shanghai's Zhang Garden in March 1901. Theodore Huters, *Bringing the World Home: Appropriating the West in Late Qing and Early Republican China* (Honolulu: University of Hawai'i Press, 2005), 128. I am very much tempted by the possibility that one of the speakers may be a tongue-in-cheek caricature of the author himself, but I am not confident in making any such assertion. At the very least, however, we may perhaps imagine Wu to be an audience member at the same time as Baoyu and Bohui.

CHAPTER 18

1. This refers to Yu Xian 毓贤, the former governor-general of Shandong, who was executed after the Boxer Rebellion for his encouragement of the Boxers and his role in the execution of a number of foreign missionaries. See James Hevia, *English Lessons: The Pedagogy of Imperialism in Nineteenth-Century China* (Durham, NC: Duke University Press, 2003) 288–89.
2. This is likely a reference to reformer turned revolutionary Tang Caichang 唐才常 (1867–1900), an intellectual with connections to both movements. After the failed Hundred Days Reform, Tang founded the Independence Society (*zili hui* 自立会), whose militant arm, the Independence Army (*zili jun* 自立军), mounted an uprising in Hankou in 1900; however, in spite of the society's stated goal of protecting the emperor, Hao Chang notes that Tang also espoused more radical "anti-Manchu revolutionary" sentiments as well. The uprising was easily crushed by Governor-General of Hunan and Hubei Zhang Zhidong, and Tang was executed. Hao Chang, *Liang Ch'i-ch'ao and Intellectual Transition in China, 1890–1907* (Cambridge, MA: Harvard University Press, 1971), 140–41; Stephen R. Platt, *Provincial Patriots: The Hunanese and Modern China* (Cambridge, MA: Harvard University Press, 2007), 95–97.
3. Wu Sangui 吴三桂 was a former Ming general, infamous for having intentionally allowed invading Manchu forces into the empire via the Shanhai Pass in 1644 and thereby contributing to the ultimate downfall

of the Ming. He would go on to serve the newly established Qing dynasty, but in 1678 he rebelled against the Qing and declared himself emperor of his own state. Jonathan Clements, *Coxinga and the Fall of the Ming Dynasty* (Phoenix Mill, UK: Sutton Publishing, 2007), 2–4, 97–108, 252–55.

4. *Daxue* 大学 (The Great Learning) is a treatise that dates at least to the former Han dynasty (2nd c. BCE) but is possibly older, since it is claimed by some to have been written by either a disciple or descendant of Confucius in the 4th c. BCE. Wm. Theodore de Bary and Irene Bloom, *Sources of Chinese Tradition, Vol. 1: From Earliest Times to 1600*, 2nd ed. (New York: Columbia University Press, 1999), 330. In the Song dynasty, *The Great Learning*, along with *The Analects*, *The Mencius*, and *The Doctrine of the Mean*, was canonized as one of the foundational "Four Books" of Confucianism. As a part of Confucian educational canon, it would have been included in Baoyu's own education; as a result, Baoyu, who is hoping for novelty, finds the lecture that follows clichéd and uninspiring.
5. The translation is adapted slightly from James Legge, *The Shoo King* (*Shujing* 书经), *The Chinese Classics* (Taipei: Wenxing Shudian, 1966), 3:168–69. Legge uses "renovate" rather than "reform" to translate *weixin*.
6. This line appears in the Major Ode *King Wen* 文王 from the *Shijing* 诗经 (Classic of Poetry).

CHAPTER 19

1. In the famous "East Window Plot," Song grand councilor and "notorious traitor" Qin Hui used deception to have "patriotic" General Yue Fei executed. Tang Xianzu, *The Peony Pavilion*, trans. Cyril Birch (Bloomington: Indiana University Press, 2002), 333n10.

CHAPTER 20

1. Again, Beiming's misapprehensions present difficulty to the translator to render fluidly. Beiming has heard the name "Sir Liang" (where Liang 梁 is simply a common surname); however, he has once again made a muddle of things and says he heard someone mention either a "Sir Liang" (凉大人, Sir Cold) or possibly "Sir Re" (热大人, Sir Hot). As with the previous punning about Grand Secretary Gang, I have decided not to change the name of a historic personage just for the sake of making the joke work better, and so I have settled, somewhat unsatisfyingly, for a simple mishearing of

similar surnames, Liang and Jiang. However, this approach also means that the translation must very directly state the man's name ("Sir Liang") rather than giving the more oblique pun ("Sir Cold") in the original.

In this case, I suspect our superintendent, "Sir Liang," to be Liang Dingfen 梁鼎芬 (1859–1919), a close associate of educational reformer Zhang Zhidong, who would have been governor-general of Hubei and Hunan at this time. (This connection would explain the superintendent's outsized influence.) Liang occupied a series of important educational positions during Zhang's tenure as governor-general; he would also play a role in persuading Zhang to suppress the activities of the Independence Army, which led to the execution of Tang Caichang. See Wu Zengfeng and Han Chunying, "Shilun Liang Dingfen yu Zhang Zhidong de guanxi" (On the Relationship Between Liang Dingfen and Zhang Zhidong), *Lishi dang'an zazhi* (Historical Archives) 1 (2005): 63–66.

Given Wu's sympathetic portrayal of Tang's case in chapter 18 (see the notes to that chapter), his feelings on Liang Dingfen are not altogether surprising.

2. Here, Beiming has misunderstood *baimen* 拜门 (to become someone's disciple; lit., to go pay one's respects at someone's door) as "to pay respects to a doorway." Unable to make sense of this, he muddles it further into "pay respects to a door or a window."
3. Liu Xuesheng 刘学笙 is a pun for "overseas student." This character is intended to embody the author's criticisms of those Chinese who studied abroad and returned with new, foreign ideas of "freedom" and the like. Maoming 茂明 literally means "lush enlightenment," but it can also be taken as a pun for *maoming* 冒名, "false name" or "impostor."

CHAPTER 22

1. Time in the Realm is always measured in native Chinese *dizhi* 地支 units (Earthly Branches, a system of twelve named units, each of which represents two hours of time). The time given here translates to 8:15 a.m. See the following note for more information on *dizhi*.
2. As mentioned above, this system of time notation uses the twelve names of the Earthly Branches as names for two-hour periods of time (called *shichen* 时辰) during the day. The hours are as follows: *zi* 子, 11:00 p.m.–1:00 a.m.; *chou* 丑, 1:00 a.m.–3:00 a.m.; *yin* 寅, 3:00

a.m.–5:00 a.m.; *mao* 卯, 5:00 a.m.–7:00 a.m.; *chen* 辰, 7:00 a.m.–9:00 a.m.; *si* 巳, 9:00 a.m.–11:00 a.m.; *wu* 午, 11:00 a.m.–1:00 p.m.; *wei* 未, 1:00 p.m.–3:00 p.m.; *shen* 申, 3:00 p.m.–5:00 p.m.; *you* 酉, 5:00 p.m.–7:00 p.m.; *xu* 戌, 7:00 p.m.–9:00 p.m.; *hai* 亥, 9:00 p.m.–11:00 p.m. The first of the two hours is designated *chu* 初 (early); the second of the two hours is designated *zheng* 正 (proper). The consistent use of the *shichen* chronological system in the Realm illustrates the Realm's dedication to native Chinese epistemologies. Given its significance to the novel's political message, I would have liked to preserve this usage throughout this section; however, referring to notes for each instance that a time is mentioned would likely have proved cumbersome for the reader, so I have reluctantly adapted *shichen* times into European hours in all mentions that occur after this introductory scene.

3. Hua Xing 华兴: the scientist's name means "China rises." His courtesy name, Hua Bizhen 华必振, likewise means "China must arise." "Supply aid to each individual" 人人而济之: literally, "help people ford the river one at a time," a quote from the *Mencius* speaking to the idea that a good government fixes systemic issues (like flooding) before they become problems, since ad hoc relief, while showing goodwill, is inefficient. See Robert Eno, trans., *Mencius: Translation, Commentary, and Notes*, https://scholarworks.iu.edu/dspace/handle/2022/23423 (May 2016), 80.
4. The ability to control the seasonal weather has precedent in ancient texts, again suggesting that the Realm is steeped in native epistemological tradition: for example, the ability to control the weather as depicted here is reminiscent of a phenomenon described in the *Classic of Mountains and Seas* (*Shanhaijing* 山海经), in which the god Luwu is responsible for controlling "the cycle of four seasons in the Supreme God's garden." *A Chinese Bestiary: Strange Creatures from the Guideways Through Mountains and Seas*, ed. and trans. Richard Strassberg (Berkeley: University of California Press, 2002), 107.
5. "Remaker of Heaven" (再造天): this name obviously harkens back to Baoyu's mystic origins in *Story* and his feelings of desolation at not having fulfilled his purpose. As the reader may recall, he was originally a magic stone whose purpose was to be used by the goddess Nüwa in the "mending of the heavens" (补天); that Hua Bizhen has successfully "remade" or mended Heaven clearly inspires admiration in Baoyu.

6. The words chosen as names for the districts reflect a range of key Confucian virtues. I have made a few emendations to this paragraph to facilitate understanding of the organization of the regions and districts.

CHAPTER 23

1. Lao Shaonian's condemnation of Liu Xuesheng echoes language from Liang Qichao's "Lun ziyou" 论自由 (On Liberty), one of the essays Liang wrote as part of his larger *On the New Citizen* project. Liang writes: "What I mean by 'liberty' is the liberty of the collective, not the liberty of the individual. In an age of barbarism, individual liberty flourishes while collective liberty languishes; in an age of enlightenment, collective liberty is strengthened and individual liberty is weakened." Liang Qichao, "Lun Ziyou" in *Xinmin shuo: Shenwei jiedu ben* (On the New Citizen: A Deep Exegetical Reading), ed. Kang Xue (Beijing: Zhongguo wenshi chubanshe, 2013), 93. Translation mine.
2. The name of each family member bears ideological significance. Dongfang Qiang 东方强 translates to "Eastern Strength"; Dongfang Wenming 东方文明 to "Eastern Civilization"; Dongfang Ying 东方英 to "Eastern Heroism"; Dongfang De 东方德 to "Eastern Morality"; Dongfang Fa 东方法 to "Eastern Law"; Dongfang Mei 东方美 to "Eastern Beauty"; and Hua Zili 华自立 to "China Stands for Itself."

CHAPTER 24

1. Units of length: in addition to li (roughly equal to one third of an imperial mile), length in the novel is usually given in one of two other units: chi (尺, slightly larger than an imperial foot), or zhang (丈, equal to ten chi, or around eleven imperial feet). I have left li untranslated throughout but have expressed chi and zhang in terms of "feet" for readability, in spite of their not being perfect equivalents.
2. That is, the flag of the Qing dynasty.

CHAPTER 25

1. "Vertical propulsion drive rotor": this is my translation of *shengjiang ji* 升降机, literally an "ascent-descent drive." Wu seems to envision this

drive as encompassing both the functional lift mechanism (which can be started, shut off, or turned up or down to a desired setting) as well as the rotor (which rotates or stops); I refer to it as either "the drive" or "the rotor" throughout, depending on which component seems to be the object or subject of the verb in a given sentence.

2. *Jinghua yuan* 镜花缘 (Flowers in the Mirror): a novel written by Li Ruzhen 李汝珍 (c. 1763–c. 1830), which predates the current text by roughly eighty years. (As such, Baoyu can have read it only at some point during the action of our novel.) A substantial portion of that text follows the protagonists' travels through a number of foreign countries populated by unfamiliar peoples and often relates the strange customs, values, social structures, or physical attributes of the peoples visited by the protagonists. These depictions are often satirical takes on contemporary mores. In the text, a flying car lent by the Zhourao 周饶 to the sovereign of the Country of Women is described thus: "This car can fit two passengers and can travel two or three thousand li in a day; if one encounters favorable wind conditions, it may even travel as far as ten thousand li in one day." Li Ruzhen, *Jinghua yuan* (Taipei: Shijie shuju, 1965), 266. Translation mine.

   The Zhourao people Baoyu mentions here are not just the fictional invention of Li Ruzhen but are in fact mentioned (sometimes as the Jiaoyao 僬侥) in entries in much older texts such as the *Bamboo Annals* (*Zhushu jinian* 竹书纪年, ca. 3rd c. BCE) and the *Classic of Mountains and Seas*; see *A Chinese Bestiary: Strange Creatures from the Guideways Through Mountains and Seas*, ed. and trans. Richard Strassberg (Berkeley: University of California Press, 2002), 166. Li Ruzhen was obviously drawing on historical texts and knowledge of native legend in his creation of a landscape full of curiosities in *Flowers*, just as Wu does in turn in this half of the current novel.

CHAPTER 26

1. Lao Shaonian is quoting two different adages, from the classical texts *Liji* 礼记 and *Hanfeizi* 韩非子, respectively, that refer to a lack of criminal activity.
2. Constitutionalism (*lixian* 立宪): it is important to note that Wu Jianren seems to be envisioning constitutional monarchy in particular when he mentions constitutionalism.

CHAPTER 27

1. Duo Jianshi 多见士: this name is a pun for "vast knowledge."
2. *Peng* 鹏: a symbol invoked in the Daoist *Zhuangzi* 庄子 to represent the vastness and unknowability of the universe. In the death of the *peng* we see the triumph of the Realm's Confucianist rationalism over Daoist mysticism. The abstruseness that the *peng* formerly symbolized is rendered mundane, tamed by rational metrics and measurements: in its death, the sublime vastness of the *peng* is reduced to mere "largeness"—a clerk measures it and finds it "to measure fifty-two feet from head to tail and thirty feet across at its widest point," demonstrating the mastery of the Realm's efficient scientific bureaucracy over the *peng*. Once the *peng* is mounted in the Realm's museum, placards placed in the exhibit ensure that this specimen, once the symbolic embodiment of "unknowability" is rendered fully legible and "knowable" to the Realm's museum-going public. As such, this once majestic "metaphor for understanding the sublime and ineffable quality of the universe" is reduced through the civilizational goals of the Realm and practical technologies of the hunt, into "a symbol of sovereign power and a tool of cultural education." Nathaniel Isaacson, *Celestial Empire: The Emergence of Chinese Science Fiction* (Middletown, CT: Wesleyan University Press, 2017), 78–79.
3. The texts named here are all seminal works in the Confucian tradition. The *Classic of Music* 乐经 is mentioned in other texts but is no longer extant, having been lost centuries before the writing of the current novel. According to Wing-tsit Chan, it had already been lost by the 3rd century BCE. Chan, "Exploring the Confucian Tradition," *Philosophy East and West* 38, no. 3 (July 1988): 236. It is of course remarkable that the Realm has originals of all of these texts, purporting to be compiled (or dictated) by Confucius himself. That the Realm is in possession of the original *Classic of Music* is particularly impressive.

CHAPTER 28

1. Religion vs. teachings: Wu uses the same word here, *jiao* 教, which means both "religion" and "teaching." I have chosen to translate it differently according to context to make the point of Lao Shaonian's argument clear.
2. Zhang Daoling 张道陵: a master in the Daoist tradition.

CHAPTER 28

3. As noted in the previous chapter, according to the *Zhuangzi*, the *peng* and the *kun* 鲲 are different transformations of the same creature.

CHAPTER 29

1. Liu Yueshi 刘越石: a poet of the Jin era. The quoted line is from Liu's poem "Chongzeng Lu Chen" 重赠卢谌 (Presenting Another Poem to Lu Chen). See *Xinyi Gushi yuan* (Sources of Ancient Poetry with Modern Translation), ed. and trans. Feng Baoshan (Taipei: Sanmin shuju, 2006), 2:593–96.
2. The literal translation of the original *haima* 海马 would be "sea horse," but Wu clearly intends a larger, much more vicious animal than the seahorse, and one that is comfortable both on land and in water to boot. Given that *haima* is semantically very close to *hema* 河马 ("river horse," the generally accepted translation for "hippopotamus"), and the fact that the woodblock print that accompanied the 1908 illustrated edition of the novel depicts something very hippo-like, I have decided to translate *haima* as "sea hippo." Huang Heqing has identified a few instances of *haima* being used as a direct translation for "hippopotamus" in the nineteenth century, which to my mind makes the idea of a hippo possible, if tentative. Huang, "Hema tanyuan" (Traceability of "*Hema*"), *Zhongguo keji shuyu* (China Terminology) 20, no. 1 (2018): 72–73.
3. The idea of fabricated wings that work underwater has precedent in ancient text: the same Zhourao people that Baoyu mentions in chapter 25 as inventors of flying machines (as depicted in the Qing novel *Flowers in the Mirror*) are also, according to Richard Strassberg, credited in the *Bamboo Annals* with having "presented [to sage-king Yao] a device called 'Underwater-Wings' as an example of their technical skills." *A Chinese Bestiary: Strange Creatures from the Guideways Through Mountains and Seas*, ed. and trans. Richard Strassberg (Berkeley: University of California Press, 2002), 166.

CHAPTER 30

1. Man-fish: here, the Chinese is *renyu* 人鱼, which might be translated to "fish-man" or "merman"; however, according to Richard Strassberg, within the world of the *Classic of Mountains and Seas*, the *renyu* "is not a

merman but a fairly common fish." In Strassberg's translation, the "Human-Fish"—his rendering of *renyu*—"resemble catfish with four legs and make a sound like a baby." *A Chinese Bestiary: Strange Creatures from the Guideways Through Mountains and Seas*, ed. and trans. Richard Strassberg (Berkeley: University of California Press, 2002), 99, 130. Tian Chun, in his cataloguing of various textual and visual representations of *renyu* over time, states that the *renyu* of the *Classic of Mountains and Seas* is something akin to a giant salamander (鲵鱼 *niyu*); however, he also points out that long before the Qing dynasty, *renyu* had come to be used to describe a part-human, part-fish "mermaid" as well and cites Li Ruzhen's mid-Qing novel *Flowers in the Mirror*, mentioned by Baoyu in chapter 25, as containing an example of this latter usage. Tian Chun, "Zhongguo gudai renyu tuxiang yu chuanshuo de hushi yu yanjin" (The Evolution and Mutual Constitution of Folklore and the Image of the *Renyu* in Ancient China), *Meishu xuebao* (Art Journal) 2 (2015): 99, 106. As translator, I have thus been faced with a conundrum. Wu was obviously familiar with both texts, but given his reliance on the *Classic of Mountains and Seas* for inspiration throughout this section of the novel, I have followed the former interpretation and rendered *renyu* as a kind of fish. I acknowledge that there is room for disagreement and that Wu may have intended something more like "mermen." It bears noting that when Lao Shaonian first sees the *renyu*, the original text says that he sees "a swarm of people" (*yida qunren* 一大群人), which may be a point in favor of the latter interpretation. I have altered this to "what appeared to be a swarm of people," on the assumption that seen from a distance, the limbs of giant salamander-like creatures would resemble human limbs.

2. One version of the source text I looked at gives the fish name here as *tiao* 鰷; another gives it as *shu* 儵. The entry quoted is identical to that of the *shu* 儵 fish in the *Classic of Mountains and Seas*, so I give the name as *shu* throughout. Strassberg renders the description as "like a chicken but with red feathers, three tails, six feet, and four heads" (119). My translation here is indebted to his, in that he takes the *chi wei* 赤尾 (red tail) in the original passage as an error for *chi mao* 赤毛 (red feathers).

CHAPTER 31

1. "Floating stones": that is, pumice.

CHAPTER 32

1. Duo Jianshi's two brothers, mentioned here, are Duo Zhi 多知 (Much Knowledge)/Duo Nengshi 多能士 (Gentleman of Great Ability), and Duo Cai 多才 (Much Talent)/Duo Yishi 多艺士 (Gentleman of Great Skill).

CHAPTER 34

1. Here Wu uses the characters 大观 *daguan*: Grand Prospect or Grand View, the same characters used in the name of the sprawling, ostentatiously appointed (and ruinously costly) garden built by the Jia family in *Story*, named for its awe-inspiring vistas. One suspects that this line, delivered by Baoyu, is an intentional choice on Wu's part to suggest an alternative source of awe—namely, the mechanized factories of the Realm, and specifically the firearms factory with all of the militaristic implications it entails. At the same time, Wu draws a stark contrast between what the old Baoyu and the new Baoyu would have considered to be marvelous. Baoyu's former sense of merely aesthetic wonder has been superseded by one informed by technological achievement.

CHAPTER 35

1. In the *Classic of Mountains and Seas*, Kuafu 夸父 dies of thirst before he is able to catch up to where the sun sets. In Richard Strassberg's translation, Kuafu is rendered "Kuafu the Boaster." *A Chinese Bestiary: Strange Creatures from the Guideways Through Mountains and Seas*, ed. and trans. Richard Strassberg (Berkeley: University of California Press, 2002), 178.
2. Lao Shaonian seems to be referring to the dirigible-flying contest that took place at the 1904 World's Fair in St. Louis, also referred to as the Louisiana Purchase Exposition. See "Airship Makes Good Showing," *New York Times*, September 7, 1904; "Baldwin's Airship Lost in the Clouds," *New York Times*, November 2, 1904.

CHAPTER 36

1. This is a reference to a passage from the *Yizeng* 艺增 chapter of the treatise *Lun Heng* 论衡 by Han-era intellectual Wang Chong 王充. In the

passage, Wang comments on a received anecdote set during the reign of sage-king Yao, in which an observer watches as an elderly person at leisure amuses himself by playing a game in the dirt of the road. Asked about the greatness of Yao, the man replies, "What are the abilities of Yao?" According to Wang's commentary, the elderly man in the anecdote is an exaggerated caricature of the ignorance of the common person, both in his childlike desire for play and in his inability to understand or express the magnitude of his ruler's greatness. The point Lao Shaonian is making is that nostalgia for the eras of Yao and Shun is misguided, because in spite of enlightened rulership, the general populaces of those times were still insufficiently educated relative to the Realm's standards. Wang Chong, *Lun Heng* (Shanghai: Han fen lou, 1922), 3:72; see also Alfred Forke, *Lun Heng: Miscellaneous Essays of Wang Ch'ung*, 2nd ed. (New York: Paragon Book Gallery, 1962), 2:267–68.

CHAPTER 37

1. I am indebted to Charles Hucker's *A Dictionary of Official Titles in Imperial China* (Stanford, CA: Stanford University Press, 1985) for the correct translations of these military titles.

CHAPTER 38

1. The 1899 and 1907 Hague Conventions prohibited the use of chemical weapons in warfare. See Gerard Fitzgerald, "Chemical Warfare and Medical Response During World War I," *American Journal of Public Health* 98, no. 4 (April 2008), https://www.ncbi.nlm.nih.gov/pmc/articles/PMC2376985/.

CHAPTER 39

1. Wu's naïve and racist characterization of enslavement and of the challenges facing emancipated Black persons during the Reconstruction and Jim Crow eras of U.S. history is either woefully misinformed or intentionally obtuse, neglecting as it does to acknowledge either the brutal inhumanity of enslavement or the fact that after emancipation white institutional power was still actively working to ensure the continued subjugation of freed Black persons. See Robert J. Cottrol, *The Long,*

CHAPTER 39

Lingering Shadow: Slavery, Race, and Law in the American Hemisphere (Athens: University of Georgia Press, 2013), 176–79.

2. Here Dongfang Wenming actually refers to Xue Pan by his courtesy name, Xue Wenqi.

CHAPTER 40

1. Successful young examination candidates were lauded as "prodigies." This led to the phenomenon of older examinees lying to conceal their own true age so that, if successful, they might claim such status for themselves. Benjamin Elman, *Civil Examinations and Meritocracy in Late Imperial China* (Cambridge, MA: Harvard University Press, 2013), 142–43.
2. This refers to real historical events, although in this dream space the novel has leaped a few years ahead in its own timeline: in the real world, a massive anti-American boycott was staged in Shanghai in 1905 as a result of the 1904 renewal of the 1894 Gresham-Yang Treaty, which had extended the terms of the 1882 Chinese Exclusion Act. The boycott generated a substantial amount of nationalist and anti-imperialist discourse and literature, as well as marking an important moment in the awakening of popular political consciousness in China. For more on the boycott, see Guanhua Wang, *In Search of Justice: The 1905–1906 Chinese Anti-American Boycott* (Cambridge, MA: Harvard University Press, 2001), and Wong Sin Kiong, *China's Anti-American Boycott Movement in 1905: A Study in Urban Protest* (New York: Peter Lang, 2002).
3. Wu's choice of a "World's Fair" is significant, since he likely has in mind the 1904 St. Louis World's Fair. The World's Fair was envisioned as a spectacle of Euro-American imperial and civilizational might: the Euro-American pavilions displayed the fruits of conquest and the trappings of "modern" progress. Meanwhile, now-infamous live "anthropological" installations presented colonized peoples as curiosities for the scrutiny and amusement of visitors. Though the Qing government funded the construction of an impressive pavilion—and even dispatched a member of the imperial family to serve as China's representative—in hopes that these efforts would demonstrate China's own civilizational achievements, there was no question that China was not considered by others to belong to the "civilized" echelon of countries. Indeed, racist anti-Chinese exclusionary laws in the United States meant that Chinese attendees at the World's Fair were subject to a strict set of entry rules and were closely monitored

and policed during their stay. See Carol Ann Christ, "The Sole Guardians of the Art Inheritance of Asia: Japan at the 1904 St. Louis World's Fair," *positions: east asia cultures critique* 8, no. 3 (Winter 2000): 675–709; Theodore Hardee, "China's Remarkable Exhibit at the World's Fair," *New York Times*, August 28, 1904; "The British Pavilion and Exhibit at the World's Fair," *Scientific American* 1503 (October 22, 1904); Jane Leung Larson, "Articulating China's First Mass Movement: Kang Youwei, Liang Qichao, the Baohuanghui, and the 1905 Anti-American Boycott," *Twentieth-Century China* 33, no. 1 (November 2007): 21.

4. It is worth noting that Dongfang Wenming uses the royal pronoun *zhen* 朕 throughout this speech (this same pronoun was translated as a royal "We"/"Our" in the sitting emperor's edict in chapter 35). The use of this pronoun asserts Dongfang Wenming's imperial authority in this setting, unlike in his own home, in chapter 39, where he more humbly refers to himself as 老夫 *laofu* "this old man." To avoid confusion with the first-person plural "we"/"our," I have translated into a simple first-person singular "I"/"my" here rather than a royal "We"/"Our."
5. For more on the Zhen Baoyu/Jia Baoyu meeting in *Story*, see the introduction.
6. The quoted line is from a version of Tang dynasty poet Wang Bo's "Preface to 'King Teng's Pavilion'" (Teng Wang ge xu). It has since achieved the status of common idiom, commenting on the random nature of meetings in life. (While an article by Sheng Dalin was helpful for identifying and interpreting the original source of the quote, I should note that Sheng's article is actually focused on identifying textual corruptions in received versions of Wang's text and posits this particular line as one that has likely deviated from Wang's original poetic intention as a result of mistransmission.) Sheng Dalin, "Xiangkao Wang Bo 'Teng Wang ge xu' zhong de jichu ewu" (On Some Errors in Wang Bo's 'A Tribute to King Teng's Tower'), *Shangqiu Shifan Xueyuan Xuebao* (Journal of Shangqiu Normal University) 38, no. 8 (August 2022): 56–57.
7. Mind and Spirit Mountain 灵台方寸山 and Cave of Slanting Moonbeams and Three Stars 斜月三星洞 are sites in the Ming-era novel *Journey to the West*. The cave is home to the sage Master Subodhi 菩提祖师. It is here that Sun Wukong begins his quest for immortality and learns, through cultivation of his mind and the teachings of Subodhi, the magical techniques that make him so formidable. See Anthony Yu, ed. and trans., *Journey to the West*, vol. 1, chs. 1–2.
8. The text of this poem is given in English in the original.

GPSR Authorized Representative: Easy Access System Europe, Mustamäe tee 50, 10621 Tallinn, Estonia, gpsr.requests@easproject.com

www.ingramcontent.com/pod-product-compliance
Lightning Source LLC
Chambersburg PA
CBHW020225110726
47898CB00004B/1145

* 9 7 8 0 2 3 1 2 0 3 4 7 0 *